PATIENCE
IS A
SUBTLE
THIEF

PATIENCE
IS A
SUBTLE
THIEF

A NOVEL

ABI ISHOLA-AYODEJI

HARPERVIA

An Imprint of HarperCollinsPublishers

HarperCollins books may be purchased for educational, business, or sales promotional use. For information, please email the Special Markets Department at SPsales@harpercollins.com.

FIRST EDITION

Designed by SBI Book Arts, LLC

Library of Congress Cataloging-in-Publication Data

Names: Ishola-Ayodeji, Abi, author.
Title: Patience is a subtle thief : a novel / Abi Ishola-Ayodeji.
Description: First edition. | New York, NY : HarperVia, 2022.
Identifiers: LCCN 2021044319 (print) | LCCN 2021044320 (ebook) | ISBN
   9780063116917 (hardcover) | ISBN 9780063116924 (trade paperback) | ISBN
   9780063116931 (ebook)
Subjects: LCSH: Nigeria—Fiction. | LCGFT: Bildungsromans. | Novels.
Classification: LCC PS3609.S49 P37 2022 (print) | LCC PS3609.S49 (ebook) | DDC
   813/.6—dc23/eng/20211208
LC record available at https://lccn.loc.gov/2021044319
LC ebook record available at https://lccn.loc.gov/2021044320

22 23 24 25 26 LSC 10 9 8 7 6 5 4 3 2 1

For the ones waiting on proof that their lives matter,
and that their dreams are possible.

And to my dear Kunle,
you said that I should finish . . . that I would finish.
And here we are.

1

IT WAS A DAY TO CELEBRATE HER FATHER, BUT BY THE time Patience walked into the white party tent on the massive lawn of his two-acre mansion, she was twenty minutes late.

Another staid party to celebrate yet another of his professional victories.

She looked down at her dress, a short and flirty frock made of thick lace in an ugly shade of brown. *A color only Modupe would love*, she thought when she had first seen it a week before.

As she made her way through the crowd, she caught a glimpse of Modupe's penetrating gaze.

"Where were you?" Modupe said. "We looked for you in the house. The ceremony is about to start and you're just coming?"

"Sorry, Mummy. I was getting dressed," Patience said with the same pointed dip in her voice that came whenever she called her step-mother Mummy. In her mind, she was merely Modupe, and purely Margaret's mother, not hers.

"Why is this dress so short?" Modupe said, looking Patience up and down. "You ruined the dress I gave you? Did you lose your head, ehn, Patience?"

"Mummy, it's not ruined, it's just—"

"We will talk later," Modupe said, before hurrying to the high table to greet the VIPs.

Patience expected Modupe to scold her, but she had taken the risk willingly. She had shortened the hem of her dress and smiled each time she tugged the needle to secure a stitch. When she had put it on and looked at her reflection, gone was the bush Ibadan girl she often saw staring back.

"She is about to implode," Margaret said as she dragged her chair closer to Patience, bringing the half sisters shoulder to shoulder. "You've really outdone yourself."

"Long dresses in this heat? She wants us to melt." Patience looked up at the tent's towering ceiling. Tall industrial fans powered by her father's massive generator spun uselessly, only churning the day's thick heat. Women attendees fanned themselves with her father's ceremony booklet to make up for the lack of air.

She surveyed the crowd further—the usual cast of Ibadan's who's who: businesspeople, politicians, chiefs, dignitaries. They arrived in Mercedes and Peugeots, driven by drivers who parked next to her father's personal fleet of Mercedes and Peugeots. The men donned heavy aso oke agbadas with coral beads dangling from their necks. Their women wore delicate lace, high tied geles, and 24-karat gold jewels.

"I wish you had made my dress shorter like yours," Margaret said.

"Next time." Patience bumped shoulders with her.

"Is Daddy really going to have us sit through this entire thing?"

"Shhh, it's starting," Modupe said as she sat back down.

"We've gathered on this fifth day of September 1992, to celebrate Oyo State's new commissioner of finance," the governor said. "He is a multimillionaire businessman, a pioneer in creating concrete blocks used at some of Ibadan's most important construction sites. He was educated in America at Howard University in Washington, DC."

Patience shifted in her seat. Her dad lingered near the stage, standing tall and proud.

"He is a devoted husband and beloved father," the governor continued.

"Beloved." Patience spoke the word softly. As it stumbled off her tongue, she wondered if she truly loved her father. He had never said "I love you" to her or Margaret, nor did she expect him to. On the off chance he ever did, she wondered if she would believe him. Love was the thing families spoke of in fictional American TV shows.

"He is a leader, and now he will proudly serve Ibadan. Ladies and gentlemen, I present Chief Kolade Adewale!"

The crowd cheered as he walked onto the stage beside the governor. The two men turned to the photographer and posed.

Snap, snap!

"My distinguished friends, it is an honor to accept this appointment as commissioner," her father said, squaring his broad shoulders, once he took the podium. "I promise to serve Oyo State in the light it deserves. I'm proud to say that Ibadan is my birthplace and my home. Thank you so much for being here today to witness this grand occasion. Thank you."

As usual: a man of few words, Patience thought as she shifted in her seat. The crowd applauded. Many stood and made their way toward him as he stepped down from the stage.

Modupe also stood but in a state of agitation.

"Fatima! Fatima!" she yelled across the aisle to her personal house girl. She turned to Patience and Margaret. "Look at this useless girl standing there like ọdẹ!"

The meek girl dressed in a stiff, khaki-colored maid's dress hurried over, squeezing past guests.

"Are you deaf?" Modupe snapped. "Go tell the caterer to have the food ready to serve!"

"Yes, Ma," Fatima said. She curtseyed and moved on with shame in her eyes.

"Girls, oya na! Go and congratulate your father." Modupe ushered Patience and Margaret toward the crowd.

They lingered behind the attendees, who hugged him, shook his hand, laughed with him, and posed with him for photos. Then the crowd grew thinner.

"Smile," the photographer said to Patience and Margaret once they were at his side.

Snap.

"Go greet my guests, o jàre," their father said to them hastily before they could utter a thing.

"Yes, Daddy." Patience pulled Margaret away.

"We have our instructions," Margaret said. They both snickered. "Maybe you can redeem yourself with Mummy if you greet enough guests."

"Oh, please. Mummy dearest will have many words for me once this party is over. I trust that."

"Don't worry, I will calm her down."

"Margaret, I'm fine."

"I know you're fine, but Mummy doesn't understand you the way I do."

"I've told you, I'm not for her to understand."

Margaret pressed her lips together and put her hand on Patience's shoulder. "Let's just get this done."

"You know I hate socializing, especially with Daddy's old friends," Patience said.

"Just talk to as many people as you can."

They walked in opposite directions.

Patience smiled and knelt slightly as a man walked toward her.

"Ah, you're Chief's daughter—Margaret, isn't it? Congratulations to your daddy."

"Thank you, Sa. I'm not Margaret, I'm Patience."

"You're not Margaret?"

"No, I am Patience, Sa. Patience Adewale. Firstborn of Chief Kolade Adewale."

"Ooohhh, oookay. Patieeeenceee. You are the elder sister. Modupe is not your mum."

"Yes, Sa, that's me."

There had been a time when she felt a gut punch whenever someone expressed the vagueness of her existence within her family. But over the years the feeling had been reduced to a dull pinch. Patience had come to understand it more as confusion than as outright disregard.

She grew anxious as the man began to brag about his son and how people should now call him Engineer Abidemi Adejobi, because he had finished his studies in Scotland, and he was ready to come home and work and build his first house, possibly on Victoria Island in Lagos, because Ibadan had become too small for him.

"Excuse me, Sa, I need to find my sister." Patience walked on and didn't wait for his response.

No more greetings, she thought.

She made a swift turn toward the exit of the tent, then started toward the house. She could no longer ignore the dampness under her arms. She decided not to wait for her stepmother's permission. She was going to change her clothes.

"Patience," she heard an unfamiliar voice call out. *Who the hell is this now?* she thought. She turned to find out. A tall, slender woman dressed in English attire—a lavender double-breasted skirt suit that looked like it was plucked from Princess Diana's wardrobe—walked toward her.

"Patience, how have you been?"

Patience squinted as the woman came closer.

"Do you know who I am?" the woman said in a slight whisper.

"Oh . . . hello, Ma."

The woman smiled again. "I'm Aunty Lola."

Patience hesitated, still confused.

"I haven't seen you in so long. Don't worry. I know you don't remember."

"I'm so sorry, Ma."

"Your mother, Folami, she was . . . she is . . . my best friend."

Patience's chest shuddered as she took a long breath.

"How are you?" the woman said.

"I'm . . . fine . . . I'm okay." Patience smiled, hoping to conceal her shock. The woman leaned in to hug her. Patience softened into her embrace. The woman's voice, her bouffant hairdo, the smell of sticky hairspray, her floral perfume—it was true, Patience had known her once. She hadn't seen the woman since her mother's departure ten years before.

"Wow, I'm surprised my father invited my mother's friend to his party," Patience said.

"Well, my husband is now commissioner of health in Lagos, and he's known Kolade for years. We moved to Lagos a few months ago, so we are just here for the party."

"I'm moving to Lagos next week to go to UNILAG. I finished SS3 this year."

"Wonderful. My daughter, Bimpe, just finished at University of Lagos. Maybe you can meet with her when you arrive. She can tell you all about the school, I'm sure."

"I don't mind."

"I want you to visit me at home so you can tell me about how you've been getting on. Please come and see me," the woman said, now in a hushed tone. She dug into her purse and pulled out a pen and an address book, scribbled something, and tore the page out. "This is my address." She placed the paper in the palm of Patience's hand and clasped her fingers shut.

Patience felt like she was in a dream, standing with a person who had acknowledged her mother after all the years of her absence and all the years of her father and Modupe acting as if she didn't exist.

6

"My father told me my mum went back to America. Is it true? Have you heard from her?"

"Patience, that is quite a long story. Please, when you get to Lagos, come to my house and I will tell you all that I know."

"Aunty Lola, we can go to my room and talk if you prefer."

"I know you must be anxious to know more, but this isn't a good place for me to tell you anything. By now you know that your father doesn't like to discuss your mum. We will talk." The woman placed her hand on Patience's shoulder and walked on. Patience turned and watched her approach a man. She stared as they mingled, then as they made their way along the path that led to the parking area.

Patience followed.

She peeked from behind a wall and saw them enter the back seat of a black Peugeot. The car pulled out of the driveway and pressed toward the exit of the compound. Patience looked down at the paper the woman had given her. Written with her name was her Ikoyi address. She tried to picture herself navigating the intimidating streets of Lagos alone in search of it. She would find her way there even if it killed her.

"So, how many people have you greeted?" Margaret said as she crept up behind.

Patience stuffed the address into her bra, then turned to her half sister.

"I hope you knelt down for people," Margaret said.

"Yes, I did my greetings. But *please*, let us get out of these dresses. Aren't you hot?"

"Very hot. Let me go find Mummy to let her know we're going to change." Margaret walked back toward the tent, braving the crowd of people again. Patience thought about her encounter with Aunty Lola. She needed a moment alone.

She decided not to wait.

She walked toward the back door of the house, climbed the winding staircase, and dashed into her room, locking the door behind her. She rushed into her walk-in closet and pulled the large quilt off a medium-size box, finding behind a thin sheet of plastic her mother's jeweled black sweater, one meant for Christmas in cold American cities.

Then there were her mother's books: *To Kill a Mockingbird*, *Things Fall Apart*, *Oliver Twist*. Patience read the title of the thinnest book: *Becky*. It was about the little Black girl who went out shopping with her mother and found a doll that looked just like her. Patience sat down and held the book against her chest. She flipped through the pages and remembered listening to her mother recite each word as she sat on the side of her twin-size bed in her parents' former apartment in Washington, DC—her birthplace.

She dove back into the box and pulled out newspaper clippings: NIGERIAN SPRINTER TAKES HOWARD UNIVERSITY TO THE TOP; FOLAMI BAYONLE SETS NEW RECORD FOR HOWARD.

She searched through the box and pulled out her favorite photo of her mother—a lean and muscular woman dressed in a red, white, and blue track uniform, holding up one finger to indicate her victory. Patience remembered it displayed in the sitting room of the Ibadan bungalow where she and her parents had lived after they had left America behind.

She had thought of that photo when she joined her own school's track team.

Her plan then had been simple: make it to the Olympics, so her real mum would see her on TV and locate her. But once practice had begun, Patience was startled by her own clumsiness and sluggish pace. She had quit after two weeks.

She shoved her hands back into the box and pulled out the letters, handwritten by her mother, the paper wilted and oxidized. Patience remembered her fallen tears sitting where the words had bled slightly from the page. One letter was addressed to her four years after she last saw her mother, the other to her father. No envelopes. No return address. Just folded pages.

March 5, 1987

My dearest Patience,

I really tried, but sometimes in life we have to accept when we lose. But like my own mother used to say, one loss doesn't quantify a total journey. I named you Patience because you took your time. Twelve hours of labor before you arrived. Can you imagine? There was no other name for you. Please understand that the same patience you had in my womb and the endurance I had the day I gave birth to you will remain our link. One day we will meet again, and when we do, you will know what I've added to our lives. Let your daddy keep you for now.

Love,
Mummy

Patience had combed over every word each time she read the letter. What did she mean by accepting loss?

"I really tried," her mother wrote so plainly with no further explanation.

What had she tried to do? Patience didn't know, and her ignorance had devastated her time and again.

Patience unfolded the letter her mum had addressed to her father and began to read:

March 5, 1987

Kolade,

Please give Patience my letter to her. Please, for the love of God, let her read it. My errors were my errors. But I know who I was to you. I know I did my best when I was at my best. And you know what you did to damage me, even after I changed the

9

course of my life to be with you and to be a mother to Patience. You made your choice long before we moved back to Nigeria. If you don't give her the letter, please, I beg you, at least tell her I'm in America.

Most sincerely,
Folami

"Patience! Patience! Where is this girl?" Patience heard Modupe's footsteps approach from the hall. She gathered her mother's things, threw them back in the box, and pushed it into her closet.

"Yes, Mummy?" she called out. She ran to the door and unlocked it. Modupe burst in. Margaret trailed behind.

"Patience, kini o n ṣe? Today is an important day for your daddy, and you're in here doing nothing. What is wrong with you?"

"Sorry, Mummy. I was looking for the skirt and blouse you made me." She went into her closet and leafed through her clothes.

Modupe came in beside her. Patience hoped she wouldn't notice her mother's things spilling from the box.

"Look at it here," Modupe said, picking the skirt and blouse out of Patience's closet. "I wanted us to look elegant today, but you cut your dress. You young-young girls, you wear these short dresses and think you've achieved something. Patience, when you get to University of Lagos I hope you won't be showing all your legs. Those men in Èkó, they are easily tempted." Modupe tugged at her earlobe.

"Mummy, you talk like you were never young before," Margaret said.

"And short dresses can be just as elegant," Patience said under her breath.

Margaret met Patience's eyes. She spun around playfully, deliberately twirling her long dress, which was once identical to Patience's. "Can you imagine what they would say at school if they saw us wearing this?

'Keep Lagos Clean!'" Margaret was mimicking the mean girls from their boarding school. "Mummy, seriously, dresses like this are only good for sweeping the floor. Patience made it look better."

Patience tried to remain unenthused, but Margaret's humor broke through her hard edges. She thought about how freely her sister expressed herself with Modupe. The reward of a true mother-daughter union, a luxury she did not have.

"You girls are not serious." Modupe moved toward Patience and patted her cheek firmly, her usual gesture that demonstrated annoyance rather than tenderness. "People are calling this the party of the year. We need to make a good impression."

Patience held her breath, refusing to take in Modupe's favorite fragrance: Elizabeth Taylor's pungent White Diamonds. She still didn't understand why a woman would want to smell like that on purpose.

"I won't tell your father about how you ruined this dress. Make sure you do as I say for the rest of the night."

"Thank you, Mummy. We will change now," Patience said.

"Just hurry up."

"Yes, Mummy," Patience said. Patience grimaced when Modupe left her room.

"Why didn't you wait for me outside?" Margaret said. "We were supposed to change together."

"Do we have to do everything together?" Patience snapped.

Margaret's head ticked back in shock.

"I just needed a break from the heat," Patience said, realizing her own unease. "I knew you would come upstairs when you were ready."

"You could have saved me from those meaningless conversations, actually." Margaret paused and looked down toward the edge of Patience's bed. "What's that?"

"What's what?"

"That," Margaret said, pointing. "It looks like a children's book."

Patience looked to her side and saw the book her mother used to read to her. Somehow Modupe had not noticed it. Margaret knelt down and picked it up. She leafed through the pages. "Is this yours?"

"Yes. It's mine." Patience suddenly felt the thumping of her heart.

"Why are you reading a child's book? I can get you some romance novels if you want, o Patience."

"My mother used to read it to me."

"Wow. It's beautiful . . . I mean the illustrations are beautiful." She closed the book and handed it to her. "Where did you find it?"

"Oh, I saw it in one of the storage rooms." Nobody but Patience knew about the box filled with her mother's things, and she intended to keep it that way. They were things her father had forgotten to discard after her mother left, things Patience had found in bits and pieces around their old house over the years—including the letters from her mum.

After a persistent silence, Margaret cleared her throat. "Bisi taped the new episodes of *A Different World* for me when she went to America. Let's watch tonight after the party," Margaret said, finally cutting the tension.

"Let's see how we feel by the end of the night," Patience said. She wasn't in the mood to watch anything, though she usually loved watching American TV with Margaret. It was how she groomed and rehearsed the American accent she coveted.

"I'm going to miss you at school when you're off in Lagos living the high life at UNILAG," Margaret said, then tensed her slender lips the way Modupe sometimes did. "Who will make sure those silly SS3 girls don't disturb me for being my natural self?"

"You only have three years left, then you'll be at UNILAG with me," Patience said, masking the mixed feelings she had about being away from her sister. She knew she would miss her, but she welcomed the idea of having time away from her to discover herself, to create herself, to morph into the person she couldn't fully see but she knew had a right to exist.

Because for too long she had belonged nowhere and to no one in particular.

She loved Margaret, but she was exhausted with trying to ignore how her half sister's existence sometimes caused her pain.

And in Lagos, she would finally find out where her mother was. The thought made her anxious.

"Just don't go to Lagos and grow a big head," Margaret said.

"I promise I won't. Now let's change our clothes and go downstairs before Mummy kills me."

2

CHIKE FELT THE SWEAT BEADS ON HIS FOREHEAD DRIP AS the searing Lagos sun smothered his face. It was noon, and the parking lot of Iya Tina's Buka was crowded with dozens of okada drivers who stood propped against their parked motorcycles eating beans and bread. Chike didn't have much cash to buy anything special, so he opted for the cheapest thing he could find: roasted plantain and groundnuts.

A few of his fellow drivers were drinking stout and other brews and complaining about their bosses, about Lagos traffic, about women.

Chike looked up from his scanty meal and noticed a bright red V-Boot Mercedes drive toward the exit of the parking lot a few feet from where he stood. He thought he was in a daze when he saw Ekene Nwigwe sitting in the back seat, being transported by a driver.

Chike looked closer. It was definitely Ekene. He could never forget the face of his former classmate. His arch nemesis.

Chike looked around for a place to hide. He dreaded telling Ekene that he hadn't been able to find a job once he got to Lagos, and that his degree in petroleum engineering was going to waste while he endured the sun pounding on his back as he labored each day.

It was too late. Ekene saw him and gestured to his driver to slow down.

"Chike, is that you? Really?" Ekene said, rolling down the window.

"It's me o, wow, Ekene Nwigwe," Chike said, approaching the shiny car.

"Why are you on that okada? Are you a driver?" Ekene wore a disgusted smirk, a look Chike remembered well from the days when Ekene would compare his lesser exam results with Chike's high marks.

"Driver? No . . . I'm here . . . for my cousin who drives. He asked me to look after his bike."

"Shouldn't you be on an oil rig somewhere doing important business?" Ekene said, interrupting. "I mean, kai, tell your cousin this is a disgrace. A whole UI graduate, a petroleum engineering graduate sitting with okada drivers eating plantain and groundnuts."

"I know, sha, I will give him his bike. Me, I'm still looking for work, so we'll see . . ."

"I'm working with Shell now. My mum has a friend who knows the director."

Chike remembered his own interview with Shell. The manager had barely spoken a full sentence to him before telling him he wasn't ready for such a job. Hearing Ekene brag about what was likely the same position was a Lennox Lewis fist to the gut.

"Well, I have to be on my way back to the office. You take care, sha, and good luck finding a position that suits you."

Chike nodded and forced a smile as Ekene rolled up the window. Chike was so stunned he barely noticed one of his fellow drivers approach him.

"How you know that bobo wey dey for dat Mehcides?"

"Na my old classmate. Hey dey work for Shell."

"Shell? Na wa o! Why you no get job like that? Dis okada na hard work."

"I still dey look for a betta job now," Chike snapped at this illiterate man. And yet the truth was that the only thing that separated them was the university degree his mother displayed in a slender aluminum frame in the family room of his childhood home in Enugu.

His mother had sacrificed so much to get him through secondary school. Always making a way even after his father died. And now he could barely take care of her.

When he had spoken with her over the phone the night before, he nearly broke down. How could a doctor turn her away as she suffered?

Peter Edozie sped into the parking lot, honking his horn, and Chike remembered he wasn't the only university graduate forced to ride an okada to make a living. Peter had started driving one after two agonizing years of combing the city for work with his accounting degree in tow.

Peter's tires let out a rocky screech as they skidded on the pavement. The group of drivers jumped several steps back as he came to an abrupt stop.

"Look at this useless boy," one driver shouted at Peter.

"No vex, no vex," Peter said as he got off the bike.

"Why do you insist on driving like a crazy man?" Chike said.

"Am I not still in one piece?" They slapped hands and snapped their fingers simultaneously, their greeting since secondary school days in Enugu.

"This job is a nuisance," Peter said.

"You suggested I become a driver and now you dey complain?"

"Well, what were your options? Your mother is not well and you have a girlfriend."

"I'm done with that girl. She's crazy."

"Ah, now, I thought you would walk on water for Chichi." Peter slapped Chike's shoulder playfully.

"Mehn, I thought we were having fun. Then she started talking about marriage."

"You knew she was in love with you, so I blame you," Peter said.

"Shut up."

They laughed, and Chike thought about how love would have to come later. He had too many problems. Why add more baggage to his load?

"Any engineering job prospects?"

"No, sha. And something must come soon. My mum's condition is worse."

"God will provide."

Chike looked up and noticed a thick gray cloud forming, essentially signaling the end of lunchtime. Peter was the first to start his engine as a few raindrops fell from the sky. The drivers revved their bikes and sped against the drizzle, hoping to outrun it. Chike rode toward the rear of the pack.

What was the point of speeding? None of them was headed for shelter. Instead they combed the bustling streets of Lagos for passengers seeking an escape from the downpour.

Soon they would all be drenched.

3

"WE CAN TAKE CLOSE TO ONE MILLION NAIRA."

That was all Emeka heard Kash say as they sat in his smoke-filled flat watching Jackie Chan fling his legs toward seven foes.

One million.

The idea of making that much money filled Emeka with the kind of hope that desperate men clung to.

And desperate he was.

He dreamed of wearing European suits and driving the red BMW he had always wanted. Ever since he had read in a foreign magazine that BMW sports cars were "every speed demon's dream," he thought of himself as a speed demon looking to get his next set of wheels.

He refused to start driving an okada like his junior brother, Chike.

He despised that his own flesh and blood would stoop so low, especially after their mother had practically enslaved herself to pay his way through school. There would be no perfect job thrown at his feet, no company car, no stable salary. It was time for Chike to wake up and see how people like them really made money.

"It won't be easy. This is the most money we've ever dealt with," he said, watching Kash pump his fists in the air, imitating Jackie Chan's moves.

"Of course not. But it's all about assembling the right team," Kash said. Quickly out of breath, he plopped his stocky frame down on the floor. "We need people who need money, who are willing to start off with small pay, and who are not afraid to take money. That's it."

"You know Chike. It will be hard to convince him to do this. Maybe we should think of other people," Emeka said.

"We need a woman," Kash replied.

"What about your ex-girlfriend? Bose?"

"That one? No way," Kash said, waving him off.

"Why not?"

"That one dey craze. I will find the right girl."

"Your cousin? You said your cousin will be moving to Lagos. What of her?"

"Ah, Patience? No, no. Her papa get plenty money," Kash said. "How can we expect her to do 419? This is not regular 419. This is bank fraud."

"I can't think of anybody else."

"We must find somebody quick, quick. Oga said if we do this, he will give us more work," Kash said.

"Oga. Oga. All you do is talk about Oga, but when will I meet him, ehn?" Emeka said.

"Soon. You know Oga is not a normal person. These things take time."

Emeka had lost count of how many times he had asked Kash to introduce him to the man behind all the petty schemes he did to feed himself. He wanted to meet this Oga, who supposedly had five cars parked in his compound in Ikeja, and find out if it was true he drove around Lagos with large travel bags full of cash. He had heard that Oga came off as nonthreatening but still strong and in charge. Emeka felt a connection to him despite never having laid eyes on him.

"Don't worry, I will introduce you when the time is perfect," Kash said. "Me, I'm tired of sending letters abroad requesting money from these mugus. If we can do this bank job, I know he would want to meet you anyway. It takes time."

Emeka looked at the cracked clock hanging on the wall in the sitting room.

Seven p.m.

Chike was due to come home. He didn't want Chike to meet Kash there. He wanted to propose the job to his brother alone.

"You should be going. I will call you. We will talk more."

"Okay, but try to convince Chike. That one . . . he's too honest. Since the time we were at University of Ibadan, he won't take kobo from nobody."

"Go now, before he comes." Emeka pushed Kash out and shut the dusty wooden door. He walked back to his couch, once a gold and burgundy color, now dingy with stains ten years in the making. As he sat down, he heard the loud voices of the middle-aged couple who lived next door.

"This pounded yam is like water! How will this hold me! You will send your husband to work like this?" his neighbor yelled.

Emeka ignored the ruckus and focused on the fight happening on his mini-television. Jackie Chan was mid-kick when a roar of static and gray fuzz replaced the fight scene that was just about to heat up. He sucked his teeth as he jumped up to bang the top of the television.

"Useless, cheap contraption," he yelled as he tried to adjust the VCR's cord. He switched the tube off and noticed Chike standing in the doorway.

"You and this TV," Chike said as he shut the door.

"Chike. Welcome. Sit, sit."

"Emeka, you want something, don't you?"

"No, no, not like that. I have a proposition for you," Emeka said as Chike sat down on their couch. "You know Mama's arthritis is getting worse and the Secretariat forced her to retire. We're grown men now. We need to make real money."

"Emeka, I beg, I don't have time for this. I'm driving a bloody okada. Don't you think I want money? But I can't do what you and Kash are planning."

"Ah-ahn, what do you mean?"

"I've known Kash longer than you've known him. Why wouldn't I know how he's been feeding himself? I hear when you talk to him."

"Okay. Continue to work as a slave. So it wasn't enough to see Mama wake up with the roosters, even with her arthritis, just to go to her yeye job at the Enugu Secretariat, for barely any money? My brother," he said, patting Chike on the back, "that's not how people like us succeed. We have to take our share."

A knock at the door startled him into silence. Mayowa barged in wearing a blue button-down shirt with sleeves that barely touched the wrists of his lanky arms. Emeka rolled his eyes and walked back to the television to turn it on.

"My friend," Chike said.

"Emeka, how now? You're never excited when I come to your place," Mayowa said.

"Why should I be?" Emeka mumbled under his breath as he adjusted the TV. He had decided he wasn't fond of Mayowa when Chike first introduced them. Emeka noticed right away that Mayowa was the kind of person who was always smiling and hopeful. Emeka refused to believe that people like him were sincere.

"Don't mind him," Chike said, waving his brother off. "He wants me to join him on an illegal job he and Kash are planning. As if the petty-petty stealing they do isn't enough of a shame."

"Why are you telling people my business?" Emeka yelled.

"Oh, please. Mayowa is not stupid. Everybody knows what you and Kash are doing."

"No more stealing after Abiola takes office next year," Mayowa said. "Chike will find a real job after that." He laid a hand on Emeka's shoulder and clutched his own narrow waist with the other.

Emeka laughed. "When Abiola takes office? Just because your father is Abiola's friend, you think he's going to take office?"

"Not that I think. I know he will. He asked my dad to manage his campaign. Military dictatorship is dead, sha. The pro-democracy movement has shaken the military to its core. You will see, Nigeria will be a democracy come next year. Abiola will rebuild when he becomes president," Mayowa said.

"Ne-va! They will never allow a civilian to take over. And if Abiola wins, it's because of his business with the military. How did he make his money? Is it not contracts with the military for ITT? Why did Fela call him international thief? Use your common sense."

"Abiola is an honest man. He's a philanthropist. Just because he made money doing business doesn't make him a thief. The military is head of state. Who else will he do contracts with?"

"You talk as if Abiola is the inventor of Western democracy. He's a figurehead for the military. And people who have any sense know a Yoruba man can never be trusted," Emeka said.

"Stop that nonsense," Mayowa said, waving Emeka off. "Abiola is for the people: Igbo, Yoruba, Hausa, everybody. Why do you think he chose 'hope' as his campaign message?"

"University of Ibadan really led you and my brother to mental insanity," Emeka said. "Kash came out with better sense."

"Kash who didn't finish school?" Mayowa said.

Chike, visibly annoyed by the conversation and the static coming from the television, stood up and gave it one big bang on top. The picture cleared slightly. The sound of Jackie Chan fighting off his opponents silenced Mayowa and Emeka's debate.

"Ah, actor never dies." Mayowa watched as Jackie Chan kicked a group of men simultaneously. "That Jackie Chan will always win."

"Bruce Lee is the best anyway," Emeka said.

"Na lie! Jackie Chan is better than Bruce Lee."

"Look at this ignoramus saying Jackie Chan is better. Jackie Chan doesn't have the skills of Bruce Lee," Emeka said.

"Look at him jump and stay in the air at the same time!" Mayowa pointed at the television excitedly.

"That is not real. It's an effect for the movie, idiot!" Emeka said.

"There is no effect. This is one hundred percent authentic fighting!"

"Chike, what do you think? Which actor is the best: Jackie Chan or Bruce Lee?"

"You know my preference is Sylvester Stallone, Van Damme, and Chuck Norris. They are better fighters," Chike said.

Mayowa waved off Chike's answer, then backed away from the television, barely taking his eyes off the screen.

"Actor never dies," he repeated, gazing steadily at his kung fu idol. "Actor never dies."

Then, like a chain reaction, the television fell silent before it blinked off completely.

The overhead light flickered.

The room went dark.

"NEPA!" Chike yelled, as if the National Electric Power Authority were a thief he had caught stealing. "They done take light."

"Will your friends Abiola and Jackie Chan give us light?" Emeka said. He pushed Mayowa's shoulder, his laughter filling the entire room.

"Shut up!" Mayowa yelled.

Emeka felt his amusement fade as they all sat in front of the blank television inside the dark room.

4

"PATIENCE!" MARGARET YELLED OUTSIDE OF HER DOOR, startling her out of half sleep. "Time for breakfast!"

She knocked hard and twisted the knob repeatedly, as if twisting it would somehow unlock the door.

"I'm coming, Margaret." Patience sat up in bed, still groggy. She got up and strolled toward the door, then flung it open.

"So you like locking doors these days?" Margaret said.

"Why do you care?"

"Just asking." Margaret screwed up her face. "Are you okay?"

"Why?"

"You've been acting different since we got back from school, and even at Daddy's party."

"Sorry, I'm just tired. I was up all night packing for Lagos. I will be down soon."

"Aren't you the one leaving today to start university life? Abeg, Patience, shouldn't I be the moody one?" Margaret shook her playfully. "I'll be in the kitchen helping Mummy." She backed away from Patience's door, softening her gaze, then made her way down the hall. "Daddy's in the sitting room. He wants to see you, so hurry up."

Patience closed her door softly and thought of the night before— packing her belongings for the next chapter of her life while obsessing over her recent encounter with Aunty Lola. Was the woman serious?

Why hadn't she come to her sooner? Had she spoken to her mum recently? Did she ever visit her mum wherever she lived in America? Her ceaseless thoughts were like self-inflicted abuse.

When she attempted to sleep her pain away, what had taken place the very last time she saw her mum played in her mind on an endless loop—her mother frantically running toward the front door of the house; Uncle Timi dragging her back to the lawn, where he tossed piles of her clothes and shoes; her father cursing her in Yoruba.

Patience had seen diseased goats handled better.

Once sleep finally came, she dreamed that Aunty Lola died before she made it to her house, leaving her with no new information about her mother. Patience woke up in a cold sweat to find herself loathing her father.

"She went back to America," Patience remembered him telling her days after he kicked her mum out of the house. "She's not well."

That was all he gave her—an explanation that explained nothing, a claim with no proof. And for years, he was a massive brick wall that stood between her and the truth—a wall she feared scaling.

Was it time for her to ask him again?

No. She couldn't. He would scold her. Dismiss her.

He could at least tell her where she was in that massive place called the United States of America.

Then there was the letter her mother wrote her—and how she found it inside his desk drawer on a day she was looking for a pen. She rustled through his papers and there it was, tucked away with the one her mother had addressed to him, both dated four years prior.

"Let your daddy keep you for now," her mother had written.

It was the part of the letter she hated most, because her daddy did nothing special to *keep* her.

Patience took off her house clothes and put on the Levi's jeans and Guess T-shirt her former classmate had given her as payment for mending her pants with a simple needle and thread.

She left the room and made her way down the hall. At the top of the staircase hung a large portrait, and she gazed into her own eyes. She wondered what she was thinking the day she had posed for it, standing next to her father, Modupe, and Margaret.

Her family—the people so close but from whom she felt so removed.

She walked down and stopped in the foyer. She looked around as she often did, hoping to absorb something she couldn't name. She imagined it was a sensation that came from feeling completely at ease in one's home. Instead, she felt the same sense of absence she often felt in the compound. Unlike Margaret, nothing here was completely her own—her sister, half hers; her father, barely present; her step-mother, merely a presence.

Patience walked into the sitting room and found her father seated on his large burgundy chair watching television, with his legs propped up on the matching ottoman. She sat down on the chair facing him.

"Good morning, Daddy," she said, interrupting his intense focus on CNN. "Did you sleep well?"

"Yes, o," he said, barely looking away from the television. Patience glanced at the newspaper beside her. It was covered with headlines about Nigeria's impending democracy.

"I hope you're prepared for UNILAG. Accounting won't be easy. But I expect you to excel in your studies."

Of course accounting wouldn't be easy, because it was a course her father had chosen for her, like a blind man trying to color-coordinate clothes in a closet. She preferred the arts.

"Yes, Daddy, I'm prepared for Lagos."

"I'm not telling you to focus on Lagos. I'm telling you to face your studies," he said gruffly. "I don't want to hear that you are roaming around the city like those silly girls looking for rich men who are old enough to be their fathers. What are you young people calling these men now? Aristos," he said sarcastically.

Oh, the irony, she thought, remembering the steady cast of university girls her father had had on rotation over the years. He was the truest definition of an aristo. Then one day, without warning, her stepmother and her half sister, just three years her junior, whom she had not known existed, moved in with them and never left.

Patience thought about Aunty Lola and how she had made her mother's presence in the world feel real again. The questions she had for her father began to bubble up in her throat.

"Oya, let us sit and eat!" Modupe called out, interrupting her thoughts.

Patience stood and walked into the dining room, leaving her father still transfixed by his television. She sat in her usual seat across from Margaret.

"After we eat, *A Different World*, right?" Margaret said.

"I'm busy today. I have to pack more."

"Busy? Patience, I saw what you packed. How much more can you take to a university hostel?"

"I have a few more things," she said. Her sister was always so persistent.

"So you're just going to go upstairs after we eat and literally pack until you leave?"

"Okay, just two shows, but after that I'm done."

"Yes!"

Modupe stood over the table, giving orders to Fatima and Mr. John, the chef.

"Fatima, remember to put the yam on the right-hand side for Daddy. John, where is the fried egg? Eh hen, put it there. I hope you put in enough pepper." She sat down when she seemed somewhat satisfied with their work.

Kolade walked in, prompting Modupe to stand again. "My husband, sit. Come and eat."

Patience gritted her teeth. She looked at her father and wondered how he had been able to banish her mother with no remorse.

"Ifemi, people are still talking about your party. The celebration of the year. Ekú ìnáwó," Modupe said.

"Yes, yes," Kolade replied as he watched Mr. John pile more slices of yam onto his plate. "John, that's enough. Oya, put egg, put egg."

"Patience, make sure you go see Kash when you get to Lagos," Margaret said.

"I told this girl to focus on her studies when she gets to UNILAG and you're telling her to visit Kashimawo? That boy is too unserious," her father said coldly. "He has turned out to be as lazy as my brother. Make sure you don't follow him. He is doing absolutely nothing with his life, just like his father before he died."

Patience had already decided Kash's place would be her first destination in Lagos. In her mind, she had the logistics sorted: Kash would calm her nerves as he always did with his humor and unrepentant crudities.

He would help her navigate the intimidating streets of Lagos.

He would take her to Aunty Lola's because he would want her to know the truth.

He would do so because he knew that she was one of the few people who revered him.

"Kash has been living in Lagos for some time now, Daddy. Don't you think he can help her get around?" Margaret said, reading her mind as she sometimes did.

"That Kash. I heard he's in Lagos doing petty-petty theft," Modupe said. "How can a boy go to a school like the University of Ibadan and fail during his final year?"

"His father died that year," Patience said under her breath.

"Ifemi, did you see Commissioner Omotayo at the party?" Modupe said, changing the subject.

"Yes, yes, everybody was there."

"Ah, your speech was perfect."

Her father didn't respond. Instead he began to eat. As he chewed his food, the gray hairs in his beard gleamed in the sunlight that poured into the dining room from the backyard.

"Commissioner Omilana and his family, they wore a very nice lace, sha."

Kolade continued to chew. His eyes rolled back as they normally did when he was tired or uninterested. The room fell silent. Modupe took two pieces of yam and looked at Patience. She rested her fork on the plate, then clasped her hands together.

"Patience, making your dress shorter than your sister's was very silly of you." Modupe wiped her mouth with the white cloth napkin beside her.

"But, Mummy, you said . . ." Patience stopped and held her anger in.

"I know I said I would not report you, but you're leaving for Lagos today, and I don't want you going there dressing like those yeye girls. And for you to cut that dress without my permission is just rude. What do you think, ọkọ mi? Patience must know that those short-short dresses can get her into trouble."

Patience closed her eyes and imagined being teleported to Lagos straight from the dining room table.

"Ehn, ifemi, what do you think? Talk to this girl about her clothes and rudeness."

"I have spoken to her. She knows what I expect from her. She will not disgrace my name."

Modupe looked at her husband as if she wasn't satisfied. Then she turned back to Patience. "Did you pack your toiletries?"

"Yes, Mummy." Patience thought of her real mother, once a star runner who broke records during her time at university in America, a place so coveted, a place Patience was desperate to run away to.

Patience began to feel buried by the weight of her questions again. What had happened to her mum? Where had she gone? She took a bite of her yam and chewed slowly to avoid smacking her lips, a sound her father hated.

"Daddy, what was it like when you were at Howard University?" she said.

"Ah, Howard." He stared at the wall that faced him as if it would reveal the details of his college life to him. "Howard was good, but it was also a bit challenging. Being away from Nigeria, I had to adjust to America. And that Washington, DC, is too cold."

Patience found it ironic that he spoke of his experience in a new environment rather than his studies, yet he warned her to only be concerned with her studies.

Typical, she thought.

"Ah, ifemi, America is too cold," Modupe said, shaking her head. "I couldn't cope there after university."

"Did you have many friends on campus?" Patience said, ignoring Modupe.

"Oh, yes. As you know, I was the president of the African Student Union. I was a leader then as I am now."

"Were there a lot of members?"

"Ah, plenty." He still looked tired, but he softened his gaze. He grabbed a toothpick and began to dig food from his back teeth.

"Ah, you should have been at the University of Virginia with me. We had no leadership," Modupe said, shaking her head. "But at least when you came to my school, God brought us together. I was finishing my last year when your daddy came to recruit for the company he worked for at our job fair," she said, turning to Margaret in particular. "When I arrived at his booth, I told him my name, and we started talking about Nigeria. I said to myself, 'Look at this sharp fellow from Ibadan.' We laughed and laughed. Then he asked me to lunch that day. So he would come and visit me there in Virginia from DC. The two places are so close, sha. We had fun. But Nigeria is home, so we had to leave that place."

"Yes, Mummy, you've told me this story," Margaret said. She flashed her usual coded smile at Patience, a playful gesture to lighten the mood as she always did. But this time Patience didn't entertain her sister's diplomacy. She too had heard the story plenty of times, and each time she heard it, there was always a big piece of it missing: her own mother.

"Daddy, how did you meet my mum?" Patience said. She clasped her hands together as they started to shake.

The room fell silent. Kolade continued to slide the toothpick down the creases of his teeth.

"John, come and give Daddy more yam and egg," Modupe yelled as she flashed Patience a look of sheer disgust.

"I'll take more too," Margaret said.

"Was my mother a member of the Student Union too?" Patience said. She was surprised by her sudden boldness with her father. He kept digging into his teeth with his wooden pick, showing no sign of alarm.

"Yes, your mama was one of my members," he said.

Patience was surprised he answered. She decided to try her luck with her most burning question.

"Where is she now?"

He put his toothpick on his plate. Patience's stomach leaped into her chest.

"In all the years she has been gone, have you seen her come to this house to ask for you?"

"No, Daddy."

"So why are you asking me about a woman who has not looked for you?"

"I'm asking because I wonder, Daddy." She hated her response, but her father, with his distant and unfazed tone, had a way of making her want to turn off every working part of her body.

"I told you that your mother went mad. She went to America to get herself together."

"Where, Daddy? Where in America?" Patience's voice had started to quake.

"I said your mama went mental. I don't know where in America."

Her father stood up from the table, as he usually did when he had finished ahead of everyone else. "Patience, I'm telling you, make sure you focus on UNILAG. You should be preparing yourself for university, not thinking about a ghost from the past. Let this be the last time you ask me about her, sho gbo?"

Patience hesitated. Her father was calm, and she couldn't understand why. How could he tell her so casually to forget about her own mother?

"I said, do you hear me?"

"Yes, Daddy."

Modupe looked at Patience and shook her head. She got up and followed Kolade into the living room. Margaret looked at her and smiled a nervous smile similar to the one her mother often forced. She saw their resemblance—their perfectly straight teeth, their slender lips, their small, sunken eyes. She thought about the resemblance she knew she shared with her mother. Margaret put her spoon on her plate and took a sip of water.

"If you want, we can watch TV now. I really don't need all this food."

"No, Margaret. You eat. I will be in my room until I leave for Lagos."

5

THE AIR WAS DIFFERENT IN LAGOS. THE STENCH OF BURNING trash; the steady pulsation of heat bouncing off dusty tarred roads; the vibration of countless people hustling to get every which way, to be every which way, to conquer every which way—it all reeked of both victory and defeat.

The wild mood in Lagos was the first thing Patience noticed on her ride through the city. As Mr. Shonuga, her father's driver, steered the car toward UNILAG, she wondered how the city would steer her in the coming months.

The atmosphere shifted when Mr. Shonuga pulled into the gated campus, leaving behind the magic and madness of the bustling streets. She observed the quiet blocks of homes where lecturers likely lived. There were buildings that students came in and out of with books in hand and bags in tow. There was beauty, greenery, and a massive UNILAG marquee.

There was life and ease.

And yet Patience wished Mr. Shonuga could drive her back out into the city, then straight to Kash's, then to Aunty Lola's. But her father would know.

She would have to find her own way.

"That's your hostel," Mr. Shonuga said, pointing toward a two-story, clay-colored building. He turned and parked the car adjacent to it.

"I will carry one bag up. You carry this one. It's not too heavy."

"Thank you, Sa."

When they reached her room, she knocked on the door lightly, then opened it. There was a girl inside. Two wooden bunk beds sat headboard to headboard, creating an L shape without an inch of space in between.

"Good afternoon," Patience said.

Her roommate turned and nodded. "Good afternoon." She turned back to putting her clothes on hangers inside the slender wooden wardrobe.

"Mr. Shonuga, thank you so much. Safe journey back to Ibadan."

"Okay, o, Patience. Face your studies well o," he said, slightly wagging his finger.

"Mr. Shonuga, I will," she said.

She watched as her father's driver walked out, and thought about how the man who had given her life couldn't be bothered to come to see her off to a new school in a new city.

"I'm Tolani," her roommate said. "You?"

"Patience."

"Patience, okay. We have one more roommate. Her name is Ayanti. She went out somewhere, I don't know."

Patience tried to picture three women moving about on an average day in such a small room. Her secondary school hostels held more beds, but the space was larger, freer.

"Where are you from?" Patience said.

"I'm from Lagos here. You are from Ibadan, right?"

"How did you know?"

"You just told that man he should have a safe journey back there."

"True. Where in Lagos are you from?"

"Surulere. Ijesha. Not too far."

"You know, I have a cousin who lives in Mushin. Do you know how I can get there?"

"Ah, Mushin, you can go there by yourself?" she said. She rolled her eyes and pressed her lips together firmly, as if going to Mushin was like going to hell.

"I heard it's not the best area. My cousin's father died, so he's been on his own for a while now."

"Sorry o. If you want to go to Mushin, you can take the bus that goes straight there. But honestly, I think okada will be quicker for you."

"Your parents allow you to ride bus and okada?"

"Why not? I was a day student, so I found my way around," said Tolani.

"I was a boarder in a school in Ogbomosho."

"Na wa o, from Ibadan to Ogbomosho. One village to another."

Patience looked sternly at Tolani. "I was born in America, actually. I came here when I was eight."

"Oh, so that's why you talk like that."

She had never been good at making friends. She thought of boarding school, where she had spent years cultivating a persona that made her only somewhat acceptable to people, and how she had used her meager sewing skills to get what she needed.

Tolani had begun the same "show me who you are" initiation that the girls there had done so well, though she wasn't the type who had room to dismiss anyone. Her dusting powder was several shades lighter than her face. Her hair was relaxed straight, but the thick cotton-like roots suggested she was in desperate need of retouching.

"Honestly, though, that's the best way to get to Mushin, and I'm sure you can handle it," Tolani said encouragingly, likely reading Patience's irritation.

"I can take the bus, but I don't think I can take okada."

"You can adjust to okada. It's nothing."

The door opened. In walked another girl—tall, lanky, fair skin.

"This is Ayanti—our roommate who I was telling you about. Ayanti, this is Patience. I was just telling Patience that she can take okada, no big deal."

"Patience, okada is a necessary requirement in Lagos unless you have your own car or you have a driver," Ayanti said as she made her way to her bed. Patience marveled at how her legs took up half her body.

"Honestly. Even if you have a car, okada is good at times," Tolani said.

"And the best way to get to Mushin," Ayanti said.

"Unless she takes the danfo going to Mushin straight."

"Ah, that bus? Really?" Ayanti scrunched up her face in confusion. "Why not?"

"Ooookkayy. Yes. If she's too afraid of okada, that's what she can do."

They spoke like longtime friends, delivering each phrase as if they were swatting a table-tennis ball.

"My daddy said riding okada is dangerous," Patience said, not mentioning the fact that she herself was afraid of riding on one.

"Is your daddy here?" Ayanti said amused. "Anyway, I suggest if you want to go today that you start going in the next hour. Traffic even on an okada will be something when you're coming back."

"What about going to Ikoyi? Is it far?"

"Yes, o. That is in the opposite direction," said Tolani. "That's Lagos Island. Really, haven't you been to Lagos before? Ibadan is not far."

"I have with my stepmother and father, but it's not like I have taken public transportation in Lagos. I have in Ogbomosho, but Lagos is busier, and I don't know the roads here."

"Well sha, you will need to learn your way around if you want to enjoy Lagos," Ayanti said.

"My cousin who I'm going to see, he will show me around, I'm sure. He's like my brother," Patience said. She watched as Tolani unloaded the rest of the clothes from her suitcase and piled them on her top bunk. Ayanti took out a bag of toiletries and wandered around aimlessly. Patience decided to start unpacking too. She unzipped her bag and found her mother's jeweled sweater on top. She pulled it out and held it against her chest. She wondered what her mother was doing in America. Then she envisioned her as a madwoman in some insane asylum, foaming at the mouth, rocking back and forth, chattering to herself.

She hated the thought, so she allowed it to leave like a dark cloud passing through a crisp blue sky. That is not what had happened to her mum, she told herself firmly. She knew it. She felt it.

"What is that?" Tolani said, gazing at her mother's sweater still cradled against her chest. "I don't know if it's cold in Ogbomosho right now, but you can't wear that in Lagos. It's even too thick for harmattan. And if you think you will get on a bus wearing that, just expect to pass out right there. Where did you even buy it?"

Patience looked down at the sweater, gripping the heavy wool tighter. "This is very important to me. I don't wear it, I just keep it with me."

"Okay, so you know better."

Patience took more clothes out of her suitcase and plopped them on the bottom mattress on the bunk opposite Tolani's.

WHEN LUNCHTIME APPROACHED AND PATIENCE DIDN'T think of food, only the city outside her campus and what Tolani and Ayanti had told her about traffic and travel, she knew she needed to make her way to Mushin to see Kash.

She would have begged her roommates to escort her there if they weren't out taking a stroll around campus. She couldn't wait another day to see him.

Patience got up, stuffed her purse with the pocket money her father gave her, and slipped on the beige pantsuit that she had Modupe's tailor in Ibadan create with inspiration from an advertisement in a foreign magazine. She pictured herself dancing next to Mary J. Blige wearing the one-button blazer and loose flared-leg pants.

Patience caught the school shuttle to Yaba, as Tolani had explained. When she got off the bus, she stepped directly into the world she had observed earlier from the safety of her father's Mercedes.

She walked along the side of the road and watched cars and okadas zip by as her long, pencil-thin braids spilled over her shoulders in different directions.

She walked on.

Hawkers were selling, people were yelling, and a grungy stench hung in the air like an omnipresent menace to the thousands of bodies pacing the sweltering streets.

She kept going.

"Excuse me, Sa, where is the stop for Mushin?" she asked a man who had just zipped up his pants after pissing on the side of the road.

"There," he said, pointing a few feet away on the opposite side. The danfo pulled up, and she heard the conductor cry out the destination.

"Mushin!"

Patience gripped her purse and dashed toward it.

Just before boarding she noticed a large green-white-green sticker that read, "MKO Abiola for President," fixed on the side of the vehicle, which had once been yellow but had morphed into an ombré of hues formed by layers of dust.

Every seat was filled except the one behind the driver's seat. Patience thought twice about sitting there. She knew the car battery right beneath the seat would roast her bottom the entire way. It was the seat she avoided whenever she and her classmates in Ogbomosho would sneak off campus to take the bus into town.

She decided to take her chances after looking over her shoulder at the countless other passengers who had gathered, struggling to board the already crowded bus.

Patience held her knees closed and clutched her purse to her abdomen. A man holding a torn, faux-leather briefcase stood over her and grinned as he looked down at her chest. She held her purse closer.

When the driver took off, the fifty or so standing passengers shifted in all directions, flinging out an assortment of pungent body odors. Two women sitting near Patience, carrying red, blue, and white checkered Ghana-must-go bags, chattered loudly about the inflated prices in the market.

"Can you imagine, plantain, twenty-twenty naira!"

"O ti won ju."

Patience began to feel the heat beneath her seat as the driver tried to maneuver his way off the crowded expressway. She looked ahead, past a man dangling his arm and part of his head out of the window frame to create more room for other passengers. She looked to the side and noticed traffic was completely backed up.

The bus began to rattle. A muffled roar rang out from the vehicle's front hood. The wheels came to an abrupt halt.

"Oya, everybody, get out!" the conductor shouted.

"What do you mean get out?" Patience heard a woman yell.

"No petrol! Comot for here!"

"No petrol?"

"Kai!"

"Kini gbogbo nonsense?"

"When Nigeria no get petrol, how bus go run? Ask de gov-ment why we no get petrol."

Patience watched as some passengers quickly made their way toward the exit as if they encountered buses that ran out of fuel all the time. Others continued to complain to the conductor.

She followed the former.

What would her father say if he saw her hustling out of a bus packed with people he considered domestic help?

She got off and peered through crowds of people. She hailed a little boy selling water in clear plastic bags.

"Ice wata! Buy ice wata!" he yelled after taking the large bucket of water bags off his head to serve her.

She paid him, pierced the bottom of the bag with her teeth and squeezed to drink it. She thought of her dad again and his warning to her not to "consume such dirty local water." She rolled her eyes and squeezed the bag harder until there was no more.

Patience looked around as the crowd began to move toward the next bus stop. Some whistled for okadas to stop as the sun hammered down. A man dressed in gray slacks and a button-down with soiled armpits stood next to her, blocking the sun from his eyes with his hand as he looked out into the distance, past the cars that raced by.

"Excuse me, Sa, how can I get to Mushin from here?" she said.

"Ah, Mushin, you need bus. The next drop, it's somewhat far. Get okada. The driver will take you straight to Mushin."

Patience remembered what her roommates had told her about the convenience of riding an okada in Lagos. Before she could turn to ask the man another question and linger in the relief of his presence, he had begun negotiations with a driver on a motorcycle.

"Oya, you have to call for them," the man said to her. He hopped onto the back of the bike with his driver. She watched as they sped off.

Patience spotted one and waved the driver down awkwardly with both hands flying in the air just before more stranded passengers got off the bus. The driver steered his motorcycle toward her, almost running over her feet.

"I'm going to this place at Mushin Junction," she said as she fumbled through her purse for Kash's address. She showed him the address she had written on a folded sheet of paper.

"Oya, let's go," the driver said.

She straddled the bike.

He slammed his foot on the gas before she could settle onto the ripped leather seat.

Patience felt her stomach plummet as the driver squeezed through bumper-to-bumper traffic at full speed.

Her long braids flew forward as the driver made a sharp turn and stopped near a roundabout, a lounging spot for three crippled homeless men, one armless, one legless, and the other with half a face—his forehead caved in on one side, his eye socket crushed, and his cheekbone nonexistent.

"This go-slow, na wahala," the driver yelled, complaining about traffic.

Patience panned her eyes to observe thousands of cars and people on the road: Mercedes, Toyotas, Peugeots, Volkswagen Beetles, overly packed buses, street hawkers, and a sprinkling of other motorcycles squeezing between lanes.

Patience's driver pumped the gas and squeezed past several cars when he noticed the far right lane cleared an inch. She caught a whiff of alcohol on his breath. She fumbled silently through an awkward prayer.

She held her eyes shut for what felt like hours until the driver made a sudden stop. "Ṣebi, you say this place?" her driver said, pointing to the building beside them.

She paid him, then stepped off onto the road and stared at the grimy dilapidated structure accented with corroded metal balconies where hand-washed garments hung like ornaments.

She walked up the steep, poorly constructed staircase, then approached Kash's door, which vibrated to the pulse of the music blasting from inside. She knocked hard. Kash opened swiftly.

"Ah, Patience!" he yelled. He grabbed her and lifted her off the ground.

"Kashimawo, how are you?" she said. When he put her down, she hugged him again.

"Ah, you know me. I dey do my ting no matter de place. Come in jàre."

She entered the tiny, smoke-filled one-room efficiency, greeted by Kash's friends and the sounds of Fela Kuti's jazzy Afrobeat arrangement pumping through the dented speakers of a small portable radio with missing knobs. Fervent vocals accompanied the jazzy musical arrangement.

"Zombie oh! Zombie! Zombie no go think unless you tell am to think!"

She adjusted her eyes at the sight of Chike, Kash's former roommate from the University of Ibadan. Her heart began to pump a rhythmless beat. He was just as striking as he had been on the day they first met.

"Everybody, this is my cousin Patience. She is at UNILAG now from Ibadan."

"You are welcome," she heard.

"Patience, look how you're flexing in this suit. This is Lagos. Take it easy, o."

"Kash, what do you mean? This suit is in vogue in America," Patience said, confidently showing off her American lingo.

"Hmph, Patience, you haven't changed. Still chasing America," he said. "This my cousin. If she talks, you will think she just came from Yankee."

Patience sat and watched him take a puff on his cigarette. He exhaled and pointed toward one of his friends. "That is Mayowa there, our very own politician," he said. "Emeka is our money guy. And Chike, you know Patience, jàre. You met her at our hostel in Ibadan."

"Yes, yes. I remember. Patience, welcome," Chike said. Their eyes met, then he looked away.

"We meet again." She blinked, hoping to release the sparkle from her eyes.

The same sensation had come over her the day they met in Ibadan, because by some miracle, the air around him was a whirlwind that pulled her in and stirred every inch of her. He was tall, his body well defined. She wanted him to look at her again so she could sink deeply into his eyes the way she had when he uttered his first hello at UI.

"As you can see, Lagos is treating us well," Kash said. "I am here in the ghetto, and Chike is looking for work, though I think driving okada suits him well." Kash laughed his signature belly laugh.

"Useless man," Chike said playfully. He bit down on his lower lip, and Patience felt her body go limp.

"Don't mind him. Lagos will be better soon," Mayowa interjected.

"You dey start. Better for who?" Kash stood abruptly.

"Better for us with Abiola in office."

It was as if Mayowa had set off an alarm. They yelled and debated, but Patience could barely make out what they were saying—something about MKO Abiola creating jobs and fixing Nigeria's problems. Emeka and Kash seemed to wave off such claims as they puffed Benson & Hedges between delivering their impassioned points, flicking their ashes into empty Coca-Cola bottles. Chike stayed calm, as if he had heard the same argument too many times.

Kashimawo's long, brawny legs and a bottle of Guinness stout rested on an almost broken stool. Above his head, against the dingy wall, hung a large, withered poster of Sade Adu that read "Smooth Operator."

Somehow their heated conversation moved on to soccer.

"Me, o, I blame Rashidi Yekini. He allowed the goalkeeper to intimidate him," Kash said. "When they enter the World Cup next year, he can't do like that."

His loud, husky voice filled the room as he spoke at fierce speed. Patience remembered then how much she had missed his magnetism.

"Patience, Ah-ahn. You're not my guest. Take water or minerals there."

Patience looked at Kash's old burgundy kitchenette, the steel handles corroded, the wood cabinets decrepit. Plastic red cups, plastic stew-stained plates, and a tattered sponge made of straw floated in a large pail of murky water that sat in the middle of the floor. Patience imagined Kash bent over the filthy water, cleaning what he used as tableware.

Then she remembered how just a few years ago Kash would leave school on breaks and return to Uncle Timi's two-story house in Felele, the one her father had built for him not far from his compound. But after Uncle Timi died, her father sold the property, leaving Kash with no walls to inherit. When Kash failed all his classes at UNILAG, her father felt even more justified.

"That's why Nigeria will never flourish. Our leaders are corrupt and people follow-follow," Mayowa said. "Ah-ahn, when the head doesn't function, how can the rest of a man's body do the job?"

"Mayowa, you done start. How can we go from soccer back to politics?" Kash said.

"Don't mind him!"

Patience got up and walked over to Kash's kitchenette to treat herself to the bottled water he had offered her. She noticed then that he had no stove. She opened the water, took a gulp, and peered out the window. Outside kids were playing soccer with a half-deflated ball.

"I think we should open the window," she heard a voice say behind her despite the boisterous debate that went on in the room. She turned to see Chike standing there.

"I was thinking the same."

Chike leaned over and shook the window to slide it up.

"Where is Kash's stove?" she said, no longer able to tame her curiosity. She hoped she didn't sound as abrupt and awkward as she could at times.

"Oh, you don't know the setup of face-me-I-face-you living?" Patience felt the urge to slap his hand flirtatiously.

"Everybody with a room on this floor shares one kitchen. One stove," Chike said. He peered at her suspiciously. "Kash mentioned that your father is rich, so this is not the kind of life you're used to, I'm sure."

"Trust Kash to leave out the part that my daddy doesn't spoil me. You're not smoking like your friends," she said, eager to change the subject.

"Beer is okay in moderation, but smoking is like making arrangements for your own demise."

Patience's skin prickled as Chike gripped a beer, bringing it up to his mouth. She wished her lips were the bottle tip, pressing against his.

She was startled by a loud and firm knock at the door.

"Enter," Kash yelled out above the music and the chatter. In walked a young woman, likely the same age as Kash, tall with healthy hips and breasts. The braids packed into a bun at the top of her head made her look royal.

"Kash, please, can you turn this music off or at least turn it down. Those of us who work don't want to hear your nonsense."

"Bose, you complain too much, ah-ahn. Don't you see I have guests here?"

"Bose, please o, no vex," Emeka said.

"Kash, just turn the music off," Chike called out.

How endearing, Patience thought. And with that, she wanted him as intensely as she craved the truth about herself.

"Listen to your friend," Bose said sternly. She looked around the room, then locked eyes with Patience. Stunned, she seemed.

"That's Patience. She's my cousin from Ibadan," Kash said quickly. "She just moved to Lagos to attend UNILAG."

Bose kept her eyes locked on Patience. "Welcome, Patience. So Kash is your cousin? Okay," she said. "Since you have guests I will just go and bury my head to find my peace."

Kash stood and turned the radio down. "Is that okay?"

"Yes, thank you," she said, though she still seemed annoyed. She walked out and closed the door firmly.

"Your neighbor?" Patience said.

"Yes, my neighbor."

"And his former girlfriend," Chike said.

Patience then understood the tension. She looked at Kash. He seemed embarrassed, a rare emotion for him to display openly. She would ask about Bose later.

"If you're going to be around," Chike said, leaning in closer to her, "you have to get used to Kash's women and loud, good-for-nothing debates." He looked at his brother and his friends, who started up yet another discussion about the country's leadership. She sensed Chike was avoiding eye contact with her on purpose.

"So . . . do you really drive okada?"

"Yes, for now." He shifted his weight from one leg to the other, rest-lessly. "I'm still looking for work."

Patience thought about her okada ride here—the haste, the stress, the fear it had brought her. She wanted to ask him how he was coping with such strenuous work.

"Look at you talking about greed!" Kash yelled at Mayowa, killing her chance to extend her conversation with Chike.

"Yes, greed and power! Army officers beat my father at the bank for not lining up! Can you imagine? And you're telling me we don't think it's time for a civilian president!" Mayowa yelled back.

"Sorry about your dad, but if anyone in this place had the oppor-tunity, they would rob Nigeria blind." Her cousin snickered and blew out a long puff of smoke through his nostrils. "Forget this debate. My cousin is here."

Kash looked at Patience from across the room and smiled his usual infectious smile. She smiled back, wondering why his crassness often amused her.

"You know, Patience is a real Americanah," he said. "She can carry her passport and go to the airport and leave this Nigeria tomorrow and go anywhere. All because of American passport. Small blue booklet like that."

Patience was flattered by how he painted her as a true American and intrigued by the power he claimed she had by being born there.

"Is it that simple? I can go to America right now if I have my passport?" she said, stressing the *r* in *passport* but letting the *t* fall, the way an American would.

"Of course. You don't even know yourself," he said, shaking his head.

"Modupe always talks about how Daddy keeps our passports locked in a safe in his closet. Daddy would never give it to me."

"Just go get another one," Kash said. He spoke casually as if he were well versed on the process.

"So I can just say I'm American-born and they will give me a passport?"

"I don't know everything about those foreign things, sha," Kash said. "I know one guy who paid plenty money to get his visa, but if you are American, maybe you can apply for your passport instead of a visa."

"There is no maybe. Any American citizen can go to the American Embassy and apply for their passport," Emeka said confidently. "Just go there and ask."

"Why do you need it? What of UNILAG?" Mayowa said eagerly. Patience was surprised by his concern for her.

"Daddy said my mum is in America somewhere. He won't say where, though, and I haven't seen her in ten years." The room fell completely silent. She felt her hands tremble. She had never discussed her mother, or anything that personal, so openly with strangers.

But the room felt safe, and they made space for her to unload her pain alongside their own—Chike's lack of engineering work, Mayowa's dad's encounter with army officers, Kash admitting to his poor living conditions. It was as if their burdens hung in the air like the haze from their cigarettes.

"Daddy won't tell me anything, really. He just keeps saying she went mad and went back to America, but he won't say where in America. That place is big. But I met one of my mum's old friends who lives here in Lagos. In Ikoyi. I need to visit her. I think she knows where my mum is." Patience hesitated and looked down at her trembling hands. "Kash, can you take me to her?"

"Why not? We can go by bus. How did you get here?"

"Okada."

"Okada? Kai! If Daddy knows you took okada . . ."

"How will I get around in Lagos? Do you see a driver here waiting outside for me?"

"True. All your ajebutter no fit for Lagos."

Kash and his friends laughed. Patience was softened by their amusement.

"I can take you to Ikoyi on Saturday," Chike said. Patience felt her body stiffen. "Just pay me half the fair since you're Kash's cousin."

"Look at this useless man. You would take money from my cousin?"

"You go pay for my mum's hospital bill?" Chike said.

Though Chike spoke in jest, Patience felt he was serious.

"Business is business. I understand," she said, interrupting them. She turned to Chike. "Meet me in front of UNILAG on Saturday at noon."

"I will be there."

"Trust that he will get there even before noon," Kash added. "Chike operates by the book."

Chike waved his friend off, and Patience kept her gaze steady on him. The sparkle in her eyes returned, but this time she didn't bother to blink.

6

PATIENCE FELT HER CHEEKS WARM WHEN SHE SAW CHIKE
parked across the street from the entrance of her school.

She wanted to stand there and keep her gaze fixed on him as he sat gripping his bike's handlebars with his lean muscles jutting through his blue polo shirt.

Fine boy, she thought as she smoothed her braids down at the roots, then pulled them to rest on her left shoulder.

She looked down at her watch: 11:58. He was two minutes early. Kash was right about him.

She waved her hands to get his attention. He revved his engine and drove closer to her.

"Good morning," she said.

"It should be good afternoon at this point," he replied as he fiddled with his rearview mirror.

"You're a little early, so it depends on how you see it."

"Put this on." He handed her a helmet, though he wasn't wearing one himself.

She obeyed and thought of how she hadn't been wearing one when she took an okada the previous day. Neither had the driver.

"Won't you wear a helmet?" she said.

"I forgot it at home, sha. You're Kash's cousin, so I need to keep you safe."

She pressed her lips together to stop herself from smiling. She hopped on the bike and held on to his slender waist gently. His cologne, a pleasant light musk that smelled of new leather and rain, made her want to hold him closer. Tighter. She wondered if he wore it to impress her.

"Ready?" he said.

"Yes. Ikoyi, here we come."

"Actually, if you don't mind, I need to make a quick stop. It's on the way there."

"That's okay," she said.

Chike drove off, gliding steadily against the winds that whipped by. She noticed that he avoided the kinds of abrupt turns and dangerous maneuvers that her driver had managed the day before. For a petroleum engineering graduate, driving an okada must be a disappointment, but somehow Chike's ride made her feel free.

She wondered if he felt the same.

About ten minutes had passed when Chike pulled into a lot where other drivers were parked. He steadied the bike and turned off the engine.

"Peter!" he yelled. "Peter!"

"Chike. How na?" Peter said as he ran toward them.

"I dey, o. This is Patience. You know my friend Kash? Patience is his cousin. She's starting UNILAG."

"Ah, Patience, welcome. Will Chike show you around?"

"We shall see," she said, working to conceal her delight.

"Peter is the person who got me into this crazy business. I should kill him, but I will spare his life."

They laughed.

"Is Mr. Chimezie around?" Chike said.

"Ah, of course now. He is here worrying people. I don't have his full money for next month, sha. Let me go pick up some work so I can pay him. We will chat?"

"Yes."

"In fact, we should go to that bar next weekend to watch the match. I will buy you a beer," Peter said.

"I will let you know."

Peter revved his engine and fastened his helmet. He sped off recklessly.

"That guy, ehn. Driving safely is not his thing," Chike said. He looked toward the other end of the parking lot and let out a deep sigh. "Wait here," he said to Patience like he was about to be disciplined by someone. He got off and walked toward a partially bald man wearing dark sunglasses, jeans, and a long-sleeved shirt, as if he was somehow immune to heat.

"Chike, you get my money?" the man yelled out before Chike approached him fully.

"Mr. Chimezie, I get your money here. Chike calmly handed the man a bundle of naira. The man counted it.

"I hope you no dey cheat me, ehn, Chike?"

"Ah-ahn, why would I?"

"Because I no dey for road when you dey drive my okada."

"I don't cheat."

"Okay, o. That's why I'm giving you special agreement to drive first and pay after."

"Mr. Chimezie, listen," Chike said lowering his voice. Patience saw him speak, but she couldn't make out what he said.

"Increase? Ah, look at you!" Mr. Chimezie said, making no attempt to meet Chike's slight whisper. "You asked me to share a percentage instead of paying one fee. I agree. Now you wan make I give you more percentage?"

"Mr. Chimezie, if I don't pay her bill, her doctor won't treat her again," Chike said, no longer whispering.

"How can ten percent be too small? All dese youth, you dey chop money too much. All you need in life: food and wata. You can even sleep on de roadside and survive. You get house and you belle full, but you no get money for your mama."

As Chike continued to plead, Patience picked at the cracks in her blue nail polish and pretended she didn't hear the conversation. She couldn't believe Chike took home only 10 percent of the money he collected from passengers all day. She hoped that he wasn't actually giving Mr. Chimezie his fair share.

"Listen, because I neva get problem with you, we go do 85–15 percent split. Thas it," he said, lowering his tone, though Patience still heard. "And make you no tell any other driver."

"Thank you, Mr. Chimezie," Chike said, though he still seemed unsatisfied. He walked back to the bike, avoiding eye contact with Patience. He hopped on, started the engine, and drove off without a word.

AFTER A HALF HOUR OF DRIVING, THEY REACHED AN AREA jam-packed with cars.

"This is Martins Street," Chike said. "We are not far from Ikoyi."

The ride became more forceful as he maneuvered through tight traffic.

"Hold on, o," he said. She welcomed his invitation and squeezed his waist tighter.

"Olòdo!" she heard a driver yell out as Chike cut him off with his bike. The minutes passed, and Patience noticed the streets transform. There were mansions much like her father's sitting on roads paved with cobblestones and tar, protected from the outside by large iron gates.

"This must be Ikoyi," she yelled above the motorcycle's engine.

"Yes. That is her house there."

Patience looked up at the two-story mansion, its shade of yellow offering the street a subtle joy even behind its black gate. Chike parked the bike. She stepped off.

"These people are rich, ehn."

"Her husband is a commissioner."

"I wonder how much of the country's money he used to build this house," Chike said sarcastically.

Patience realized then that Chike might have never been inside a home like this.

"High government official. Serving Nigeria means securing himself."

Patience thought of her father. Was he planning to do just that as commissioner in Oyo? She was sure Kash had told him about her father's position.

"Anyway, sha, I will be around in the area, but let's meet here in one hour."

"What if I'm delayed?"

"Then I will circle back every thirty minutes after that to see when you return. But try to keep to time."

"Thanks for the ride," she said as she locked eyes with him. His lips curled into a smirk. He looked down and broke their connection.

"No problem," he said as he put on the helmet she had taken off. He revved his bike and drove away.

Patience took a deep breath. She knocked on the gate. A man appeared.

"Who are you?"

"I'm here to see Aunty Lola."

"What is your name?"

"Patience. Patience Adewale."

"Okay, she has been expecting you."

Patience walked through the gate, then approached the front door and rang the bell. A young woman dressed in a maid's uniform opened the door.

"Good afternoon."

"Good afternoon. I'm here to see Aunty Lola."

"Patience, is that you? Wow, come in, come in."

Patience felt a sense of warmth flood over her when she stepped inside Aunty Lola's home. She wasn't sure if the feeling came from the woman's natural kindness or the decor in the entrance, where palms sat inside bone-colored clay pots and slender marble vases cinched bouquets of long-stem roses. The opulence reminded her of being at home in Ibadan, but Aunty Lola made her father and Modupe's decorating seem gaudy.

Patience admired a large portrait of her holding her two young girls close, with her husband standing behind.

"Patience, you're looking so beautiful," she said as she reached to hug her.

"Thank you." Though she hardly felt beautiful. When she hopped off Chike's okada in front of the house, she had caught a whiff of her own stench. She decided then that her life in Lagos called for a new deodorant.

"Please, feel at home here," Aunty Lola said, walking her into the den.

The place felt inviting, even with its fancy trimmings. Patience watched as four house girls bounced around like flies, sweeping the buffed marble floors, dusting crystals that dangled from the slender chandelier, fluffing the matching throw pillows on chairs upholstered with a gold paisley print, and spraying mosquito repellent onto the plush burgundy drapes.

"I am still decorating, but so far I like how everything is looking. I hope you were able to find us without much problem."

"Yes, the journey wasn't bad."

Aunty Lola smiled. It was the same smile she had flashed when Patience saw her at her father's party in Ibadan.

"Are you hungry? Of course you must be, look at the time. Let us eat." She led Patience down a long hallway without waiting for her response.

"Kike, go and tell Augustin to bring out the food for our guest." She patted the house girl gently on her shoulder. Patience thought of her stepmother, Modupe, and how she usually berated and manhandled house help in front of guests.

When they reached the dining room, Patience was struck by its charm, with its display of antique china in cherry wood cabinets, floral seat cushions and curtains, and a large shiny birch wood table. She imagined her mother trading decorating advice with her best friend when her life had been less complicated.

"Please sit," said Aunty Lola. The woman sat next to her and stared at her intensely, barely allowing her eyes to divert.

"Thank you so much for inviting me into your home," Patience said timidly. She felt herself shrink from Aunty Lola's penetrating gaze.

"I am so happy you're here. Your father has hardly let anyone visit you over the years. When I saw you at that party, I knew it was you immediately. You know, Folami and I started calling each other 'best friend' in secondary school. You look exactly like her."

"I think so too. I have a few photos of her, and I can see how we look alike." It excited Patience to hear that she resembled her mother. Her father only told her that she had inherited what he deemed her mother's faults—she was too headstrong for a woman and too irresponsible.

"How is your half sister? She must be in secondary school by now."

"Yes, Margaret is now in SS2. She's doing well."

"Wow. So have you explored Lagos yet?"

"Just a little on my way here today."

Patience decided not to tell Aunty Lola, a woman married to a man with a lofty position in government, that she, the daughter of another man of prominence, had caught a bus to Mushin of all places.

"Welcome to Lagos. My daughter Bimpe finished at UNILAG last year. She lives at home now, trying to decide if she wants to work in Nigeria or move to London to maybe do her postgraduate degree. I told her she should go abroad, but she has all her friends here. What are you reading at UNILAG?"

"Accounting, Ma. Daddy thought it would be best for me, but I would have preferred journalism or marketing. I like making clothes too."

"Journalism . . . Marketing? Making clothes means you would be a tailor, no?"

"Yes. I mean, no. Something like that. I want to be a designer."

The woman frowned. "Patience, people will tell you you're doing a hobby."

"In America, being a designer is a high honor. I wouldn't mind going there if it means I can find my mum."

Aunty Lola took a deep breath and looked away. Patience's heart quickened.

"Aunty Lola, I haven't seen or heard from my mum since she left. Daddy told me she went back to America. I don't know anything else. Have you heard from her?"

The woman sighed and gently placed her hand on Patience's. As she worked to form her words, Augustin walked in, balancing two food trays on his upturned palms. Aunty Lola rested her back against her chair and smiled as if she welcomed the distraction.

"Oya, serve our guest." They watched quietly when he carefully lifted the top of each silver dish beautifully trimmed with gold, then placed white rice and stew, along with cubes of meat, neatly onto Patience's plate.

"That's enough, thank you, Mr. Augustin," Patience said.

"It's okay, madam."

"Ma, have you heard from my mother?" Patience said again once Augustin left the room.

Aunty Lola took a deep breath. "I have, but it's been a long time. She stopped calling me years ago."

"Where is she? What is she doing?" Patience tried to keep her composure. This was a sign, she thought.

"The last I heard from your mother, she was in New York. She always wanted to live there."

Patience had often thought of visiting New York City. Any place dubbed the fashion capital of the world was where she needed to be. She had also read about stage plays on Broadway and how New York City was as energetic as Lagos.

"When your mum and Kolade moved back to Nigeria, she told me she wasn't ready to come back, but your daddy insisted. Later I heard that it was Modupe who wanted to move back to Nigeria, and your daddy followed. Modupe had already had your half sister when you were all living in America."

Patience thought of her mother's letter to her father: "You know what you did to damage me . . . You made your choice long before we moved back to Nigeria."

There was a prickly silence. Patience wished Aunty Lola would offer more about Modupe. She didn't.

"Modupe—I mean my stepmum—she wanted to move back to Nigeria?" Patience said.

"I'm sure you know by now what Modupe was." Aunty Lola reached out and stroked Patience's hand gently.

Patience pondered over her family's muted history, the bits and pieces she remembered, the things she had figured out on her own.

"I thought being in Nigeria would be good for your mum so she didn't lose touch with home, but being with Kolade in Nigeria . . ."

"What do you mean, Ma?"

"His family. They didn't give her peace. Folami had her own way of thinking."

"I remember the day Daddy threw her out of the house," Patience said. "My uncle Timi was there too, but I don't know why they put her out. Do you know what happened?"

"Well, I don't know the full story. When I asked her, she was too embarrassed to tell me the details. All I know is that she fought to stay with you. She went to court even, but it's hard for a woman going up against a man like Kolade."

Her father had never mentioned anything about a court case. He had painted her mum as a woman who had picked up and left her responsibilities because she was too crazy to cope with life. Patience had reconciled that it was her father's empty excuse.

Her mother's letter to her. She remembered her words: "I really tried, but sometimes in life we have to accept when we lose."

Finally, she understood. Her mother had tried to regain custody of her. Of course she didn't just abandon her without a fight.

"Let your daddy keep you for now." Were those the words of a woman who had gone mad?

"Did my mother lose her mind?" Patience said after taking another deep breath. "Daddy said so."

"Lose her mind?" Aunty Lola chuckled. "A man will always say a woman is crazy when he wants to ruin her. But it wasn't like that. She went to New York to get away from everything. There was too much going on with her in Nigeria, and on top of everything Kolade did, her mother died. You know, stress can kill our elders quicker than anything. Imagine an old woman like that seeing her only child disgraced by her in-laws. She was all the family your mum really had. Your mum didn't keep relations with her half siblings."

Patience felt a bubble form in her chest.

"It was too much all at once," Aunty Lola continued. "She called me when she got to New York. She called me several times after, but then she stopped calling. I tried to reach her, but her number was disconnected. I assumed she needed to start a new life without a reminder of what happened."

"So how do you know she's still in New York?"

"Patience, I *don't* know."

"Why didn't she ever come back to Nigeria?"

"I . . . don't know."

Patience had a bad thought. What if her mother was dead? Why would she have just stopped calling her best friend? "Aunty, I need to find her. I have to go look for her. I need my passport. How do I get it?"

"Ṣebi you have your old passport?"

"My daddy has it."

"Well, that's what you need, your old passport, to get a new one, and money for your plane ticket and of course spending money when you get to America," she said. "That place is not like Nigeria, where your daddy will send you out with a driver. You have to have money." Aunty Lola stroked Patience's hand gently. "Take time, finish school, then think of seeing your mother. You are too young to be going to America alone with nothing, because you know your papa is not going to sponsor this."

"How can I get my passport without asking Daddy for it?"

"Well, you are a citizen of the United States, so you can go to the American Embassy in VI and apply for it. Do you have your birth certificate?"

"No, Daddy has it, I'm sure."

"My dear, as I said, take time. I am telling you about your mum because I want you to know that she didn't just abandon you. But wait until you finish school. I'm sure your daddy will give you everything once you become a woman. Because unless you steal it from him, I know there is no way you will get it from Kolade."

Steal it.

Aunty Lola had spoken those words as if it would be a treacherous act, but what Patience had heard was a viable option, a great possibility. How could she wait another four years to find out if her mother was still breathing?

"Aunty, please, if you can help me get some of my identification, I promise you I won't go to America right away. Daddy doesn't want me to see her, so he may never give me my American documents."

The woman hesitated. "Okay . . . I can ask around to see how we can apply to get just your birth certificate. But, Patience, be careful.

I think you should look for her one day, but you also have to be prepared for any outcome."

The door began to rattle, then in walked a young woman. Patience was taken aback by the allure of her tight black jeans, her red form-fitting bodysuit, and her black suede choker. Here was a true Lagos babe.

"Mummy, what did Augustin cook? I'm so hungry."

"Bimpe, where are your manners? This is Patience. She is the daughter of an old friend of mine. You may or may not remember each other because you were so young. Patience, this is my daughter Bimpe, the one who just finished UNILAG. Patience is at UNILAG now, Bimpe."

"Yeah, I would have finished a year ago if not for the lecturers being on strike so much," Bimpe said as she rolled her eyes.

University strikes, Patience thought. If she listened to Aunty Lola's advice, she would have to wait even longer than four years to reunite with her mum. "Patience, welcome," Bimpe said.

"Thank you." Patience could feel Bimpe staring at her. She wondered if her makeup and the floral baby-doll dress she was wearing impressed her.

"What brings you to see my dear sweet mother?" she said sarcastically.

"You should pray to get to my age and have the youth in your life visit you," Aunty Lola quipped.

Patience was delighted by the idea of Aunty Lola claiming her as one of the youth in her life.

"Your mum and my mum were best friends before my mum moved to New York." Patience felt a sense of pride in knowing more about her mother's path.

"Wow, New York," Bimpe said as Augustin put food on her plate.

"Yes, New York. I was just telling Aunty Lola that I will go there to see her once I get my passport."

Out of the corner of her eye, she observed Bimpe, who was sitting next to her, putting scoops of rice in her mouth and tearing away at her meat.

"Of course you would be this hungry when you don't eat breakfast," Aunty Lola said.

"I'm fine without breakfast. It's Augustin who didn't boil this meat long enough. It's too hard."

Patience imagined herself discussing things that were meaningful yet meaningless with her own mother.

"Bimpe, why don't you take Patience up to your room," said Aunty Lola once her daughter took the last bite and wiped off her mouth and hands with a white cloth napkin.

"Sure, why not?"

She stood and led Patience up the steps. Patience felt herself growing anxious to see where Bimpe laid her head at night and where she got dressed for social functions.

"That's my room," Bimpe said, pointing at the very first door at the top of the stairs. She leaned in to whisper. "It's a great spot to be in when I need to sneak out of the house, you know what I mean?"

"Yes, of course," Patience said, still mesmerized by Bimpe, though she had no clue what it felt like to sneak out. There was hardly anywhere for her to sneak off to in Ibadan. Her new life in Lagos posed no barriers. She was free to come and go as she pleased.

Walking into Bimpe's room made Patience fall for her even harder. The walls were covered with posters of American R&B artists—En Vogue, Toni Braxton, Jade, TLC, Jodeci, Mary J., Bobby Brown.

"Take a seat on my bed if you want. I'm going to change my clothes."

Bimpe disappeared into her walk-in closet.

Patience scanned the room: Bimpe's Covergirl makeup was laid out on a small vanity; her bed, a beautiful white wood canopy; her dresser, the same color. Some of her shoes formed a pile in a corner of the room—high-heeled canvas sneakers, wedge platforms, and Keds tennis shoes.

"Where do you buy your clothes?" Patience said.

Bimpe chuckled as she emerged from her closet wearing a white T-shirt and baggy denim shorts, her laugh similar to her mother's.

"Mostly abroad. I love a few other smaller boutiques here in Lagos, but Mummy gets me the things I want when she goes to London and America. Whenever I go on holiday, I come back with loads and loads of things. What about you?"

Patience was startled by her question. Surely her clothes weren't anything to discuss, especially with Bimpe.

"I love clothes, but my father doesn't buy me any stylish things from abroad."

"Yeah, I can tell by your mufti," Bimpe said, looking Patience up and down. "It's not the best."

Patience's heart fell into her gut.

"Well, you're welcome to take a look in my closet. There might be a few things I don't wear anymore that I can give you one day. But not today."

"Really?"

"Of course. If not you, the house girl will get them."

If Bimpe were anyone else, Patience would be offended by her grandstanding. But all Patience felt was an intense need to embody her, because Bimpe and girls like her, who enjoyed foreign things the way they did and moved about with privilege the way they did, had the know-how to become whomever they wanted to become, even when they set cruel intentions. Patience knew her kind well. She had encountered girls like Bimpe in boarding school.

She had befriended the daughters of lawyers, accountants, military officers, and business owners. The worst of them had figured out how to rank one another based on their parents' amassed wealth, their beauty, and their overall appeal. For Patience and Margaret, their father's financial status never saved them from being socially inept. She and Margaret were insignificant because they weren't well traveled, despite their father's money. They weren't overly pampered, despite his success. They were the children of a rich man who did the bare minimum for them.

"Your father hasn't even come to pick you up. Did he lose all his money?" Patience remembered being asked the time she and Margaret didn't get a visit from him when Modupe traveled for a full year for the last job she had before she settled on being a rich man's wife.

Throughout their stay in the boarding school, she felt like she was standing on the outside of a chain-link fence, gazing through spaces that revealed the joys of others. All the while, girls like Bimpe moved with a kind of self-assurance that felt like sorcery. Patience wanted in on it. Even if it only gave a limited sense of self, it was assurance nonetheless.

"Go ahead. You can take a look inside my closet," Bimpe said.

Patience walked in, willing herself to stay cool. She hoped she didn't seem too overzealous as she sorted through skirts, jeans, body-suits, and belts. Patience studied the labels to find out which brands Bimpe preferred.

"Patience, come. Let me style your braids."

Patience observed Bimpe in the mirror as she pulled a few braids up, crisscrossed some in front, gathered a few in back, straightened some, and let a few hang loose.

"I don't understand how you can be American, and your mum is in America, and you have no baffs from America."

"I haven't been back since I was eight, and I haven't seen my mother in ten years."

"I see," Bimpe said. She paused and stared at Patience's reflection in the mirror. "Why haven't you seen her?"

"Honestly, I don't really know. I just know that she was forced out by my dad."

Bimpe paused again. She worked on Patience's braids quietly, her expression unreadable.

"I'm going to find my way to New York to see her," Patience said.

"I've been there a few times. Going to New York is nothing for me."

"I'm sure."

"Do you have a boyfriend?" Bimpe said.

"No, I don't. Not yet."

"Me and my boyfriend, Ade, have been together since UNILAG. See his photo." Bimpe rolled her eyes playfully as she handed Patience the four-by-six picture.

Patience studied the photo. He was dark, tall, fresh-faced, handsome—the kind of guy who fit perfectly into the life map of a babe like Bimpe.

"See your new hair," Bimpe said when she was done styling her braids.

Patience looked in the mirror. Her long plaits sat on the crown of her head in a crisscrossed ponytail. If she took a photo of herself, she would be at home on Bimpe's wall alongside the American R&B girl groups.

"All you need are some hoop earrings, and you'll look so fine." Bimpe stuck a pair in Patience's ears. Without warning, she grabbed a tube of burgundy lipstick and smeared it on Patience's top and bottom lips.

"Nobody does the one lip thing anymore," said Bimpe. Patience should have known not to take makeup tips from Modupe of all people, the same Modupe who lined her lips with black eyeliner before adding an obnoxious shade of gold on her pout.

When Bimpe finished, Patience looked at herself. This was the start of the transformation she had always imagined. She wondered what Chike would think of it. She looked down at her watch.

Chike!

"Wow, I need to be going. I'm supposed to be meeting someone who will take me home."

Patience gathered herself, and they left her room and walked downstairs.

"Mum, Patience is leaving!"

"So soon?" Aunty Lola said as she approached the bottom of the staircase.

"Yes, Ma, I have to get going."

"Well, Patience, we look forward to seeing you here again. If you ever need anything, don't hesitate to ask."

Patience felt comforted by her invitation.

She walked out of the door and into the front yard, then out of the gate, back into the world of Ikoyi's quiet streets. She felt encased in loneliness brought on by her departure and the thick haze in the afternoon sky. She looked out into the street. The bouquet of fog in the distance parted slowly, revealing Chike riding his okada with ease.

He was a beautiful man—more beautiful than Bimpe's Ade.

He sped up and stopped a few feet away from her.

"Wow, you look . . . different," he said as he stared at her, almost frozen.

"Thank you. But is different good or bad?"

He ignored the question and took off his helmet. "So, did you find your mum?" he said. Patience wasn't sure whether to be pleased that he cared to ask or to be annoyed by his brash demeanor.

"No, it's a little more complicated than that." She hesitated. "So do you actually pay Mr. Chimezie the right amount?"

Chike ticked his head back in shock and squinted. "You were listening."

"It was hard not to. Mr. Chimezie isn't exactly the most discreet person."

Chike's eyes darted around, landing on each part of her face.

It was as if he was first discovering her. "I'm not going home right away. Do you need to get back to UNILAG now?"

"Not right away. My lectures begin on Monday. I'm sure that's when I will start getting pounded with work."

"Your instincts are correct. I remember those days at UI."

They laughed, and he softened his gaze. Patience realized then that it was the first time since arriving in Lagos that she had gotten a full look at him.

All of him.

He had changed from the day they had met in Ibadan two years before. She remembered Kash introducing them when she walked into their room at UI's hostel for a visit. She shook his hand and hoped he didn't notice any sign of her heart doing the Running Man across her chest. He didn't. He barely noticed her at all.

She, on the other hand, noticed everything about him, so she could see how Lagos had changed him. She knew how the bronze complexion he had in Ibadan had become slightly dull and scorched by the sun in Lagos; how the big city had put a new bend in his back that whittled him down at least an inch; and how in Lagos his penetrating eyes were punctuated underneath with circles a shade darker than his skin.

And despite it all, he was still the most handsome man she had ever seen.

"I'm going to Allen Avenue. There's an arcade there that I go to whenever I need to stop thinking about whatever I'm thinking about. You can join me if you want."

"I haven't really been to an arcade."

"Okay, well, I can take you to UNILAG if you don't want to come," he said quickly.

"No, I want to come." And she did.

7

WHEN PATIENCE WALKED INTO THE ARCADE BEHIND CHIKE, she was pleasantly surprised by the scene.

"This or that!" the members of Black Sheep belted from the sound system, their voices and the beat almost drowning out the loud computerized noises the games made.

People stood with their faces glued to consoles, while others queued up for a turn. Chike walked toward the back of the room with his hands stuffed in his pockets. Patience followed.

They stopped in front of one machine, and Chike gave it a pat. "This is the game I usually play back to back," he said.

"'Mortal Kombat,'" Patience read from the top of the machine as Chike inserted his money. "Sounds deadly."

"Deadly and fun. There's always a long queue to play, but I think there's a challenge on the game we saw in the front there."

Chike put a few kobo into the machine, then two fighters named Scorpion and Sub Zero appeared on screen and began their battle—flipping, punching, kicking.

"Finish him!" she heard one of the characters from the game say.

Chike bent his elbows as he pressed hard on the controllers. His opponent fell, and he clapped his hands to celebrate the victory.

"Yes!" he yelled. "Do you want to try a round?"

"Why not?" she said.

He explained each button to her, then she chose her fighter: Sonya Blade.

"Fight!" the computerized voice from the game announced.

Patience pressed the buttons and leaned in as she had seen Chike do. Sonya Blade took a generous share of blows from Sub Zero, only managing to return a few before she was knocked out.

"I have to do that again," Patience said after her defeat.

Chike laughed. "It looks like you'll become as addicted as I am."

"Well, I'm sure you can do more to help me sharpen my skills." Her flirting surprised her. Chike seemed unfazed.

"Let's play again. I will show you some moves."

Chike inserted more money into the machine and played a round himself, calling out each of the buttons he pressed and the moves they created.

Patience took over after seeing him win several more times. She lost again. "This game is broken," she said.

"If it's broken, how did I win?" he said, amused. "Let me show you again. This time, I'll hold your hands." He towered behind her, wrapped his arms around hers, and placed her fingers in the right places. He started the game and pressed her fingers on the buttons. Patience felt her body go warm.

"You see, you're winning," he said.

That she couldn't see, because the game no longer concerned her. She wanted to turn around and put her arms around his waist and bury her head in his chest. From there, she would lift her head and move her lips toward his.

"Ah, madam, victory!" he yelled. He let go of her hands, grabbed her biceps, and shook her gently with excitement. A sensual ache shot through her lower abdomen, and suddenly she felt her heart pumping between her legs.

"That was great," she said, hoping he didn't notice her silently managing her desires. She wondered if he was doing the same.

"Maybe we can get to a point where we can play each other," he said, tapping the second set of controls on the game.

"Maybe."

The two took a break from Mortal Kombat and wandered around the arcade. Patience ran to the Pac-Man console and began a round. She won and jumped up yelling. Chike's laugh echoed behind her.

"Yes! Yes!" she yelled. She regained her composure and ran over to the Tetris game.

"I think I've found my calling in life," she said. "My first time playing and look at that score."

"Okay, beside Tetris and Pac-Man, what is really your calling in life?" he said as she geared up for another round.

"I'll be studying accounting. My dad decided it's best." She rolled her eyes.

"They do say Daddy knows best. But what do you want?"

"Nothing . . . I don't know. Just . . . something."

"You won't tell me, and you see what I'm doing after studying petroleum engineering?"

"I like clothes," she said, flattered that he pried for the truth. "My daddy brought my stepmum a *Vogue* magazine from America one time, and I read it so much the pages started to tear. The best articles were about the designers. And I started thinking, what if I could become a designer? What if I could make the best clothes and wear the best clothes?"

"Yeah, I'm sure your father would say something like 'My daughter will not become a bloody tailor! Nonsense!'" he said, exaggerating his words. Their laughter felt synchronized. Patience couldn't stop herself, but it was as if he caught himself. He stared at her with nothing in particular in his eyes. Then he looked away.

Patience looked back at her round of Tetris and realized she had gone below her highest score.

"Okay, this game is finished with me."

"Do you want to walk down Allen Avenue? That's what I do after I play."

"Of course," she said, hoping she didn't sound desperate.

As they walked down the road, Chike stuffed his hands into his pockets.

"Do you really remember me from the time I came to visit Kash at UI?" Patience said.

"Of course I do. Why wouldn't I?"

"No reason." She decided not to point out that he treated her like Kash's baby cousin rather than the woman she wanted him to see. "You did something that day that I never forgot," she said instead.

"What's that?"

"When we took a stroll around campus—you, me, Kash, and Kash's girlfriend—what was her name?"

"Kash and his many girlfriends. Who can keep track?"

"Anyway. When we were walking, we saw two girls together buying food at the canteen. Kash said one of the girls was a girl you liked and had been trying to toast."

"Oh, I remember!"

"Well, I remember how Kash told you to talk to her, to ask her out, to offer to buy her food. But you said no, not there. You said you didn't want to because you didn't want her friend to feel like she wasn't important, like she wasn't fine enough to be toasted by a guy."

"I remember."

"Most guys don't care about that kind of thing when they want a girl."

"Well, it's just the way I see things," he said.

"It's a good way to see things." She turned to him and looked into his eyes as they strolled slowly. He held her gaze with his, then let go.

There was a silence. Patience wanted to change the subject. She couldn't bring herself to tell him that what he had said that day made her want to know him. All of him.

"That Mr. Chimezie, he's really a nuisance, right?" Patience said.

"Well, I rent his bike, and he sees me as a small boy. He agreed to do a special deal with me, so I try not to complain about him."

"But what about engineering?"

"We live in a country that is one of the largest suppliers of oil, but a petroleum engineering graduate can still struggle to find work if he doesn't have the right connections. So you can say, I have to wait like every other jobless person."

"Wow."

"Anyway, we do what we can, sha. What about you? Your mum's situation?"

"Aunty Lola told me she was in New York the last time they spoke. She thinks she's still there." Patience was too afraid to mention that the thought of her being dead had crossed her mind.

"New York. You're really an American girl."

"Yes. A little. I mean, I've been living in Nigeria since I was eight."

"And you still talk like an American all this time?"

"I try to keep my accent," Patience said. She thought fondly of the endless hours she spent watching *The Fresh Prince of Bel-Air* on video. "When Daddy told me my mum went back there, I became obsessed with the place."

"So he told you she's in America, right?"

"Yes, but he never said where."

"So you think you can go to New York?"

"I have to. I need my passport. The money for a plane ticket—that's another thing entirely. But if I can get my passport from Daddy, I will have some hope."

"Hope is good when there's nothing else."

"My dad is a difficult man, you know. He's even cruel at times."

"And he's a commissioner now, which means he will take his share of money from Oyo State contracts that he will give to his friends. Can you imagine that a man contracted by the government to tar a road would take the money to buy a Mercedes? Then he will drive it on the same broken street he was supposed to fix. Your papa will chop from that money. You're not a baby. You should know how it works."

"Yes, I know how it works, but you're saying it like I'm my dad."

"No, you're not him," he said, his tone apologetic.

She accepted his indirect apology, because she wanted him, though she wasn't supposed to want someone like him. He was the kind who couldn't mingle with her father's kind. He was lucky to go to school and get a degree, and yet, with the chance he was given, he still hadn't become somebody her father would consider worth wanting.

But she imagined Chike would never understand that she didn't feel like her father's type either. She was an accidental version. Aspirational. She often wondered if she was supposed to feel lucky that her father had kept her, since he didn't keep her mother.

They stopped walking, and Patience realized that they were back in front of the arcade.

"What's ailing your mum?"

"She can barely walk with her arthritis," he said, taking an audible breath. "Her doctor has been treating her, but he stopped. Emeka and I have to settle her bill before they give her any more treatment and any further diagnosis. Her job forced her to retire because of it."

"So settle her bill."

"What did you say before? It's a bit more complicated than that, right?"

"I did," she said, slightly embarrassed. "Your mum must be in a lot of pain."

Chike let out another audible breath. "We will go to Enugu to see her in a few weeks' time after I gather more money."

Patience thought about her father and the amount of money he'd made in his lifetime. A man like him could pay for Chike's mum's hospital bills as if he were spending petty cash. She hoped the increase Mr. Chimezie had agreed to would be enough.

"I was the first to graduate from university out of all of my cousins. Emeka didn't go to university either. It's my time to take care of her."

"What about your dad?"

"He died before I started university."

Patience hesitated. She wanted to tell him sorry, but she felt her silence spoke enough. "Does Emeka have a job?" she said.

"Listen, my brother is a good man, but he doesn't always make smart choices. I won't give up on him, though."

"You shouldn't. You know, my sister, Margaret, she is the one person in my life who I can honestly say loves me genuinely," she said. "Everybody else is a question in my mind. But Margaret, she's different. She's only my half sister, you know?"

"So I assume you love her the same."

Patience fell silent again. Did she love Margaret the same? Questioning this made her wonder if she loved Margaret solely because Margaret loved her. Suddenly she felt selfish.

"I think I should take you back to UNILAG now to avoid the traffic on my way home."

"Yes, I should be getting back," she said, relieved that he didn't wait for her answer.

WHEN CHIKE PARKED HIS BIKE CLOSE TO THE ENTRANCE of UNILAG, Patience got off, unstrapped her helmet, and gave it to him. She dug in her purse and pulled out a small bundle of naira.

"Don't worry about the money," he said.

Patience shook her head and pressed the money onto his chest. She had been yearning to touch him there the whole night. "Put this toward your mother's health funds. Please, I insist."

"No, really. I never wanted your money. You're Kash's little cousin."

Patience felt deflated when she heard the word *little*. After all the progress they had made at the arcade, it was as if he was pulling away from her. She refused to allow it. She came closer to him on the bike.

"If you're not going to take the money, I have to at least say thank you," she said. She leaned in and kissed his lips. They were as soft as she imagined. She felt the throbbing in her underwear again as he slipped his tongue into her mouth.

Finally.

She had done something she had wanted to do since she left the partial freedom of boarding school life. No Daddy there to dictate. No Modupe around to scold her, then recant with a false truce.

Chike pulled away slowly.

"Okay, so this ride wasn't a free ride," he said. He smiled hard as she pressed her hand on his shoulder, still holding the money.

His words became their running joke, as he kissed her each time she hopped off his bike, each time he took her on a ride to show her around Lagos after his shift and after she was done with school, or when she would come back from his place after watching *Scarface* and kung fu movies she could hardly remember the names of, and each time they returned to UNILAG from playing Mortal Kombat and Pac-Man at the arcade.

"This wasn't a free ride," he would say, and she would lean in and kiss him just as she had the first time.

8

"GOOD AFTERNOON, SA."

Patience greeted her professor along with her classmates at the start of the lecture. She looked around at the seemingly eager faces in the room as she always did. She wondered if she could spot her fellow imposters. After all, there had to be others who were there only to satisfy familial expectations.

"As I've said before, I expect most of you to understand the basics of accounting by the end of the term. Some of you will not. Some of you will be utter failures." The professor curled his upper lip in disgust. "That is to be expected. Nobody has ever gotten an A in my course."

"He is a difficult man, but I don't care," Tolani whispered. "Let him challenge us." Patience thought of how Tolani had locked arms with her and spun her around in their room the day she realized they had the same course, same day, same time. Patience, however, couldn't return the enthusiasm in any sort of authentic way.

"Many of you are distracted by different things," the professor continued. "Do not allow anything or anyone to derail your studies."

Patience looked at the board as he scribbled "Accounting Principles," and she wondered if he could smell her discontent from where he stood.

Weeks dragged on, and each time she entered that class she had to beat back the urge to gouge her eyes out. Then one morning, she didn't want to get out of bed. When she finally did, she had her bath, then gazed at her reflection in the mirror. She felt different. Deflated. Emotionally sore. She knew then that she was no longer interested in following a forced rhythm.

She walked back to her room. Tolani and Ayanti were still there, idling about. She had hoped they would have left without her.

"Ayanti, let me borrow your brush," Tolani said.

"Which kind borrow? Like when you didn't return it that other time?" Ayanti said.

"Ah now, Patience, Şebi you saw me use that brush and put it back?"

"No . . . I mean yes, I remember."

Ayanti and Tolani were like two quarreling cocks constantly try-ing to pull her into their meaningless spats. Patience walked toward her wardrobe and almost tripped over Ayanti's pile of stuff—clothes, handbags, books.

"Sorry, o, Patience. Ayanti, keep your clothes to your side!" Tolani snapped.

Patience looked at the empty bed not being used by anyone, and she was thankful she didn't have a third roommate. Somehow life in her boarding school had been far less hectic. Then she remembered she was in a notably different frame of mind here. Back then, there had been no Aunty Lola. No new information about her family's past.

"Patience, you're just finishing your bath. I won't be late with you," said Tolani.

"Just go on without me. I will be there."

"Late again?" Tolani shook her head in disbelief.

"I will rush," Patience said with little eagerness.

"Okay," Tolani said suspiciously before she and Ayanti walked out. Patience leafed through her wardrobe and pulled out a pair of jeans and a T-shirt. She slapped cream on her forearms and face, grabbed her bag, and hesitated. She was officially late but still in no hurry. She dug inside her wardrobe where she kept her mother's things, pulled her Becky book out, and looked though it slowly.

She looked at the clock.

She was fifteen minutes late.

Patience smoothed out the bent edge of the book with her thumb, then put it back in her wardrobe. She put on her shoes, walked out toward the staircase in the hallway, and stopped. The emptiness came over her like dew settling on an open plain.

She reached the bottom of the staircase, walked in the opposite direction of her typical route to class, quickened her feet to a near jog, then boarded the shuttle bus. A distance from UNILAG, she deboarded.

She passed the stalls where treats were sold, passed houses, passed the usual cast of street hawkers. Then her eyes settled on a site she had never noticed in the area: a tailor who had set up shop on the roadside next to a stationery printing shop. He sat in front of his sewing machine, which rested on a table held up by two large wooden planks above an open gutter, his face buried in his work. Patience listened to the motor of his machine and wished she were him. She stared as he worked on bright green Ankara, the fabric moving through the machine, piling down at his feet. He looked up and met her stare. Startled, she looked away and continued walking toward the bus that would take her to Kash's.

If Chike wasn't working, she would head to Chike's place instead.

9

"KASH, IT'S ME. LET ME IN," PATIENCE CALLED OUT AS SHE knocked on his door.

Kash swung the door open and ushered her in. "Another unannounced guest," he said.

"So that's how you greet me . . . and what do you mean, unannounced?"

She walked in and was shocked by the sight of Chike sitting on Kash's chair, gripping the key to his bike. He looked up at her, surprised, then seemingly relieved to see her.

"You're here too," Patience said.

"I'm here," Chike said.

Patience sat down across from him, then for a moment they stared at each other as if Kash weren't there walking back and forth, going on about something she couldn't hear. She was too lost in Chike—too charmed by the thought of his lips on hers. They had done so much of that during their alone time together, she could hardly see him without wanting to kiss him.

If only Chike would tell Kash and the others about how they'd been spending time together, there would be no need for them to be coy.

"Patience, don't you have lectures at this time?" Kash sat next to Chike on the couch, holding a bottle of Malta.

"I tried to go."

"You tried, ehn? I can't wait to hear what Daddy says when you tell him you *tried* to go to your lectures."

"This accounting thing, I don't know." She let out a deep sigh and adjusted her braids.

"So you and Chike are having a bad day and you've come to dump your sorrows on me."

"What happened to you today?" she asked Chike, hoping she didn't sound as concerned as she was.

"One idiot jumped off my okada and didn't pay. It happened down the road, so I came here to clear my mind."

"Did you catch him?" Patience said.

"He ran. I let him go, but I wish I had chased him down and slapped the nonsense out of him."

"Letting him go was the right thing to do," Kash said. "For a man to steal like that, he must be a desperate somebody."

"So, because he's desperate, Chike should suffer the consequences of his lost time? His lost pay? Kash, please. The man was wrong."

"Don't mind him," Chike said. "He will always defend a thief."

"So that's what you think of me?"

"No, that's what I know of you, and I've known you for a long time," Chike said, amused.

"So, the two of you can't judge the situation for what it is? A poor man needed a ride but he was too ashamed to ask you to do it for free, so he took the ride from you," Kash said.

"How do you know the man is poor?" Chike said.

"And why don't you understand why the man was wrong?" Patience said.

"Because my thinking is too far ahead," Kash said. He took a gulp of his drink.

"My dear cousin, you've been insane for too long. It's time for you to admit it," Patience said.

"I will never admit to such a lie. What I will admit is that I've only had egg to eat all day, so I am still hungry and this Malta can't hold me, so Patience, go and buy suya for me near the market. There's one guy there who starts selling at this time."

"So on my bad day you send me to get suya for you?"

"Let me go with you," Chike said.

"Yes, go with her. Show her the place." Kash stood and walked toward his kitchenette and put his Malta bottle in the moldy bucket he used as a trash bin. Chike looked at Patience and tilted his head toward the door.

"Yes, Chike, you *should* come," she said, then she pressed her lips together to mask her excitement.

AS SOON AS PATIENCE AND CHIKE REACHED A COMFORT-able distance from Kash's place, she slipped her hand into his large, smooth palm and clasped hers around his. The area was especially active with crowds of students trekking about. When Chike squeezed her hand, she felt at one with a pack of secondary school girls who giggled as boys called out to them.

"So accounting is giving you wahala?" he said. He loosened his grip on her palm and let go.

"You know what I wish I was doing instead."

"Oh, yes, *our* designer. So what exactly makes a designer different from a tailor?"

Patience turned to examine his face to make sure he was joking. The curl of his top lip gave him away.

"What kind of silly question . . ." She pushed his shoulder.

"I actually don't know the difference, to be honest. Most clothes are made over and over again, so how does a designer really invent anything?"

"That's like me asking you, why do we need another petroleum engineer? Can't they just keep digging regular holes in the ground to get oil out? Or what is it that you are trying to do again?"

"Ha! You still haven't answered me. What does a designer actually invent?"

"You think because I let you kiss me you can ask me nonsense questions?"

Chike was quiet, and she wondered why he didn't respond to her mention of how they'd kissed. What was he thinking?

"You should try and concentrate on your studies," he said finally. It wasn't what she wanted to hear.

"Chike, I think you should try and concentrate on finding passengers who won't jump off your bike without paying you."

"Patience, you're really something else," he said. He shook his head, amused, then put his arm around her waist and rubbed her side gently, melting her frustrations. When they made their way beyond the side streets, she stopped and turned to face him. She gripped his forearms, inviting him to kiss her.

He looked at the crowd of people they were approaching, then pulled away.

"We can do this somewhere else. Too many busybodies around here. I'm sure Kash knows somebody here, and if he knows somebody here, that somebody knows you're his cousin."

"And so?"

"You know Kash. He'll just exaggerate this whole thing, and we haven't even established anything really."

Patience turned away and walked ahead casually, hoping she had masked her hurt enough.

Let it go, she told herself. It was true, they hadn't established anything.

When they arrived at the suya stand, the seller placed several skewers of raw meat onto his open grill.

"Excuse me, Sa, give us two cow, one goat."

The man nodded and added more meat to the grill.

"We should wait for him to finish cooking the fresh one," Chike said.

"Of course. Although I doubt this suya can come close to the one from my favorite suya place in Ibadan."

"Ibadan suya? No way. This is Lagos, my dear. You're a student at UNILAG and you're not boasting about the suya there? I'm shocked."

"There's no way it's better than the one in Ibadan. And to be honest, I haven't tasted suya at LAG."

"What do you mean? What have you been doing there?"

"Thinking about my mum. Running away from lectures."

"I understand how you feel . . . to some degree, but you're in UNI. Just enjoy it for now."

He stared at her, and she felt his eyes draw her in. She felt the urge to kiss him again, but she knew better. Neither of them knew what they were to each other, but what Patience did know was that Chike's affection for her was like the force of motion—a constant pull and push that she had no control over. *Why?* she often wondered.

"Okay, Chike. I will try," she said.

They watched as the suya seller packed their meat in newspaper. Chike pulled money out of his pocket.

"Chike, I can pay."

"Nonsense," he said. "How much is suya that I can't buy it for you?"

It was what he had always done every time they were alone together. She was flattered because she knew his struggles.

They walked a few steps away from the suya seller and picked out pieces of meat.

"Now taste it and see if it's good enough to make you forget about that suya in Ibadan."

Patience bit the meat and eyed Chike as she chewed.

"It's good. I'll give this one a high mark, but the one in Ibadan is still better."

"Wow. So you still won't bend."

"No, never."

They ate more meat, saved some for Kash, then walked through the rest of the market.

THEY ARRIVED BACK AT KASH'S PLACE AND WATCHED HIM devour the suya, which he topped off with a bottle of Guinness.

"Patience, this na correct suya, abi?"

"Patience thinks Ibadan has the best suya," Chike said before she could respond.

"Well, as a true Ibadan boy, I can't fault her for saying so."

"She hasn't tried suya at LAG."

"Ah-ahn, Patience, why na?" Kash said, his mouth agape, revealing evidence of meat. "LAG must have good suya."

"I'm so sorry I haven't had time for enjoyment at school," Patience said, peeved by their prying.

They were quiet, and Patience wished she hadn't snapped at them. It wasn't their fault that she wasn't happy at school.

"It's getting late." Chike stood and stretched. "I should be going . . . but Patience, if you need me to take you back, I can."

"Chike, isn't UNILAG out of your way?" Kash said.

Chike ignored the question and looked at Patience instead.

"Thank you, dear cousin, for making the decision for me," she said sarcastically. "I was going to say no anyway. I'm going to stay here tonight."

"Oh . . . no problem," Chike said. He seemed disappointed. Patience felt bad that she had let him down even though he had done the same to her during their stroll. But she knew she would see him again soon. Just not that night. She needed time away from campus.

"I'll be seeing you," Chike said as he walked out and shut the door.

"Seriously, Patience, you should be enjoying being away from home—being away from Daddy. Why are you acting like this?"

"I can't stop thinking about what Aunty Lola told me about my mum. I need money to get to America. I need my passport."

Kash gazed at her intensely. "You know Daddy will never give you the money to go to America," he said finally.

"Yes, I know."

"So you have to take care of yourself. Look at me. I do the impossible, but I'm surviving."

Patience looked around at his room. She couldn't believe that was the result of his so-called surviving. But at least he was on his own, he was eating, and he had nobody to answer to. She needed that sort of liberation.

"I have to start making my own money," she said.

"The solution to your problem could be right in front of you."

Patience looked at Kash, confused. She decided not to ask him what he meant.

10

"WHY DO THEY CALL THIS PLACE LOVE GARDEN?" CHIKE slid his hand down Patience's back and rested his palm above her seated backside.

"Because people like us come here." She slipped her hand into his and peered beyond a row of trees. "And people like them."

Chike turned and looked at another couple locked in a lingering kiss. "I know people come here to cuddle, but calling it Love Garden just seems so exaggerated."

"Chike, you're so tight about everything." She nudged him.

Love Garden had become one of her favorite places at UNILAG. She had first stumbled upon the quiet corner of her school during one of her many solo tours around campus. The garden's air and its parade of young adult coupledom had a way of easing the anxiety that had harassed her since she met with Aunty Lola. In the garden she could forget about the nagging of her roommates and her agonizing coursework. Most days she walked aimlessly around campus, through the parks and hostel parking lots, where she observed the crowds of students. At UNILAG's Lagoon Front, she often stared out, wishing she could magically shift large bodies of water to get to her mum.

"Have you made any friends here yet besides your roommates?" Chike said as he massaged her hand with his thumb.

"No. But I like watching people." She decided not to mention that she didn't consider her roommates friends.

"So you won't make any friends here? I thought you liked clothes. What of the big girls here who love fashion too? You should find those people. And you haven't gone to any parties or all those cultural events people from UNILAG talk about. You're supposed to do those kinds of things in UNI."

"I just got here."

"It's been more than a month."

"I will go to a UNILAG party one day, if it makes you happy," she said. She didn't want to tell him that she had no desire to move beyond the comfort that isolation gave her. She had thought she would be different at university, but she was the same recluse from secondary school. "I feel like I shouldn't be here. I don't know . . . I feel like I'm in jail at times."

"You still need friends, even if you won't be here long." He grabbed her waist, prompting her to stand, then pulled her onto his lap.

Patience looked to her left and saw another couple French-kissing. "I have you, no?"

"Yes, but . . ."

"What? Say what you want to say, Chike." She pecked his lips.

"Isn't this when you're supposed to form long-lasting friendships?"

"Won't we last?" She kissed him softly again.

He was quiet, just like on all the other days when she had asked him concrete questions about what he wanted to be in her life. He pushed her braids to one side and stroked her bare neck. She felt then that she finally knew love, that his was like an electric current that awakened her.

She had always imagined that her mother had hated her father when they were together. She wanted the opposite for her own life. It was a must that Chike be the opposite.

She shifted her body and looked into his eyes to match the intensity she felt from his touch, but he lifted his gaze. And it was like he pulled a plug from her and left her lifeless.

"Why do I feel like you treat me the way I treat this school?" she said, keeping her tone even as she stood up and resettled in her spot next to him.

"Meaning?"

"You treat me as if you know you won't be with me long."

"So you admit that you're afraid of being here at UNILAG."

"You didn't answer."

"Patience. Let us just be."

She tilted her head and rested it on his shoulder and searched for a way to refill the space inside her body from which he had removed himself.

"Abiola is giving a speech at the National Stadium tomorrow. I heard my roommates talking about it. It's supposed to be a big deal," she said casually.

"Yes, o. He's officially SDP's candidate. National Stadium will be on fire tomorrow."

"What of all the people who say he was planted by the military?"

"That was before he started speaking everywhere. He's been saying the right things. His critics are turning into believers."

"Will you be there?" she said.

"No. I'm working. Mayowa will be there. If you see him, beg him to introduce you to Abiola."

Patience was more excited about the idea of getting to America than waiting for Nigeria's democracy, but she pictured herself watching Abiola break ground.

"I will go. I'll look for Mayowa."

"Good. It will be good."

THE NEXT DAY PATIENCE FELT THE ENERGY OF ABIOLA'S impending rally all around her—first among her roommates, who were planning their patriotic attire. Tolani wore white jeans and a green-and-white polo. Ayanti tied a small Nigerian flag around her neck as if it were a silk scarf. Patience hadn't even had her bath.

"Patience, where are your colors?" Tolani said.

"You're like a ghost. It's as if you're here but you're not," said Ayanti.

"You didn't tell me to wear green and white."

"We've been at LAG for over a month and you've hardly shown your face. If you're not with Chike, you're roaming around campus doing nothing. You already missed two impromptu tests. Don't miss the next exam."

"Thanks for your concern." Patience felt touched that Tolani seemed to care about her performance in school, but she didn't need her judgment.

"When you first came, you were afraid of okada. Now you are on okada practically every day with your boyfriend who drives okada. Patience, na wa o."

"But that Chike, he's fine o," said Ayanti, prompting her shared laughter with Tolani.

"Anyway, I think you should go ahead to the rally," Patience said. "It will take me some time to get ready. Chike's friend Mayowa is the son of Abiola's campaign manager. He may introduce me to him, so I have to look decent."

"Why is it that the people who put in no effort get more?"

"I don't know if I will actually meet him," Patience said, ignoring Tolani's comment.

"It's a chance, abi? Just make sure you look for us in the crowd so we too can talk to Abiola up close," Ayanti said.

"I will try."

By the time Patience got off the bus near the National Stadium, her heart stirred from the electricity that had taken over the entire area. Music blasted from cars, bus drivers shouted chants of solidarity, and paper fliers that bore Abiola's face littered the ground.

As she walked into the stadium, the DJ for the event cut in on his microphone, shouting celebratory chants. The crowd, over a thousand deep, fashioned a sea of green and white—a steaming pot of diplomatic hope. And thanks to the food vendors who worked the area, it all smelled of grilled meat and party rice.

Patience remembered Ayanti and Tolani, who were somewhere in the crowd. She looked around, hoping to spot them quickly. Finding them would be near impossible.

"Excuse me, is Abiola here yet?" she asked one woman.

"No, but people are there setting up."

Mayowa should be somewhere close, she thought.

She squeezed her way through the spectators, keeping her eyes on the stage where Abiola would stand. She noticed a lanky guy climb onto the platform to test the microphone with his back facing the crowd. When he turned around, Patience called out to him.

"Mayowa, Mayowa!" she yelled. She waved her hands once she reached the side of the stage.

"Ah, Patience. Thank you for coming." Mayowa came down the steps of the platform. "Chike told me to look for you, but I told him I would be busy," he said.

"No problem. When is Abiola coming?"

"Soon, sha."

"Will you introduce me to him?"

"Ah, that's a tall order. We shall see," he said, the corners of his mouth curling with pride. "Anyway, pass these around to the people." He handed her a stack of leaflets that bore Abiola's campaign message.

She was happy he had asked. She walked on, carrying the fliers and feeling a new sense of purpose, though still somewhat detached from the whole affair.

"Hello, take one," she said to one man.

"Good work," he said, patting her on the back.

Patience thanked him, shook her head awkwardly, and moved on.

She began to move quicker, handing fliers to people at random. "Please take one. Please take one," she said repeatedly.

When she approached a large group of men, they grabbed several fliers from her, threw them into the air, and cheered.

Moments later the crowd exploded into climactic applause that startled her.

She turned and saw Abiola on stage, pumping his hands in the air, clapping, and yelling back at the spectators through the microphone she had seen Mayowa testing earlier. He was taller than she had imagined—darker too. His presence was arresting, yet his wide, toothy grin gave evidence of compassion. She wondered if the stories people told about him were true—how he paid his son's classmates' school fees when their parents could not, or how he handed out cash to people who frequented the area surrounding his compound.

"The election will determine the future of our country. You are the future of Nigeria," he yelled, his voice husky and commanding. The mob began to chant part of his campaign jingle: "My brother, wetin you dey think, o? My sister he-lep o done come!"

Patience looked around at the mob. There were more people cheering and waving the Nigerian flag than she had ever seen in her lifetime.

"We represent progress. We represent prosperity. Will you support our ticket? Will you vote for us?" Abiola bellowed.

"Yes!" The crowd yelled back in unison, and it was as if the roar of their voices shifted the ground beneath Patience's feet. She turned to take in the mayhem from the crowd, then she looked back at Abiola—a snapshot of hope, a living promise of good fortune.

"We will appoint not just one, not just two, not just three, but several women to the government of Nigeria. Nigeria has the most enterprising women in the whole world."

A shriek of female voices in the crowd pierced the ether.

"I believe in the people, all the people. Not just those who agree with me. I value the truth, and truth means trying to understand things from another person's point of view. We will make Nigeria a nation for the people."

The eruption from the crowd made the cheers from Abiola's initial entrance seem like a murmur. Patience's chest grew tight as she began to envision a stampede.

She pushed her way through the swarm and headed toward the back. As she reached the edges of the crowd, she felt the stress lift from her chest. She took a long, deep breath and looked around, as Abiola's voice still echoed behind.

Patience regained her bearings, and she was energized. She was ready to steer herself toward whatever goodness she had and the kind she would create.

She didn't look for Mayowa or her roommates or anybody else at the end of the event.

She didn't meet Abiola that day.

She took the bus back to campus knowing she didn't need to.

His electricity had already filled her body.

And Patience wondered how she, too, could bend the world in her favor.

SHE WENT TO HER LECTURE THE NEXT DAY. IT WAS THE first time in two weeks.

"Ah, Patience, don't be like these yeye boys who only come to class when exam time is coming," Tolani said as she sat next to her.

"Didn't you tell me yesterday to come and to make sure I don't miss the exam?"

"I did, but I honestly can't believe what you're doing. Listen, I don't have a rich father, so I will never understand this kind of thing. Why na?" Tolani tapped her press-on nails on her desk.

"Didn't you hear what Abiola said yesterday?" Patience said. "He said the election is about the future of our country, and we are the future. So I will try here. Just let me copy your notes."

"You're lucky the lecturer has not questioned you," Tolani said just as he walked in.

"Good afternoon, Sa," the class said in unison.

"Good afternoon. I'm seeing some familiar but unfamiliar faces," he said as he surveyed the room. "Maybe those people think they can use juju to pass the exam next week, because they don't think they need to come to my lectures."

The professor faced the board and began to write the notes for the day. Patience looked around at her classmates, many of whom began writing eagerly. She decided she wouldn't gouge her eyes out, but her brain felt like loose àmàlà.

11

"SO YOU'RE DATING MY COUSIN, THIS USELESS OKADA driver with a head like a coconut?"

Chike, Emeka, and Mayowa burst into laughter. Patience felt disconcerted, but at the same time Kash made her feel attended to.

"I mean, really, don't you know your place?"

"Shut up!" Chike said, finally catching his breath.

Kash was their sole source of entertainment as they sat crammed inside Chike and Emeka's dim apartment drinking beer. Since NEPA took light some hours ago, the acrid smell from kerosene lamps competed with the bitter stench of cigarette smoke.

"Can you imagine, an Igbo man gelatinizing with a Yoruba man's daughter? If my uncle finds out, he will hate me more than he already hates me. In fact, he will curse my unborn children."

Laughter filled the room again, and though Patience couldn't really see Chike's face as she sat next to him, she could sense that he was embarrassed too.

"Chike, my guy, you have been missing the past few weeks," Mayowa said. "I've been wanting to bring you to Abiola's campaign headquarters. But I told myself I will let you remain on your honeymoon with your new babe. We didn't know the babe was Patience."

"It's not like Patience and I are getting married. We are just good friends."

His response was like a quick poke at her ribs.

"Friends?" she said.

"For now, I think so."

Patience shifted her body away from him, but she decided to leave the matter there. She had no desire to discuss her feelings for him in a room full of silly men. She knew she was in love with him, and she was certain he loved her too. She could sense it in his sudden need to adjust his stance whenever she entered a room, the flicker in his eye that he would sometimes try to blink back, or how he would come straight to her hostel after work. "I'm just coming to check on you," he often said, whether they went somewhere or not.

What they were—it had to be love.

Kash made another joke related to them, and this time Chike put his arm around her neck. His hands smelled of the èbà and egusi she had made for them earlier.

Emeka shook his head at the sight of his brother's display of affection. "Chike, you really know how to lie to yourself," he said. "You cater to Patience as if she's so fragile. And anyway, there's a lot the two of you can do as a pair besides gelatinizing and fraternizing. What about making money together?" He and Kash exchanged looks of solidarity.

"Shut up," Chike said, waving his brother off.

"What do you mean by 'make money together'?" Patience asked.

"Why would Patience join in such nonsense?" Mayowa said.

"Because this would allow her to make the money she can't ask her daddy for. The money she needs to go to America."

"What do you mean? Why is everybody ignoring my question?" Patience said.

"So your dearly beloved Chike never told you about the job Kash and I have been commissioned to do? We need a team. We need you. I mean, your American accent alone will help us."

"Emeka, go away," Chike said stiffly.

"Patience, all you have to do is go to a few banks, deposit some money, then withdraw some here and there. Simple. I told Chike to go to the library and find out everything we need to know about big-big deposits and withdrawals, since he likes to read. But he's still here telling me he'd rather drive okada."

"I never said I'd rather drive okada."

"Chike, please o, you must continue to block out such nonsense. You will find work soon," Mayowa said.

"The money we can get from doing something so simple, mehn, you will have your ticket money quick, sha," Kash said as he lit another cigarette. "Since you've come to Lagos, all you talk about is going to America to find your mum."

"Emeka, Kash, wait a minute, slow down. Who would I be depositing money for?"

"For yourself."

"What do you mean? What money do I have to deposit?"

"Patience, please don't mind Emeka. He and Kash are madmen," Chike said, squeezing her hand.

"No, jàre, let her hear it," Kash said. "Do you see money dancing around here anywhere?"

"Patience doesn't need the money. She doesn't need to go to America right away. She can wait a bit."

"Can somebody explain this money that you're all speaking of?" Patience said.

"Well, you can't tell anyone, okay?"

"Okay, I won't tell anybody."

"There's a guy that everybody calls Oga. He wants us to take a big check to open a business account, then do a regular withdrawal to take some of the money out. Part of the money will be our payment."

"Where is the money for the check coming from?"

Emeka chuckled. "Chike, you really didn't tell her about the job. Wow."

"I didn't tell her because she's not going to do it."

"Patience, the money is imagined, then stolen," Mayowa said, stressing the word *stolen*. "The check will probably be fake, but the bank won't realize. That's how these wayward men make their money."

"So brother Kashimawo, *this* is what you've been doing in Lagos all this time?" Patience leaned forward and slapped his leg.

"Noooo, I've only done petty-petty work here and there," he said. "I do enough to stay alive. It's Emeka who wants to work with Oga fully."

"Of course, just like Kash to do something half-half," Mayowa said.

They laughed, including Kash, whose booming voice overpowered everyone else's.

"This job makes sense when you think about it, because where does money really come from anyway? Is it not all from our dreams? It's up to us to make it real in our lives. We are just speeding up the process of getting it," Emeka said.

"Ah-ahn, Emeka, you talk like a crooked pastor," Mayowa said.

"Or a thief," Chike said. "What kind of foolish talk is that? Speeding up the process? If money comes that simple, why are we here sitting in the dark? Why is my mummy in pain? And you, your father died, and now you're struggling." Chike pointed at Kash.

"Chike, you're becoming just like Mayowa with all this yeye talk," Emeka said, disgusted.

"You too. You're yeye," Mayowa quipped.

"Patience, the money will come from the bank, if you want to look at it like that. Doesn't all money come from the bank?"

"Yes, Kash, but if the bank gives the money to a person who steals it, they are at a loss," Chike said.

"Ṣebi the bank will find another way to reap that money? I've told you before, this system takes from people like us," Emeka said. "We have to learn to take our own share, or we will be sitting in the dark like this for the rest of our days. Me, o, I will be somewhere in VI while the rest of you sit here."

"Patience, if you want to see your mum anytime soon, you better start gathering the money now. No be small-small money you need for America," Kash said.

"Patience doesn't even have her passport, and you're telling her to gather money," Chike said. "And Kash, didn't you say she's here to study at UNILAG? Now you want her to start doing 419?"

Patience felt ashamed because she pictured herself saying yes, completing the job, and settling in New York City. She had been hoping to find a way to make quick money. This was it.

No, it can't be. She shook away the thought. Being thrown in jail for fraud wasn't exactly the life she was longing to create for herself. There had to be a safer way to get to America. "I can't do that. We can get into serious trouble, and my dad will completely disown me."

"Exactly!" Chike said.

"So what other solutions do you have, ehn, Patience?" Kash leaned toward her in the darkness, waiting for her response.

"Don't worry. She will find a way," Mayowa said.

"Patience, you don't have to feel bad about telling my brother no," Chike added as he squeezed her hand.

"Kash, what I really need is for you to come with me to take my passport from Daddy's safe," she said. "At least I should do that—get my passport."

"What about the money? What is a passport with no money?"

"Kash, I know where he keeps it. It's in a black safe in his closet. He locks it with a key. Can't you break into it?"

"Does he keep money in that safe? That's what we need."

"You know Daddy loves money. If we take money, he would notice. But he has no need to check for my childhood passport."

"I cannot go back to Daddy's house after all he said to me," Kash said.

"We can go when he and Modupe are out."

"So the gate man and the house girl won't see you and say something to your dad?"

"You, Kash, you're talking as if you haven't bribed or even threatened your way back into your father's house." Patience remembered how he had done just that when he was in SS2, after he had spent a night on the town drinking. He paid the gate man but didn't know his father was watching the transaction and waiting inside to flog him.

Kash stopped talking and took a long drag from his cigarette. He exhaled, and white ghost-like swirls of smoke danced in the dark room. He hesitated and took a mouthful of beer. He burped and wiped his mouth with his hand.

"Patience, go to the embassy and apply for your passport, jọ. I can't go back to that house."

"Kash, please," she said, ignoring his dismissal.

"I don't know, Patience. I don't know. Just think about the money."

"Just think about my passport," she said.

She did think of the money again, along with the job proposal. She could never do it.

She pictured her father's cold gaze. He would shame her for even considering such a thing. "You have disgraced my name," he would say.

The risk, the danger, the uncertainty—such a thing could only end in defeat.

12

CHIKE FROWNED AT THE ROYAL BLUE SHIRT PATIENCE HELD against her chest in one of his favorite clothing stalls at Tejuosho market.

"Get this. It's bright, and you will stand out," she said.

"I need a shirt in case I get an interview, and nobody should wear bright colors to an interview."

"And why not?"

"It's not proper. I'm an engineer, not an artist. I should wear a white shirt to be safe."

"Why be safe when you haven't found a job?" Patience put the shirt back on the rack and leafed through more of the store's inventory.

"Did you read about that in one of your American magazines?" he said.

"Speaking of America, can you imagine how much I've still been begging Kash to come home with me to help me get my passport?"

The determination in her eyes turned him on. He grabbed her waist, twisted her from side to side, and kissed her forehead. Smart, beautiful, yet naive, he thought, and the combination tickled him.

"How are you going to get in and out of your popsie's safe without him seeing you? Have you really thought about it?"

"Yes. If I'm going to America to see my mum, I have to get my passport from my dad."

What if her mother didn't want to be found, Chike thought.

Or what if her mother was dead?

With all her desperation, Chike hoped she wouldn't consider the bank job.

No, not Patience, he thought. *She would never.*

He shook the worry out of his mind and picked up a white button-down, the very thing he had come to get. "Let me just buy this today, sha. I want to be prepared in case I do get an interview soon."

"That's a good plan," she said.

He had decided not to tell her about the interview he was going to have with Chevron the next day. He would tell her whenever he got the official offer. He knew the job was his. He had never been so confident about a job prospect. This time he wasn't entering as a nobody. The dean of UI's Petroleum Engineering Department knew the chairman of the board and had called to tell him that Chike was one of the top graduates from the program.

This time, he had a connection.

All he needed to do was impress the manager of the department during the interview and wait for his offer.

An eager salesman approached Chike and Patience holding a long, slender mirror.

"Chief, you wan try am? I go give you good price," he said, pointing at the white shirt Chike was holding.

"No, chief, I go take it now."

Chike paid the man. Patience left the stall and walked ahead. Chike followed and gazed at her body from behind. He loved how her slender waist dipped just above the curve of her round hips. When she had walked into Kash's flat the day she moved to Lagos, he couldn't believe she was the same secondary school girl he had met in his UI hostel. This Patience—Lagos Patience, UNILAG Patience—had blossomed into a woman.

"I need this watch," she said as she approached a stall that sold counterfeit name brands. "I'm buying it today. I know it's fake, but I don't care."

Chike grabbed the watch and surveyed the words *Tommy Hillfiger* etched boldly across its strap.

"It has two *l*'s but Hilfiger is spelled with one *l*. I still want it, though."

"Why don't you buy the real thing with your pocket money?"

"Oh, please. You don't know my dad. In secondary school I used to do minor alterations for my classmates whose parents actually spoiled them. They would pay me or give me things in exchange."

"You and your American labels. Why?"

"What can I say? I'm drawn to them."

"Do you think your mum would really care that you wear American designs?"

"I don't know," she said, staring off. She hesitated, then shook her head as if she were rejecting a new revelation.

Chike grabbed her waist and kissed the back of her neck. She turned to face him and placed her hand gently on his cheek. He smiled, then pulled away from her abruptly to check the price on a Cross Colours tee.

He wondered who he was becoming, showing affection to a woman so openly. He hadn't felt like that since he'd been with his first love, Nneka, the girl he thought he would marry one day.

But he was a teenager then, and he had barely touched Chichi, his last girlfriend, in public.

Yet what he felt for Patience hovered over him like a swift-moving squall that drove him to run for cover.

"If I haven't told you before, I hope you get an interview soon. These bloody oil companies, they need you."

A master of flattery, he thought. He couldn't wait to tell her in a matter of days that one of those "bloody oil companies" had finally hired him. His chest rose. Then it dawned on him: once he had the job, he could finally yield to the thing that made him weak for her.

"There's an eatery that is the talk of Lagos right now. Let me take you there tomorrow evening," he said.

"Of course."

"Wear one of your favorite designers. It's supposed to be a place for you and your fellow ajebutters."

"Oh, please," she said, slapping his shoulder.

They walked on.

"AS A DRILLING ENGINEER, I BELIEVE I CAN LEARN FROM your example."

Chike rehearsed for his interview as he looked in the mirror and adjusted his navy-blue tie on his new white button-down. He grinned when he thought of Patience and how serious she had been about him wearing a bright blue shirt. He decided he would surprise her with a real Tommy Hilfiger watch once he had saved up enough money. But first, he had to pay the whole of Mama's hospital bill.

The thought made him whistle as he brushed his closely trimmed hair. He rubbed cream on his face. He smeared balm on his lips. He sniffed his armpits, hoping he hadn't forgotten to put on deodorant, though on most days he used it sparingly since he was running low and looking to cut expenses. *Today is different*, he thought. He un-tucked his shirt and smeared more on.

The phone rang.

He ignored it when he heard Emeka pick it up.

He grinned in the mirror to make sure there were no remnants of the bread he had eaten with tea for breakfast. He grabbed his tooth-brush, put toothpaste on it, and swirled it in his mouth for the second time that morning. It was better to be safe than sorry. When he fin-ished, he smiled again. Emeka appeared in the doorway holding their secondhand cordless phone.

"It's for you. From Chevron."

Chike grabbed the phone.

"Hello."

"Hello," said the woman on the other end. "I am calling from

Chevron. Mr. Tinuola would like to inform you that he no longer needs you to come for the interview. The position has been filled."

He froze. He looked at the clock on the wall. Nine o'clock.

"What do you mean? I'm scheduled to be there at eleven o'clock."

"They hired someone for the job, Sa."

"Well, that can't be. I was recommended by—"

"Sa, Mr. Tinuola wishes you well, but he cannot offer you the job right now, so there's no need for an interview."

When Chike heard the line click off, he continued to hold the phone to his ear in disbelief—the same phone they couldn't afford but got because of his need for a direct line that would allow potential employers to reach him; the same phone they decided to keep so that Mama could call and talk about her mounting doctor's fees.

A single tear dropped from his eye.

He walked to the room, pulled off his tie, unbuttoned his proper white shirt, then collapsed on his bed.

"What happened?" Emeka said, standing above the bed.

"They gave the job to someone else." Chike kept his face buried in the pillow, hoping Emeka wouldn't hear him clearly.

"Brother, don't forget about that bank job. All these useless interviews are a waste of time anyway," he said as he walked out and closed the door to their room.

By now puddles of tears had formed in his eyes. When he blinked, he felt the wetness seep into the pillow. The weight of slumber began to bear down on him as he thought of Patience and the plans they had made to meet that evening. He brushed the thought away and allowed sleep to take over.

IT HAD BEEN FOUR DAYS SINCE HE AND PATIENCE WERE supposed to meet. He had promised to take her to a new eatery in Lagos, but he hadn't visited her. He knew she would be worried, but for the past four days he felt he was nothing to worry about. He was merely a crumb in the vast city. A manager at an oil company had tossed him away, again, with a flick of a finger.

Who gave anyone the right to disregard him and his connection to Chevron?

It was the question that burned at his core for four days. But on the evening of the fourth day, he was confronted with a deep longing to see Patience. He gave in and decided to go to her.

So there he sat, in front of UNILAG, for over an hour, waiting for her to come out as she normally did when she had the urge to take a walk off campus. When she finally came out, she and her roommate looked like typical university students. Seeing them reminded him of the late nights he had spent laboring over chemistry problems and studying for exams, dizzy with exhaustion and hunger as he skipped meals to cram. Food was scarce, and provisions were a luxury. While his friends from well-off homes munched meat pies, buns, and fish rolls for snacks and ate complete meals from local eateries, he retreated to his room to drink garri in water. On rare occasions he would scrounge up enough money to buy cabin biscuits and Peak milk from the school's tuck shop, put the ingredients in a bowl of garri, then let the concoction soak. When it came time to dig in, it was the sweetest thing he had ever tasted.

"Well, good evening. To what do I owe such an honor?" Patience said, stone-faced but smug, when she approached him.

"Don't do like that," he said, attempting to mask the urgency he felt around seeing her. He decided to stay on his bike. It was a barrier that made him feel less exposed.

"Tolani, I will see you later," she said.

"Okay, o, Patience," Tolani said, staring at Chike suspiciously.

"What happened to you? It's been four days. This is not like you. Did you forget?"

"Nothing happened. I didn't forget, sha. I was just tired."

"I waited for you," she said.

"Don't you ever get tired of me?"

"No, I don't, actually. Are you tired of *me*?"

"I don't know."

Patience blinked, and her large eyes grew wider.

Instead of saying he didn't know, he wished he could tell her what he really felt, how his job had been taken away from him, and how he was told just two hours before his interview. He wished he could cry on her shoulder the way he had in bed every night for four days straight. He wanted to hear from her that everything would be fine, but he didn't know how to have her without having his dignity too.

"If you need space, you're free to have as much as you need."

"I think four days was enough. Let me take you out now."

She hesitated and looked into his eyes. He felt her reading him, and for a moment he welcomed it. For a moment he wanted her to discern his truth. But he folded. He blinked and looked away.

"Chike, you know you can tell me things."

"Tell you what? Abeg, let's do what we do. What about the arcade?"

She hesitated. She looked back at the entrance of her school. She looked at him again. She sucked her teeth and hopped on the back of his bike. He revved the engine and sped off.

13

COURSE: INTRODUCTION TO
FINANCIAL ACCOUNTING

EXAM INSTRUCTIONS: COMPLETE ALL
QUESTIONS IN SECTIONS A AND B

1. Which is a liability?
   A. Machinery
   B. Accounts payable for goods
   C. Motor vehicles
   D. Cash at bank

PATIENCE KNEW THE ANSWER, BUT SHE DIDN'T WANT TO know it. Her stomach began to flutter when she thought of how dull her life would be if she became an accountant.

She felt no joy from knowing the answer to that question.

Only contempt.

She hated it. She hated her life. She hated sitting there.

She got up.

She felt their eyes—her classmates. She knew they were confused.

Why was she headed for the door? Meanwhile, the lecturer was laughing. As she walked out, she heard his assessment of her abrupt exit.

"That is what happens when you don't read your notes. When you don't come to my lectures."

D. Cash at bank.

She knew the answer to the question on the test. It was cash. She didn't want to know it, because the things she wanted to know had been taken from her. They had been made to seem small: her mother, her desire to become a designer—a desire she couldn't reveal to her father.

But those were not small things to her.

Patience caught the bus off campus. When she stepped onto the street, she looked at the usual scene of shops and people hustling about. She walked on and approached the tailor who had set up shop on the roadside—still seated atop two slabs of wood held above an open gutter. Bundles of fabric were draped on another table beside him, and his finished work hung on the concrete wall behind him. She had stared at him, amazed by his self-restraint. None of the goings-on moved him off his axis.

She walked closer, then approached his station.

"Excuse me, Sa. Good afternoon. I want to learn to sew," she blurted out. "I want a machine, but I only hand sew."

He looked at her, his skin like tree bark, the whites of his eyes a pinkish red. He looked down and kept his machine running. She was sure he had noticed her on other days.

"Sa, I really want to learn. Please. Please teach me."

"I am not a teacher," he said, his voice raspy as if he hadn't spoken to anyone in hours.

"Can I watch and ask questions?"

"Time na money?"

"Sa, my money is running low, but I can give you five hundred naira to learn."

The man looked at her again, and his eyes looked even redder than before. "Five hundred? You insult me."

"Please, Sa," she said, making sure she didn't switch to her American phonetics. "I am a student."

He continued to sew quietly. Several minutes passed. Patience stood her ground.

"Sit down," he said finally. "Just be looking at what I'm doing. No questions for now."

She did. She watched how he threaded the machine again and placed new material under it, how he positioned the fabric, how he guided the fabric along the needle to complete the stitching. She watched for hours. Then she remembered that her time was supposed to be spent taking her exam.

She had chosen this for herself.

When the man was done, he fluffed out a long Ankara skirt. Patience couldn't believe how quiet they had been the whole time. "I have a machine there that I can sell to you. It's better you go home and practice what you saw me do here. You can buy patterns for simple styles."

"How much is it?"

"Three thousand naira. Electric machine," he said, pointing to a discolored and outdated contraption that sat on a table behind his workstation with its long cord wrapped around.

"Ah-ahn, I told you, Sa, I'm a student, and my money is running low."

"Okay. So leave the machine there."

"Sa, please. Take one thousand."

He said nothing. Instead, he sorted through bundles of fabric. He chose one and laid it out on another table. He took his scissors and cut the straightest line she had ever seen. She would practice that too.

"Okay," he said finally. "Drop one thousand for the machine and the five hundred for sitting here," he said before she could thank him and rejoice.

PATIENCE ARRIVED AT KASH'S DOORSTEP CRADLING HER new sewing machine as if it were a newborn baby. On her wrist, she carried a plastic bag with scraps of material the tailor had given her to use for practice. She shifted the machine to one arm and used the other to bang on his door.

Kash opened the door. "What is this?" he said.

"It's my new sewing machine," she said. She pushed past him and put it on the table that Kash jokingly called his imported dining set. It was even more beat up than the tailor's table.

"This machine is not new. It looks like something that belongs in the bin. And why do you need a sewing machine?"

"I'm going to teach myself how to sew. I will start making clothes that I can sell to make money for my ticket to America."

"Patience, don't be silly. If you want money to go to America, you have to think big. You have to do that bank job!"

"I have this now." She patted her machine.

"Patience, this is an electrical one. Why do you think most tailors have a manual machine? What will you do when NEPA takes light? Do you see a generator here? This is not your daddy's compound or your private secondary school."

"Okay, okay. I know electricity is scarce. It's scarce at UNILAG and it was scarce at my secondary school, but it always comes back eventually. This is my life's calling. Now I can do it better and make money."

"So you brought the machine to my place? Why not your hostel?"

"Kash, I can't take it there. I can work from here, sha."

"My dear cousin. You are always up to something."

Kash watched, bewildered, as Patience worked to set the machine up. There were so many things she didn't know since the tailor didn't allow her to ask questions. She would just have to teach herself.

After Kash went out to the local bar, she started poking around the machine to see what things did, like the lever that controlled the contraption that resembled a foot. She felt ready to start on a piece of fabric. She threaded the machine, held the fabric steady, and she started sewing. When she finished, she noticed the stitching was crooked. She tried again.

Same result.

Then again.

Crooked.

Hours had passed before a breakthrough came: two straight lines of stitching that brought together two pieces of Ankara. She held it up with amazement. It didn't look like the kind of skirt she would buy, but she had made progress.

She moved on to putting together a buba. She cut the fabric—the line not as straight as the tailor's but not terrible. She placed the fabric under the needle and began to stitch. She stitched and cut and stitched and cut until she was ready to survey the final product. She held out the shirt. One sleeve was longer than the other, and the sizing looked suitable for a child, but still she was proud. Again she had sewn fabric together on a machine she was teaching herself how to use. She would move on to using rulers to make sure her measurements were correct.

She placed new fabric under the needle, then pedaled.

Suddenly her machine stopped, and her body went stiff.

The lights flickered off, and she realized that NEPA had cut her lesson short.

She hated to think Kash was right. She would resume in the morning. "There will be light again," she told herself.

THE NEXT MORNING PATIENCE DISCOVERED THAT THE electricity hadn't returned.

By afternoon, still no light.

She decided to cook for Kash to avoid his criticism about her putting her trust in a "rubbish" sewing machine. When she served him a plate full of ẹ̀bà and egusi, he gobbled down the food as if chewing was too burdensome.

When his room fell dim, he pulled out a kerosene lamp. Patience knew then that there would be no light that day.

"Dear cousin, this is Mushin. As you can see, ko si luxury nibi. When light goes, it goes. We can only pray for it to come back."

"Maybe by tomorrow, Kash. I was just making progress. I will stay another night."

"Okay, o, Patience."

She looked around the room aimlessly and suddenly realized she hadn't eaten all day long. She remembered the egusi stew. She went into the communal kitchen and lifted the lid on the pot she had left there on the stove.

Empty.

When she had left it there after serving Kash, there was enough to feed two more people.

She looked again.

Even the sides of the pot were smeared clean. She looked around frantically at the empty kitchen as if she would discover the thief hiding somewhere.

She thought of the time it had taken her to make the stew: the long walk to the market, the money she paid to grind the peppers, onion, and tomato, the moment she nearly sliced her finger off as she cut the spinach, her useless efforts to fan herself in a kitchen with no ventilation.

She stared at the empty pot and fought back tears.

She grabbed it by its black plastic handle and stomped back into Kash's room.

"Kash! Look! Look!" she said, waving the empty pot at him. "I left this on the stove there in your kitchen, remember? Now there's no food inside. Somebody ate it all."

"Patience, that's how people do here. I should have warned you before."

"Who would do such a thing?

Kash hesitated as if he was hiding what he knew to be the answer.

"Well, Bose, my former girlfriend who lives right there—she loves egusi." He shrugged.

"That means nothing. A lot of people love egusi."

"I know her."

"So you think it was her?"

"I'm thinking so."

"I should go talk to her."

"No, no, no . . . about what? Patience, please o, if you want peace, just consider it done."

Patience bit her short, stumpy nail and walked back over to her pot. "How can a person just take another person's stew like that?"

"Maybe she was hungry," Kash said with a shrug.

"*I'm* hungry!" Patience yelled before plopping down on his stool and pouting.

WHEN LIGHT DIDN'T COME ON THE THIRD DAY, PATIENCE decided to go back to her hostel that evening, though she didn't want to face her roommate, who had witnessed her walk out on an exam. She opened her room door and flipped on the light switch.

No electricity there either. She didn't have the energy to care.

At least my roommates aren't around, she thought. She walked carefully in the dark to her bed, climbed in, and pulled her cover over her head.

14

"TWO WEEKS, NO POWER. CAN YOU IMAGINE? IF YOU SEE how I was sweating at night. See how mosquito just come dey take ovah. Kai! NEPA is so useless."

Patience had no time to listen to Kash's complaints about NEPA. She only cared that the light had finally returned to Kash's place, and it was time for her to refocus on sewing. She had waited with bated breath as she thought often of the day when she had made progress with her machine—a tête-à-tête with her new tool cut far too short.

"I have so much to do," she said as she sorted through her scrap materials.

"Patience, you and this machine. I hope you thought about that job Emeka and I told you about. That is the only way you will get quick money to see your mum."

Patience ignored him as she sat at her machine. She removed the black thread and rethreaded it with white. She lifted the foot and lowered it on the white lace she had chosen. She peddled. The sound of the stitching elated her. She kept sewing. She pictured herself making perfect dresses to sell to the fashionable babes at UNILAG.

Then she heard what sounded like an engine on the verge of collapse. She continued peddling her machine, then the needle stopped.

The motor stalled.

The machine shut off.

She looked around the room. Kash's fan was still going. His overhead light was on. NEPA hadn't betrayed her again.

She looked back at her machine. She flipped its switch off, then on. Nothing.

"This machine wants to kill me!" she yelled as she firmly smacked it.

"What do you mean?"

"I was just sewing, and then it just switched off. It won't come on again."

Kash came over and surveyed it. He put his hands on his hips, then touched it with ease as if sewing machines were his forte. He turned the machine off and on as she had done.

Nothing.

"Well, it looks like your machine is broken."

"How do you know? It can't be broken. That tailor just sold it to me."

"How much did you pay him?"

"I paid him one thousand naira. He wanted three."

"Did you have to price it down much?"

Patience thought of her exchange with him. "He didn't object much when I came down on the price."

"Yepa! Patience. The guy sold you a nonsense machine. I told you this thing looks like it belongs in the bin."

"Why would he sell me a bad machine?"

"Because that's what people do when they need to make money with the little they have. They sell you what you wish to be true, and because you want it so much, you won't question if it's a lie. This na simple 419."

Patience got up. She sat, dumbfounded, in Kash's favorite armchair.

"I will take it back to him."

"It's better you just leave it. You don't know the man. He can cause commotion as if it was you who broke it. Just accept it as a loss."

"What if he didn't cheat me?"

"Abeg, this is Lagos. You better start using your brain, o, Patience, before you continue to get duped."

The tailor had seemed so direct. Like no-nonsense, yet he had sold her a nonsense machine? She couldn't believe it. She hated him. She hated that she had tried to sew. She felt as though she were back at her school library cramming for a test she didn't want to take. How would she get the money she needed?

"Patience, that bank job . . . we, too . . . we can sell a whole bank the kind of truth they expect. Are you in?"

15

"OKAY. YOU WERE RIGHT. THIS IS GOOD," PATIENCE MUM-
bled with her mouth full of the most delicious suya she had ever
tasted—UNILAG suya.

"Better than your favorite Ibadan suya, right?"

"I won't say."

Chike nudged her shoulder, and she was happy to see him happy.

She, too, was delighted and still on a high from the adrenaline she
had felt when she snuck him into her room before anyone noticed.
By some form of miracle, both her roommates were away. After the
complete failure of her sewing venture, she needed to be in Chike's
company.

"You know, there is still so much about you I don't know," she said
as she bit into another piece of the suya.

"What else do you need to know?"

"Little things . . . what's your favorite song?"

"'Jump Around,' House of Pain," he said swiftly.

"You already know I can't choose between Janet Jackson 'That's the
Way Love Goes' and 'Baby' by TLC."

"You mean 'Baby-Baby-Baby.'" Chike pinched her thigh.

"Of course, you must correct somebody about their own favorite,"
she said, amused. "What is your favorite book?"

"*Animal Farm*," he said quickly.

"Ha! So, I assume you read that one in secondary school too. Why would you choose that one?"

"Why not? The book is about power, manipulation, and wickedness by those who govern the people. We can relate in Nigeria, no? What's your favorite book?"

"Too many to name, but if I have to choose one, I would say . . ."

"I know you will say a romance novel," he said, cutting her off.

"No! I mean yes! I love romance, but I was going say a book my mum used to read to me when I was young. Whenever I read that book, I can hear my mum's voice."

Chike didn't respond. Instead he gazed at her, then looked away. He bit another piece of suya.

Patience decided to interrupt the awkward silence. "I know your favorite food is egusi. Speaking of egusi, somebody at Kash's place finished the entire pot I made. Kash said it was Bose."

"Really? Somebody actually finished it?" He gripped his chin, confused.

"What? Do you think it was her too?"

"No, I'm just surprised because . . . you can't really cook egusi well. You know Yoruba girls can't cook like Igbo girls."

She slapped his shoulder, and they laughed.

"It's true. You're lucky you're beautiful."

"You're lucky you are too," she said. He leaned in and kissed her, and the rhythm of their lips shifted by the second—tender, deep, then passionate. Patience pulled away. She wanted to know more of him. She needed to know more. She took a breath.

"What is your goal . . . what do you want this whole engineering thing to amount to?"

"I want to take care of my people. That's it. I want my mum to be okay," he said with his voice taking on a new depth. "I want Emeka to have better choices than stealing. I don't know if I can support him completely, but I will try. I want to send my children to good schools and spoil their mum." He dropped his gaze, putting the mood on pause. Patience couldn't bring herself to ask him if she was the woman on his mind. She couldn't face being rejected by him again.

"What is your most important possession?" she said.

"Nothing, really. I don't know."

She thought of her mother's things that she had kept and wondered how a person had nothing to treasure—no tangible thing sustained by hope and dreams.

"Let me show you something," she said. She walked to her wardrobe and pulled out her suitcase. She rolled it over to the bed where he sat. She pulled out her mother's sweater.

"Okay. Of course it's something designer."

"No . . . it was my mum's. She left it behind, and I found it at our old place."

"So you kept it?"

"Yes, I kept it, and I look at it often, and I try to picture her wearing it or maybe wearing something like it."

"You know what? Whenever I think of my dad, I think of him wearing the only suit he had," Chike said, staring off. "He was so sharp even in his one suit."

He gestured as if he wanted to say something else but thought twice. Then he spoke. "My dad used to tell me, Oge adighi eche mmadu. That is, time and the tide waits for no one. It's not easy, but we have to make sure we are moving forward and not living in the past."

Patience looked at him and wondered if that advice was for her. *Move forward?* Was he telling her to forget about her mum? No, she thought. Surely he understood why she couldn't. She decided not to ask because she feared he would confirm her suspicions.

She dug back into her suitcase and pulled out her mum's letter to her. "I've never let anyone else read this," she said as she handed it to him. "Be careful with it."

Chike unfolded the pages gently. While he read the letter silently, Patience recited it word for word in her head.

My dearest Patience,

I really tried, but sometimes in life we have to accept when we lose. But like my own mother used to say, one loss doesn't quantify a total journey. I named you Patience because you took your time. Twelve hours of labor before you arrived. Can you imagine? There was no other name for you. Please understand that the same patience you had in my womb and the endurance I had the day I gave birth to you will remain our link. One day we will meet again and when we do, you will know what I've added to our lives. Let your daddy keep you for now.

Love,
Mummy

"Your mum still loves you wherever she is."

"Aunty Lola said the same thing. She helped me fill in the gaps . . . she said my mum took my dad to court to get custody of me again. That explains why my mum wrote that she really tried. Aunty Lola promised to help me get my birth certificate at least."

"Patience, don't put too much hope in another person. If you can't do it yourself, well . . ."

"We all need help from time to time."

"Yes, but people make promises, then they act like you are crazy when you come to collect what they promised."

Aunty Lola was her mum's best friend. She had to come through for her.

"What do you think my mum meant in her letter—'you will know what I've added to our lives'?"

"I don't know. Only your mum can answer that question."

"Exactly," she said.

It's the reason she'd held herself in place. There could be no forward movement without answers.

She decided not to say anything else, because she knew Chike understood differently.

"So, are you finished quizzing me? Did I pass? Is my taste good enough for you?" he said.

"You did okay."

"Just okay?"

"Just okay," she said.

They kissed again, and this time she did not pull away.

16

"INNOCENT, PULL SOME OF THE HIBISCUS TO PUT INSIDE the house."

Aunty Lola wafted the air with her large straw fan as she and Patience sat in the middle of her flower garden in back of her home. Patience watched as she gave occasional orders to Innocent, her houseboy, who weeded the plants and hacked away at the surrounding grass and hedges with a large machete.

"You really love flowers," Patience said.

"I do. I really do. In my former life I was probably a florist." She smiled, and Patience admired her perfectly positioned teeth. She tried to remember her mother's teeth. She couldn't.

"What about my mum?" she said. "Did she like flowers too?"

"Ah, Folami. I don't think so," she said as she smiled tenderly. "She liked fashion like you. She liked winning, of course."

Patience beamed when she thought of her mother as a symbol of victory.

"That was one of the things your father didn't appreciate about your mother. He thought she was too ambitious."

"Aunty, can I ask you? My dad . . . do you know . . . ? Why is he so . . . ?"

"Why is he so *hard*?"

"Yes. Why is he so hard?" Patience wasn't sure if *hard* was the right word, but it was close enough.

"I only know what your mum told me. I know his parents died. His aunty raised him—that same aunt who gave your mum hell. He grew up poor. You know . . ." she said as she began to fan herself again, "poverty can be like a mental disease that affects people in two ways: either you succumb to it for the rest of your life or you spend your days searching for ways to be rid of it. And for those lucky enough to escape poverty, there can be an obsession to never return there."

"But why ruin other people with ambition? Ruin my mum?"

"Some men cannot accept a woman who wants to do big things. Or they want to be the first to achieve something." Aunty Lola's face fell. Patience wasn't sure what to make of her expression. Aunty Lola turned her gaze toward Innocent, who had moved on to watering the soil with a large silver canister.

"Not too much water, ehn, Innocent," she said. "Patience, just focus on UNILAG, get your degree, and God will reunite you with your mum one day."

"But, Aunty, what about my birth certificate? Have you started looking for it?"

"Innocent, trim that area there," she said. "My darling Patience, I'm trying. Just remain focused."

The sudden sound of heels hitting the backyard pavement made them turn toward the walkway. It was Bimpe and Mr. Shola, Aunty Lola's driver, making their way toward them.

"Patience, you're here again?" Bimpe said.

"She came by to see me, and so?" Aunty Lola said playfully.

"Good afternoon, Sa," Patience said to Mr. Shola, not knowing how to respond to Bimpe.

"Good afternoon, Patience. Madam, mo n lọ."

"Before you go home, Shola, ẹ jọ, carry Patience back to UNILAG. I don't want her taking that bus today."

"Yes, Ma."

Patience was relieved.

"Bimpe, you go with Patience so the two of you can catch up in the car."

"Okay, Mum, because I have nothing else going on," Bimpe said. She smiled and turned to Patience. "Shall we?"

Patience nodded.

As they sped along an open road in Ikoyi, Patience thought about her talk with Aunty Lola. She had said she was trying to find her birth certificate. What did that mean? How far had she gotten?

"Did your mum really start looking for my birth certificate?" Patience tried not to sound too eager.

"I don't know. I think so. Oh, your birth certificate? Yes, yes! I heard her say something like that."

Patience felt her heart jump. "What did she tell you?"

"Patience, let's go to one boutique there before we take you back to UNILAG, ehn?" Bimpe said, ignoring her question.

"Okay, but I told you I don't have money. I can only look at what they have."

"Yes, you told me you don't have any money, but I really just need you to come help me pick out a few things. Mr. Shola, please, can you take us to Arewa Boutique up the road there? Patience wants to help me choose a dress."

"Madam said we should take Patience straight to UNILAG."

"Please, Mr. Shola. She won't know we went. I won't tell her."

The man gazed at her in the rearview mirror and rubbed his brow. "Okay, you must make haste so we don't worry madam."

"Yes, Sa," Bimpe said, grinning.

Patience felt uncomfortable as they continued on toward the boutique. All she wanted to do was discuss her birth certificate.

"Have you decided to go to London to get your master's?" she asked instead.

"Patience, I don't know. All I know is my Ade is not going so why should I? I can get a job here. Daddy can get me something. But Mummy thinks London would be best. Ade's dad just started a new telephone company, and Ade is his right-hand man. Why would he leave all of that behind?"

"Can't you come visit Ade when you're off from school?"

"You're full of advice, aren't you?" Bimpe said as she rolled her eyes.

"If Ade won't leave Nigeria for you, why should you stay for him?"

Bimpe stared long and hard at Patience, as if she wanted to burn a hole through her. Patience looked away, uncomfortable.

They arrived at Arewa Boutique. The bright red-and-black store awning was large and imposing. They got out of the car and walked inside. Patience surveyed the slick black-and-white chairs, the black-and-white walls, the silver racks, the black velvet hangers.

"This is nice," she said to Bimpe.

"Of course it is."

Ripped jeans, overalls, and floral babydoll dresses hung on the store's back wall. Patience was so consumed by the display, she hardly noticed the fair-skinned woman with long, heavy braids who drifted in from the rear of the store.

"Bimpe, darling, how are you?" the woman said. She walked over and gave Bimpe two air kisses on her cheeks.

"Oh, Tayo, I'm well. How are you? This is Patience," she said without allowing the woman to answer how she was doing, as if it was a rhetorical question.

"Patience, welcome, ehn."

"Thank you."

Bimpe began to sift through the racks. "Patience, try this on," she said.

Patience hesitated, wondering if she had heard her correctly. "Bimpe . . . I told you . . ."

"You're trying it on for me."

"What do you mean?"

I want to see how it fits on the body." She stared at Patience with a slight smirk.

Patience hesitated. She loved the dress—the fiery red color, flirty sleeves, and short hem. She knew if she put it on, she would love it even more. She would want to take it home and even brainstorm how to make a copy by hand.

"Listen, if you ever want to borrow it, we can talk," Bimpe said, reading her.

Patience ignored her. She took the dress, entered the dressing room, and drew the curtain back. She looked at herself in the mirror. Her black bodysuit and jeans were cool enough. If she bought that dress, her pocket money would be depleted completely.

"Hey, Bimpe, so you were telling me before . . . what did your mum say about my birth certificate?" she called out.

There was no answer.

"Bimpe, are you there?"

Bimpe ignored her again.

Patience slipped into the dress and yanked the dressing room curtain open. She gazed around the store, then spotted Bimpe across the room, looking through racks and laughing with a salesgirl. Patience raised her arms to get her attention. Bimpe looked up. Patience waved again. Bimpe looked away, then looked up again and put up a finger as if to say "Wait."

Patience idled around awkwardly. She looked in the mirror and fell in love with the dress even more when she touched the fabric, soft like silk but not quite silk. Then she began to feel uncomfortable. She turned to get Bimpe's attention again, but Bimpe was still looking through racks.

When Bimpe finally walked over to the dressing room area, Patience felt as if she had been stripped bare.

"Turn around," Bimpe said with little enthusiasm. Patience turned around, confused. "Now bend over a little so I can see if it's too short."

Patience obeyed, though self-consciously.

"I don't know. What do you think?" Bimpe said.

"I love it."

"I actually hate it. Never mind, take it off. Maybe I'll find something else for you to try on for me."

Patience was slightly stunned. Luckily the salesgirl came over before she said or did anything she would regret.

"That dress looks good on you. You should get it," the salesgirl said.

"She doesn't have money," Bimpe said, her tone reeking of forced compassion. "She was trying it on for me. Patience, just change. Let's get you back to UNILAG."

Patience looked in the mirror. She didn't want to change. She wanted information. But she knew, just like the dress, she wouldn't be getting it that day.

17

THE GRIDLOCK FRIDAY NIGHT TRAFFIC DIDN'T ALLOW Chike to drive as fast as he wanted. Instead of taking a swift ride on his okada, he inched his way toward the Serenity Hotel in Aguda. Feeling the time pass, he looked down at his watch and noticed he was almost an hour late to his outing with Peter.

When they had gathered at their usual spot for lunch earlier in the day, Peter had insisted that they meet that night to drink beer and watch soccer. *I should be saving money for my trip to see Mama*, he thought. He and Emeka could no longer put off assessing her medical condition in person.

But Peter had offered to pay for the first drink. He couldn't remember the last time he was treated to anything, and he couldn't wait to talk to Peter about Patience. Peter could talk about women for hours.

Almost two months had passed since he and Patience had started kissing and spending time together.

She called it dating. He didn't.

Driving an okada and getting serious with a woman at the same time had never been his plan. He needed time to get himself together.

But did he already love her?

Peter would tell him what he needed to do.

When he approached the front of the parking lot, he saw Peter sitting on his bike, talking to a woman with a baby strapped to her back with a colorful Ankara wrap. It appeared they were in deep negotiations.

"You will pay two hundred," Chike heard Peter say.

"I beg, take a hundred," the woman said, reaching down into her bosom to reveal a few crinkled bills.

Chike parked next to Peter's bike and flashed a confused expression his way.

"My friend, no vex. Traffic was just too much," Chike said.

"No wahala. Let me quickly drive this woman to Ijesha."

Chike rolled his eyes. "You're still working?" he said.

"My friend, I was waiting for you when this woman came. Should I not make money? Just drive behind me. We can go to that beer parlor at Adeshina Street."

Chike started his engine as the woman boarded the back of Peter's motorcycle. Her baby's head dangled when she shifted her body to get comfortable. She grabbed Peter's waist after he sped off without giving word. The baby's head jerked back. Chike drove quickly to catch up, this time on the opposite side of the gridlock traffic he had just conquered. He never understood why Peter insisted on driving so recklessly.

Speeding was one thing; driving like Peter was another.

After cruising for two miles, they ran into a minor traffic jam. Chike watched Peter intensely as he weaved through cars. He thought about how he had learned the dangerous driving technique from him.

His friend's haste became even more apparent when he had to brake suddenly to avoid slamming into a car ahead of him. Chike could hear the female passenger on Peter's bike yell a few cautionary words, but Peter resumed his normal speed toward the lane on the far right, then made a swift turn onto Adeshina Street. Chike tried to keep up, but he reached the corner and slowed down.

Then the sound of skidding tires and a loud crash went off like a minor explosion. Chike turned onto the street, but he didn't see Peter anywhere ahead. He slowed down and came to a stop, watching as the crowd gathered above a steep gutter. The mob of people looked down, pointing and cursing. A woman's screams echoed from below. Chike inched closer to the crowd and heard the screams of a baby.

"Useless okada driver! Ọdẹ! See him inside gutter," an elderly man explained. "Can you imagine? Carrying a woman and pikin, he dey drive like dat?"

The words paralyzed Chike, but he managed to gather his composure as he parked his bike, then pushed his way through the crowd toward the edge of the gutter. Just as he suspected, he saw Peter moaning and rolling around in a deep open sewer with a shallow pool of murky water inside. A dark substance, maybe feces, maybe dirt, stained Peter's face and arms. The red Superman shirt he wore was unrecognizable.

Chike noticed the woman a few feet away from Peter struggling to stand with her baby still tied to her back. They both cried hysterically while covered in the same questionable filth.

"My God o, my God o," she cried. "Dis man wan kill me! He wan kill my pikin!"

The mob grew bigger, and more people stared down at Peter, shouting insults. By then, Peter was sitting in the gutter, cradling his legs in the fetal position. He kept his face buried between his knees, likely avoiding eye contact with the angry observers.

A man arrived with a rope and a large wooden plank and pushed his way through to the gutter. He stepped into the murky water in the ditch close to where the woman and baby lay helplessly. He pulled the baby girl out of the cloth that held her in place against her mother's back, then handed her to a woman standing in the crowd. People clapped and cheered.

Everyone turned their focus back on the Good Samaritan as he rolled the woman onto the wooden plank, then signaled for someone to hand him the rope he had brought. He tied it around her waist and around the plank with several fragile knots. Then he signaled for the other men to help lift her.

Chike couldn't bear to watch. He looked down at Peter, who by then was lying next to his crashed bike again. Peter tried to use his forearm to stand, but he shouted some obscenities, then settled back into the murky water.

Chike knelt at the edge of the gutter. "My guy, let me help you," he said as he extended his hand. Peter waved him off. Chike wondered how bad his injuries were and what Mr. Chimezie would say about his smashed okada.

"My guy, I don't think I can treat you to a beer tonight," Chike heard Peter say.

"Don't worry about that. I will help you get to a hospital." And he did.

18

PATIENCE POKED HER SLICE OF PIZZA WITH A PLASTIC fork and tried her best not to stare at Chike, who sat across from her eating his food wildly.

It was their first time dining at an eatery of this caliber as a couple. The restaurant, Maxwell Burger, was located in an outdoor bungalow in the parking lot of the UTC market in the trendy Eric Moore section of Lagos. The venue's DJ kept the crowd entertained with the sounds of the latest tunes.

Patience wanted Chike to feel comfortable, so she ate daintily. Tope, her school mother from her days as a junior student, had told her to be demure around a man taking her out to a nice place. It sounded like good advice. But she really wanted to devour her food the way he did.

"This place is nice, sha."

"It's okay," Chike said, unenthused.

Patience let this slide. She knew he was still sad about his friend.

"How is Peter? Have you checked on him?"

His sigh was deep and long, and he pressed himself against the back of his chair.

"Yes. Even with his broken arm and twisted ankle, he's just happy to be alive. And he's lucky the baby was fine. The woman, sha, she suffered. Cracked ribs, broken leg, broken arm. Too much."

Patience shuddered at the thought of the pain, and she hoped that Chike would never experience anything of the sort. She brushed the idea away, then looked around.

Dozens of university students and recent graduates populated the area. Groups of guys huddled together like ants in a pile.

"Why aren't the guys dancing?"

"Girls dey form too much so guys have to choose their steps wisely. Nobody wants rejection so we gather for protection."

"That is ridiculous. If a woman is not attracted to a man, why should she give him face?"

"Just to be polite."

"Did I form with you?"

"No, you practically threw yourself on me."

"What?" Patience slapped his hand. "You know, I liked you from the day I met you, but believe me, if you were daft enough to let me get away, I would not have stood in your way."

"I am enjoying you," he said, amused.

"What does that mean?"

He hesitated and looked out into the crowd. The DJ switched records and blasted a familiar mid-tempo track into the parking lot. The crowd responded almost immediately as the people spilled into the eatery to dance.

"Send down the raaiinnnn," people sang in unison.

She took a bite of her pizza while bobbing her head to the music, her eyes fixated on the crowd. A guy with a high-top fade and silly flip-up sunglasses approached one of the prettiest girls on location. She gave him the cold shoulder. *Chike's point proven*, Patience thought.

"This place is bubbling," she said, shifting her gaze to a group of well-dressed youth who were sharing a roasted chicken. Their sense of style suddenly made her self-conscious. She looked down at her short-sleeved T-shirt and old jeans. She was happy she had finally gotten them patched up by Modupe's tailor in Ibadan after the crotch area gave out from wearing them too much.

She looked across at Chike's fake Cross Colours tee. She remembered when he had gotten it from the bend-down market on their last trip there. It still looked somewhat wearable despite the color being a bit faded.

Though she never felt like a rich kid, she was an American citizen. There had to be a place for her among the cool. She thought of Bimpe and how she would fit right in at Maxwell Burger.

"You say this place is bubbling. I say it's okay, sha," he said. "For me it doesn't live up to all of the talk."

She watched as he stuffed a little less than half of the gyro he had ordered into his mouth.

"Has your salary increased?" she said.

"Increased? I'm driving okada," he mumbled with his mouth full of food.

"So the increase from Mr. Chimezie didn't help much?"

"I still need to find a job as an engineer," he said after taking a pause to swallow. "I didn't go to university to be driving people around on a motorcycle. The job is just too stressful." As he squared his shoulders and lifted his chin, Patience remembered that look of pride from one of his graduation photos.

"I'm proud of you," she said, touching his knee beneath the table. "You're strong and you're kind. If not, you wouldn't be doing the job just to support your mum."

The praise seemed to settle him. He relaxed his shoulders and propped his back against the wooden bench. He grabbed a few fries that had come with his meal and stuffed them into his mouth.

Patience thought about how she always knew exactly what to say to calm him down. She had mastered the art of stroking his ego.

"Chike, what if we do the bank job?" she said. She spoke in a hushed tone. She was sure none of the cool rich kids had to discuss doing illegal jobs to get what they needed.

"Why would you ask? There is no way I'm going to sacrifice my reputation just for quick money," he said.

"Well, it sounds like good money that could help you support your mum better," she said, realizing she was breaking her rule of staying on his good side.

"Wow, so you're considering it."

"Well, I need like twenty thousand naira for a ticket to New York. Then I'll need a return ticket if my mum is nowhere to be found and money for a place to lay my head and for food, of course."

"That's at least like eighty K. You're crazy."

"It's a lot, but I've been fooling myself trying to come up with ideas to raise that kind of money."

"You and this America. When will you let it go?"

"Would you let go of a chance to see your mum? I'm just considering different options."

"I don't want to be a criminal. I want to be an engineer."

"Yes, you're right. It's risky. But I was just thinking, what if we can actually do it without getting caught?"

"No," he said as he let his fork drop onto his plate. "I'm not doing it. I will just continue to suffer until I find a real job."

Patience began fiddling with the straw in her Fanta bottle.

"Kash finally agreed to go with me to my dad's to get my passport out of his safe. We leave tomorrow."

"So what are you—now a robber? How do you expect to get your passport without your popsie knowing?" He looked away from her.

Patience also looked away and watched how—like magic—Chaka Demus and Pliers's "Tease Me" summoned everyone to the dance floor. Even the posh girl she had seen earlier finally gave in to dancing with the guy she had previously turned down.

Patience didn't expect Chike to understand why she needed to get to America. She just wished he would see their lives as they truly were.

They were unlucky.

Even with her father and his wealth and his status, she was just as unlucky as he was.

"I'm tired of waiting for my life to make sense."

"I know, but I can't do that kind of thing."

After dinner, Patience begged Chike to take a stroll in the UTC market. She knew he didn't want to go because he couldn't afford to buy anything. She was surprised when he spent so much at Maxwell Burger on two meals.

"Let's just go in and browse."

"Who goes to a supermarket to look around?" he said, trailing a few steps behind her as she entered the store.

Chike caught up to her in the aisle stocked with foreign chocolates. Her eyes scanned a few of her favorite candy bars and assorted delicacies made of milk chocolate, dark chocolate, and white.

"These truffles remind me of Daddy."

"Chocolate?"

"One time he went to America on vacation and came back with a box of these. I looked at them, and I wished I had been with him on that trip. He dropped the box on the dining table like they were nothing."

Patience grabbed the truffles. She turned the box over and noticed the price tag. Chike leaned in.

"Chineke! For one box! This stupid store and its inflated prices."

"Chike, it's foreign. Of course they have to factor in the shipping costs and all that. Many Nigerians would pay this price without hesitation."

"Not this Nigerian man."

Patience dropped the truffles on the shelf and walked toward the next aisle. As Chike followed behind, she felt herself becoming irritated.

She scanned the shelves in the next aisle and was captivated: Oreo cookies, Chips Ahoy, Aunt Jemima pancake mix. Then she noticed a familiar product.

"Oh my God, I need this!" she said with excitement. "Jell-O. I've been looking for this brand."

"American brand," he said sarcastically. Chike grabbed the box of Jell-O to check the price.

"Wow, I guess you have three hundred naira to blow on this small thing."

"Yes, I do," Patience said defensively. "I will buy it and make some for Kash. I'm sure he would appreciate it."

"Kash is all about cash," Chike said. "If you can find a way to serve him money instead of Jell-O, I'm sure that would make him happier." He let out a lingering obnoxious laugh.

Patience took the box, then walked toward the front to check out. Chike followed behind her quickly. She handed the cashier the box of cherry-flavored Jell-O, then dug into her purse, pulling out several twenty- and fifty-naira notes. Though she had money saved, she knew spending that much on one item wasn't the best idea. She still had to buy food, along with her feminine products and have money for transportation. But she couldn't help herself.

Jell-O was a reminder of her mother, and having it made her picture their reunion. Her mother would see her face and know her instantly. They would share a long embrace. Then they would rekindle their old affection right away.

That was why she needed the Jell-O.

"Three hundred naira, madam," the cashier said. "You only gave me two hundred. We don't haggle at UTC."

Chike shook his head and rolled his eyes.

Patience rustled back through her purse. She pulled out a hundred-naira note. She held the money up, then extended it to the cashier. She squared her shoulders and lifted her chin, remembering Chike's prideful pose.

"Thank you, sir," she said. "I will come again."

They walked outside and made their way to Chike's okada.

"I want to go home with you tonight," she blurted out. "I'm not in the mood to see my roommates."

"Okay. Well, I can sleep on the floor. Emeka can take the couch."

Patience was delighted by his quick suggestion for sleeping arrangements, because it meant he was just as eager to spend the night with her.

They hopped on his bike and sped away.

PATIENCE AND CHIKE WALKED INTO HIS FLAT AND FOUND that they were alone.

"Emeka must be out. That gives us time to watch this Van Damme film." He flicked the television on and sat on the couch next to her.

Patience scrutinized him.

She didn't want to watch a film. She wanted to hear him say he would consider the bank job. She didn't feel like discussing Van Damme's fight scenes.

She wanted him to kiss her passionately and take her into his room.

She didn't understand it—how he could frustrate her and ignite every cell in her body at the same time.

"How many times have you seen this film, Chike?"

"I can't count." He put his arm around her and pulled her close. He kept his eyes on the screen as Van Damme crept around slowly in a dark warehouse, AK-47 in hand.

Patience turned her face toward him and bit his earlobe gently. She remembered when a female character in a foreign film she had watched did the same thing. It was as if the male character were her prey and that single sensual gesture made him come to her instantly.

Chike pulled away slightly. She took the side of his face and turned it toward hers. She kissed him and slid her hand down to his shoulder, down his chest, onto his lap. She knew how he felt when she placed her palm ever so slightly on his swollenness.

"Can we go to your bed now before Emeka comes back?" she whispered in his ear.

"Yes," he said with surprise in his eyes. "How did you learn how to seduce a man?"

"I guess from watching the films you wouldn't watch."

He chuckled under his breath. They stood. The sound of gunshots and men grunting from the television leaked past the room door. He kissed her neck, her earlobes, her lips. The sound of his breath began to mix with her own. He undressed her, and as her clothes came off, fear settled upon her.

"You're trembling a little. It's your first time, right?"

"My first time with you . . . yes."

He paused and looked into her eyes, shocked. "Okay," he said finally.

She felt him go limp. She grabbed his face and kissed him passionately until his fullness returned.

He took the lead, kissing every inch of her body. Soon she felt her body settle into bliss as he sank into her.

AFTER A LONG WHILE OF NESTLING AND KISSING AND GOING in and out of sleep, Chike finally asked her what she knew was on his mind.

"When did you lose your virginity?" He interlaced his fingers with hers.

"You want to talk about that now?" She hadn't kept track of time, and she was thankful Emeka still hadn't come home.

"I didn't expect that from you."

"Well, it happened in secondary school."

"With who? Your school was all girls."

"Yes, true. But I met someone."

"Who? Where?"

"I met someone who taught at the boys' school near ours," Patience said.

"You had sex with a teacher?"

"Yes." His tone made her feel as exposed as she had when she first got her period. She had stared nervously at the gush of blood in her panties, wishing she had the power to shoot bleach from her pupils. When Modupe caught her stealing pads from her top drawer, she questioned why Patience hadn't informed her, then told her father begrudgingly.

"Why? Why a teacher?"

"Why not? He was a man I was attracted to."

"He must have been at least ten years your senior," he said, seemingly holding back his true level of shock. "What happened?"

"No big story to tell, except that I thought I was pregnant afterward. Even after getting my period I still thought I was pregnant."

"If you got your period, why did you still think you were pregnant?"

"I was afraid. I didn't have anyone to tell. Was I supposed to tell my dad that I allowed some teacher to penetrate me?" She laughed, but Chike didn't. "I didn't even feel comfortable telling Margaret."

"Why?"

"What would she think of me? She's my little sister. And anyway, it was my decision. I wanted to do it."

"And now?" he said. He looked around the room as if the space explained their union.

"This feels good."

Silence lingered between them.

"Have you ever wished you to belonged to someone, anyone, but you just don't really?" Patience said, avoiding eye contact with him.

Chike paused and stroked her arm. She could sense his pity. She wished she hadn't asked.

"No, I can't say that I've ever felt that. Is that how you feel?" he said.

"No, not like that. I think I'm being too deep right now."

She laughed lightly. He didn't join her.

They fell silent, and she scolded herself again for baring that part of herself.

What did he think of her now?

"Should I be surprised that *you're* not a virgin?" she said, finally breaking the silence again.

A roar of laughter burst through Chike. "No," he said, trying to tame his amusement.

She waited for him to catch his breath.

"Chike, there's so much I know you hold back from me," she said finally. "Hopefully, in time you'll be more open."

"That's how you see me?" He sat up and looked into her eyes deeply, confidently. How rare of him to do so, she thought.

"Yes, Chike, that's how I see you."

19

FINALLY, PATIENCE THOUGHT WHEN SHE AND KASH stepped onto the bus heading toward Ibadan.

"Brother Kash, thank you for doing this."

"Doing what? Nothing has been done yet. I wish we could just slip in and slip out of the house. Staying with Daddy for two whole days? Mehn."

"We can't just slip in and out. You know Daddy's gate man will tell him we came. But we are going at a good time. Modupe should be out when we get there, so let's just get the passport quickly. Remember to tell them we came home because I think I have malaria, so you had to escort me."

"I hope we don't get caught."

"We won't. But if we do, I will be the one he throws away next," Patience said, recalling how her father tossed her mother's things out of the house.

She turned to Kash. His expression turned blank. "So you're still worried?" she said. "When you came to me and said you would do it, I thought you weren't afraid anymore."

"It's not like that."

"Why would you be afraid of Daddy? Your current job isn't exactly risk-free."

"Listen, a man has to eat."

Patience couldn't completely fault him for his fear. Everyone told them they would get caught. She too was petrified, but she was willing to take the chance, because no passport, no New York.

Stick to the plan, she thought, no matter how precarious it was.

"Remember, his black safe is all the way in the back of his walk-in closet. You brought the tools you need to open the lock?"

"Yes. My guy showed me a few tricks. I will get it open. That is not my concern."

"You're worried about seeing Daddy."

"Of course," he finally admitted. "The last time I saw him he said things that were just . . ."

Patience remembered how her father had called him "olòdo" and how he had told him he would no longer "support a stupid fool" after Kash failed all his classes the year his father died. She, too, thought it was cruel.

"Kash, do you miss your dad?"

"What kind of question is that? You miss your mum, right?"

"I do," she said. "I know my dad wasn't good to you, but your dad wasn't good to my mum," she said. "I told you I saw how they put her out. He was there helping my dad throw her things outside."

"A man cannot apologize for another man's wrongdoing. But I'm sorry on his behalf anyway."

"That means something to me. I'm sorry for my father too."

They were quiet. Patience stared straight ahead at nothing in particular. She was happy that she and Kash didn't allow their fathers to put a wedge between them.

"Remember when we started locking Margaret in the bathroom in the boys' quarters when she and Modupe first moved in?" Kash said.

"And she would scream," Patience said, shaking her head. "We were so wicked. And she never told Modupe."

"Margaret really loves you."

"Maybe she just feels sorry for me."

"I said she loves you, jàre," he said, waving her off.

Patience felt warm as another memory formed. "Kash, remember when you came to stay with us when your dad traveled and you put that blue dye in the bucket that Mr. Olayo used to wash Modupe's clothes? Poor Mr. Olayo. He was almost sacked that day when Modupe saw her clothes."

"That was my only regret. He was good guy." Kash stared bemusedly into the distance. "We were bored, and Modupe and her scattered brain were too easy to disturb."

"Mummy Bukky, she flogged you well that day, ehn. Ah, that woman was a tyrant. Aunty Lola told me she gave my mum hell when she and my dad moved back to Nigeria."

"I'm not surprised," Kash said. "But why didn't you let Modupe be like your mum? She's a little crazy, yes, but she's not horrible."

"Kash, you know I really tried with Daddy's women. Remember Sade?"

"Ahhh, Sade. Daddy, he fucked up with Sade. That one was fine, o."

"Not only fine. She was good to me. She would weave my hair for school. She made my favorite foods all the time. She was teaching me how to cook. She was genuine."

"Genuine and beautiful," Kash said, curling his lip up mischievously.

"I was young when my mum left Nigeria. I needed somebody like her. Before Sade, Daddy would pick me up hours late from school."

"That's Daddy," Kash said, snickering.

"When Sade was with Daddy, she picked me up on time every day. Even my primary school headmistress loved her."

"Ah, it was when she moved into Daddy's house that everything just fucked up with her and Daddy." Kash shook his head.

"When he brought that other girl home while Sade was there in my room doing my hair, Sade cursed him that day and left. She was only half done with my hair. I thought she would come back. Come and see people at school laughing at me, calling me iroko tree head."

Kash seemed highly entertained, though she was certain she had already told him the story.

"When I was there stranded after school, I knew I would never see Sade again."

"Daddy. Original play-ah."

"But honestly, it's not about Sade or Modupe. My mother didn't die. How can a person just disappear? How am I supposed to know myself without my mum in my life?"

"You are Patience Adewale, daughter of the most high," he said playfully.

"And you are completely useless." They laughed until their laughs melted into a long, steady silence. She thought about how she had never told Kash that she had stopped believing in God. Her total denouncement happened after the reverend mothers who ran her secondary school forced her and her classmates to read Revelations as punishment whenever they disobeyed. She looked at Kash and wondered if his convictions had been shattered like hers.

"Kash, really. How do you feel? Your father is gone. He's dead. Your mother has been dead for a long time now. You finished three years of university, but you're barely surviving. Should I be more worried about you?"

"Listen, in life, we are given what we are given, and whether we accept it or not, what we are given is our truth. Like all this petty stealing we're doing—will it change who we are? Emeka wants to become rich from this thing, but this kind of work can never remove a person's destiny. We are who we are, and we do what we need to do to survive. My father is gone and I'm here. I'm getting by."

"Does that mean you don't want to do the job?"

"Of course not, o! We need money! What I am saying is that you will always be Patience, my cousin Patience, daughter of a wealthy man who banished her mother. I will be Kash through and through. What came before will remain. And what is destined will take place."

"You must be sprinkling grass in those cigarettes you smoke."

They shared the delicate nature of the moment, and she thought about how she didn't understand a word Kash said. Indeed, because it was Kash, she knew she might never fully understand.

BY THE TIME PATIENCE OPENED HER EYES, SHE SAT UP and saw the familiar landscape of her hometown greet her from the bus window.

Ibadan—the ancient city built on seven hills and several plains. Patience stared out into the distance toward the bundles of red roofs propped unevenly above dilapidated, cream-colored houses littered across Oke Mapo Hill. Ibadan was the place that had birthed both her parents. She was proud of that.

Later, as she strolled, the sun beamed, and rays of white light kissed the faces of Ibadan residents. It wove itself through their bodies, increasing the collective energy they had shared since daybreak. Market women scurried to sell their goods to shoppers who flooded their stalls. Workers trekked and caught rides to local eateries. Women carrying babies on their backs and heavy inventory on their heads walked cautiously as they balanced their entire lives in one trip. Street hawkers wearing their merchandise around their necks like jewels weaved through traffic, hustling for the next transaction. Patience noticed two quarreling like true Ibadan people who could cut at one's soul as if cursing were an art form.

"Ko ni dara fun ẹ, bastard," shouted a street hawker wearing a ripped shirt and plastic slippers that were two sizes too small. "Ìyá baba ẹ," his opponent replied, pressing his palm against thin air to dismiss the curse.

Ibadan faithful, she thought.

After a long trek up the road, they arrived at her father's house. Kusa, her father's gate man, approached, looking confused.

"Patience, why are you not in school?"

"Mr. Kusa, I'm not well. I think I have malaria."

He peered at her, then at Kash, clearly suspicious.

"Kash, I thought you and Daddy dey quarrel."

"No, Kusa. Daddy and me are okay."

Kusa stepped aside, still looking skeptical. They rushed up the long winding pavement toward the entrance, then knocked on the door. The house girl opened it.

"Fatima, báwo ni? Mo ni malaria, and I need to get something in my room."

"Ah, Patience, your Yoruba is terrible," Kash said. "You spend too much time trying to talk like an American."

Patience pushed him playfully.

"Fatima, ṣé a lè wọle," Kash said.

Fatima stepped aside, and they walked in. Somehow the furniture seemed even more gaudy.

"Fatima, did madam go to her club meeting?"

"Yes, ó ti lọ. She has gone."

"Come, help me in my room," Patience said to Fatima. "Kash wants to check something in the storage room." She flashed Kash a coded smile, then looked at her watch. Modupe wasn't due back home for another three hours or so, and her dad, another five hours. Plenty of time to take what was hers.

An hour had passed, and Kash still hadn't returned to her room with her passport. She kept busy and stalled Fatima as they rearranged and folded the clothes she had left behind in her closet. "Thank you, ehn, Fatima. I go give you pocket money," Patience said once they were done.

Had something gone wrong? she wondered. Then he knocked and opened her room door.

"Fatima, I am hungry, o."

"What do you want to eat?"

"Iyan. I beg."

"Patience, will you eat pounded yam too?"

"Yes, thank you, Fatima."

She left the room, and Kash collapsed onto Patience's foldout cushion.

"Did you get it open?" Patience said in a loud whisper.

"Yes, but there was no passport there. There was this." He flashed her a wad of cash.

"How much?"

"Five K."

"You took five K but no passport. Not even enough for a plane ticket."

"It's pocket money for now. I said there was no passport there, and there wasn't much cash there anyway."

"It has to be there, Kash. Modupe said it over and over again. That's where he keeps our documents."

"I didn't see any documents. Maybe he put them somewhere else."

"Patience!" The sound of Modupe's voice rang out through the hall. She was two hours earlier than she expected. Kash quickly stuffed the money inside Patience's backpack. They sat on the bed and braced themselves for her to enter.

She flung the door open. "Patience, they said you're not well. Ah, Kashimawo, why are you here?" she said, startled at the sight of him. "If Daddy sees you here, he will not be happy."

"Mummy, I wasn't feeling well, so Kash came with me."

"Yes, Ma, I wanted to make sure she got home safely. I think she needs a chemist."

"So there's no chemist in Lagos?"

"Yes, Mummy, but it's hard to care for myself alone in the hostel."

Modupe paused and tightened her lips. She grabbed her purse and dug inside. "Okay. Kash, take money. Take her to the chemist now. You can stay until she's ready to go back. But when Daddy comes home, I don't know what he will say about this. Your school is not on holiday yet. Less than three months and you're already back home."

"Thank you, Mummy. Don't worry, I will catch up with my studies."
Modupe walked out and left Patience's door open.

"I can't believe the passport wasn't there and now we are stuck
here," Patience whispered.

"At least Modupe gave us more money. We can add it to what I took
from Daddy."

"What about my passport? That's why we are here."

"Maybe you should just forget the passport for now."

"Why would I do that?"

"Because only God knows where it is. There was no birth certificate
either. If you want it, you have to check with the embassy."

"I will find my passport, Kash."

Patience and Kash continued their debate, ignoring how time
moved on.

"Patience, your daddy is here," Modupe announced on the other
side of her door. She and Kash stood frantically.

"Why is Patience home?" she heard her father say as she and Kash
moved carefully downstairs.

"Daddy, I wasn't feeling well," she called out. They made their
way into the hall where he stood. Her father looked at Kash, and his
expression melted into one of confusion. "I think it's malaria. Kash
brought me home," she added quickly.

Her father stared them both down and walked into the sitting
room without another word.

Patience and Kash hesitated, then made their way into the sitting
room too. Patience sat across from her father, and each time he glanced
at her, briefly but piercingly, she felt herself wilt.

"Patience, why didn't you call from school to let us know you are
sick? You came all the way to Ibadan with Kashimawo. Why?" he said.
She knew then that he didn't believe her story.

"Daddy, no wahala, one of my friends, he was coming so we took a
ride with him," Kash said.

"My darling, I've given them money for a chemist," Modupe said as she sipped the tea that Fatima had brought her. "They were supposed to go there before you came home."

"A sick person would have run to the chemist," he said as he turned on the television. "Kash, I hope you have not been showing Patience any of your foolishness in Lagos. I sent her there to study."

"No, Sa. Patience is very, very focused."

"Patience, is that true? Are you focused?" His tone matter-of-fact.

"Yes, Daddy. I am." She hoped he didn't notice the quiver in her voice.

He peered at her. "How have your studies been?"

"Fine, Daddy. I've been doing fine."

"Fine, ehn?"

"Yes, Daddy. I'm doing my best. Mummy, have you visited Margaret?" Patience said. She turned to Modupe, desperate to change the subject.

"Yes, she's getting on well, though she misses you. That is to be expected. You've been with her all these years."

All the sound left in the room was the chatter of NTA news coming from the TV and the clank of Modupe's porcelain teacup each time she put it on its saucer.

Modupe looked up at Patience uncomfortably. Patience shifted her gaze to Kash, who was tapping his foot nervously.

"Patience, you said you've been doing your best."

"Yes, Sa."

Why is he back on this topic? she wondered.

"We had a few impromptu tests."

"Impromptu tests," he said, then paused for what felt like hours. "Did you sit for those tests? Be very careful before you answer."

Patience was stunned. She wondered then who had told him she had been missing classes and tests. Was it the professor she despised?

"Daddy, I missed some of my lectures when I wasn't feeling well, but I've been trying my best."

"So you're saying you've only missed a few lectures since you came down with malaria?"

Patience sank into clear defeat and tuned in to the effects it had on her body—limpness, vacantness, sluggishness.

"So it's true. You didn't go to several of your lectures. But you say you're trying your best. Who told you to *try* anything? You are there to *do* as I told you to do. You should have known that I would have someone there to monitor you. And still you disobeyed me. You will not disgrace my name."

"Daddy, I am not disgracing you. I will do better when I go back."

"You will not go back."

"Daddy . . . what do you . . ."

"Kashimawo, was it you who put this in her mind—that she can dismiss her lectures and exams?" her father said.

"Sa? No, Sa." Kash waved his hands, objecting to the thought.

"Patience, I have told you that your only concern should be your studies. I cannot allow any daughter of mine to become a wayward child. It's good you came home. You saved my driver a trip to Lagos."

"What do you mean?" she said.

"I already enrolled you at University of Ibadan last week. You should know by now—I know everybody in this Ibadan, including UI's chancellor. From today, you are no longer a student at UNILAG. You will stay right here in Ibadan. You will attend UI, and you will not live on any campus. Your room upstairs will be the only hostel you know."

"Daddy, no! Please!"

"Patience, don't shout at your daddy," Modupe interjected.

"Look at you. You're just like your mum. Behaving as if you are a man."

"Daddy, I promise I will do better. Please! I beg you," she said, struggling to tame her emotions.

"I've made up my mind. I will call UNILAG and tell them to rescind your acceptance there. Tomorrow morning, Kash will take you to the chemist down the road. When you come back, you will go to UI to find out about your lectures. Do you hear me?" he shouted with the ferocity of a beast.

"Yes, Daddy!" Patience ran upstairs into her room as her father shouted obscenities. She sat on the edge of her bed and sobbed. Kash appeared in the doorway.

"That wasn't the plan," he whispered as he sat beside her.

"Plan? When do I ever get to have a plan?" she said.

PATIENCE HELD TIGHTLY TO THE STRAPS OF HER BACK-pack as she and Kash walked up the road to the local chemist.

"We should go to Mr. Biggs to eat. We can pay with the money Modupe gave us for your medicine," Kash said. "You don't have malaria, but I get empty belle syndrome."

"I'm not hungry," Patience said.

"Patience, you have to eat. You can't punish yourself over this thing."

"I'm not punishing myself anymore. We just can't eat anywhere right now. We have to get back to Lagos soon."

Kash stopped in the middle of the road as Patience picked up speed. "Patience!" he called out. "What do you mean, get back to Lagos? Daddy said you can't go back to Lagos. He said no more UNILAG. Patience!" he called out.

She kept walking. He ran after her and grabbed her arm when he caught up.

"Kash, I'm going back to Lagos with you, and I'm going to stay at your place until I find my way to New York," she said. "How will I ever get to New York with Daddy monitoring my every move? I don't need UNILAG, I just need money and my passport, and I know I will get both." She stared at him and felt her eyes adopt her father's piercing gaze. Kash let her arm go.

"If you go, Daddy will kill me," Kash said.

"Daddy already washed his hands of you. Let's go."

"You know if you run away you will have disgraced yourself in Daddy's eyes. You can never come back."

"That would be the first good thing to come from this whole situation."

"Patience, why na? Have you seen my place? You want to live like me?"

"Kash, you have your independence. Do you know how important that is? Help me find mine."

He paused, and she knew she had touched him with her words. She started walking again. He walked silently beside her.

"Patience, what if you can't find your mum?"

"What if I never try?"

"You have no money."

"I will do the job."

"Ehn? The bank? Na lie."

"Yes, I will do the job."

Kash ran in front of Patience to stop her from walking. He stared into her eyes.

"We need Chike too," he said.

"Don't worry, I will talk to Chike again."

With Chike, she would have to be firm because Chike would smell the stench of what existed beneath all her toughness—pure fear. She, with all her doubts, could take money from a bank?

Take money from a bank and not get caught?

Take money from a bank, then walk around the next day as if she had earned the money? She was not a thief.

She didn't want this.

She had no choice.

"Daddy left me no choice."

A woman without a mother is empty. The irony—needing to do something unlike herself to actually find herself.

Would she get caught?

She remembered that she had long been acquainted with uncertainty.

"One day we will meet again," her mother had said in her letter, but her mother had not come for her, her father gave her no explanation, and she could no longer wait.

For her mother's words to stand, *she* would have to make them true.

20

BY THE TIME THE BUS REACHED ENUGU, CHIKE WAS exhausted—maybe from the nine-hour drive or the mental drain of listening to Emeka criticize his job as an okada driver.

"That could have been you who crashed into the gutter like Peter," Emeka said.

"When will you stop discussing Peter's accident?" Chike said.

"I won't stop. The accident should have opened your eyes to the dangers of driving okada. You need to start thinking of real ways to make money."

"So it's not dangerous to walk into a bank and open a fake account?" Chike said sarcastically.

Though Chike was quick to defend his position, inside he knew he was now afraid of driving. Every time he got back onto his bike, he saw a vision of Peter struggling to emerge from the bottom of a filthy gutter.

Chike stared out the window, realizing they were a short distance from his mother's house. He was nervous about seeing her in so much pain.

He was also uneasy about how much her care would cost.

His earnings just barely covered the food in the house, petrol for his bike, and his everyday needs. His savings were next to nothing.

Chike and Emeka stepped off the bus at their stop. Emeka walked a few feet, then let out a loud kissing sound when he saw a cab driving toward their destination.

"Emeka, we can walk. Why are you hailing a car?"

"You cheap man, I'm too tired to walk. We need to get to Mama's place as soon as possible."

"Where is the money coming from? You always expect me to pay for the things you want."

Emeka ignored Chike and walked over to the driver. He told him their destination and worked out a price. He opened the back door and climbed in, leaving it open for Chike.

As they drove on, Chike looked out the window at the familiar streets of his hometown. The common smell of burning refuse filled his nostrils, but somehow the air seemed cleaner than it did in Lagos. Chike looked into the distance at the tall hills spread out like giant funnels turned upside down. It was a calming sight as the driver moved the car up a busy paved street. Beautiful clay roofs atop two-story homes, grass, and bushes lay stretched across the landscape's wondrous peaks and dips.

Chike marveled at the beauty of his hometown. He remembered the days he and his friends would climb to the top of one of the hills above an old coal mine, then stare down, astonished by the sprawling valleys they had left below.

The driver turned onto the street leading to his mother's residential neighborhood. The untarred road made their ride a roller coaster. As the driver slowed for ditches, Emeka held on to the handle above the passenger window. Their bodies shifted from right to left and jerked forward as the car struggled to move on. Chike felt his stomach bubble midway through. His body was no longer accustomed to being a passenger on uneven, untarred roads. Lagos was ahead of Enugu in that regard.

Chike unclenched his stomach muscles at the sight of Nneka's house in the distance. It was the same brown color with beige trim.

The lanky coconut tree they had sat under the first time he stole a kiss from her was still a few steps from her house. He wondered if she was home, if she had gotten married, if she had moved away for school.

To Chike's surprise, Emeka paid the driver when they arrived at Mama's house. The light pink bungalow was covered in layers of brown dust. Weeds grew from the cracks in the large, exposed brick gate that surrounded it. Their father had commissioned workers to build the gate when Chike was eight years old, but he couldn't afford to have it sealed with cement and painted. Year after year, he had promised to have it done, until he passed away just before Chike entered secondary school.

Then they noticed their mum's rickety table propped against the gate, the same table that had once held her inventory of corn and sweets—an income she relied on whenever the Secretariat in Enugu withheld her salary for long stretches. Since her arthritis had kicked in, she had been sidelined from both the Secretariat and her little business.

Emeka opened the gate and stood before his childhood home with all its imperfections. The cracks in the paint made it look as if the entire structure would crumble from the slightest push. The mosquito mesh on the screen door was bandaged with a nylon bag.

Chike and Emeka were startled when their cousin Adama burst out of the house and ran to hug them.

"Welcome, Brother Chike and Brother Emeka," she said, stepping back to survey them timidly. "Mama is inside resting. I was helping her cook the stew that we will offer you."

"Adama, you're a woman now o," Chike said.

Before he went off to university, her breasts were buds. Now they rivaled the most endowed girls he had dated in Lagos. He hoped she wasn't sleeping around like many of them were. Adama was too good for that, he thought.

"Please o, if you have a boyfriend make sure I don't see him while I'm here," Emeka said, almost reading Chike's mind.

Chike and Emeka followed her inside.

"Where are my children?" Mama said with excitement.

Chike's grin stretched across his face like a rubber band pulled to capacity.

"We're here, Mama, we're here," Emeka said.

Chike walked over to where she sat. Both her legs were propped on a wooden stool. He bent over and gave her a hug. Emeka followed his lead but embraced her robust frame a little longer.

"My children, o. I'm so happy, my God."

Chike's smile disappeared when he noticed the swelling of her knees. Parts of her light caramel skin looked bruised and pulled.

"Mama, we should get you to a doctor right away," Chike said as he sat on the stool next to her.

"You just arrived. Won't you eat something? Adama has been cooking for you all day." She smiled at her niece, who stood in the doorway. "That girl was sent to me by God. She has taken care of me so well. Please, take care of her for me the way she has pampered me."

Chike felt a thumping pressure in his head. He had forgotten to budget pocket money to give Adama. They were lucky to have her, since they couldn't afford house help for Mama.

"Mama, I think Chike is right. We should get you to the doctor before he leaves," Emeka said finally.

Chike, Emeka, and Mama arrived at Enugu's National Orthopedic Hospital just an hour after they arrived in town. When Chike handed the taxi driver the fare, his heart sank.

On this trip, every bit of cash mattered.

A nurse greeted them at the hospital entrance, as they held their mother by her forearms.

"Madam, you've returned. Have you come to settle your bill?"

"Yes, my children have come to assist me. They live in Lagos," she said proudly as she walked toward the waiting area, arm in arm with her sons.

"Wow, Lagos boys, you are welcome. The receptionist will assist you with your payment. Then you can see the doctor again."

Chike and Emeka held their mother as she sank into one of the rickety armchairs in the waiting area. When they released her arms, she adjusted the back of her short-cropped wig.

"Your mum is Comfort Okonma, correct?" the woman at the desk asked Chike and Emeka.

"Yes, Comfort Okonma is her name. What is her bill?" Emeka said.

"Let me check."

Chike looked around the room as the secretary flipped through her files. The last time he was in a hospital was when he had typhoid fever in primary school. Despite the old furniture in the waiting area, he was happy the place was kept clean. He had heard horror stories about unsanitary rooms, limited medical equipment, and incorrect diagnoses.

"Ah, Mama, your bill has gotten high," the receptionist said, looking at her over her slender eyeglasses. She shifted her gaze to Chike and Emeka. "Your mum owes five thousand naira," she said.

Chike was stunned. It was no small sum, yet he thought it might have been a lot more.

"We will pay it right now," he said as he pulled his wallet out of his front pocket.

Emeka brought out a few bills held together with a rubber band. He placed half the money on the table. Chike was surprised that he didn't complain.

The nurse reemerged from one of the hospital rooms to check if the payment had been settled. She grabbed hold of a copy of the itemized bill as if she was coming to collect a personal debt.

"The doctor can see you now, madam," she said, seeing the money exchange hands.

Chike and Emeka helped Mama into the room a few feet from the waiting area.

"Kedụ, madam, how are you feeling today?" the doctor said.

"I'm still in pain. My knees have gotten more swollen since my last visit."

"Madam, we're happy you were able to settle your bill so we can continue with your care. We've assessed your situation, and we now know you're suffering from septic arthritis."

"I know I have arthritis, Doctor. You explained it before. I need more physical therapy."

"No, madam. Septic arthritis is quite severe. It could lead to disease or even death if it's not treated properly. We will continue the therapy with you, but you need surgical drainage to really see better results in your health."

The word *surgical* made Chike's heart plummet into his groin. Surgery could cost a fortune. How were he and Emeka going to pay for this and keep their place in Lagos? Pretty soon the landlord would be knocking at their door for his yearly rent.

"After the surgical drainage, we may keep you here for one day to observe your progress," the doctor continued.

Chike looked at Emeka, who was fidgeting and playing with his fingernails.

"How much will this cost?" Emeka put his hands on his hips.

"The secretary will give you the price."

"Tell her to come now to let us know the price, Doctor," Emeka said, flailing his hands, then crossing his arms over his chest. Chike knew he was annoyed.

The doctor walked out of the room, then came back almost immediately with the secretary, who was holding a calculator and a clipboard. She began typing numbers into the machine and then wrote down several figures.

"For surgical drainage, one night stay over, and therapy, fifty thousand naira," she said.

The brothers looked at each other. Chike knew what Emeka was thinking. Chike was the first to turn his attention to their mother.

"Don't worry, Mama," he said, rubbing her hand. "We will find a way."

"DRINK MORE," IKE SAID.

Chike, already on his fifth beer, didn't want another, but he didn't want to kill the fun for his friends.

"Okay, I will have one more," he told the waitress.

When Ike had come by Mama's house just an hour before to invite him to the local bar, Chike couldn't have left home any quicker. The news of Mama's medical expenses heightened the stress he had already been hauling around since he arrived. He was ready to decompress with Ike and Nnamdi, though he was hardly prepared for the amount of alcohol they were consuming.

"I'm sure you do this every day in Lagos. You're a big man now," Nnamdi said.

"No, actually, I'm not a big man. I told you I'm still looking for real work," Chike said as he fiddled with his empty beer bottle.

"Nonsense. You're an engineer now. How can you not be a big man? Even if you no get job, you dey for Lagos. That place is expensive."

"That's the point," Chike said with frustration. "It's more expensive, so when you have a degree with no real job, you suffer," he said.

"What are you saying? Lagos get plenty jobs, na."

Chike couldn't believe how naive his friends were. It had been only two years since he saw them on his last visit, but it felt like decades. He couldn't totally fault them, since they weren't privy to the realities of living in a big city. They barely left Enugu at all.

Chike wanted to change the subject. He had been dying to get an update on his first love.

"How's Nneka?"

"Hmmm, look at this man, still thinking about Nneka. She has married," Nnamdi said. "Her husband is very rich."

"Married?" Chike said, trying to mask his disappointment. Then he thought of Patience. He told himself he was fine with Nneka being married.

"Yes, she married one businessman from Nsukka. He get two private schools," Nnamdi said.

"No, na architect," Ike said.

"Architect? I don't know, o. I just know he get plenty money and plenty cars," Nnamdi said.

Chike couldn't believe Nneka was married to a wealthy man—yet another punch to his battered ego. There was a time when he had pictured himself marrying her in his future life no matter how much time and space came between them.

"Beer, Sa," the waitress said, handing the unopened bottle to Chike.

"Please, give me one more," Ike said.

"Me too, give me one more," Nnamdi said.

"Na wa o, you guys can really drink," Chike said after opening his bottle of stout. "That's like the tenth beer for both of you."

"Ah-ahn, it's not every day our guy comes home to visit. When you're here, we have to enjoy," Ike said.

"True, it's good to see your scattered faces," Chike said through a burst of laughter.

"Scattered face? Look at this useless man," Nnamdi replied.

"Anything else?" the waitress asked as she returned with two beers.

"How about some suya," Nnamdi said.

The waitress turned and headed out the back door to get the suya meat from the grill outside. The pepper and smoky aroma filled the room when the door swung shut.

Chike took another sip of beer, then suddenly got a bad feeling.

Nnamdi was unemployed, and Ike was barely making a living as a new fish dealer. How were they going to pay the bill?

"I don't think I will eat suya," Chike said, putting them to the test. "I will finish this beer and go home. But don't let me spoil the celebration. Stay and continue to eat. My head has not been correct since I heard about my mama's condition."

"So you won't pay the bill?" Ike said.

"Pay the bill? Is it not me who should be pampered? I'm your visitor."

"Look at this man," Ike said. "He has moved to Lagos, but when he comes home he dey count his money. Look at us here struggling."

"Me too, I'm struggling. I told you that," Chike said. "But you're ordering food and drinks as if I'm a rich man."

The waitress returned with a large plate of barbecued meat and diced peppers spread on a platter. All three of the men looked at one another. The tension was thick enough to slice with a machete.

"Ah, madam, I don't think we can eat this suya anymore," Nnamdi said.

IT WAS PITCH-BLACK AND THE MOSQUITOES WERE ON THE hunt for human flesh, but Chike decided to sit outside on the front porch after Ike dropped him off.

The sounds of crickets chirping and chickens cooing around Mama's small plot of land provided the ease he needed. He couldn't believe the evening he had spent with Ike and Nnamdi.

The audacity.

How could they just assume he could afford such a bill? He paid it anyway because he knew they had nothing.

Then he thought of Adama. He didn't have much to give her. He began to regret the money he had spent on Patience at Maxwell Burger. But he had promised to take her when he thought he was getting his first engineering job.

"What are you doing outside?" Emeka said as he emerged from the house.

"Nothing." Chike stared wide-eyed at the gate surrounding the house. "I just needed some fresh air."

"You should be thinking about how we're going to pay Mama's hospital bill," Emeka said in a whisper. "Chike, I know you're a noble man, but we need money and we need it fast."

"I know," Chike replied without blinking. As he kept his focus on his mother's unfinished gate, he thought of his father. A rush of sadness came over him.

"Chike, we need to do the bank job. It's the only way we can handle our duties as men. Mama needs us."

"I know."

"You know?"

"Yes, I know . . . I will do it."

There was a long pause. Chike could sense his brother's delight.

"What about Patience? We need Patience," Emeka said.

"Don't worry, she's already in."

21

PATIENCE TUGGED ON HER BLACK TAILORED SKIRT AS SHE walked into the UBN Bank in Ikeja. She took off her sunglasses and stuffed them into her faux-leather tote.

She scanned the room.

A host of financial advisers sat at large tables beyond the queue of customers waiting to be called by the next available bank teller. That was where she needed to be, she thought.

She was somewhat startled when a short, chubby banker approached, smiling a wide smile, showing off uneven bottom teeth that resembled the aerial view of a metropolis.

"Madam, can I help you with anything?" he said.

"Yes, you can help me, sir," she said, stressing her American phonetics, allowing *sa* to become like *sur*. "I'm here to open a business account."

She tugged her skirt down again. She knew she should have bought the suit one size bigger, but Emeka had insisted she dress like a professional woman who was not afraid to be a little sexy.

Beyond her clothes, Emeka had coached her on what to do, how to look, and how to handle emergency situations. He had explained how he had assessed the bank when he walked in a week before to appraise the security guards, the bankers, the layout of the room. He had pretended he wanted to open an account, asked several questions, then made up a phony reason why the bank wasn't well suited for his needs.

"You've come to the right bank. I can assist you. I'm Mr. Kolawole. And you are?"

"Ms. Da Silva."

"Ms. Da Silva, please follow me," he replied as he walked to his desk. He pulled out a padded chair for her, then sat on his large black leather seat. He opened the drawer on the left side of his workstation and handed her a card from a large stack.

"Madam, please fill out your personal information." He gave her a pen imprinted with the UBN logo.

Patience pulled out the fake identification card that Chike had one of his former classmates create. Though Emeka made her recite her fake identity over and over again, she was afraid she would forget something. She placed the card on the banker's desk and glanced at it.

"Ms. Da Silva, can I please see your ID card?"

"I'm sorry, what for?"

"I just want to start putting your information into our system," he said.

"Oh. I see. Here . . . here you go." She gave him the card, and he placed it in front of him and began typing into his computer. Patience smiled, then handed him her completed bank slip. She wondered if he saw her bottom lip quivering.

"Ah, so you're here to open an account for your boutique, Sade's Fashions. So many women are making a lot of money doing this clothing business."

"Yes, sir, it's very lucrative. I've done well for myself so far," Patience said. She felt her confidence rise. She knew a boutique would be the perfect phony business to present since she had visited a few with Bimpe in Lagos.

"I can see that you're very fashionable yourself. What kind of clothes do you sell?"

"For now, I sell native wear, but I'm expanding to sell foreign designer brands."

"My sister is always talking about the latest fashions."

Patience sat back in her chair watching the banker type more information into the computer. She wiped her moist hands against her snug skirt, hoping he didn't notice her nerves.

"Madam, I need to see documents for proof of business. Also cash or a company check that you want to deposit."

Patience opened her briefcase and pulled out a manila folder. She rustled through the papers inside, then gave the banker a few documents. She went into her purse, then her wallet, and pulled out the check Oga had given them. She glanced at the handwriting—the date, December 14, 1992. By this time she would be home, doing whatever she could to avoid helping Modupe prepare for her holiday gatherings. She and Margaret would watch taped episodes of one American show or another or listen to pirated CDs they'd buy from Gbagi Market. She wondered how her sister had taken the news that she had left home.

Patience slid the check across the banker's desk.

"Okay. For your business account for Sade's Fashions, you're depositing two million naira," the banker said.

"That is correct, sir," she replied. She folded her hands together on the banker's desk. She smirked flirtatiously.

The banker returned her smile and then looked down at her documents. He leafed through the papers and then started typing more information into his computer.

"Ms. Da Silva, if you're looking for someone to manage your boutique, I can recommend my sister. She is very hardworking and very fashionable," he said with a cheeky grin. Patience looked around at the other bankers. The security guard standing in the doorway made her uneasy.

She remembered Emeka's advice: deflect if the banker got too personal.

"How long have you been in banking?" she said.

"For ten years now, madam. My sister studied chemistry, but if she can get a job with you for now I will be happy. We just need her to work. Can you imagine . . . I'm taking care of my grown sister, my mother, and my elder brother? I have my own children."

Patience glanced back at the security guard, still battling her nerves. She pictured herself being set up by the chubby banker. What if he was making her think everything was going well so he could stall until the police came? She looked down at her watch.

"Wow, it's three thirty already. I have to send the driver to pick up my mother. I'm sorry to rush you, but I must be on my way soon," she said, sitting up in her seat.

"Madam, we are almost finished. Just one moment." He typed faster. Patience sat back in her chair, looking toward the entrance. The banker looked up at her. He gathered her documents, as if he noticed her uneasiness.

"Madam, I'm so sorry for the delay. Here is your receipt for the money deposited. Patience looked down at the slip. Two million naira deposited from a bogus check. She felt relieved.

"Your check should clear in the next five days. At least 80 percent of the funds are available," the banker said. "But please, madam, consider my sister for a position with your company."

As Patience grabbed for her documents, Mr. Kolawole held on to them. He stared at her. She felt her body begin to shrink.

She was caught. She knew it.

"Madam, it's just that, I know my sister can do great work for you." He began to fidget.

She sensed his sincerity and released her grip on the documents. She put her hand out as if to say, "Give them to me."

He did. He placed her papers in her hand and let go. She felt like a sorceress who was still somewhat unsure of the weight of her power. She gathered the papers as she worked to keep her composure.

"I thank you, Mr. Kolawole. I will be in touch if I am in need of another employee," she said, shaking his hand.

She made her way toward the exit and searched the security guard's face for any sign of suspicion. She couldn't read him. She kept moving until she had walked out of the bank and returned to the heat of Lagos. She dug into her tote, found her sunglasses, and put them on. She strode toward the bus stop to catch the one to Mushin.

This time, she knew the way.

22

"NOW WE MOVE ON TO THE REAL JOB."

"Emeka, what do you mean 'the real job'? Did I not just risk my freedom in that bank?"

"Remember, you're not free until you're paid. We're not free."

"Where is my money, Emeka?"

"You have to go back to that same bank next week and take the money out of the account. I explained everything before. We have to do this fast, fast."

"I just put it in the bank! That's too soon."

"Leave the planning to the people making the plans. Remember, you ran away, your daddy disowned you, you have no money, you're sleeping on a filthy mattress on Kash's floor. Do you want to go to America? Do you want to see your mum?"

"Yes. Of course."

"Finish the job and everything go work out."

Emeka's words stayed with Patience and gave her new confidence when she walked back into UBN Bank the following week to make her withdrawal. No, she did not want to stay with Kash forever. In her mind she could catch a flight to America that same day. This was her work now, and it left her feeling hopeful and depleted at the same time.

She was ready because she had to be. There was no turning back. No other opportunities.

She watched with vigor as Mr. Kolawole counted bundles of naira and placed each stack inside a large duffel bag.

She was at ease when she thought of Chike's extensive research on the amount she could take from a business account without igniting any suspicions.

The banker gathered the one million naira she had requested, half the money she had deposited. She envisioned herself landing in New York City.

"I look forward to doing business with you again, Ms. Da Silva."

"Yes, sir," Patience replied. She made her way toward the exit.

"Madam, have a nice day," the security guard said as he stared at her chest.

"Likewise."

She walked out of the bank holding on to the bag for dear life.

23

HAPPY FACES WERE ALL CHIKE SAW AROUND HIM.

Inside his flat, Patience and Emeka reveled in the glory of their first successful job.

"My girl," Emeka said as he threw his arm across her shoulder. "Chike, make sure you marry this girl, o."

Chike tried to seem excited, but Patience's demeanor distracted him. Instead of showing signs of fear, she sipped her Coke and welcomed Emeka's praises.

Emeka paced the room like a grown child, giving him handshakes and body taps.

"Emeka, sit down and lower your voice before our neighbors hear what we've done," Chike said.

"Ah-ahn. Wetin be your problem? This is a celebration."

Chike wondered why he couldn't bring himself to be overjoyed. What they had done went against his principles, but he and Emeka could now afford to pay for their mother's operation.

Why wasn't he at least happy about that?

He wanted to be relieved that Mama would be able to walk with no pain. But he couldn't. Instead he faked a grin so as not to bring down Emeka's and Patience's spirits.

He bit his tongue when he thought for a second that Kash wouldn't show up with their money. He was irked by the fact that he was the only person given responsibility for picking it up.

"I will buy my plane ticket to America soon," Patience said with passion in her eyes.

"Yes, you're almost there. We should get at least a hundred K each. You'll be on a plane to Yankee soon," Emeka said.

Chike continued to force a smile. He wanted to be happy for Patience, but he still wondered if she was planning her meeting with her mother the right way.

"Where is Kash?" Emeka said, flicking his cigarette into the wooden ashtray that sat on their rickety table. "I hope this boy didn't run away with our money, o."

"Kash would never do that to me," Patience said.

Chike was happy that Emeka had said what he himself was thinking. They had been waiting for over an hour for Kash to show up. Kash told them he was coming from Oga's girlfriend's house in Adeniyi Jones, where Oga would distribute their share to him. It should take less than an hour.

"Let's not worry," Emeka said. "He's coming. My guy is coming. I trust him."

The room fell silent as if a switch had been flipped. Chike thought about how trusting Emeka could be. It wasn't a good trait to have if he was going to ever be a professional thief. Even he knew that.

Kash walked into the room. He was carrying a black duffel bag. Patience and Emeka rushed toward him. Emeka grabbed for the bag, but Kash didn't release his grip.

"Ah-ahn? You think say I go cheat you?"

"No, of course not. Oya, bring the money out," Emeka whispered.

Kash sat on the dusty couch and pulled the rickety center table closer to him. The wood from the table let out a cracking noise that suggested an impending collapse.

"Hey hey, be careful now," Chike said, annoyed. And in that

moment, he realized it would have been a relief if Kash had left town with the money, because he alone would bear the burden of stolen money.

Now they all had to face the thing that had turned them into thieves.

Kash reached into the bag and placed several bundles of naira on the table. Emeka's eyes grew, and Chike knew then his brother had been seduced. Kash separated the money into four rows.

"Now here we go," he said picking up the first three bundles. "Ten thousand for you Emeka." He handed him a single stack of money. Emeka looked confused but remained silent.

"Ten K for you, Patience," Kash continued. "And ten K," he said to Chike.

"What do you mean ten K is for me?" Emeka said. "Shouldn't we be getting at least a hundred thousand?"

"Hundred? You think we should be getting half the money?" Kash said, then belted obnoxiously, "You people are mad if you think Oga would split the money with us like that. He is the boss. Emeka, I explained it to you before."

"You said we can make one million naira," Emeka said.

"Yes, we *took* one million, but we get paid what we get paid. Emeka, you've done those small-small jobs with me. You think Oga gave us equal share with him? Your head has scattered." Kash laughed harder.

Chike searched his brother's face. Emeka bit his top lip as he usually did whenever he was wrestling with anger.

"Believe me, this is good money, and we can make more. He was very happy with the way we arranged the entire job, but we can't go in expecting to get equal profit."

"Kash, this is serious. You told us we would have all the money we need to do what we need to do after this job," Patience said as she paced up and down. Chike was somewhat pleased she had allowed her fear to show. "I just risked my entire life going into the bank twice—fake check, stolen money. We can't even get the money we need? We can still get caught even."

"Patience, don't be simpleminded. We will not get caught, and this is not like going into business with your friend as a partner. We are workers, you get? We have to earn every kobo."

"What do you mean we have to earn every kobo?" Chike said, feeling as if he had just stood up after being body slammed. "We planned and executed a bank scam. What more should we do to have an equal share of stolen money?"

"Oga is a professional. It was his check we deposited. He knew which bank we could take, and he instructed us to complete the job. He is entitled to more. We just have to continue doing this until we've reached our goals."

"What kind of nonsense are you talking?" Chike blurted out. He could no longer keep his composure. "We were lucky this time, but if we keep going, we will get caught."

"Listen," Emeka said, breaking his self-imposed silence. "Let's not get too agitated over this. If Oga wants us to continue with him, I think we should continue."

"We could make even more money next time," Kash said.

"You people are not serious. You expect me to do that again?" Patience said.

"Emeka, you said we would only have to do this once. Now you're agreeing to do more?" Chike said.

"Don't be a mumu," Kash said. "Listen to your elder brother."

"My elder brother has gone mad."

"I haven't gone mad. I'm just being realistic. We can either do a few more jobs or go back to struggling and making no money. Think about Mama. Patience, what of your mum you're trying to see? We all have plans."

Chike tried to ignore the blood rushing to his head, but he couldn't. He sat on the couch and grabbed his temples. As he massaged them, he felt Patience sit next to him. She rubbed his arm.

He pulled away.

24

ON NEW YEAR'S EVE, PATIENCE WOKE UP WITH PAIN IN her neck and a stiff back. She thought she had gotten used to sleeping on the thin mattress on Kash's floor.

The pain she felt proved otherwise.

It had been two full months since she had moved in.

Two full months of a different kind of torment.

She looked at the time. Six o'clock. She went to the bathroom, twisted her head to stretch away her aches, and turned on the faucet. There was water but only a steady flow the width of a needle. She let that stream of scarcity run down her finger and wished for supernatural powers to make the water gush out the way it did whenever she turned on a faucet at her father's compound. She kissed her teeth when she remembered no such thing was possible—at least not at Kash's place. Even UNILAG had had a better water supply for the short time she was there.

She walked back into Kash's efficiency. She could hear his loud snores beyond the thin sheet he had nailed from one wall to the next to create privacy for her. She pulled a pair of jeans from her suitcase and put them on, then grabbed a bucket. She pushed her feet into slippers that had become dusty and worn from Mushin roads, grabbed her head tie, and walked out.

When she arrived at the nearby well, there was a queue. She estimated a thirty-minute wait.

"You're Kash's cousin?" She turned and saw a familiar face. It was Bose, Kash's ex whom she had met her first day in Lagos; Bose who lived a few steps from Kash's room because all of their neighbors were just a few steps away in their respective rooms. Bose whom Kash had accused of stealing her egusi stew straight from the pot she had left in the kitchen.

"Yes. I'm Kash's cousin," Patience said.

"So, is it true? Did you leave UNILAG to come here?"

"Something like that." Patience still wasn't used to her new neighbors. Sometimes she felt like she was still living in the hostel. Instead of being surrounded by fellow students, she dwelled in the same breathing space as an electrician, a plumber who boasted about his loud farts after dinnertime, a woman whose job was to grind pepper in the market, and another who hawked Gala sausage rolls up and down the road.

And then there was Bose, a primary school teacher and an accused egusi stew thief, according to Kash.

"Why na? Why did you leave school?" Bose said.

"It's a long story."

"Make sure you go back."

Patience ignored her and walked ahead as the line moved.

"Education will increase your life. Or do you want to be like Kash?"

Patience thought of Chike. His degree. His current job. She walked on.

"I'm sure he told you we used to be together. I had to let him go, sha. He's too unserious."

"Kash is just different," Patience said.

"Yes. He is different from me. All he does is lie and cheat."

"It's true, Kash is no saint, but he told me how you finished my pot of egusi," Patience said, appalled by Bose's hypocrisy.

"Is that what he told you?" She laughed.

"Yes, he did. Why didn't you just ask for some?" Patience said, still sickened.

"While he was telling you stories, did he tell you he stole money from me? Did he tell you that's why I left him?"

Patience fell silent. She knew it was possible. He had stolen money from her father's safe when he was instructed to take only her passport. Patience shook the thought away when she considered her own involvement in it.

"I'm done with him. I'm engaged now, and we will do our introduction for our families soon."

"Congrats," Patience said.

"After that I want to get my master's."

"Your master's? Wonderful," Patience said, still with little enthusiasm, too tired to care.

Patience looked ahead and noticed the line was dwindling faster than she had imagined it would. She thought of Chike. They had plans to go to his friend's place to create another fake ID card for the bank. The thought of taking money again sent waves of fear through her.

Would she get caught this time?

Don't think like that, she thought. She couldn't continue living like this. She needed the money. She needed a chance.

Speed would have to remedy her fear and her guilt. If she worked fast and got to America fast enough, she could rid herself of trepidation without spending much time troubled by shame. That or accept her life—no parents, no answers, no future.

She needed out.

She and Bose walked ahead. Women in line began to sing:

"He has made me glad. He has made me glad. I will rejoice for he has made me glaaaad. Hallelujah!"

Patience felt uneasy.

"You know, this is actually not a long queue," Bose said, likely noticing her annoyance. "Haven't you seen it longer than this?"

"A queue longer than this?" Patience said, realizing she hadn't seen the worst of what she already considered suffering.

"Yes, o. Even longer. But what can we do? We need water."

By the time Patience reached the well, she felt as if she would pass out from the early morning heat. She lowered the well's bucket all the way down into the borehole. She lifted it and poured the water she collected into her own bucket. She repeated it several times until her bucket was full. She grabbed the head tie she had brought, curled it into a large ring, and plopped it on her head.

"Let me help you," Bose said, reaching for Patience's bucket.

"It's okay, no need."

"Why are you like that?"

"Like what?"

"Like you don't need somebody?"

"I didn't say that."

"So let me help you."

Bose grabbed one end of the bucket, and they both lifted it. Patience hadn't balanced anything on her head since secondary school, when fetching water had been like a rite of passage (no matter who your parents were). Here it felt arduous.

She wondered if she was expected to wait for Bose, since they were headed the same way.

"Bose, thank you, ehn. I will see you later. I have to meet my boyfriend soon."

"No wahala." Bose shrugged. "Happy New Year in advance."

"Same to you." Patience walked on. Upon each step, she lost small amounts of water.

Each bit that fell pained her, as if gold were being swallowed into the ground.

Patience kept her head as steady as anyone could walking on an uneven road while carrying a fifteen-pound bucket on their head.

Finally, she arrived home.

She walked up the stairs, keeping the bucket steady. When she reached the corridor of their place, she saw two queues of people with their buckets in tow: one by the bathroom, another by the toilet. She walked into her room, dejected.

"Kash! Wake up!" she yelled after putting her bucket down.

"What is it, na? I'm sleeping," he said, his voice husky from recent slumber.

"I just woke up to fetch water. There was a queue at the well. And now there's a queue for the toilet. I need to relieve myself."

"What do you expect?" Kash sat up in his bed and rubbed his eyes. "If you need to relieve yourself, go outside to the bush. Brush your teeth there too."

Patience kissed her teeth.

"I'm glad you are a smart girl. You have seen for yourself that nobody will come and save us. We have to work."

"What I need is to get myself to America."

"You and this America. You're here right now, and we have to eat, abi? That should be your concern. Or go home and beg Daddy to take you back. You're the child of a rich man and you've chosen this life for yourself? You could be a student at UI right now."

"So it's okay for Daddy to keep me under his foot because he's rich? Kash, I have a mum that I haven't seen in ten years." Patience rolled her eyes. She hated to be reminded of her father's wealth. His money had never been a remedy for her.

She took out her toothbrush, spread green toothpaste on it, and began to clean her mouth. She spat into the empty plastic cup that she kept at her bedside, then dipped her washcloth into her bucket of water and wiped her face, her neck, her armpits.

"Rub and shine," Kash said, amused.

Patience pulled her braids into one. She grabbed another plastic cup from their nonfunctioning kitchenette, then drew her curtain for privacy. The sound of her piss filling the cup echoed throughout the room.

"So you've learned to pee in a cup here? It's not your fault," he said.

"I know you do it too." She put the cup down, threw her clothes and shoes into a bag, then pulled the curtain back to face Kash.

"Where are you going?" he said as she pushed her feet back into her slippers.

"To Chike's for the day. They usually have water, and they have their own washroom. I can have my bath there."

"You said you would cook another soup today. So you will leave me here with no food tomorrow, the first day of the new year?"

"Kash, I will cook when I come back." It was all she had done since she moved in: cook and clean for Kash—a consequence of being his younger cousin who was now squatting in his tiny efficiency.

"Well, at least I don't have to fetch water, because you're leaving this bucket for me. Don't forget to throw that outside."

Patience grabbed her cup of urine and her bag, and walked out without another word.

"CHIKE, I HAVE TO GET OUT OF KASH'S PLACE. IT'S TAKING too long to put the money together," Patience said as soon as she got off Chike's parked okada. They walked on, then headed toward a compound of flats.

"Your mum named you Patience for a reason. Things don't just come right away because you want it. Or you can always go back to your daddy's place."

Patience noticed he rolled his eyes. She decided to ignore him. She was already managing her own fears. But it was as if their first bank job preordained the second. Done it before, do it again, even if she had to convince herself this was the way things had to be.

They approached a door on the second floor and knocked hard. Chike's former university mate, Ayodele, flung it open. He was dressed in an undershirt, jeans, and brown leather Hausa slippers.

"Look at this useless man trying to break his own door," Chike said.

"Patience, how you dey?" Ayodele said, ignoring Chike.

She nodded subtly. "I dey," she said in her dainty way of speaking pidgin.

When they walked into his flat, she admired his furniture: a large dark brown ottoman, a glass center table and matching side tables, a bright red rug, and his massive television. It was an abode adorned by a bachelor who had money to play with. Patience smelled the authenticity of his leather couch when she and Chike sat down.

"So you need a new ID card? How much does Oga want you to handle this time?"

"Three million," Chike said, almost whispering.

"Ah, you're a big boy now," Ayodele said in Yoruba. He rubbed his large hands together.

"Will the bank be alarmed by a three-million-naira deposit?"

"Ah, you can never know. But when you do the deposit for Oga and wait for the money to clear like you did before, you will be okay, sha. Listen, this method will decrease suspicions about the account's authenticity. If you listen, nothin' go happen."

Patience looked at Chike. He seemed concerned, but if anyone had inside information on the average bank, it was Ayodele.

"How long did you work at the bank?" Patience said.

"Like six months mehn."

"Only six months because you stole money." Chike snickered.

"To this very day they never showed proof of any theft." Ayodele smirked.

"How much of the three million can she withdraw first?"

"If you take about one and a half or even two million naira, you will be fine."

"Oga said we should do GTE Bank. Why GTE?"

"Ah, Chike. Settle your mind. Oga's checks are so solid. No bank can detect any foul play."

"Why do you think his checks are like that?"

"Because when the big men do their work, they use checks that are made of money, not just ordinary paper."

"Meaning?"

"I mean, there's probably an account associated with it. A dormant one."

"So why doesn't Oga just steal all the money from the account?" Patience interjected.

"Ah, now. If he takes everything now, what will he have later?" Ayodele said.

"And anyway, it's better to spread it round to different people to reduce the risk of getting caught. You pay me for the ID cards, you do the job, Oga gets his money, you and your people chop too. That's how to spread the money round. Something that our yeye politicians are only doing among themselves, isn't it?"

Patience imagined that the account connected to his forged checks belonged to some multimillionaire—billionaire even—who didn't notice when his or her money left its nest.

"Madam, are you ready to take your new photo?"

"Yes. Let's take it." Patience pulled her hair tie out and allowed her braids to hang. She sat in the chair Ayodele had set up in front of his expensive-looking camera—the kind one would find in a studio. *His fake ID hustle must be earning him good money*, she thought.

"So, what name did you choose as your latest identity since Sade Da Silva is dead?" he said.

Patience thought for a moment about who to become next. What name would she remember on the day of—a name that would help settle her fears. "How about Oyinkansola?" she said.

"That's a good name."

"It's my mum's middle name. I will remember that name. I can do Oyinkansola . . . and . . . Afolabi as the surname."

"Your mum's name . . . she would be so proud," Chike said, shaking his head.

Patience ignored him and smiled for the camera.

Snap!

The front door opened, and a woman walked in carrying three aluminum food trays stacked high. Patience could smell the stew and jollof from where she sat.

"Chike, Patience, this is my girl, Peju." She comes bearing the food for our party tonight," Ayodele said.

"Welcome. You're staying for the party?" she said as she placed the trays on Ayodele's dining table.

"Yes, o! Stay," Ayodele interjected. "We will have plenty food, plenty drinks."

Patience looked at Chike and gave him an approving nod.

"We will stay," he said.

"Patience, when you're finished with your photos, you can help me fry the plantain so I can concentrate on the puff-puff," Peju said.

"No problem."

"We will celebrate tonight. Nineteen ninety-three will be a memorable year. New democracy, new philosophy," Ayodele said.

"We can only hope. You know the military dey flip-flop," Chike replied.

"Ah, no. They have to honor their promise this time or we will take it to de streets."

Patience thought of the prospect of a clean slate. Nineteen ninety-three—a new era. Would she mark it as the best year she'd ever known, the year she reunited with her mum, the year of Nigeria's new democracy? *Nineteen ninety-three will be good*, she thought.

"Oya, let's take another photo." Ayodele shifted his camera's lens and peered into the viewfinder. Patience adjusted her posture.

Snap!

That night at the party, Patience and Chike ate, danced, and mingled with the small group of friendly attendees who chatted about their alma maters and hometowns.

"This is Patience and Chike. Patience is a student at LAG, and Chike did petroleum engineering at UI."

Patience wished Ayodele would stop repeating the same introduction to people Chike didn't already know from UI. Each time he described her as a student, she was reminded of what she really was—a bank thief, a university dropout, a disowned child.

Near the back of the room was a different kind of crowd. The group of guys dressed just as flashy as Ayodele—satin shirts, square-toe leather shoes, belts with exaggerated buckles that tagged top designers (two shiny Gs welded together meant Gucci or a large D and G for Dolce and Gabbana). Some of the men wore dark sunglasses embellished with golden Medusa heads near the hinges. With every move they made, they resembled models posing for an editorial.

Proper olodu boys, Kash would call them.

They were the perfect archetypes of successful scammers who spent a good part of their money on high fashion and fast cars.

Patience noticed how Chike steered clear of them, as if ignoring them would make him less guilty of their own crime.

When House of Pain's "Jump Around" came on, Chike, Ayodele, and a few other guys leaped around the room and yelled out the lyrics to the song. Patience wondered then how many drinks Chike had had.

The song faded, and Ayodele put on a slow tune that shifted the mood.

Chike went up to Patience and put his hands on her waist, prompting her to dance with him.

"I don't know this song," she said.

"I'll be back," he said, somewhat slurring his words.

She watched him as he walked toward the stereo where Ayodele stood. He whispered something to him, then waited as his friend dug into one of his shoeboxes filled with CDs and cassettes.

Patience looked around at the small group of partygoers and wondered what secrets they were carrying. Had any of them walked into a bank, deposited a fake check, and withdrawn a large sum of money?

She doubted that even the 419 boys in the corner bothered with such work. She imagined them appointing someone else to the task—someone who was as desperate as she had become.

Let it go and enjoy the party, she thought.

The music stopped and started again—this time with Janet Jackson offering allusions on how love goes.

Chike made his way back to her and wrapped his arms around her waist.

"So you asked him to play this one for me."

"Of course, now. It's your favorite."

They grooved a bit, then she turned her back to him and twirled her hips, sending her butt bouncing against his groin. He pulled her in closer and rested his chin on her shoulder. She turned her face toward his. She ignored the strong stench of stout on his breath and puckered her lips to kiss him. But his weight began to bear down on her, and their sultry dance morphed into a burden.

"Are you falling asleep on me?" she said.

"No, no. I usually drink only three," he said, seemingly embarrassed.

She drew away and looked around the room. She noticed a spot on Ayodele's leather couch and pulled Chike over to sit beside her.

"I understand," she said. "It's New Year's Eve. What else would we be doing anyway?"

"Are you afraid?" he said. "Are you afraid of what we are doing? Of what we did?" His eyes darted to the back of the room where the 419 bunch stood chatting.

She hated that he brought it up here. She had tried all night to push her worries beneath the beat of her favorite songs, under the plate of rice and moi moi she had devoured, and below her dancing feet.

She told herself over and over again that it was the start of a new time and somehow that newness would chip away at their distress.

"Of course I'm afraid," she said. "But I don't really want to discuss this here. We *shouldn't* discuss this here."

He looked at her and buried his head in her chest. She stroked his head.

"I'm looking forward to the new year. I think it will be good for all of us," she whispered to him.

Chike sat up and pressed his lips together. "I just hope nineteen ninety-three won't be the year we go to jail," he said.

"Me too."

He gazed at her, and she was surprised by his sudden shift from nervous to sweet. The wonders of alcohol, she thought.

"You're right. Let's continue to enjoy." He sat up, facing the other attendees, and put his arm around her shoulders. As their bodies melted into new comfort, Ayodele stopped Janet Jackson mid-tune, causing an abrupt silence.

"We are one minute away from midnight!" Ayodele called out. "Shall we count down?"

"Yes, o!" people called out.

And so they did—they counted down to midnight, and when the newness of the new year settled in the room, Chike and Patience welcomed nineteen ninety-three with a kiss.

25

"ARE YOU SURE THIS CHIKE GUY REALLY WANTS YOU?"

Bimpe sat up in her bed with a scowl.

Patience struggled to respond. "Chike is just having some problems right now." She hated that she sounded weak.

"Really?" Bimpe said.

"Yes, he is a good man, an honest man. Handsome too."

"Did you have sex with him?"

"No! Why do you ask?" Patience didn't feel safe enough to tell Bimpe that she and Chike had finally done it.

"Because whether it's decent sex with a handsome man or good sex with a broke man, somehow sex makes a woman blind to foolishness," Bimpe said as she ran her emery board over the corner of her thumbnail. "Most women experience this at least once in a lifetime. Like right now, my mum is annoyed with my dad because he didn't come home last night."

Patience was taken aback by Bimpe's revelation, and by how she didn't seem fazed.

"Does your dad stay out a lot?"

"Sometimes. He might have another family," she said with a shrug. "He told Mummy he doesn't. He claims he's been working. But would it be hard to believe he has another family out there somewhere? Most women take what they can get and cry about it when they're in the deepest part of the wahala it brings. I told my Ade the one thing he can't do is take another wife or family. That would just be too humiliating for me."

Bimpe stopped and pointed her emery board at Patience.

"This is why you have to be careful about who you sleep with," she said. "That's when they put juju on you. I started having sex in JSS3. Believe me, I know."

Patience was shocked by the way Bimpe spoke about sex. The girls at her secondary school who were having sex had kept the info to themselves, and those who weren't having sex had spoken about their so-called purity.

"If you had sex with Chike, you can tell me."

"I said we haven't had sex," Patience said. She would keep the truth about this to herself for as long as she could, because sex with Chike made her feel safe—safe from his mercurial way with her, safe from the uncertainties of her life, safe from their new line of work.

"Well, this Chike found a way to put juju on you without sexing you. That's impressive," Bimpe said, then began to file her nails again in silence. "You know my mother used to be an interior designer?"

"Aunty Lola?"

"Yes, my mum. She had a business. But she let it go for Daddy. He told her it was a hobby, and he needed her to be home more. And now they're trying to force me to go abroad to make something great of myself," she said with her voice fashioned like an exaggerated parent. "What does that even mean?"

Patience pictured Aunty Lola manning her own desk, taking calls, looking at samples of upholstery. The picture was so clear.

There was a knock at the door. Aunty Lola let herself in.

"Patience, darling, you're here?" Aunty Lola walked over and kissed her on each cheek as if they had bumped into each other on a street in Paris.

"Yes, Ma. I came by to say hello. Bimpe and I are just here gisting."

"How did you get here? Have you been taking the bus?"

"Yes, Ma, I have."

"Be careful on the bus," she said, bewildered. "But anyway, I'm glad you're enjoying Lagos, sha."

"Who wouldn't enjoy Lagos after living in Ibadan their whole life?" Bimpe said with a snicker.

"You this girl," Aunty Lola said, slapping Bimpe's shoulder. "You and Patience, come to my boudoir. I need your opinion on what I should wear to an event with your father."

Inside Aunty Lola's dressing room were towers of fragrances, stacks of geles on shelves, and silk nighties draped over the closet door. Patience noticed then how Aunty Lola's natural elegance was a nice contrast to Bimpe's cool.

"Ayobami, Patience is here," Aunty Lola said to her younger daughter, who was curled up on her mother's queen-size bed.

"Aunty Patience, good afternoon," the little girl said. She hopped off the bed and gave Patience a hug.

"Ayobami, every time I see you, you're taller."

"My birthday is coming. Mummy said I can invite anybody to my party. I think you should come, sha." The little girl placed both her hands on her hips.

"Are you sure you're not turning nineteen?" Patience said as she giggled and watched Ayobami climb back on her mother's bed.

"Mum, you know after a while all this lace starts to look alike," Bimpe said, gazing inside her mother's closet, where she kept large bundles of materials that formed a rainbow of hues.

"Just choose one from this row."

Bimpe grabbed a stack from her mother's bed and began leafing though it. "What about wearing something English instead?"

"The dress code called for native."

Patience stood back and was reminded of the feelings she had whenever she watched Modupe and Margaret together.

"Patience, come here," Aunty Lola said, breaking her brief moment of melancholy. Come help me choose a fragrance."

Patience scanned the shelves. "Aunty, I'm surprised you don't have White Diamonds. Isn't that the reigning perfume?"

"Oh, I had it, and then I gave it to my sister. It's just not me."

Patience smirked and began opening the bottles.

"How is school?"

Patience felt her body stiffen. "School is good, Ma," she said.

"More exams are coming soon. Be prepared," Bimpe said. "Do well for your dad. Then when you graduate, do what feeds you."

"Bimpe, how is anything you're doing feeding you? You should have a job by now or go abroad. Make a decision, jàre," Aunty Lola said.

"Mum, don't worry. Ade and I are just making sure we are on the same timetable."

"What yeye timetable?"

Their minor disagreement activated Patience's usual yearnings, then she realized she was in a room with the right person—a person who could ease her curiosity. "Aunty, what about my mum? Was she a good student?"

"She was so curious," she said. "She would walk around the school to learn every inch of the place. She knew every single teacher, every student, down to the junior students. Everybody loved her."

Patience listened, rapt.

"When she started track and field, she would practice so much. She wasn't the fastest girl, but day in, day out she practiced. And she studied so hard for exams. When she got a scholarship, I was amazed. Not many girls went abroad for school just like that, talk less of getting a scholarship. Many women had to stay behind and wait for their man who traveled abroad to send for them once they were situated. Folami was a special girl. Make sure you study hard like your mum."

"What did you think when she came back to Nigeria?"

"It surprised me," she said, speaking over the crinkling sound of the gele she attempted to tie on her head. "She never talked about marriage. We all had boyfriends from the local boys' school, but she was so focused on the Olympics. Your father, hmm, he found his way into her life . . . well, anyway, she loved you."

"When did she find out about Modupe and Margaret?" Patience said.

Aunty Lola hesitated, her eyes bulged a little, and she looked over at Ayobami, who was still curled on her bed, minding her cartoons.

"That I'm not sure, but a woman always knows," she said.

Patience glanced at Bimpe, who was sorting through her mother's shiny purses. Patience was surprised by her silence and wondered what had happened to all of her radical opinions about relationships.

"Honestly, there's nothing unique about a man having another woman and having another child," Aunty Lola said as she glanced at Ayobami again. Patience suspected then that Aunty Lola didn't want her young daughter to hear her discuss the realities of a family formed by a man's recklessness. Her tone read as if she wanted Patience to believe it was no big deal, though she felt the contrary.

"How many of your friends have half siblings?" Aunty Lola said.

"Many."

"Exactly. But you, you've been raised by a woman who is not your mum, and you barely know your own. Kò da now," she said, her expression full of compassion.

Patience felt anxious. She wanted more. She needed more.

"Aunty Lola, my birth certificate?"

"Ah, I've asked around. You know, these things take time. Just be as patient as your name, my darling."

She was tired, ironically, of being patient, especially with their next bank job coming. She was happy she was getting closer to the amount of money she needed, but without her passport, she couldn't travel to America freely.

It was time to look for answers on her own, she thought.

"Lola!" a voice called from the hallway, then there was a slight knock at the door. Bimpe's father opened it.

"Daddy!" Ayobami yelled as she jumped off the bed and grabbed hold of his leg.

"I'm home o." He picked her up, kissed her forehead, and plopped her back onto the bed. "Lola, I'm here," he said as he pulled his wife close and kissed her on her cheek. Aunty Lola tensed her lips.

"Welcome, ọkọ mi. How was work?"

"Work has been busy. Patience, how are you? I hope you're getting on well in Lagos." His voice echoed, filling the quiet spaces of the room as if he spoke through a megaphone. Patience looked at Bimpe, who grew quiet and tense as she paid closer attention to choosing lace and geles. It was as though his wife and children stood still for him, in both admiration and slight scorn.

"Good evening, Sa. Yes, Sa, I am enjoying Lagos."

"That's good. Will you stay with us to eat tonight?"

"Yes, Sa."

"What of you? Will you be here to eat tonight?" Aunty Lola asked him, her tone matter-of-fact.

"Of course, now," he said, tapping her shoulder.

"Me, I'm always here, o. I was here yesterday. I'm here today," Aunty Lola said, her delivery turning sarcastic.

"I'm here now," he said, amused.

Aunty Lola's expression melted into one of uncertainty. He grabbed her shoulders and squeezed.

"Settle your mind, woman."

Bimpe rolled her eyes, and Patience felt like an outsider for the first time, as if she was hearing something that wasn't meant for her ears, though nothing was completely spoken. A man like that, who commanded the room each time, could very well maintain two households at the same time, and yet Patience sensed that he loved

Aunty Lola by the way he pacified her with his smile and how he instructed her to settle her mind.

"Make sure you pick something elegant for your mum to wear."

"Daddy, when do I ever get these things wrong? Mummy, here's what you can wear," Bimpe said as her father left the room. She held up a unique aṣọ oke dress that resembled a man's agbada.

"Bimpe, that is too . . . it's too much for this event."

"Mummy, if it's too much, why did you have it made? It's beautiful. You will turn heads."

"Silly girl," Aunty Lola said. "Let me just fit in with the rest of the old folks at the party. What do you think, Patience? Ṣebi I'm a woman who turns heads no matter what I wear?"

"Yes, Ma, you are."

"Excuse me, o, I won't taint your elegance," Bimpe said. She laughed. Aunty Lola slapped her hand, and Patience felt herself slip into another mother-daughter daydream.

She became even more transfixed by their world during dinner.

They all laughed when Mr. Akanbi cracked silly jokes, and she noticed how Aunty Lola remained tickled longer than everyone else. Patience was surprised by how her mood had shifted from the time they were in her room. There at the dining table, she didn't have to wonder where her husband was having dinner that night. Her apparent happiness pleased Patience.

Such an elegant woman deserved joy.

"How is everything at the office?" Aunty Lola asked her husband.

"Well, with Abiola's campaign gaining traction, my colleagues are worried about their future prospects."

"Why, Daddy?" Bimpe said.

"Ah, Ṣebi a new president will bring in his own cabinet of people. Me, I'm not worried. Abiola will be good for the country."

Patience was impressed by his altruism. She thought of her father, who she knew wouldn't be as diplomatic.

"I was actually at Abiola's rally at the National Stadium," Patience said. "I thought I would meet him because my friend's father is his campaign manager, but I had to leave early."

"That's wonderful, Patience," Mr. Akanbi said. "They say the event was a complete success."

"Patience, who knew you had such important friends," Bimpe said, her tone almost underhanded.

Patience sipped her water and remained quiet.

When they had finished dinner and dessert, Patience looked down at her watch. Six o'clock.

"I should be going soon. Thank you so much for dinner, Ma . . . Sa."

"Patience, I think it would be best if you stay tonight," Aunty Lola said with a concerned glare. "I can't have you traveling by bus at this time all the way back to UNILAG, and it's Friday anyway. No school tomorrow. You can sleep on the guest mattress in Bimpe's room."

Patience pictured herself sleeping on a comfortable portable bed next to Bimpe's grand white canopy, in an air-conditioned room, with a generator outside on standby if the electricity was taken. Kash's place offered nothing of the sort.

"Thank you, Ma. I will stay."

"I was thinking I need to style your braids again," Bimpe said.

"Aunty Patience is staying? Yes!" Ayobami said in celebration.

"Thank you, Ma. Thank you for your hospitality."

"Patience, this is your home too. You are always welcome."

"I HOPE THIS IS COMFORTABLE ENOUGH," BIMPE SAID AS she pulled out a plump folding cushion.

Patience plopped down and worked to conceal her joy. "This is quite all right," she said, remembering her own mattress again.

"Here is a nightie you can wear. You can even take it home, sha. I don't wear that anymore. In fact, I think I can give you a few things I'm about to throw out."

They stayed up for hours, trying on different dresses, jeans, and tops. Patience kept a straight face as Bimpe bragged about her wardrobe. Bimpe could boast all she wanted, as long as Patience had something tangible to keep in return.

26

PATIENCE RUBBED HER EYES AND GLANCED DOWN AT HER fake Tommy Hilfiger watch. Six forty-three in the morning. Almost time for the American Embassy's gate to open.

She stood and looked at the crowd that stretched beyond the block. Some sat on raffia mats spread out on the road, others on portable plastic chairs they had rented from unofficial vendors.

There was sweat dripping from men's foreheads and soiled armpits, and women fanning themselves and their children as they waited in the merciless heat.

When the embassy gates finally opened, the mass of people waiting outside cheered and poured into the building's grounds like a tidal wave breaking over a tranquil seashore. Patience managed to take in the beauty of the luscious green lawn with its myriad trees and bushes of purple heart, pink roses, and white orchids. Her musing was cut short once the guards emerged from inside the stone-white building.

"If you're here for visiting visa, join this queue!" one guard shouted in a curious mélange of Nigerian and British accents. Like all the embassy guards, he prowled amid the crowd with his neck stretched like a giraffe's.

"Student visa, stand here! Work visa, here! We will come round to look at your documents. Make sure you have an appointment!"

Patience resented how the guards behaved like gods. One looked down at her over his disproportionate gut. He puffed up his chest, accentuating the large breast pockets on his khaki uniform shirt. "Why are you here?" he said.

"I came to apply for my American passport," Patience said, using her American inflections. *Maybe she could teach him how to really speak foreign*, she thought. "I have an appointment, but I don't have all my paperwork. Where should I wait?"

"Just join the student visa queue and explain yourself to the consular."

Her heart tensed. The student visa line was the longest. She would have to bear it. She was tired of hanging on to Aunty Lola's promises. Then there was bank job number two, which she would have to do the next morning. Same crazy mission—walk into a bank and walk out with a large amount of cash as if it were rightfully hers.

Thoughts of her new work often pushed her into a pit of regret. She only managed to pull herself out with the kind of obscure justification she never knew she would need.

Isn't the money rightfully mine?

I am doing the work to take it.

Why did I ever agree to become a thief?

"Just focus on getting your passport today," she mumbled.

Patience looked up and noticed a newspaper salesman walk toward her area of the queue.

"My name is Mr. Nkereuwem. I'm here every day by God's grace to bless you."

The crowd chuckled. Patience turned to face him.

"Yes, my newspapers will bless you. If you buy one, you will get your visa."

He lifted a few newspapers from his aged, overstacked wagon, each with a bold headline celebrating Nigeria's African Cup of Nations win.

"This time tomorrow, you can be in America. The money you

spend on my newspaper will multiply tenfold. America is where you will become rich. This newspaper is your ticket to wealth."

The crowd laughed louder. "Give me one!" shouted one man. "Bring me two!" someone else yelled.

He gathered the money from his sales and approached a man in the visiting visa line dressed in stained jeans and a faded black T-shirt with a droopy neckline.

"Are you here to apply for yourself?" Mr. Nkereuwem said, looking down at the man's plastic slippers. He clasped his short, stumpy fingertips together, making his query seem more pressing.

"No, Sa. I dey queue for one woman."

Patience noticed other hired stand-ins in line, bearing the sun's blaze. Those who employed them sat comfortably in their air-conditioned luxury cars.

"Make your money, my good man," Mr. Nkereuwem said as he moved toward another man dressed in an oversize suit.

"Ah, you're looking sharp, sharp." He patted the man on the back before pushing his small, round-framed glasses up the bridge of his nose. "What will you say to get your visa?"

"I will say, 'My elder brother in America has a green card. He is hosting a very big wedding for his daughter in Texas. I want to go to that wedding.'" The man fidgeted and looked down at his black square-toe shoes.

"Hmm . . . be careful," Mr. Nkeremuwem said. "You have to make eye contact."

Patience thought about everything he said. She needed her own script.

"My name is Patience Adewale. I'm here to apply for my American passport so I can look for my mother who is missing."

No, she thought. *I won't say she's missing.*

"I have to go to America to reunite with my mum who I haven't seen in ten years."

"That sounds better," she mumbled.

After about forty-five minutes, the line moved forward again, bringing her to the front entrance of the embassy. She walked in with ease, shoulders back, chin up. Others bowed their heads and spoke in hushed tones like parishioners entering a holy space. She was relieved when the cool air inside the building wrapped itself around her sticky body. She walked through a long hallway, then into the waiting area, where a crop of consular officers sat behind stations protected by thick glass. She looked up at the fluorescent overhead lighting, then around at people seated in black plastic chairs. She wasn't surprised that the seats were all taken. Those who had nowhere to sit crowded around the perimeter of the room. Patience found a spot in a corner and sat cross-legged on the cold marble floor.

"NUMBER 503!" A CONSULAR OFFICIAL SHOUTED.

Patience glanced at the clock on the wall. Eleven o'clock. Four hours of waiting. She couldn't believe it was her turn.

"I'm here, I'm coming!"

She sprang up and clasped her purse to her chest. Her long pencil-thin braids spilled over her shoulders in different directions.

She approached the consular officer's station. His desk was piled with a clutter of files, documents, and a stack of US passport booklets.

"Hello, *sir*," she said, remembering to pronounce the *r* like a dog's growl like Americans do. "I am here to apply for my American passport." She slid her application through the slit in the glass window. "I'm here to have it reinstated." She looked him in the eye just as the newspaper salesman suggested.

"Ms. Adewale," he said after taking a deep breath. "You only wrote your name and birthday on this application. Do you have documents to support your claim that you are an American citizen?"

"I still haven't found my particulars, but I was born in Washington, DC, in 1974. My mother is in America. I'm going to look for her. I haven't seen her in ten years," she said. She scolded herself for deviating from her script. "Can you look up my records?"

The caseworker rustled through a stack of papers, then slid a page through the opening in the glass window.

"Ms. Adewale, here are examples of some items you can bring in to report your passport lost or stolen. And if you're an American as you say you are, you won't have to come on the days we see visa applicants," he said.

Bewildered, Patience looked at the paper. She had no idea what a social security card was. She didn't have an American driver's license. She had no clue where her father kept her birth certificate. And she had failed at getting her old passport.

"Without some information, we wouldn't even know where to begin with your case. Until you can prove you are an American with legal documents, there's nothing I can do for you."

"Just take my name and birthday and enter it into your computer system." she pleaded. "Isn't this the American Embassy?"

"Do you know your passport number?" the consular said after taking a long and deep breath.

"I don't."

"Have you ever registered with the embassy if you were born in Nigeria to American parents?"

"I told you I was born in America."

"Do you at least know your birth certificate number?"

"I don't. I just know that I was born in America."

"If that is true, then you'll need to contact the vital records office in your birth state to have your birth certificate sent to you."

"Oh, yes, let's do that," Patience said through a wide grin. It was the thing Aunty Lola was supposed to do for her. "Let's contact my birth state. When can we begin the process?"

"That is not the responsibility of the embassy."

"I paid for this appointment. How can you just send me away with a paper?"

"Madam, we are not in the business of gathering people's documents unless there is some proof. Please excuse yourself from my station."

She was shaking with anger. She sucked her teeth for what seemed like a full minute. She stomped toward the door clutching her purse under her arm, almost tripping over its long, tattered shoulder strap.

"This place is so useless, but mark my word, I will get my passport," Patience said.

She couldn't believe it—being rejected by the embassy of her homeland. She remembered how Kash and Emeka spoke of her being entitled to her passport, and yet *her* embassy had turned her away.

Wasn't this her birthright—that they help her, that they get her to her mum in America, who had birthed her on American soil?

Wasn't it so—to be American born meant problems were mere misunderstandings? Hardship to the American born, a foreign concept?

They wanted papers as proof of her Americanness, but they wouldn't help her gather them.

It was her father, she thought. Why else would her embassy turn her away?

Maybe he had eyes on the place like he did at UNILAG. It wasn't enough that he had taken her mother. Now he wanted to hold her hostage in Ibadan. Take her last shred of hope. She had run away, and so he did *this* to her. He made sure she would lose on her own.

She wanted to crumble. She imagined herself crawling out of the building because walking out would take too much energy. She had already lost enough.

"Why is this so hard?"

After she managed to find her bearings and walk toward the building's exit, the thick blanket of Lagos air settled across her face as the automatic door slid open. She pushed through clusters of people still waiting in the heat. The singing voices of the flock of white-garment-wearing worshippers floated above the crowd's chatter. They belted praise songs and prayers for people desperate for a successful visa interview. Patience stopped and watched as they collected money from the crowd.

"Give your offering to the Lord and *He* will bless you with permission to travel abroad," she heard.

Nonsense, she thought as she walked on.

When she reached the end of the embassy block, away from the long queue, she turned to get a full glimpse of the building. She swallowed her anger and marveled at how pristine it was. One of many gems on Victoria Island.

A rare Lagos wind danced, causing the flower beds to spit out an aroma of sheer bliss. Patience looked at the street sign that marked the embassy's block: Eleke Crescent.

She gripped her purse and dashed toward a bus conductor who yelled her destination.

"CMS, CMS!"

She boarded the small white bus headed across the freeway. As the car inched closer to the Lagos mainland, Patience watched Victoria Island's modern waterfront skyscrapers trail off into the distance. As the beauty faded, she was reminded of the day her mother was taken from her. The view of the mainland ahead boasted shorter, less imposing buildings overlooking a litter of yellow danfo buses and dullish gray streets punctuated by potholes and packed with pedestrians.

Looking forward never felt grimmer.

PATIENCE WAS STARTLED BY THE SIGHT OF EMEKA AND Chike when she walked into Kash's efficiency.

"Where did you go?"

"I hope she's ready for her job tomorrow," Emeka said before she could respond.

"Patience, where were you? You were gone all day, and Chike is sitting right here," Kash stressed.

"I went to the embassy to see if they would give me my passport."

"You and this passport. Patience, let's focus on the money," Kash said, waving her off.

"Money, money. All you think about is money," Chike said.

"Did they give it to you?" Kash said, irritated.

"No. They said I need proof."

"Eh hen, now. How many times will you punish yourself about a passport?"

"Kash, you know my situation. I can't stay with you forever." She pulled back the curtain and plopped onto her mattress.

"Listen, right now we need money. That money I took from Daddy— gone. My share of the money from job number one, na chicken change."

"The withdrawal for tomorrow has to be correct," Emeka said.

She wanted to tell them she couldn't do it again. The thought of going back into a bank along with her disappointment from the embassy made her want to vomit, except she hadn't eaten that afternoon. She needed to lie down. She stared at the ceiling. She wished this wasn't her job. She wished there was another way. But how could she not do it? She had agreed to this, and now her friends needed her.

And she needed the money.

She needed to know if her mother was somewhere still breathing.

"I will do it the right way just like before. I'm ready," she said, fighting back her nerves. "Don't worry," she said out loud, though she was speaking to herself.

27

PATIENCE'S SPIRIT COLLAPSED EACH TIME THE BANKER dropped a stack of money on the table.

"That's one and a half million," he announced.

She checked the time. One o'clock. She was cutting it close. She and Chike had until 1:30 to get the money to Kash, who would get the money to Oga. "Mr. Falola, can you count faster?" she said, using her American inflections.

"Ah, madam, it takes time. We cannot miss a single note. We don't want to cheat you."

She watched Mr. Falola's stumpy hands as he placed another stack in the money counter. The bills fluttered through the machine like a runaway train transporting her to the promised land.

Just half a million naira more and she'd have the two million naira she had come to withdraw—millions in cash from another phony business account she had set up with a fake three-million-naira check. *Nothing should go wrong*, she thought.

Nothing will *go wrong.*

"Madam, I've seen cases where the customer comes back to say we cheated them, so it takes time," Mr. Falola explained.

Patience wondered what Oga would do to her and the crew if his money was short. Beat them senseless? Resort to torture tactics such as breaking their fingers and toes like they do in all the American gangster movies? She looked at the table of money. Seeing it there in physical form in one space made her tremble. She told herself there was no reason to be afraid, but in her heart she knew there was.

When she first walked into Bank of Èkó in Ikeja that afternoon, she had been taken aback by Mr. Falola's casual questioning.

"Ah, madam. Back so soon for a big withdrawal? Didn't we open your account last month?"

"I need money for business expenses," she said, though it was none of *his* business.

"Please sit," he said, gesturing toward a seat in front of his desk. "Your identification?"

She dug into her purse and pulled it out.

When he looked down at her fake Lagos State ID card, she thought about the important details of her new alias:

Name: Oyinkansola Afolabi

Age: 28

Role: Owner of Yinka's Fashion Boutique that employs five people

Mr. Falola gave her back her ID along with a withdrawal form. She grabbed a pen from his desk.

She wrote Oyinkansola Afolabi's information, because for this job, and the others, she had suspended her true self.

A half hour had passed since she began watching Mr. Falola count out the cash she had requested.

As he reached for another wad of money, Mr. Okwu, the bank manager who had introduced himself to her earlier, approached.

"Excuse me, madam," he said, barely looking her in the eye.

He leaned in and spoke in Mr. Falola's ear.

Mr. Falola's gaze went blank.

He looked at his manager, stood up straight, and put his hands in the pockets of his brown polyester pants.

"Madam, please, I need to go and check something with Mr. Okwu before I complete your transaction."

Her chest tightened. "Is there a problem?"

"No, no, no. Just wait for me right here."

Her eyes followed the men as they walked toward the back of the bank's office, then entered a room encased in glass. Mr. Okwu paced as he spoke. Mr. Falola leaned over and put his hands on the desk in front of him, as if to support himself from passing out.

"Don't get caught, don't get caught," she repeated under her breath, though she often wondered what it would feel like if she did get caught. What would her father say or do? She remembered that she shouldn't care. Just make it out of that bank with the money. Another victory. *This money will carry me straight to America, straight to my mother,* she thought.

Mr. Falola closed the door behind him and walked toward her.

"Madam, can I ask you, you just opened this account, correct?"

"Yes, sir, I did. You asked me when I came in today."

"Is this an urgent withdrawal?"

"I need it for business expenses. Why am I being questioned about my money?"

Was he stalling for the police? The sweat from her palms could have wiped a smudged mirror clean. She glanced around the room and saw no sign of police. *What if they were on the way to pick her up, arrest her, and give her hell?* she thought.

"Mrs. Afolabi, understand that it's only that . . ."

"Madam," Mr. Okwu interrupted as he walked toward them.

What was he doing back here with his melon head? If she was going to jail today, it would be because of him acting as if the bank's money was his own.

"I'm afraid that we . . . I know that we cannot support your transaction . . ."

Patience shifted in her seat.

"We can't support your request comfortably because we are running low on funds."

Patience felt her shoulders rise.

"Can we please ask you to forgo withdrawing so much today? It has been slow for us at the bank. Maybe we can have the funds for you tomorrow, but if we do it today, we would have to close right now."

"Maybe?" Patience inquired.

She thought about the choices he presented: leave with the money to save her own nyash or leave the money at the bank to save them.

"I am so sorry for your problems, but it's a must that I get the money today," she said.

Mr. Okwu dropped his head. He looked at Mr. Falola and nodded.

"Okay, we will continue to count your funds."

Mr. Falola put another rubber-banded bundle of cash next to the other stacks that he had arranged in uniformed rows. A fresh feeling of power overtook her, and she wondered why she had worried herself in the first place. She was doing what she had to do.

"That's two million naira, madam," Mr. Falola said as he placed another stack of bills on the table. The room smelled of new bank money, crisp and plant-like. "How should I pack it for you?"

Patience froze as she felt her confidence leave her again.

"Madam, how do you want to carry your money?" he said again.

"Oh, yes. Pack it up for me." She handed him two large bags. Her hands trembled.

As he packed the stacks of money, she thought about how another job was almost done. She looked around the room and adjusted her gaze so she wouldn't seem suspicious. Mr. Falola zipped her two bags shut.

"Please, just sign here that you received the money." She scribbled her signature, remembering to write *Oyinkansola Afolabi* and not *Patience Adewale*. She stood, straightened her black slacks, grabbed the bags off the table, and thanked Mr. Falola. She stumbled from the weight of the load as she made her way toward the door. She had told Emeka that wearing heels wasn't the best idea for her, but he had insisted.

"Have a good day," said the guard standing next to the entrance.

"Yes, sir, you too."

She walked out into the city, put on her sunglasses, and tightened her grip on the bags.

Her grip created a stream of power that flowed from her hands into her body.

She looked at the streets of Ikeja, where buses and cars competed for space on the narrow roads and the sound of countless car horns pierced the air in every direction. In the distance she saw Chike on his okada approaching until he turned into the bank's parking lot and stopped near her. She hopped on, cushioned the bags between their bodies, and grabbed hold of his waist.

"Did you get it?" he said.

"I got it all. Do you think we'll make it in time?"

"We will."

He put both feet on his bike and sped away.

28

EMEKA TRIED TO KEEP CALM, BUT HE COULDN'T BELIEVE
the day had finally come. After Kash told him that Oga had asked to
meet with him in person, he ran in place, jumped, and somersaulted
off his couch.

"I have arrived, o!" he yelled. He never thought his idol from afar
would request to meet *him*.

"I reminded Oga how you led our two successful bank jobs," Kash
said. Emeka jumped up and embraced his friend.

On meeting day, Emeka dressed in his best wares. He was especially excited about the brand-new, crisp white shirt he had gotten
from Tejuosho market. His slender-cut slacks were a pair of Chike's
old trousers he had mended and altered.

When he and Kash arrived at the Sichuan Chinese restaurant on
Allen Avenue, he felt his palms dampen. He wiped them on a handkerchief already soiled from the sweat he dabbed from his forehead.

"Relax," Kash said after taking a deep breath. "You look like you've
seen a ghost. Oga is quite smooth. You will like him."

"I want him to know how much I respect him," Emeka said, stuff-
ing the handkerchief into his back pocket.

"Don't worry. Everybody respects him. We don't have a choice in
the matter."

When Kash opened the door to the restaurant, Emeka's eyes gleamed as he admired the red and gold textures that decorated the entire room—from the furniture to the walls. It was a Monday afternoon and the place was quite empty, so he imagined that most of the people who could afford to eat there were at work.

Kash led him to the back of the restaurant, and he was impressed by how Kash knew exactly where to go.

"You've been here before," Emeka said.

"Of course, this is Oga's number one place to have meetings."

Emeka straightened his back as they walked toward a table where three men sat.

"Oga, how na?" Kash said as they approached the large rectangular table where his boss was seated. Emeka noticed that Oga's workers stood around him as if they wouldn't dare to take a seat in his presence.

"Kash. I dey, jàre," Oga replied.

He was dressed in the way Emeka pictured himself as a rich man—gray double-breasted European suit, stylish satin necktie, and a matching pocket square. His hair and goatee, black like coal and shaped to excellence.

"I see you're still wearing this same shirt of yours," Oga said to Kash as he fiddled with his gold pinkie ring. "Why can't you buy yourself some nice clothes with the money I'm paying you? Must I beg my guys to look decent?"

"Ah, Oga, you know we try, o," Kash said with a light chuckle that sounded tame compared to his usual obnoxious laughter.

Emeka looked down at himself. He didn't feel so dapper in his shirt anymore. He hoped Oga wouldn't detect that such a plain shirt had come from the market.

"Who is this?" Oga said, pointing at Emeka.

Didn't Oga remember he was coming?

Hadn't he requested for him to come?

Emeka began to fidget.

"Oga, this na Emeka. He was in charge of the last bank jobs. Both were a success."

"Yes, yes, you told me about him. Have a seat," Oga said, gesturing to Emeka and Kash.

Emeka almost tripped over his own feet as he hurried to claim the chair across from Oga. Kash flashed him a look. Emeka could almost hear him saying, "Relax yourself."

"An eager worker, I see," Oga said, noticing the exchange.

Emeka was embarrassed, but not enough to flounder in the moment. He noticed Oga had his legs crossed, so he shifted to the left side of his chair and crossed his too.

"Yes, I'm eager, Oga. I've been wanting to meet with you for a very long time," Emeka said.

"I've heard you've made me quite a bit of money."

"Yes, and I know we can make a lot more," Emeka said.

"Phillip, bring me that Cuban cigar," Oga said to his assistant.

Phillip hurried over to the table opposite them, where three large bags sat. He opened one and revealed stacks of naira. Emeka imagined it might have been at least a million.

"Don't be an idiot," Oga said, noticing Phillip fumble through the wrong bag. "Didn't you just pack these this morning? It's the other bag."

Phillip opened the other bag and revealed packs of Cuban cigars, cigarettes, lighters, and a bag of white dust. *What is Oga doing with a bag of talcum powder?* Emeka thought.

Then it dawned on him.

He remembered a friend from years back had told him how some of Nigeria's biggest hustlers dabbled in the cocaine trade. Emeka had never suspected Oga to be one of them. This made him even more mysterious.

"Would you care for a cigar? Chuks, bring this boy a cigar, jàre," Oga called out before Emeka had accepted the offer.

He was comfortable with cigarettes but had never even held a cigar. Refusing one would expose all his greenness.

"Ah, Oga, thanks," he said, taking it from a tray Chuks put in front of him.

Emeka hesitated. He watched as Oga ran his cigar across his nose, taking in its aroma. He bit the end off, then gripped it between his middle and index fingers. Then Chuks lit it, not with a match or a lighter but with a soft flame that crept up some sort of long brown stick. He wondered why it had to be done that way. He imagined that Oga was particular about how things were done.

"Won't you prepare your cigar?" Oga said, blowing smoke toward Emeka.

"Oh, oh, yes, Oga. I was just looking around the place." Emeka bit the end, hoping to imitate his idol, but when a large chunk came off in his mouth and the wrapper began to unravel, he knew he had done something wrong.

"Na wa o," Oga said. "This is how the average man ruins a good Cuban cigar." Laughter echoed through the room. Emeka felt himself shrink, but he rebounded.

"Oga, it's you who we're all striving to be like," he said, disguising his shame by matching their amusement. "Just give us some time."

"Well said. Now let's talk business."

Emeka felt his skin prickle from the excitement.

"My boy, are you ready to move on to other ventures?" Oga said with the cigar balanced between his teeth. Emeka wished he hadn't disfigured his cigar so he could do the same.

"What other ventures are you thinking?"

"I like to work on spontaneous projects. There's a house I need you to sell. The owners will be away in their village for their daughter's wedding. I need someone to stand as the owner. Can you handle that?"

Emeka was confused. If the owner wants to sell his house, why didn't he arrange for it to be sold by a broker? Couldn't the owner do it himself after returning from his hometown?

Then he understood.

"The owner doesn't really want to sell."

"Look at this man. He thinks fast, o. You men, take notes. You have to think fast to be in this business," Oga said. "Yes, we are going to sell a house that isn't for sale. We will make the profit and move on. We don't have much time, since the owner will only be away for a few weeks."

Emeka knew selling an actual house was another level of fraud. He wasn't sure about Patience or even Chike being able to pull it off. His brother was still naive enough to think he would get an engineering job, even though they were so close to paying for Mama's surgery with the money they made with Oga.

"We will do it. I will tell my guys tonight," Emeka said.

"I like your style. You know, I like to groom sharp workers like you," Oga said, pointing his cigar toward Emeka. "If you want to come and stay in my boys' quarters for some time, I will allow it."

"Wow," Emeka said, not knowing how to respond. "I will think about it. Right now I live with my brother."

"Let us get through this job first. We will give you the details by next week. Stay alert," Oga said with a slight grin. "And make me one promise."

"What's that?" Emeka said.

"Burn your market shirt after you've completed this job."

Emeka hung his head, giving in to the shame. He surveyed his shirt and his mended pants. With renewed courage, he looked up.

"I will burn it tonight."

29

WHEN CHIKE ARRIVED AT THE BUS STOP TO MEET MAYOWA, he saw his friend propped up against his father's shiny new Peugeot. Mayowa stood out from the crowd, wearing a patriotic green-and-white T-shirt. As Chike got closer to the car, he noticed the words *Hope '93 MKO* stamped across Mayowa's chest.

"My friend, wetin be your problem?" Mayowa said, amused.

Chike knew Mayowa would excuse his lateness because of the nature of their intended trip. He had finally agreed to go to Abiola's campaign headquarters after weeks of avoiding his friend's invitation.

"What's my business there?" was the question that looped in his mind.

He was sure his new line of work wasn't what Abiola meant by "hope" and "progress."

"Please, no vex that I'm late. I had to stop at one place like this," Chike said.

"Place ke? You're just late, my friend. No wahala though," Mayowa said. "Let's be going."

As they stood talking, a man pointed at Mayowa's shirt.

"MKO for president!" he called out to them.

Mayowa responded with an impromptu dance. He bent his knees, stuck out his buttocks, and grooved in a circle.

"MKO, MKO, MKO, Action! MKO, MKO, MKO, Progress!" As he shouted the words of Abiola's campaign jingle, Chike felt awkward.

"MKO, Kingibe, Action! MKO, Kingibe, SDP, Progress," the man continued.

Passersby joined in.

"Abiola will serve Nigeria well," one man said.

"No more corruption under Abiola," Mayowa shouted, still grooving to the music in his mind.

"My friend, stop that nonsense," Chike said, pulling Mayowa up from his dance by his shirtsleeve.

"Ah-ahn, don't ruin my shirt," Mayowa said.

When they got into Mayowa's father's car, Chike thumped the tassel shaped like a tree that dangled from the rearview mirror. The sweet-smelling air freshener it held filled Chike's nostrils.

"So what's going on with you?" Mayowa said.

"Same thing. Emeka is still up to his 419 things. In fact, he has a brand-new job for us to complete."

"Which kind job be dis one now, ah-ahn?" Mayowa said.

"The short answer is we will sell a house."

Mayowa looked confused for a moment, then his eyes rounded out to the size of table tennis balls.

"I've heard of this one before, o," he said. "Will you do it?"

Chike felt himself fidget through his silence.

"This is risky business you've now entered," Mayowa said.

"Riskier than taking money from two banks?"

Mayowa poked his lips out and didn't bother to answer.

"The money is double what we've been making," Chike said. "Kash will pretend to be like omo-onile who built the house on the land he inherited."

"Ah, those useless omo-onile. How can a person step foot on a piece of land and say they are the owner only because they are natives of Lagos? They are thieves, and everybody knows," Mayowa said. "If

Kash presents himself as omo-onile, why would anybody trust him and buy a house from him?"

"I don't know how this thing will work, but Emeka and Kash say it will be a guaranteed win for us."

"My guy, I dey tell you plenty times, after the election you won't need to worry yourself. You will find a proper job."

Chike wanted to believe Mayowa, but the elections were months away, and there was no way Nigeria's job force and economy would transform overnight.

"You know my mum's situation with her arthritis. We've almost raised enough for her operation. At least you're making money working with your popsie and Abiola."

"Chike, I know. I won't judge you," he said. "And Patience? Is she a part of this one too?"

"Of course," Chike said. "That girl will do anything to get to America to see her mum."

As the car turned the corner, Chike looked out the window and surveyed their whereabouts. They had reached Ikeja, and Mayowa continued toward Toyin Street. Chike always loved coming to this part of town. The houses there that were built in the '60s and early '70s weren't as fussy and overdesigned as the new houses coming up on Victoria Island—the kinds of houses Emeka obsessed over.

As the car rode on the tarred road, Chike looked at the solid black iron gates that sealed each compound off from the rest of the city. He viewed the armor as much more than a security measure. To him it was how the wealthy man who once knew poverty tucked himself away from people's misfortune, preventing such a reality from mingling with his own.

As they continued to ride, Chike tried to picture what life would have been like if his father had become rich in the 1970s. Chike remembered the stories his father had told of friends who had risked their stable jobs at banks and government offices to start companies.

Some had been successful. Some had lost everything. But his father's eyes had often been filled with regret from not riding the wave of possibility like so many of his peers had.

"We done reach," Mayowa said once they arrived at the corner of Abiola's massive compound on Toyin Street.

MKO Abiola Crescent, Chike read from one of the street signs. *How does a man feel when a large stretch of city land is named after him?* Chike wondered as they stopped to honk at the black iron gate labeled *MKO Abiola Campaign Headquarters.*

A gate man wearing a navy-blue uniform emerged.

"Muhammed, how are you?" Mayowa said with his arm hanging out the car window.

"Ah, I dey. Is this your guest?" Muhammed replied as he stared into the car at Chike.

"Yes, he is with me. I brought him here to meet Chief and see how we do campaign work."

"Okay, okay. Chief neva reach house. He go for meeting. He go reach by three o'clock."

"No problem. It's almost two thirty," Mayowa said, looking down at his watch. Is my father there?"

"Yes, your father dey for compound."

Muhammed opened the doors of the gate and waved them in. Chike wasn't surprised by the security measures. A man like Abiola needed such protection.

As they drove in, Chike was floored by what he saw. The lawn was something to behold. Each shrub and inch of grass perfectly aligned. The building itself was black-and-white and stretched across almost as far as a football pitch.

"Is that his house?" Chike said.

"Yes, that's where he lives with some of his wives and children. This is the campaign office. Mayowa pointed toward a one-story bungalow positioned on the side of Abiola's mansion. The office structure alone was bigger than his family's entire house. Mayowa parked the car behind a black V-Boot 200 Mercedes.

As they walked toward the office door, Mayowa stopped and looked at Chike.

"Make sure you don't discuss what you and Emeka have been up to. If anybody asks, just tell them you're looking for a job as an engineer."

"Why would I tell people I'm a thief?"

Chike felt a rush of excitement when they entered the office. The room appeared to vibrate from the sound of ringing telephones and the deep voices of men discussing the news of the day. Mayowa motioned for them to go and greet his father, who stood across the room talking to a group of men, but Chike was distracted by a large painting of Abiola that hung above the corridor of the space. In the portrait he wore a gold-and-white aso oke agbada with bright green *Newbouldia laevis* stuffed inside his high black-and-gold embroidered cap. His large, toothy grin befitted a newly crowned chief.

"Won't you greet my father," Mayowa said.

"Yes, yes. I was just wondering who painted that."

"I don't know. Chief is a rich man, and he knows a lot of people." Chike could tell Mayowa didn't like not knowing the answer to a question about his idol.

As they approached, Mayowa's dad welcomed them with a smile. The gap between his two front teeth complemented his dark, slender features.

"Good afternoon, Sa," Chike said with a slight tilt forward. Igbos didn't have to prostrate for their elders, but since Mayowa's dad was a proud Yoruba man, Chike knew he expected it, so Chike did it as a show of respect.

"O jàre, how are you, Chike. You are welcome," his father said. "Mayowa, give Chike a Coke or Fanta now—you're there looking like he's not our guest."

"Thank you, Sa," Chike said.

Mayowa walked over to the door to another room. His father put his hand on Chike's shoulder.

"This is where we form plans and strategies for Chief MKO Abiola. Chike, I hope you've been following what is happening with the upcoming elections."

"Yes, Sa, I am. MKO—I mean Chief—has my vote."

"That's all right," the elder man said, patting Chike's back. "He should be arriving here any moment, so you will see him."

Mayowa hurried back with a bottle of Coke for his friend. Chike noticed that he had a new glimmer in his eyes.

"Chief is here," someone shouted.

All the men scurried to find their places in the office. Mayowa's father walked toward his desk and straightened up a stack of papers. He placed them in a large manila folder, then put it in his top right-hand desk drawer. He brushed the front of his suit jacket with the palms of his hands, then sat down in his large, cozy leather chair. Mayowa grabbed a chair for Chike and put it near the corner of his father's desk. Chike sat down.

As Abiola walked in, Chike froze in his seat. Everything seemed to go in slow motion as he saw him approach, greeting his workers along the way. Chike took note of his lofty figure and powerful presence as men continued to greet him, some prostrating slightly.

When he approached Mayowa's father's desk, Chike went numb. He couldn't believe his body was failing him. He watched Mayowa and his father stand to greet Abiola, but he couldn't get up. He looked up at him. Then Abiola placed his hand on Chike's shoulder.

"Who is this young man?" he said.

"He is my good friend Chike," Mayowa said after a long pause.

"Look at this boy. Stand up and greet, ah-ahn," Mayowa's dad said.

"I'm so sorry, Sa," Chike said as he found the strength to rise from his chair. "My name is Chike."

"It's okay," Abiola said with a laugh. "You are welcome."

Chike couldn't understand his own behavior. Until then, he had thought of Abiola as a rich man running for president. But being inside his compound changed his perception. Walking into his office made it all real for him.

"Chike, have you finished school?" Abiola said.

"Yes, Sa, I have. I studied petroleum engineering at University of Ibadan. I'm looking for work now."

"That's wonderful. If you are Mayowa's friend, then you must be quite sharp. You will find work soon." Abiola patted Chike on the shoulder, then he turned to Mayowa's father. Chike could hear him mumble something about the elections. Mayowa looked at Chike with round eyes and smiled.

"Did you hear that? He said you will find work soon, Chike."

"Yes, I heard him."

Abiola turned and faced Chike and Mayowa again.

"There's a camera here. Let Chike take a photo with me. Maybe he can go and show it to his father so I can secure their votes," Abiola said jokingly.

Chike didn't bother telling him his father had died. He braced himself for the photo. Abiola towered over him, put an arm around his shoulder and pulled him in closer.

Mayowa's father stood before them with the camera. "Ready?"

"Yes, take the photo," Abiola replied, his voice deep and raspy just as it was on television.

Snap.

Blinded by the flash, Chike blinked long and hard. When he opened his eyes, Abiola was already walking toward another of his employees. Chike understood—a man like him couldn't linger for too long.

To Chike, though, their exchange was a moment forever stamped in time.

30

"PATIENCE, I'M TIRED. TRY THESE ON FOR ME," BIMPE said, holding up a pair of Levi's 501 jeans in the Adeniran Ogunsanya Shopping Mall.

"Again?"

"I need to see how they fit," Bimpe said, barely looking up from the rack of clothes she was sorting through. "We wear the same size, so why not?"

It was the same belittling request she had made on their last trip to a boutique. Patience was certain that Bimpe only asked because she assumed Patience was still broke. Bimpe wanted her to suffer as she tried on clothes she couldn't afford.

"Why do you keep asking me to do this?"

Patience remembered how small she felt when Bimpe told her to turn around and bend over a bit. Now she waited for Bimpe's response.

"Why are you acting so serious?"

Patience stared at her until her eyes made clear some things she had long ignored. Right there, she saw Bimpe's thin lips and her droopy eyes and her plump nose that lacked definition. And it dawned on her that underneath her makeup and her carefully curated wardrobe from abroad, she was just like any other ordinary girl looking to dress up the parts of herself that she felt were askew.

But now Patience would not oblige her. She would not model the clothes Bimpe wanted. She had money in her bag, so she would only model clothes for herself. She had set a good amount aside to go toward her plane ticket to New York, and she would have even more cash after they handled the house Oga had given them to sell.

She was ready to spend money on a dress.

"How are you going to pay for that?" Bimpe said as Patience pulled a long burgundy slip dress off a rack. She pictured herself wearing it on a night out with Chike, then letting him take it off her once they got back to his place.

"I have money today," Patience said.

"I thought you didn't have any money."

"I have a little now."

"How did you get it?"

"My dad sent me some cash."

"Are you sure?"

"Yes, why wouldn't I be sure?"

"Don't lie."

"What do you mean?"

"Patience . . . I know you're not in school anymore. I know your father washed his hands of you."

"How do you know?"

"I know a lot of people at UNILAG. You know I practically ran that place."

In this moment, Patience looked at Bimpe and loathed her. The parts of her that she had discovered were unattractive became even more pronounced. She wanted to push her down, grab the keys to the Peugeot they had come in, and leave her there to find her way home on public transport. How sweet it would feel to know that she had to struggle to hail an okada or squeeze onto a packed danfo to get home. Patience took two deep breaths and decided to listen to her instead.

"I heard that you had to leave school and leave the dorm because your daddy disowned you. Is that true? What is really going on, Patience?"

Patience put the slip dress back on the rack. How was she supposed to respond? Aunty Lola kept telling her she would help her get her birth certificate so she could reapply for her passport. She would probably go back on her word if she knew she was dealing with an eighteen-year-old disowned child trying to travel across the world to find a mother who might not want to be found.

"Things are complicated right now," Patience said. "You know I haven't seen my mother in ten years."

"Yes, but you have a father. Why would he disown you?"

"It's too much to explain."

"My mum knows your father from Ibadan. I haven't told her, but I'm sure she could find out the real story if she asked around." Bimpe walked toward another rack of clothes and picked up a few dresses. She flung her braids from her shoulder to her back.

Patience felt her chest collapse slowly. She was like an egg that had been cracked open and splattered onto a hot pan.

"My father doesn't care, so I left home."

"What do you mean you left home?"

"I left. I'm staying with my cousin. He doesn't have much."

"Is that why you've never invited me to the hostel?"

"Yes."

"Is this the reason you don't have your passport?"

"Yes. But please don't tell Aunty Lola," Patience pleaded.

There was silence. Bimpe looked up at Patience from the rack of clothes.

"So if all this is true, why do you now have money for a dress? Did Chike give you money?"

"Something like that."

"So why didn't he give you money before?"

Patience hated hearing Bimpe utter Chike's name. She was happy she hadn't introduced them.

"Listen, if you're doing something illegal, I won't judge you," Bimpe continued. "I knew a few girls at UNILAG who did certain things to survive. I've heard so many stories on that campus. You wouldn't believe it. Just be careful."

"Please don't tell your mum anything," Patience pleaded again. "I really need help getting my documents."

"I won't tell her."

Patience felt lighter. Maybe Bimpe wasn't the enemy after all.

"You know, my mum has grown so fond of you. She really wants to see you do well," Bimpe said.

Patience was moved. She too was fond of Aunty Lola. But now Bimpe had sliced Patience open and dissected the things she tried to keep hidden, only to stitch her back up again with what may or may not have been loving counsel. Patience decided to play it cool with her.

Maybe Bimpe was being sincere.

Maybe she really didn't want her to go down the wrong path.

"What do you think of this dress?" Bimpe asked, holding up the same slip dress Patience had put down earlier.

"I love it. I was going to try it, remember?" Patience said.

"Yes, yes, try it on. I need to see how it fits on the body."

"Why would you buy the dress I want?"

"Ah now, Patience, I'm your senior. You should just let me have the dress."

Patience decided to let it go.

31

"HOW MUCH DID YOU SAY YOU WANT FOR THIS HOUSE?"

"You can have it for twenty million naira," Emeka told their potential buyer as they stood in the dining room of the Onabanjos' house in Ikeja.

"Ah-ahn, twenty million? Too expensive!"

"My broker, he knows what this place is worth," Kash said, patting Emeka on the back. "This house is practically brand-new, Sa. I built it ten years ago on the land my grandfather bought in 1971."

Emeka had reservations about having Kash handle such a crucial part of the job, but with his swift Yoruba and his meticulous bargaining skills, he acted as the perfect omo-onile born and bred in Lagos.

"It would have to be twenty million," Kash said. "Houses here go for thirty, forty, even fifty million, but because I'm moving my family to London, I have to sell this house in haste."

"Okay. Twenty million. It's not bad, sha," the man said.

Emeka thought of the sum of money, and the hairs on the back of his neck stood up. He wondered how much profit Oga would give them. They had already completed two successful bank jobs. They should be higher earners by now.

"My wife, she loves this house. It is her happiness that I am thinking about. Please let me see the deed again."

"Sa, you have seen the deed several times. It's time to trust that you've found your house. I appreciate that it will make your wife proud. I feel like my family's inheritance will be transferred to the proper hands."

"Ṣebi I'm buying the house? You're not giving me anything."

"That is so, Sa, yes, but . . ."

"And we've seen how you omo-onile have cheated people," the man said, raising his voice with each word he spoke. "I need to be sure that you're selling me a house that is your own, that you built it on your grandfather's land as you say, and that you have the right to sell it."

"Sa, if this house is not mine, how would I be here—living here? Wouldn't the owner be around? And this is not an ordinary plot of land. This is a house I built on my plot of land."

"Why is your price so low?"

"Sa, I thought you said it was expensive."

"Ehn, now. We must negotiate, but you said houses go for fifty million here."

"Sa, as I said, my family and I are leaving Nigeria in two weeks' time."

"What if you're the houseboy here and you're doing 419?"

"Sa, how can you insult me like that? I cannot be a houseboy for anybody. I am moving my family to London, and you're calling me a houseboy? If you don't want the house, say you don't want it."

"I just want to be sure I won't be cheated."

"Let me show you the paperwork again." Emeka rustled through a manila folder filled with phony documents. "See the deed." Emeka handed him the paper he was most proud of. When Patience and Chike brought it home after forging it with the help of Chike's connection, Emeka searched it closely for flaws. It was as close to perfect as perfect is.

"Sa, I know how you feel. As a broker, I am worried for my clients when I'm on the other side. Lagos has become a town of thieves," Emeka said, shaking his head.

"Yes, o. It's like we have to watch our back, side, and front when money exchanges hands," the man said.

"If you are so concerned, why don't you hire a lawyer to look at the documents?"

The man hesitated. "A lawyer will cost another something million just to read the paper that I'm reading now. I am an educated man. I don't need another man to show me how to use my common sense."

Emeka knew he had the man where he wanted him. The man loved the house, his wife loved the house, and he was willing to allow his pride to dictate how he handled a major transaction.

Typical mugu. Gullible ignoramus.

"Good afternoon, Sa," Patience said, emerging from the kitchen, looking as though she were trying to mask her astonishment. Emeka was sure he had told her they would be showing the house to their most promising potential buyer. Why would she just show up?

"Sa, this is my sister," Kash said. "She lives here with me. She will be going to London with me and my family."

"Good afternoon. So this house . . . you can attest to the authenticity of it?" the buyer said.

"Yes, Sa, I can. This is our family house. It will become your family house soon, correct?"

"We shall see," the buyer said as he grinned, seemingly satisfied with Patience's input.

"Go and start preparing for the children," Kash said to Patience, offering her a way out. "They will be home soon."

"Yes, of course," she said, then walked out.

"Sa, we have to close this deal soon. Do you want the house?" Emeka said.

"Let us take another tour before I make my decision."

"Sa, you've looked around this house several times in the last two days. Will this be the last time?"

"Yes, just one more tour."

Emeka and Kash led the man from the office to the medium-size foyer. A modest house it was—quaint with its oak doors and slightly worn tan carpet and banana-colored walls. They passed the sitting room entrance, where just beyond wooden double doors were two gold velvet couches covered with pillows that gave the room an ease and comfort.

As they made their way up the stairs, Emeka surveyed the small holes in the walls, once hidden by the framed photos of a man, his wife, and three children, the real family that lived there—photos he and Kash had taken down before they started showing the house to potential buyers.

They reached the master bedroom. It was a spacious area divided into two parts, a sitting room in front and a sleeping area in back with a king-size bed.

"My wife can find comfort here—I can see it in my mind," the man said. He sat down in a reclining chair and allowed his body to melt into its angles. He rocked and stared at the ceiling. "This is very comfortable. Can you leave it here? My wife, I know she would like it."

Emeka and Kash exchanged looks. Kash shrugged.

"Yes, you can keep the chair."

"Thank you so much. I will tell her about your kindness."

"Ah, don't worry. I've outgrown the chair anyway." Kash said.

"This would be our first house, you know? And this Adeniyi Jones area is a good place. We will be happy here."

"Yes, Sa," Emeka said, grinning. "You will be happy here."

32

"PATIENCE, MEET ADE."

"I've heard so much about you," Patience said as she peered at Bimpe's boyfriend over the large gift she had brought for Ayobami. "It's nice to finally meet you."

She walked into the backyard party with a mission to speak to Aunty Lola before carrying on a conversation with anyone else. Her profit from selling the house in Adeniyi Jones was a decent amount—enough for a plane ticket and a hotel in New York for a few weeks. Everything was starting to line up.

It was time for Aunty Lola to give her real answers about her birth certificate so she could apply for her passport. But when Patience spotted her near the cake table, Bimpe and Ade had approached her, derailing her plan.

"Ade and I were just talking about this party that his friends are having," Bimpe added, not giving her a moment to settle in. "You should come. A few UNILAG people will be there."

"Yes, make sure you show your face at the party," he said.

Patience shrugged and ignored their request. Maybe they'd stop asking if she treated the invitation like it was nothing much, though the idea of finally attending a university party in Lagos intrigued her now that her life plans were coming together.

She looked toward the cake table. Aunty Lola had moved on. Patience scanned the Akanbis' backyard for her.

No Aunty Lola anywhere.

Patience set her gift on the concrete patio and looked around at the noisy children and the inflated balloons. A man dressed like one character or another sat in the middle of the yard trying to read a storybook to kids who paid him no mind.

"Don't you think it's time for me to meet this Chike of yours?" Bimpe said as she put the flier for the party in Patience's hand.

Patience wasn't sure if she was ready to introduce her friends to Bimpe and Bimpe's friends. They were not cut from the same cloth. And if Bimpe's friends were anything like her, she knew they would make that clear.

"Okay, fine, I will come, and I will ask them if they want to come."

"Good. I can't imagine anyone saying no to this party, sha. Make sure you dress well and tell the guys to dress well too. If you come looking ras, believe me, you will be bounced. In fact, you can go in my closet today and choose a dress. Just return it after the party."

"Ade, I hear you work with your father at his new telephone company," Patience said, attempting to change the subject of her borrowing Bimpe's clothes.

"Yes. We're planning to do a complete takeover in Lagos now that the government has allowed the private sector to participate in telecommunications. One day we'll be the biggest player in Nigeria—in West Africa, in fact." He paused as if he wanted Patience to praise him somehow. She kept quiet. "I hear your dad is quite the businessman himself," he said.

Patience watched him as his eyes landed on her breasts. She had to be seeing things. She glanced at Bimpe, who didn't seem to notice.

"Patience, darling, you're here."

Patience turned and saw Aunty Lola float toward her wearing a flowing floral caftan. "I'm glad you could come."

Patience picked up the large teddy bear that she had tried to conceal with flimsy wrapping paper. "My gift to Ayobami."

"You're just a student. You didn't have to bring a gift."

Patience made quick eye contact with Bimpe at the mention of the word *student*.

"No problem, Aunty. You know I'm fond of Ayobami."

"I see you've met Ade. Isn't he just a sharp, sharp fellow?"

"Yes, he's quite interesting. I see Ayobami is having fun," Patience said.

"Yes, o. She and her friends have been running around the place with that character all day. Now her daddy is there entertaining them too."

Patience looked on at the crowd of kids. There she saw Mr. Akanbi lingering, laughing, and chasing his daughter. When he grabbed her and threw her up in the air, Patience crowned him Superdad, even despite him possibly having an affair with another woman.

"Oya, everybody dance!" a voice yelled out.

"Let me monitor these children. Patience, eat, drink, relax."

"Aunty . . . wait." Patience watched as the woman walked on. She turned back to Bimpe and Ade, hoping to conceal her frustration. He stuffed one hand in his pocket and lifted his Heineken toward her as if to say, "Cheers."

"So how are you finding UNILAG?" he said. Patience wasn't sure how much Bimpe had told him about her current state as a dropout and disowned child.

"It's okay. I don't think it's for me, though."

"Oh, really? What is for you?"

"I don't know yet."

"Patience really loves sewing and fashion," Bimpe said with a hint of humor.

"Wow. That's . . . interesting."

"Let's cut the cake," a voice called out. Patience welcomed the distraction and walked toward the crowd, which had already launched into the happy birthday song. When she reached the other side, she was pleased that Ade and Bimpe hadn't followed her.

The candles were blown out. The cake was cut. Patience took a plate and took a bite of the cake. She looked up and noticed Aunty Lola pulling party favors out of a nylon bag. Patience set her cake down on a table and went to her.

"Aunty, can I help you with anything?" she said.

"Patience, you're our guest. Just enjoy the party."

"Yes, Aunty . . . but, Aunty . . . how about my birth certificate? Have you made progress?"

"Patience, we will discuss this after the party," she said, patting her on the shoulder.

"I went to the embassy, actually."

"You did?" the woman said. She seemed surprised. "How did that go?"

"Not so good. They say I need proof. So my birth certificate is crucial."

"Of course. They won't just let you have American documents without proof. I told you that from the beginning."

"You did, Aunty. I just feel like I need to get my papers soon."

"Yes, I know. But you must take time. I will let you know when I have everything sorted."

Patience sensed hesitation in her voice. How hard could it be to contact a US office and have an application sent? Maybe she had it sent and it got lost in the mail? *Useless postal system*, she thought. She had heard stories of how mail that came from America would either arrive open and rummaged through or never come at all. She took a deep breath when she noticed Mr. Akanbi approach.

"Patience, how are you?" he said.

"Good afternoon, Sa. It's good to see you having fun with Ayobami."

Aunty Lola turned away and continued sorting through the party favors, stiff and silent.

"Ah, this is nothing. Life cannot be just about work."

Aunty Lola chuckled under her breath, as if her husband had just told a lie.

"I agree, Sa."

"How's your daddy?"

"He's fine, Sa," Patience said through her stiffened jaw.

"I will see him in Ibadan next week."

"If you see him, Sa . . . greet him for me," she said, then scolded herself for her response. Mr. Akanbi didn't reply.

"Patience!" Bimpe called out from across the yard. She turned and saw her holding a bouquet of balloons and standing near the man dressed as a character.

"Excuse me, Sa . . . Ma." Patience squeezed her way through the crowd of kids, thinking about how she had made no progress with Aunty Lola.

"Let's go to my room now. We can pick out the dress you should wear to the party."

"I'm not worried about that, Bimpe. I will look good. My friends will look good."

Bimpe ignored Patience and shifted her gaze toward her parents. "So what was my mum saying? Was she talking to Daddy at all?"

"No. She seemed annoyed when he came," Patience said.

"She's convinced he's found happiness somewhere else. But he's always been easygoing. It's like her biggest fear is ending up like her friends whose husbands left them. I told her, if she finds out he has another family, she should become a trendsetter and leave him."

"And what's your biggest fear, Bimpe?" Patience didn't know why she had asked, but the question seemed necessary.

"I fear . . . I guess I fear nothing," she said, perplexed yet proud.

"Then why won't you go abroad? What is holding you in Nigeria?"

Bimpe, stunned, looked at Patience. Patience sensed she had touched a nerve. She now started to wonder if Bimpe didn't want to leave her mum with her dad. Or maybe she didn't want to abandon the comfort of being a Lagos babe without knowing what she would become somewhere else. Patience wanted Bimpe to express her own vulnerabilities, since Bimpe had confronted her about being forced out of UNILAG and disowned.

"Let me go find Ade. He might want some cake," Bimpe said drily.

Patience watched her as she walked on. She thought of Aunty Lola being stressed about her marriage. Patience had been obsessed with getting her birth certificate from her. She suddenly felt selfish. If Aunty Lola needed time, she would just have to wait.

33

SOMETHING WAS BURNING IN ADENIYI JONES.

It was the Onabanjos' house. The area's residents found it in flames as they trickled outside looking for the source of the stench. Men ran toward the house, screaming from outside the gate to alert the family. They were likely home. They had recently taken a trip to Ekiti, where Mr. Onabanjo had married off his daughter one week before.

Mr. Onabanjo, his two teenage sons, and his wife ran out the side door of the house screaming.

"Fire! E gba mi o!" he yelled as they opened the gate.

There was no time to wait for the Federal Fire Service to come quench the blaze.

They had a way of not showing up at all.

Neighborhood men took on the challenge, passing buckets of water from the Onabanjos' borehole and a nearby well. The fire grew and spread like a fungus as they tossed water onto the flames that enveloped the two-story house. The men continued to work in vain as the fire raged on to the tune of glass breaking and wood structures from the front patio collapsing. The crisp peach color of the house blackened by the second.

"Jesu! Olorun gba wa!" Mr. Onabanjo pleaded. His wife wept and threw herself to the ground next to their sons, who stood emotionless.

Nobody was more amazed than Chike, who crept inside the gate and looked on at the scene bewildered. He had just been at that very house a few days ago. Like any other moderately expensive home in the area, it stood at a typical two-story height and worried no one.

Now the house is on fire, he thought.

Chike noticed a group of men yelling obscenities running from the side of the house dragging a man behind them. It was Mr. Olubiyi. Chike recognized him despite his black eye and blood-stained lips.

"This man said he set fire to this house! We will kill him today!" a loud voice from the mob yelled.

Police arrived and grabbed the middle-aged man from the angry flock. As they hustled him toward their car, he and Chike locked eyes. He yelled out to Chike, who at first couldn't make out what the man was trying to tell him. Then he understood.

"My life savings," he yelled. "My spirit is in that house."

A chill shot through Chike's body. It was the same chill he had felt the day he met Mr. Olubiyi at that very house one week before. He was on his okada, and he decided to visit the place he, Emeka, Patience, and Kash had just sold off to some "gullible ignoramus," as Emeka described the buyer.

Chike wanted to see what he had defrauded someone out of. He wanted to take note of the object that had become another job well done for them, another completed mission that he despised.

Their roles in the operation had been simple. Kash surveilled the house to make sure the family had left when it was time to start the transaction. Emeka called the shots as usual, so he appointed Patience and Chike to forge all the documents they needed to sell the house: a fake deed and a phony certificate of occupancy.

Emeka acted as the broker. Kash played a typical Lagos omo-onile, who claimed he had acquired the plot of land and the house built on it through family lineage.

And they had pulled it off.

Kash and Emeka bragged about how dumb their buyer was and how easy the job had been. Chike became curious. He wanted to see the house himself, so he went to it. There he found Mr. Olubiyi standing near the front gate, staring hard as if he could move the house with his mind. Chike kept his distance, fearing the man might have been the rightful owner, until an annoyed Mr. Onabanjo came out the front gate.

"Why are you still standing in front of my house?" Mr. Onabanjo said. "Wo! I will call the police!"

"Are you sure this is your house?" Mr. Olubiyi said. He seemed emotional.

"Yes, I'm sure. I've shown you all my proper documents. Now go away!" Mr. Onabanjo walked back into his compound.

As Chike prepared his bike to leave, Mr. Olubiyi called out to him. "Okada! Okada! Ebute Metta."

Chike froze. How could he give the man a ride after what he had just heard? But Mr. Olubiyi insisted.

"Okada, okada," he said, walking toward Chike's bike. "You don't hear me?"

"Um, yes, Sa, where are you going?"

"I said I'm going to Ebute Metta."

Chike tried to think of a way to turn him down, but he couldn't think of anything in the moment. "Okay, make we go," he said.

As they drove along the freeway, Chike was happy the traffic was scarce. *Get him to his destination fast-fast*, he thought. *Avoid conversation.* But as Chike hit the corner to make his way toward the bridge, they approached a stretch of stalled cars.

"Na wa o for this go-slow," Mr. Olubiyi said.

"That's Lagos for you," Chike said, hoping the chat would end there.

"Yes, Lagos is a very sad place."

Chike knew where the conversation was going. Before he could think of a way to avoid it, Mr. Olubiyi started talking again.

"Can you imagine, the house near the area where I dey hail you, na my house be dat," he said. "I just bought it with the money my wife and I have been saving for years. We wanted to build a house, but then somebody told us we could buy a ready-made house from one omo-onile in Ikeja."

"Why would you want to buy another man's house? And all these omo-onile are just 419. Build your own house on your own land," Chike said, trying to shame the man into saving his story.

"Building a house can take long. My wife is not well. I wanted to move her into a house of our own in case her condition gets worse. I found that house for a very good price, and I paid for it. Can you imagine, I put down ten million naira for that house as an initial deposit. I signed all the documents and checked them with my own eyes. Everything was correct. They even gave me the key to the house. The day I went to move all of our property there, I met a man inside who said he is the rightful owner and he made no plans to sell his house."

Chike heard the man's voice crack. He thought about how he and Patience had gotten the forged documents. It was an easy task. Oga had connected them with his lawyer friend, who had used a bogus name and seal to draft everything.

"What of your lawyer?" Chike said to Mr. Olubiyi. "What did he say about the documents?"

"I didn't use a lawyer, na. Sebi I get eyes and brain."

"Ah, this is Lagos. You can't sign documents for land if you no get lawyer to oversee everything."

"Sebi you dey drive okada. How you sabi buying and selling a house?" Mr. Olubiyi said. "As a simple okada man, what lawyer do you know?"

"Ah, you think say because I dey drive okada, I no get common sense? I am a college graduate looking for a job," Chike said, switching from pidgin to proper English. "My field is petroleum engineering."

"Na wa o, an engineer and you dey drive okada? Nigeria ti ba je," Mr. Olubiyi said, shaking his head. "Abiola, abeg, make you come save this country."

Chike thought about how he had just met Abiola a few weeks back. Afterward, he had promised himself he would tell Emeka that he wouldn't help sell the house. He was ready to make an honest living, even if he had to drive his okada a little bit after the election.

Then his mother had called about her condition and how it had worsened. They had to put together the money for her operation.

So he had given in. It would be the last illegal job he took, he had promised himself.

But this job—selling someone's house to someone for their life savings—felt different from the others. More crooked, more damaging, less impersonal.

So there he was, with his victim, pinned down by guilt. A sick wife would never live in the house her husband had bought to bring her comfort.

Chike wove through the remaining row of cars on the freeway leading to Ebute Metta. He was happy they were close to the man's destination but nervous to see where the man lived.

"We soon reach," Mr. Olubiyi said. "Just continue like this."

Chike pressed hard on the gas to get to Mr. Olubiyi's stop. As he bobbed and weaved through the other cars, he thought about Peter, who had crashed into the gutter. He slowed down.

"Right there, turn there."

They approached a tall brown-and-beige building of flats. The complex was clean, a decent place compared to other residences in the area. Chike knew Mr. Olubiyi had a good job. He felt his guilt ease a bit as curiosity set in.

"Excuse me, Sa, what do you do for work?" Chike said.

"I'm a bank manager."

Chike thought about the irony of the situation—a bank manager duped into buying a house from former bank thieves who had gone on to dabble in real estate fraud.

"Ah, with your kind of work, I'm sure you will get money again to build your own house," he said, hoping to ease the man's pain.

"Thank you for your encouragement, but the house I bought is my house. If I can't live there, nobody will live there."

The words unsettled Chike. He brushed the feeling off when he looked into Mr. Olubiyi's eyes. The man looked broken and defeated, with his slender frame humped over. The whites of his large, round eyes were almost the color of blood. The skin on his lips was chalky and cracked like the dead shedding skin of a snake. There wasn't much the man could do about the situation, Chike thought.

"What is your name?" Mr. Olubiyi said.

"My name is Chike, Sa." Chike felt his stomach seize. He had given the man his real name. "What is yours?" he said, as if knowing the man's name would make up for giving away his own.

"Olubiyi," the man said. "Mr. Olubiyi."

There was a long pause.

"Can you understand that my life savings has been poured into that house?" Mr. Olubiyi said finally. "I don't know the men who sold the house to me. I don't know where they are. All I know is that my spirit is in that house. That is all I have. Ṣe you understand?" he said.

"I understand," Chike said. "I understand very well."

34

"SOMEONE IS IN JAIL BECAUSE OF US."

Chike paced back and forth in the front room of his and Emeka's flat.

"You are behaving like a woman," Kash said with his usual chuckle, then he stumbled toward Chike as if his leg was twisted. "Money has no emotion. Money is survival. Money is energy. If one man has to rebuild his house for us to have some money to survive, so be it," he said.

"This is not about money; it's about principle."

Patience rubbed his shoulder to calm him. Her hand trembled as she slipped hers into his. At least someone else was afraid, he thought.

"Chike, you're mad! You went to that house and you met that man? You could have gotten us caught!" Emeka shouted.

"What do you mean? Did you hear me when I said a man is in jail and another man lost his house because of what we did?"

"Listen, like Oga says, there are always casualties when it comes to things like this. At least we can say nobody died."

"You've always been heartless," Chike said, rubbing back the pain he felt in his eye sockets.

"Heartless?" Emeka's shoulders dropped, and he began to breathe in and out, as if the word *heartless* was an arrow that Chike had lodged straight into his back. "This coming from a university graduate with no ambition. The favorite child. But all you did was work Mama into sickness, and now you don't have anything to show for it. Where is your big engineering job? Where is your money? Ehn, Chike? Why can't you support the woman who sacrificed herself for you?"

"Chike, Emeka, please," Patience said.

"What do you mean?" Chike said. "You've always been useless, and you want everything handed to you. You never work for anything. That's why I have a degree and you don't. You're a disgrace." He felt the blood boil in his head as his neck tensed. He knew then that the argument had escalated beyond control. He was afraid of what Emeka would say next, but his brother said nothing. Instead, Emeka walked over to Chike and hurled his fist onto his right cheek. Chike grabbed Emeka's neck and pushed him to the floor. He bent over him and swung his fists, each jab blocked by Emeka until he landed a punch onto Emeka's eye.

"Oh my God, stop this!" Patience said.

"Na wa, o. Two whole brothers fighting like animals. Does this mean we can have Chike's cut of the money from the next job we do?" Kash said as he snickered.

"Kash, you should be stopping them!"

Kash stood and pulled Chike off of his brother.

Emeka leaped up, holding his eye. He stumbled into the bedroom. They could hear him knocking things down. Patience touched Chike's cheek. He winced.

After a few minutes, Emeka emerged from the room with a suitcase, then walked out the door and slammed it behind him.

35

"HE FOLLOWED ME HOME. HE FOLLOWED ME HERE. I SAW him!" Patience said as she paced the room.

"Who followed you?"

"Mr. Olubiyi. The man who burned the house. I saw him."

"Patience, it's so dark outside. How would you see him?" Kash rolled his eyes and sat down.

"He looked at me. He looked at me, and he started following me."

"Okay, so where is he now?" Kash said.

"I don't know. I think I moved too fast for him."

"Patience, the man is in jail. You're becoming like Chike."

"He saw me. Mr. Olubiyi saw me that day. He saw you. He heard me talk. We stole his money. How will we make money now?" she blurted out.

Kash stared at her for a moment, then flashed a sly grin.

"Patience, why are you afraid?"

"What do you mean? I just said . . ."

"Why are you really afraid?"

She froze. She knew what he saw in her because she felt it within herself.

"You're not like Chike. Patience, you and me right now, *we* are the same."

He was right. She felt sorry for Mr. Olubiyi but she was more concerned with her own mission. She needed the money they took. She hated that it felt like their only option. She was sick with fear of getting caught, sick that she had to question herself about whether they had a right to take bank money and someone else's life savings.

And because of this, she feared what she was becoming.

"Patience, it is a sad story, what happened to the man, but we can't concern ourselves with that. We did what we had to do, and we will continue."

She thought of her father and blamed him. He was the one who had made her this desperate. He had done the same to Kash.

"Patience, the man burned somebody's house down. He is no longer a victim, and you don't have anybody to answer to anymore, remember? You freed yourself from Daddy."

"Yes, but is this what it means to be free?"

PATIENCE WATCHED HER BACK FOR DAYS AND FOUND HERself taking the long way home to avoid the area where Mr. Olubiyi's presence haunted her.

But on a day NEPA took light and the heat in Kash's place was unbearable, she decided to be better to herself. She took a long walk to nowhere in particular and felt entertained by the juju music that blasted throughout the area. She hailed a man who balanced a large frozen cooler of goods in front of his bicycle, paid for banana ice cream, and licked it as she made her way home.

When she arrived back at Kash's, she was startled by what she saw.

"Margaret?" Patience said as she stared at her sister, who stood next to Kash in their room. Her mouth was numb, and she wondered if it was from the ice cream or the shock of seeing her half sister in Lagos.

"Patience! I'm here. Can you imagine?" Her uniform and her short hair braided into her school's preferred style put her youthfulness on full display.

"Surprise," Kash said.

"What are you doing here? School is not on holiday."

"I know."

"She came from Ogbomosho by herself. On public trans. Can you believe it?"

"You did what?"

"I did. I needed to see you. Mummy said you're not in school anymore and Daddy isn't happy. She wouldn't tell me anything else."

"Well, that's all true. Do they know you're here?"

"Patience, I'm hungry. Let's get Mr. Biggs. They say it tastes better in Lagos."

"Margaret, answer me. Do Daddy and Mummy know you're here?"

"Of course not. Can we talk as we eat?"

PATIENCE AND MARGARET HOPPED OFF THE BUS AND made their way to Mr. Biggs.

"Can you imagine? A whole teacher having sex with a student. That is not proper. I mean, how can a girl like us look at a teacher and see him like that?"

Margaret spoke quickly as if her tongue were looking to make a permanent exit from her mouth. Patience wondered if it was the same teacher she had given her virginity to.

This was the reason she couldn't tell Margaret about it then, or ever, she thought.

"I mean, Tola should have known she would get caught. Don't you think?"

"I don't know."

"Patience, what do you think about Tola?"

"Who?"

"Tola at school. Tola in SS3. People saw her with him in the bush."

"I don't know, Margaret."

Patience wished she had the energy to entertain her sister. She had too much to think about.

"Patience, are you okay?" Margaret said.

"Yes, I'm fine. Why?"

"You don't seem to be here."

"I'm fine."

Inside Mr. Biggs, they joined the small queue of people waiting to order. Margaret requested two meat pies and a Coke. Patience ordered jollof rice, moi moi, chicken, and a Fanta. They got their food and sat in one of the booths. Margaret picked up her meat pie and took a bite. Patience stared at her as she sometimes did, searching for any sign of herself. *Not even a little resemblance,* she thought.

As they ate, she realized that Margaret was quiet.

"What's wrong?" Patience said, realizing she no longer wished for silence.

"I don't know. I was just thinking . . . about that book your mother used to read to you. Have you been reading it yourself?"

"No, I just looked through it that day," she said. She couldn't believe Margaret had mentioned her mother.

Patience unwrapped her straw and put it into her Fanta bottle. She sipped it and wished she had bought a Coke instead.

"What happened with you and Daddy?" Margaret said.

"You know him. We know him."

"Yes, I know Daddy, but why did he make you leave UNILAG?"

"Margaret, don't worry yourself. I'm okay with Brother Kashimawo."

"So you want me to just go back to school and not worry about you? I've worried about you before, but now I can't handle it anymore."

Patience hated that her younger sister worried about her. But she knew all along that it was the reason Margaret always tried to rescue her from Modupe or from their daddy, and now from herself.

"I know when you're sad, Patience. I sense it. I sensed that you missed your mum when I saw the book in your room that day, and then you asked Daddy about her when we had breakfast."

Patience sipped her Fanta again and shook her foot under the table. She thought of her mum's words: *My dearest Patience . . . I really tried, but sometimes in life we have to accept when we lose . . . One day we will meet again . . .*

"Am I right? You must be sad about your mum."

"I am fine, Margaret. Don't worry."

Margaret sat back in her chair and put a meat pie on her plate.

"So why did you ask Daddy about her before you left for UNILAG?"

"I asked because when I saw the book I thought of her, that's it. Don't worry, okay. Let's talk about something else."

"How did all of this happen?" said Margaret.

"What do you mean, all of this?"

"Why didn't Daddy help your mum if she was having problems? I mean, we know he probably cheated on your mum with Mummy, but what happened? They don't talk about it. All we've heard is that your mum is crazy."

"Maybe you should ask Modupe!" Patience snapped.

Margaret took another bite of her meat pie. She chewed and swallowed hard.

"I'm sorry, Patience. I didn't mean to insult your mum."

"It's fine, don't worry." Margaret didn't know how her mother tried to keep her, how their father put her mother out, how there was even a court case, how her mum told her they would meet again.

"No, really, I'm sorry," Margaret said.

"Margaret, please, it's enough."

They picked at their food in silence. Patience looked up at Margaret, who seemed dejected. Her sister had a right to know the truth too. But she barely knew her own truth, so she guarded the little she did know with a black iron gate that she had built inside herself.

"Turn your plate," Patience said, breaking their silence. "Let's try everything."

Margaret's lip curled at one corner of her mouth. "I know you. That's why I was eating my meat pie slooooowly." They both laughed. "Okay, first let me taste the moi moi."

"Okay, give me the second meat pie."

"Ah-ahn, the whole thing? Why not just take a piece?"

"Margaret, if you eat rice and moi moi you won't finish that meat pie."

They spun their plates around and delighted in the moment. Margaret stuck her fork in Patience's plate. Patience grabbed a meat pie from Margaret's. She hesitated and decided to break it in half after all; she gave her sister what remained of it, just as she always did.

PATIENCE STARED UP AT THE CEILING, THINKING ABOUT how exhausted she was, as she lay on the thin mattress next to her sister. She looked up at Kash's cracked clock. Three in the morning. She couldn't stop obsessing over her conversation with Margaret at Mr. Biggs. Kash's aggressive snoring didn't help.

"Margaret, you know . . . I kept a lot of my mum's things hidden in my closet. That's where the book came from." She was whispering, not sure if her sister would hear her. She felt the air in her body diminish as the words left her mouth. "So, yes, I'm sad about my mum."

Margaret shifted from her side onto her back, and Patience realized then that her sister was also awake.

"I have two letters from my mum: one she wrote me and the other for Daddy. She didn't want to leave me, but she didn't say in the letter where she was going. She just said we would meet again." Patience took a deep breath and continued. "At Daddy's party, I met one of her friends who said she had kept in touch with her for some time. My mum was in New York the last time she spoke to her."

"So what are you going to do?" Margaret turned to face her, propping her head up with the palm of her hand. Patience turned to her too. The room was dark, but still she felt Margaret's reassurance.

"How do you know I'm going to do anything?"

"Because that's you. You always know how to get what you need."

Patience thought about the bank job, the man who lost his house, the other who lost his life savings.

Was she a natural born thief?

Maybe. Maybe not.

But she had a cause that called for desperate measures. Wasn't she just as entitled to see her mother as those men were to their things and the banks were to their funds?

"Patience, I hope you find your mum."

"Thank you," Patience said. Her struggle to tame her tears made her nose burn. She rubbed it hard and held her breath. Her head began to throb.

"Why didn't you tell me sooner?"

"I don't know why. But please, *do not* tell Daddy or Mummy."

"Patience, you know I won't."

"Yes, I know."

The silence lingered between them.

"When I first met you . . . wow," Margaret said. "You had your own style and your own ways, and I wanted to be like you because you and all your independence . . . you were a star in my eyes. Like gold or honey. But then you were also a part of me. We were blood. We *are* blood."

Margaret paused. Patience was speechless. She didn't know whether to say something or just take it in. She blinked hard to hold back the tears.

"My mum . . . I know she treated you like an outsider even when she convinced herself that she treated you the way she treated me. But, Patience, that half-sister thing, I can't do that with you. You are my sister. Completely."

And just like that, Patience's tears flowed like strong currents crashing through the stone of an embankment. Margaret rested her head on her sister's chest and curled her body next to her.

"This might be the first time you've let me see you cry."

Patience wiped her face and calmed herself.

She took a deep breath and felt closer to home than she had in a long time, though still not fully home quite yet.

36

"FIRE! FIRE!"

"Chike!" Patience shouted as she jolted up. She shook him, then rubbed his cheek. He sprang up, and his body trembled.

"Chike, you had another dream," Patience said as she stroked his arm. He sat up, rubbed his eyes, and put his hand on her waist. He buried his head in her chest. She stroked his close-cut hair.

"When will you stop having these dreams about fire?"

"I don't know."

Chike looked up and kissed Patience on the forehead. When she stared into his eyes, he welcomed her gaze with a subtle smile.

"Thank you for staying with me again. I promise I will stop waking you like this."

"Chike, try to forgive yourself. I know it's hard, but try harder."

Chike fidgeted and stayed quiet. He moved to the edge of the bed. She sat up next to him. She rubbed his back, then his neck. He looked into her eyes again and kissed her shoulder.

"You know, since me and Kash moved into our new flat last week, I haven't slept in my new bed once," Patience said.

"Yes, I know."

"But I don't mind."

"I will be okay. It's just so fresh in my mind. A man has to go to jail because of something we provoked him to do."

"Chike, you and Emeka paid for your mum's surgery. Is that not reason enough to try to forgive yourself?"

"Yes. Yes . . . a little."

Patience had Kash and Margaret to thank for reminding her of why she had done what she did in the first place—though she still felt random pangs of guilt.

"I'm still thinking about what else I can do to get to America. I still don't have enough money to actually *be* in America. I still don't have my passport. It all feels like such a waste."

Chike stared at her and rubbed her back this time. It was his turn to comfort her, and she was happy he was finally taking notice.

"I don't know what to do, honestly," she said. "I can't keep living like this."

"I wish I could do more for you," Chike said. "I've always wanted to do more for you." He stroked her back again more firmly, then her shoulders.

"Remember . . . that time . . . that time I was supposed to take you out when you were at UNILAG, but I didn't come and you didn't see me for almost a week?"

"I remember."

"I didn't come because I lost an engineering job that was supposed to be mine," he said as if his saliva had turned bitter. "I got a recommendation. Can you imagine? I even practiced how I would accept the position."

"Why didn't you tell me?"

"I don't know."

Patience knew why. It was the same thing she had felt many times—first the day she watched her father throw her mother out, then each time someone probed her about her position in her family—yet Chike somehow convinced himself that he alone knew that feeling, a feeling she didn't know how to name.

"Chike, you will find your way. *We* will find our way."

"Honestly . . . I don't even remember what I need."

In the midst of their silence, Patience searched her mind for what to say to settle him, because settling him made her feel useful. It was a feeling she had come to crave.

"Shall I make you egg? I think we still have some Agege bread." It was all she could think to say.

Chike stood and pulled her up. He held her waist, then kissed her again. He slid his hand down her pants, and she felt a good kind of fire engulf her.

She had said the right thing.

37

"SEE HOW SMOOTH THIS CAR IS," EMEKA SAID AS HE
looked at Chike in the rearview mirror of the black Toyota Cressida
he had borrowed from Oga.

"It's small but correct. Not a BMW, but it's good." Emeka shifted
his gaze to the street in front of him, then again toward the rearview
mirror, looking at his brother in the back seat.

Chike shuddered at the darkness and entitlement in his brother's
eyes, and looked away. He moved closer to Patience, though they were
already cramped next to Mayowa. Their bodies were melded together
by sweat, a result of the Lagos heat that encased the car. Emeka insisted on leaving the air-conditioning off to save gas. The fuel shortage
was making everyone cut back. Ignoring the sticky humidity, Patience
rested her head on Chike's shoulder and her hand on his chest. He put
his arm around her and pulled her in even closer. Kash, in the front
passenger seat, took a long, exaggerated puff of his cigarette.

"Ah, Oga really likes Emeka. Nobody else touches his cars except
Phillip, his driver," Kash said.

"Has your dear boss heard anything about the burned house?"
Chike said.

Emeka looked at him again in the rearview mirror and rolled his
eyes. "No, he has not."

Just a few weeks ago, if anyone had told Chike he would be riding in Oga's car with Emeka at the wheel, he would have cursed their mother, their father, and their children—living and unborn. But it had been two months since his fight with his brother, and that amount of time was the only thing that could smooth over what had been broken between them, though the edges of their relationship were permanently dented.

He looked up again at Emeka in the rearview mirror of the Cressida. He hated him like he had that day. He regretted joining him for the ride. But Patience had insisted they all go to meet Bimpe at some UNILAG party.

"The place is on that street. Watch the road. Ah-ahn," Mayowa said as Emeka took a swift turn.

"Why disturb the driver from the back seat?" Emeka said, glancing over his shoulder.

"Emeka, you *can* slow down a bit," Chike said.

When his brother had called and offered to drive them to the party in one of his boss's fancy cars, he had thought about saying no. But there had been an eagerness in Emeka's voice that suggested he wanted to plant a white flag into the gap in their brotherhood.

When they were young, they had fought with their fists about petty things like Chike getting the last of the chin chin because of his good grade on an exam or whose turn it was to handwash their father's clothes. This time, they had said things they had always known they'd felt but never expressed with actual words. And now their words had found a permanent resting place in their minds. And it would take too much effort to evict them.

"You're driving Oga's car, and you're living in his house now," Mayowa said, interrupting Chike's thoughts. "Emeka, you're better than this."

"Mayowa, abeg, not tonight," Emeka said. "No talk of Abiola, politics, Naija's economy, real jobs, none of that story-story right now.

You're sitting in the car of the man you call 419, and you're enjoying the ride. What does that make you?"

"Okay, o. Me, I will keep quiet." Mayowa sat back and looked out the window next to him.

Chike wasn't surprised when he heard his brother had moved into Oga's house. He had gotten the status he craved, though vicariously through one of the most notorious crooks in Lagos. The only contact they had had during their break was when he and Emeka put their money together for their mother's surgery. That day, Chike had told his brother he was done with their illegal jobs.

But Chike missed his brother. He knew it for sure when he started having dreams about Emeka being set on fire by Oga, though he also knew he dreamed of that because fire remained constant in his mind.

He dreamed of his brother on fire, Mr. Olubiyi on fire, and even Patience on fire. Seeing her ablaze, running topless at Bar Beach, then thrusting herself into the ocean, changed the way he saw her. As she became the only person who didn't shame him for going to see the house they sold, he began to bare himself to her.

Patience shifted her body again.

"My leg is burning. When will we get to this party?" She relaxed the *t* in *party*, using her usual American accent.

"You people are full of complaints today," Emeka said.

Chike kissed Patience's forehead in response to Emeka's accusation.

"Chike, you have to test-drive this car. Why are you behaving like this?" Emeka said, looking at him again in the rearview mirror.

"I'm fine on my okada," Chike said, still wounded from his brother's claim that he lacked ambition.

Emeka rolled his eyes and looked away. "Chike, rapu okwu a," Emeka said, hoping they could move past their quarrels.

"Emeka, abeg, watch the road," Kash said as he held on to the dashboard. "Look, police roadblock. These idiot police."

Emeka slowed the car as he prepared to stop at the police check-point. There were so many around Lagos, he knew not to wait for an officer to give him the signal to brake. Emeka stopped behind the car ahead and looked at Kash before turning to everyone in the back seat.

"When this useless police sees all of us, they will expect something from all of us," Emeka said.

"I'm broke," Chike said. After paying for his mother's surgery, he was back to his okada salary.

Patience slipped two hundred naira into his left palm. He looked down at the money and put it in his pocket.

The officer walked toward Emeka's window carrying a large AK-47.

"How na?" the police officer said, peering into the front of the car, then the back seat. Patience noticed the black layer of filth on his palm when he leaned his head farther into the car.

"You're all looking sharp," he said.

"Abeg, what is it? We are going home," Emeka said, annoyed.

"Ah-ahn," the officer said, his mouth gaping open. Chike noticed his missing teeth, one on the side and another on the bottom row. His breath smelled of the hot liquor fermented by unlicensed booze makers who sold their inventory on the roadside.

"How much did he drink today?" Patience said to nobody in particular as if she read Chike's mind.

Chike whispered, "Relax."

Emeka continued to taunt the policeman until he gave in and slipped the officer a one-hundred-naira note.

"Ah-ahn, five people dey for this car," the officer said.

Chike looked at the disheveled officer with fury. "Abeg, Emeka, drive away," Chike said.

Emeka ignored Chike and continued the banter with the officer. "Just bring money out so he can let us go," he said, turning halfway to the back.

Mayowa stuffed a few naira into Emeka's hand, and then Chike dug into his pocket for the money Patience had slipped him and gave it to Emeka.

The police officer shifted his gun from across his chest to his back, counted the money discreetly, and then signaled for them to move.

"When government never pays police salary, what can one expect?" Kash said.

"Give Nigeria time, sha," Mayowa said, breaking his self-imposed silence.

"Chike, you of all people should know, to have a job has become a luxury. To have a job that pays you your rightful salary on time: that's another thing entirely," Kash said.

Chike laughed and nodded in agreement. But reality came back like a wave.

He could no longer laugh.

38

THEY APPROACHED THE ENTRANCE OF THE PARTY, WHERE
a tall, burly man stood guard and blocked them from entering.

"Who do you know?" he said.

"My friend Bimpe Akanbi invited us. She should be inside now,"
Patience said, butting in to prevent Chike from saying something that
would ruin their chances of entering.

"Bimpe Akanbi? Okay. You can enter."

Inside the venue Patience estimated there were about a hundred
people in the large single-level club, mingling, drinking, and dancing
under the dim lights. Kash gave Patience a nudge and pointed out
the man behind the turntables. It was Don G, one of the hottest radio
DJs in Lagos. Patience was already impressed. She scanned the room
before spotting Bimpe dancing.

"Well, well, look. Patience is here, and she brought her posse," Bimpe
said. "Welcome, welcome. You must be Chike." She looked him up and
down.

"Yes, I am. You're Bimpe, right?"

"Yes, that's me."

"Let me guess the rest of you. You must be Kash. And you're definitely Emeka. And . . . Mayowa, correct?"

Everyone seemed amused except Chike. Patience stood and waited for Bimpe to introduce them to her friends. She didn't.

"Hello again, Ade."

"Patience! Welcome." He flashed the kind of grin that made vaginas moist. If not for Chike and Bimpe, and Ade's wandering eye, Patience might have been smitten by his chiseled jawline and smooth, buttery skin that rivaled a baby's backside.

"Ade's father is a lawyer by trade, but he's now in telecommunications, planning to take over everywhere," Bimpe said to the group. Patience had already heard ad nauseam about his father's fully functioning law firm, where he hadn't practiced since starting a telecommunications company that was already making him more money than he could quantify.

"I'm Lara."

"Nice to finally meet you, Lara," Patience said. According to Bimpe, Lara was the poorest among them, her father the owner of several dry-cleaning locations in Lagos.

Bimpe's other two friends ignored introductions, but based on Bimpe's endless descriptions, Patience knew them well enough. There was Edak, daughter of the owner of the largest newspaper in the country; and Nneoma, whose mother was a major importer of sugar, rice, cooking oil, and flour, while her father had founded the leading bank in the country.

"This is Edak and Nneoma," Lara said, confirming Patience's guesses.

"Welcome," Nneoma said quickly.

"Can you imagine? Didn't Seyi wear that same dress to Lekan's party?" Edak said, ignoring the exchange with Patience. "Isn't she the hostess? Why would she repeat?"

"Just because you throw a nice party doesn't mean you have much," Bimpe said.

"I like the dress," Lara said.

"I think the dress is nice too," Patience said. She scolded herself under her breath for interfering. Lara gave her an approving glance as Nneoma waved her off.

"Patience has great taste in clothes, though," Bimpe said. "She picked that dress out of my closet without any help from me. It looks great on you."

Patience knew Bimpe enough to know that it was an underhanded punishment for disagreeing with her friend. Once again, the desire to ram her fist down Bimpe's throat arose just before she took a deep breath.

"Nneoma is your name, right?" Emeka said, moving closer to her.

"Yes," she said. She barely looked at him.

"So you finished at UNILAG?"

Not waiting to hear the outcome of their exchange, Chike clasped Patience's waist and pulled her in close. "Let's get something to drink," he whispered in her ear. He led her away from the group before she could respond.

They approached the bar, where bottles of beer, Coke, Fanta, and Sprite were ready to be taken. Chike grabbed a Sprite, pried open the bottle cap with his teeth, and handed it to Patience.

"Chike, please don't be so bush here," she said, watching him re-peat the action with a bottle of beer. "There is an opener on the table."

"Why are you always forming for people like this? When I told you to find friends, I wasn't talking about people like them. We should be going."

"What do you mean? We just got here."

"Bimpe's stupid friends barely spoke to us," he said. "And why did she have to tell everyone you're wearing her dress? And why didn't you just wear your own dress?"

"Oh, please, I've learned to deal with Bimpe in my own way. She's a friend. Her mother wants to help me get my birth certificate, so let's stay."

"Patience, her mother is not going to help you, and Bimpe is not your friend."

Patience knew she had to be careful with Chike. His emotions were still raw about Mr. Olubiyi and the destroyed house.

Aunty Lola would get to her birth certificate eventually. She was satisfied that she had managed to figure out how to deal with Bimpe and her subtle jabs.

"This party is really bubbling," Emeka said as he approached them. "I told Ade about the car we drove here, and now he wants to test-drive it with me. Not a bad guy, o."

"Of course you would say that," Chike said under his breath.

Patience ignored them and looked at Kash, who had found someone to dance with. Patience wasn't surprised. He looked like he fit right in with his baggy jeans with the Cross Colours logo etched on the right back pocket, his hat snapped to the back, his face handsome, his eyes alluring. Somehow he always found a way to corner a woman and make her melt.

Mayowa, who was practically dressed like a banker, was chatting with a girl who looked less than interested. Patience wondered if he was talking about the elections.

"How are you liking the party?" Bimpe said as she squeezed in between Patience and Chike, putting an arm around each of them.

Patience could feel the inevitable eye roll from Chike without seeing him do it.

"The party is good so far. Thanks for inviting us."

"Oh, it's not a big deal. We have these all the time. I will think about asking you to come to another one."

"Your friend Nneoma, she won't give me face," Emeka said. Patience was embarrassed by his revelation.

"Oh, don't mind Nneoma. She's just stone-cold, that one," Bimpe said.

DJ Don G scratched the record and stopped the music completely.

He grabbed the microphone and tapped it to test for sound. Patience was startled by the ruckus.

"All boys out! All boys out!" Don G yelled.

A group of male partygoers walked around yelling the same thing, as they pointed out several men in the crowd.

"What do they mean, all boys out?" Patience said.

"You're such a virgin when it comes to parties," Bimpe said.

"They used to do this nonsense at UI parties," Chike said, silencing Bimpe's smug response to Patience. "Party promoters want to feel important. They want some of the boys to go outside and beg to get back in."

Patience was stunned.

"Out!" one guy shouted their way.

"Can you imagine, they are doing 'all boys out' here," Kash said as he approached them from the dance floor. "This is nonsense, mehn. I was just about to dance the blues with that fine baby there."

"Yes, o," Mayowa said. "I was having a good discussion about Nigeria's growth in the agriculture sector with that girl there."

Emeka rolled his eyes. Chike gave Mayowa a sympathetic pat on the back.

"Patience, I can tell you right now, I'm not going to try to reenter this party, so let's just leave now," Chike said.

Patience didn't feel it was right to ask them to beg to reenter a party she had invited them to.

"Okay. I need to ease myself first. I will meet you outside when I'm done."

"Wow, Chike, you're just going to ruin the party for your girl. I can get you back into the party. It's not a big deal."

"Patience, we will be outside," he said, ignoring Bimpe.

"Wow, your guy is so tense. He's cute, so I can see why you like him, but he needs to relax, jàre."

Patience ignored Bimpe and turned to find the bathroom. She

walked deeper into the club as clusters of male attendees flooded toward the exit. She couldn't believe it. What was the point of stopping a party to kick people out just to make them prove they were worthy to be there?

Patience got to the bathroom and entered a stall toward the back. She locked the door, then worked to lift the layers of Bimpe's multitiered dress. She heard voices flood in.

"Nneoma, let me borrow your red lipstick."

"Are you sure you can handle this red?"

Patience was surprised that she recognized the voices of Nneoma and Edak after talking to them just once.

"Can you imagine . . . Patience and Co? And that one . . . what's his name . . . wearing secondhand designer? Yeh! We should cross-examine his Cross Colours."

"And that Chike guy—he's cute but he looks so rough."

"When Patience, their hostess, is wearing Bimpe's clothes, what do you expect?"

"Bimpe, sef, she needs to do better. She hasn't been looking herself."

"Can you imagine what she will turn into when she finds out Ade has been sleeping around?"

"Oh, please, she knows. But isn't it easier to play stupid when you want people to think everything is perfect?"

Patience emerged from the stall and stood firmly as they turned to her, startled and speechless.

"At least you can check to see if anyone else is in the bathroom before you start talking rubbish." Patience walked to the sink, turned on the faucet, and washed her hands.

"Who is talking rubbish?" Nneoma said. "Who knew you would be this irritating?"

"I'm irritating? I heard what you said about me and my friends who you don't even know. I heard what you said about Bimpe and Ade too."

"What about me and Ade?" Bimpe said. She and Lara stood in the entrance of the bathroom, puzzled. They walked all the way in and let the door slam shut. "Patience, I came to see what's taking you so long."

"Just your friends here. Or are they really? I heard them talking about me and my friends. Then they started talking about you and Ade and how Ade is sleeping around, and . . ."

"Wait, what did you say?" Bimpe asked.

"They said Ade is cheating on you."

"Oh, please," Nneoma said. "Bimpe, why did you invite this hopeless girl? She is such a liar."

"Me, a liar? I heard everything you said!"

"Look at her. She can barely control herself."

Patience looked at Bimpe, then at Lara, who looked apologetic.

"Edak, do you remember us discussing such things?"

"Of course not. Patience, you heard wrong," Edak said. She turned to the mirror and smeared red lipstick on as if the conversation wasn't worth her time.

"Bimpe, I would never lie to you," Patience said.

"Patience, I think you should find your friends and go home for now. We can talk later."

For the first time since meeting Bimpe, Patience couldn't read her. She wasn't her usual smug self. She wasn't cold. Just subdued.

"Okay, Bimpe. We will leave. I will come by your house soon to check up on you."

"I'm fine, Patience. Just go."

Outside the party venue, Patience noticed a crowd of guys yelling at the bouncer and the party promoter. Girls who had just arrived lingered about, waiting for the bouncers to move in their favor.

They all wanted in.

They longed to be among the who's who because to be denied entry would be like facing a complete denouncement of everything that made them worth knowing. Patience had longed to be in their midst because these were the people who held the power, but right there outside the club, everyone in line shrank in her eyes.

Then Patience saw Chike standing tall above the fray as he lingered on the sidelines ready to depart.

39

"OGA, WHAT ARE THE PLANS FOR TODAY?"

Emeka smiled and fidgeted. He waited for a response, but Oga didn't move the newspaper he held in front of his face. Emeka felt like his nerves were doing a dance in his gut. It was the feeling that had become constant for him in the two months he had lived with Oga. To keep cool, he read the headlines on the front page of his boss's newspaper.

ABIOLA SUPPORTERS OPTIMISTIC DESPITE OBSTACLES

ABN URGES BABANGIDA TO REMAIN IN OFFICE AS
ELECTION DAY NEARS

"All this talk of Abiola," Emeka said, finally thinking of something to say. "Our people want him, but is the military ready to give up power?"

Oga kept reading.

Emeka felt puerile. He didn't know how to be himself around Oga.

"Oga, I get your clothes for the day." Mr. Ensure, the washerman, walked in carrying several of Oga's tailored suits and native wear on his arm. Emeka found himself even more off base after the man's abrupt and dutiful entrance.

"That's quite all right. Just hang some and lay the one I will wear today out on my bed."

"Yes, Sa."

Even after two months of living in the lap of Oga's luxurious life, Emeka still found it excessive for a man to hire someone whose sole job was to wash and press his garments. It was the thing he had done for his father for free. But when he tried to picture Oga kneeling over a bucket, scrubbing his own clothes as Mr. Ensure did, he couldn't.

Having the kind of money that bought anything—it was a concept as foreign to Emeka as the contraption in Oga's toilets. Even after the Indian maid in the house told him to wash his nyash with it after he took a pooh, he still didn't understand it.

"Oga, what are we doing today?" Emeka said, trying to project his voice more. He peered over the newspaper awkwardly to make sure he was being heard.

"We're going to see a business associate," Oga said, still holding up his newspaper. "Cancel whatever plans you have so that I can introduce you to him."

Emeka wanted to pay Chike a visit. He hated being at odds with him. He felt they had made a bit of progress during their ride in the car the day before. He wanted to continue to make things right. He'd go by tomorrow, he thought.

"I don't have any plans," Emeka said.

"Good, good. You will need to be there," Oga said, lowering his newspaper.

Phillip, Oga's driver and assistant, walked in. Emeka liked Phillip. He had a genuineness about him, which seemed like an impossible trait to possess in such a cold line of work. On days when Emeka was running late to ride out with Oga, Phillip would stall for him, finding mundane things to do like check the engine oil or wash the already spotless car windows.

"Oga, I have some news. At Adeniyi Jones where the man set fire to that house, people are looking for the person responsible," Phillip said. "They are afraid it will happen again, so they hired OEC to protect them. And that man who owns the house, they say he paid police to find the person who did 419 for his house. He even paid OEC extra money to find the person."

Emeka had heard the same thing from another one of Oga's runners.

"Oga, you know the OEC, Ọmọ Èkó Congress, they are vigilant. They won't go away easily," Phillip said. "You should negotiate with them."

"So because one mugu come dey buy house out of his reach, they are afraid?" Oga said. He looked at Emeka for approval.

"Nonsense," Emeka said.

Phillip joined in. "Oga, the people there fear for their own houses. Can't you just pay the OEC and the police to settle the matter? You know it's money they want. They no go arrest you if you pay them. Give something good so they can let you go and forget the matter."

Oga raised his brows. "Phillip, what do I pay you to do? Oya, go and get my car ready." He slipped on his black-and-gold pinkie ring. "My business is my business. That house is not my business. I won't give them kobo. Don't speak of this again, sho gbo?" he said.

"Yes, Oga," Phillip said. Emeka noticed Phillip's expression go dark as he turned to walk out.

Oga stood, slipped on his Rolex watch, and put his hand out to Emeka to fasten the strap. Emeka fumbled with it. After a few tries, Oga pulled his hand away and did it by himself within seconds.

"Bush boy," Oga said.

And there, yet again, Emeka kissed poverty's nyash.

EMEKA, HIS MOUTH AGAPE, ROLLED DOWN THE WINDOW to get a better view of the massive mansion in which Oga's business associate lived. It was bigger than any he had ever laid eyes on; even Oga's house couldn't compare. The gorgeous landscape of grass, shrubs, rose bushes, and palm trees gave way to a spiraling red cobblestone driveway leading up to the stunning structure. The large water fountain performed a medley: a gush of water, a sprinkle, a spritz, another gush. The statues in front—white stone shaped like two lions in battle—filled Emeka with secondary courage.

"Your business associate lives here?" Emeka said, still in awe.

"You like this house?"

"This na correct house," Emeka said, stressing the word *correct*.

"Well, if you continue to work for me, you can have a house like this one day. Just stay focused." Oga got out of the car as he was greeted by someone at the residence.

Emeka stayed seated in the car, somewhat startled by a soft hiss. "Pay close attention," Phillip, the driver, said. His tone was hushed yet firm. Emeka peered at him in the rearview mirror. "Learn as much as you can," Phillip said.

"Okay," Emeka said, confused by his demeanor. Maybe he was jealous that Oga wasn't bringing him into the fold, he thought. He had no time to worry over his idol's ordinary worker.

The first thing they saw when they walked through the double doors was a massive photo hanging on the wall that lined a grand staircase. The man in the picture was plump with a scalp half bald. Emeka guessed he was either Indian or Lebanese.

"You are welcome. I am Sammi," said the young man who greeted them at the door. "Please have a seat here." He was tall with chiseled features, slender hands, and the same skin color as the man in the photo. Emeka wondered if he was a part of the family or just another worker.

The man from the photo walked in with a sense of eagerness.

"Oga, welcome," he said. They shook hands. "I'm Kenny. You are?" he said, turning toward Emeka, and Emeka wondered if that was the man's real name.

"Good afternoon. I'm Emeka."

"Gentlemen, let's get right down to business," he said, kicking off his slippers near the doorway. "I will have Sammi bring the product out so you can see it for yourselves. You won't be disappointed."

The pants Sammi wore were tapered at the ankles but ballooned around the hips and knees as he hurried into the next room. It was the kind of garb that made a person appear to float rather than walk. The slap-slap sound of his slippers gave him an air of ease.

He came back into the sitting room holding a large orange canvas bag. He unpacked several white bricks and placed them on the long center table in the room. Oga sat up and took off his sunglasses, a rare occurrence.

Emeka tried to contain himself.

He tried to count in his head what that amount of cocaine was worth. What would Tony Montana have paid, he wondered, trying to remember if Al Pacino ever discussed the prices of yayo in *Scarface*, and if so, how the amount would be converted from dollars to naira.

"May I?" Oga said as he reached for one.

"Yes, yes, look at it. Taste it." Oga grabbed the white brick and peeled back the plastic it was wrapped in. He placed the open cocaine on the table, then took the long, slender silver table knife that Sammi laid beside the bricks, scooped a kobo size of powder onto its tip, then snorted it. He dabbed more onto his fingers and rubbed it in his mouth.

Emeka had seen Oga with cocaine before, but he hadn't been sure it was a part of his portfolio of business ventures until now.

"Try some," Kenny said to Emeka.

"No, I need him to be focused today," Oga said. "The product is good, no doubt about that. But we have to discuss the price. This has to be mutually beneficial."

"Ah, my friend, we will come to a resolution."

"Name your price."

"For ten kilos of this product, as it is now, I expect five hundred thousand dollars," Kenny said.

They were talking US dollars. Emeka tried to contain his astonishment.

"Let's do four hundred and fifty thousand," Oga said sitting up in his chair. "That's the average going rate."

"You haven't done this before, but you want the going rate?"

"I know what I am worth. On the streets of America, one gram goes for $141. Aren't we all here to make a profit?"

"Hmph," Kenny said. "Yes, you come highly recommended, and I've been informed about some of your operations, including what happened with that house you sold." He paused and rubbed his large belly. "You know, you should leave all that petty dealing alone. You should come into this area and stay permanently, but you have to ease your way in."

"I don't believe in ease. I believe in strategy. That house is not my concern."

"What happened draws attention to everything you do. We can't have that," Kenny said, sitting up in his chair.

"This is different. I can't control the emotions of someone who has been duped. This job is not about emotions. I will hire good people to carry this into the US. They will get their money and go about their way. There won't be any emotional attachment."

"I like how you think," Kenny said as he put a pipe in his mouth.

"So do we have a deal?"

"I want to know logistics. Who will be carrying it? At four hundred and fifty thousand, I have a right to know. Your work will reflect back on me, if you know what I mean."

"Emeka has an American friend named Patience. She will be our first mule. We will send a man with her so that it looks like a couple on their way back to America. That's a kilo and a half between the two of them. The remaining eight and a half kilos will be carried by some of my guys. I want to start with an actual American for good luck."

Emeka looked at Oga, who barely blinked. He was like a lion keep-ing his eyes on his prey. Emeka wondered how he knew so much about Patience. Emeka had never told him much about any of them, yet he knew intimate details.

"You say her name is Patience?" Kenny said, smiling. "I thought you don't believe in ease. Ease is the cousin of patience."

"Patience is a subtle thief. It's a thief of time and a thief of money. See this country? People have been patient for democracy. Patient for change. All their patience will eventually steal their hope. They say fraud, and they say 419 when they speak of what *I* do, but the govern-ment is really the biggest fraud. Anyway, the girl Patience is good for the job. I don't care what her name is."

"Okay. Let's do business, but I trust you know that you can't pay me in naira," Kenny said, crossing his legs. "Your country's currency has gone to hell thanks to your military dictator." When Kenny laughed, his belly shook, and Emeka decided that it was bigger than a fully pregnant woman's stomach.

"I can get you dollars," Oga said, ignoring Kenny's supposed in-sult. He placed his sunglasses back on. "I have one more request for the day."

"What's that?"

"I need your guy to show Emeka how to prepare cocaine for swallow."

"That will cost you an extra ten thousand dollars."

"Deal."

"EMEKA, IS IT?" SAMMI'S ACCENT WAS FLUID. EMEKA WAS sure at that point that they were Lebanese.

"Yes, Emeka."

"Packing the product for swallow is quite easy, but Oga wants to make sure you have a technique that has been perfected."

"I understand." Emeka tried to hide his hands as they shook. He looked around at the room, which resembled a lab. Bricks of cocaine were stacked on top of the table. A scale sat next to Sammi. The lights were dim. He thought of where he had started with Oga and where he was now. He was happy his mentor trusted him with such an important part of the game, but he still didn't understand why.

"First you need latex. Some people use balloons. Some people use gloves. We like to use gloves because they are strong, you hear?"

"Yes, I hear very well."

"First you take about six grams of the product and put it into one finger of the glove. You can weigh it on a scale like this."

Emeka watched as Sammi spooned some cocaine the size of a cotton ball into the glove, his pinkie held out daintily. Then he cut the rest of the glove off.

Emeka was astonished by how steady his hand was and how neat the area remained after he handled the product.

"Tie the end and glue it well-well, you hear?"

"Yes, I hear." Emeka wished Sammi would stop asking if he could hear. It made him fear that he was missing something.

Sammi dipped the end of the knot in melted glue.

"After that you take another finger of the glove and put the one you just glued inside the next finger, then cut it off the rest of the glove. That way you are protecting the product with two layers of rubber. You can even do three depending on how well your mule can swallow."

"Mule?"

"You should know this already. A mule is the person who will carry the product in their belly."

Emeka had heard the stories of how people transported cocaine inside their body, but he never took the idea seriously. Why not just carry it in a secret compartment inside luggage or inside a large hat—anywhere else? Inside the body was a bold way to tempt God.

"What could happen if it bursts inside someone's stomach?" Emeka said.

"Well, they can die, of course, but that is why wrapping it like this is so important. We've never lost anyone."

It was comforting knowing that they hadn't lost a mule, so he decided then that he would no longer question the process—as tough as it was to not worry.

Sammi tied the end of the second latex layer and glued the end. The potentially lifesaving second layer gave Emeka new confidence. Sammi placed it on the table to dry. Emeka watched in awe. He wasn't sure how to ask Patience to be his mule, but considering the kind of money they could make, he knew he had a chance to sway her.

"Have your mule swallow each of these with okra soup so it can go down well-well. But make sure your mule takes an antidiarrheal pill before they swallow so they can keep this in their belly for a long time.

"So that's it, really. It's not hard. It's just a job that one has to perfect. You should practice with sugar or salt. Do you have any questions?"

"No. No questions at all."

Emeka and Sammi walked back into the sitting room where Oga was.

"So we will meet again soon once everything is solid," Oga said.

"We will," Kenny said.

Oga tapped Emeka on the shoulder, prompting him to walk. Phillip drove the car closer to where they stood, got out, then opened the door for Oga. Emeka let himself into the back seat next to Oga.

"You have to stay focused or one of these useless Lebanese will dupe you," Oga said as Phillip drove out of the compound.

These useless Lebanese. His tone had suggested he couldn't wait to speak those words.

Emeka had questions for Oga that he knew could go unanswered. "How do you know so much about Patience?" He began there.

"I know everything I want to know."

"Patience is American, but she can't find her passport," Emeka said, feeling empowered that he had more information to share. "If she can't get her passport, how will we do this?"

"Nice, my guy. I like that you say 'how will *we* do this.' That's what I want. I want you to take part ownership of this job. If she can't get her passport, we will make one for her. But it's better that she gets her real passport. This will be a defining moment for you, and you will make more money than you ever have," Oga said. "You will be able to get your own flat and build a house for you and that brother of yours and for your mother in your hometown. You just have to get your people together."

"I will," Emeka said without hesitation.

40

"SEE, CHIKE, LOOK. I'M NOT ON FIRE!" PATIENCE YELLED
at the top of her lungs as she ran and jumped across the hot white
sand at Bar Beach. Mayowa ran after her and grabbed her hand.

"Me too, we are not on fire," he said.

"Okay, I can see. I'm not blind," Chike said.

Patience wasn't sure what he had been expecting from their trip
there, but she thought it was endearing that he had insisted they
go. His recurring dream of her on fire, running naked across that
beach, then jumping into the water, had kept them up at night for
long enough.

"You see?" she said, running back toward him. "I am okay. You can
settle your mind now."

"Please, o, my guy, it is well," Mayowa said, patting Chike on the
shoulder.

"Don't mind, Chike," Kash said. He sat on a white towel that looked
like its edges had been caught in a shredder. His sunglasses beamed
from the sun's reflection.

"He thinks we're all going to die because of the house situation. Let
it go, my friend."

"You people should stop yabbing my brother," Emeka said. "Seeing
that man burn that house really got into his head, but he will be okay."

Patience was stunned by Emeka's sudden words of understanding. He was still working to make up for their horrible fight. The fact that he had taken another day off from being Oga's errand boy showed that he was really making an effort.

The calm of the ocean settled upon them as they sat side by side on the sand looking out toward the large blue sheet of water that stretched beyond their eyes' reach.

They kept their distance from the shore. None of them dared to swim.

"Look at them, swimming in the ocean like they don't love themselves," Kash said, pointing toward fellow beachgoers bobbing up and down in the water, laughing, and dunking their heads.

"Swimming is a silly thing, sha. If they all drown, that's it," Emeka said.

"They will drown, sha. That's what happens when people swim," Mayowa quipped.

"This water is rough. I will learn to swim when I get to America," Patience said.

"America, America. We can't have a day without Patience talking about this America," Kash said. "If you want to swim, carry yourself to a club right here in Nigeria where you can find a pool. Ṣebi your papa get plenty money? Go and tell him sorry, then ask him for membership at the Ikoyi club." He rolled his eyes.

Patience waved him off.

"Maybe I should go to America with you," Chike said.

"Now *you* want to go to America. My God," Kash said, throwing his hands in the air.

"Come with me," Patience said with excitement. "There is nothing here for you."

"See, I knew Patience was always a great example for you," Emeka said. "Chike, you should go! I mean the two of you should go together. In fact, I can get you both to America."

"You?" Patience said with light laughter. "How can you get us to America?"

"A new job."

"Another Oga job," Mayowa said, disgusted.

"Oga can give you a passport and a lot of money if you carry some cargo to America for him. He wants a man to go with Patience. Chike, it should be you because Patience is actually your girlfriend."

"What cargo?" Patience hated how vague he was.

"It's nothing. No big deal. Just a little bit of cocaine."

"Cocaine!" Mayowa yelled. "Now you want them to die for money. Or get arrested. How can Patience and Chike, two people who have never seen drugs, now come and carry drugs into AH-MER-I-CA?" he said.

"I'm sick of hearing your mouth, Mayowa," Emeka said.

"But it's a good question," Patience said. "When you told us we would sell a house that wasn't for sale, I thought you had gone mental. But this? You've managed to surpass your own craziness. How would we carry drugs so far without getting caught?"

"You have to . . . swallow it," Emeka said.

"Swallow? Swallow?" Patience said, bewildered. "Can't a person die?"

"Of course, if the job isn't done the right way, but Oga already paid for me to learn how to prepare my mule."

"Na wa o. Now you want somebody to be your *donkey*," Mayowa said.

"A drug mule carries drugs, idiot."

"Nobody should be anybody's animal."

"Mayowa, why are you like this?"

As they argued, Patience's mind raced. She remembered her father's tyranny. She wondered if her mother was still alive. Chike wouldn't approve of such a job. This could be her only chance to get her passport and documents. When would she have enough money to live in America?

But she could die. Chike could die. And what if they got caught? This job would end them one way or another.

She no longer felt a sense of calm as she stared out at the ocean. Instead, her father's imposing presence hovered over her like he were there, standing above her as she sat squeezing handfuls of sand.

Her heartbeat suddenly matched the pace of her thoughts.

"I can't do something like that," she said, feeling the firm thumps in her chest.

"You hear that? She said she can't do it," Mayowa shouted.

"You don't have to give me an answer now," Emeka said. "This is a big job. Just think about it for now."

Patience looked at Chike, who seemed empty and unfazed. She was surprised he didn't join Mayowa in denouncing the job. Instead, he said nothing. Then she realized how quiet he had been since they all sat down on the sand.

"Patience, carrying drugs into America is a bigger risk than the bank jobs," Mayowa said. "Don't allow Emeka to sway you."

"Yes, it is another level, and that's why you will make more money doing this than you ever have in your life," Emeka said. "Patience only has enough money for her plane ticket and maybe for a hotel for some time. But after that? This money can set her up in America the correct way," Emeka said.

"There has to be another way to make money," Patience said.

"Aren't you tired of waiting around to gather money? You have to do something big to get to America. That is the only way."

"Let's talk about it later," Chike said.

"Later? So you're actually considering this?" Mayowa said.

Patience, also stunned by his reaction, searched Chike's face for a sign of his usual reasoning, but his eyes were lifeless and his expression still blank.

"I'm just so tired," he said. "I'm tired of living like this."

"You people are always talking nonsense as if we are not about to see total change in Nigeria," Mayowa said. He stood up and brushed the sand off his pants.

Patience had come to admire Mayowa's optimism. He was just as driven about Nigeria's future as she was to reunite with her mother. In Mayowa's eyes, there was no such thing as false hope. He clung to Nigeria's potential like a parent holding their child in a crowded room.

"Maybe I should try the embassy again for my passport or maybe we can get you a visa," Patience said, still worried about them carrying cocaine.

"Patience, jọ, let that passport situation go. If you do this job, you will have a passport," Kash said.

"So as my cousin you're not worried about me swallowing cocaine and trafficking it all the way to America?"

"Patience, haven't you seen what you can do? You agreed to work with Oga before."

"Yes, but . . . it's not like I love this kind of thing."

"Just think about it. But try not to take too long," Emeka added.

"Chike, what would you even do in America?" Mayowa said.

"I don't know. I've been thinking about it," he said, staring at the waves. "Maybe I can get a visa to study there. Or get a visitor's visa but stay there permanently. People do that."

Patience remembered the line for student visa applications at the embassy and the number of people who paid so-called prayer warriors outside the embassy to offer up magical pleas to bring them favor.

"How will you work with no papers? People get deported back to Nigeria because of that kind of mischief," Mayowa said.

"That's true," Kash said. "America and Nigeria are not the same. The law there is the law."

"I don't have all the answers. But I've been thinking about it," Chike said.

"Don't worry about that. If you do this job for Oga, your visa will be sorted out," Emeka said. "We can get you an extended visa, and you can stay as long as you want. Oga has friends who are politicians who do this for the people who carry for them. Or we can get you a fake American passport."

"Politicians? They're selling drugs?" Chike said.

"Look at you, you don't know the half of this business. It's supply and demand just like any other business."

"It's only corrupt politicians who do those things," Mayowa said. "Chike, I beg, don't get yourself involved in this kind of thing."

"How long will I wait around driving okada or stealing money from innocent people?"

"Hey, hey, my friend, it's not stealing. It is controlling one's destiny," Kash said.

"I'm happy you want to come to America with me, but can we really do this kind of thing?" Patience said.

"If you do this, all of our troubles will be gone. Patience, Oga can get a passport for you without blinking," Emeka said.

"Patience, this job will be good for you," Kash said.

"How can you tell your own cousin to do such a thing?" Mayowa shouted.

"Let's calm down," Patience said.

"Okay. Do what you want," Mayowa said.

"I didn't say I would do it!" Patience said. Everyone was shocked into silence. She too was surprised by her reaction, but it felt good to yell out. She wanted to do it again, but to whom? Mayowa was only looking out for her.

Chike put his arm around her and pulled her in closer. A wave washed ashore. She thought about how open his love had become—and at the perfect time. With the burned house and Bimpe's party, she felt herself sinking further into confusion and doubt. His new affection was her balm whenever she had bouts with the blues.

"Maybe I should run into the water right now. Maybe I will swim, maybe I won't," Chike said with his eyes fixated on the ocean.

They stared, waiting for him to confess his humor. Instead he sat, void of emotion. Patience nudged him and grinned, hoping he would say something.

He didn't.

She realized then that getting out of Nigeria now meant saving Chike's life.

41

EMEKA DIPPED HIS HAND IN THE SHALLOW WOODEN COM-
partment and grabbed a handful of round, gray seeds.

"One, two three," he counted as he dropped them back into his
game tray.

"So you play Ncho?"

Emeka jerked his head, startled to see Phillip the driver standing
in the doorway of the back room in Oga's mansion. It was one of the
spaces Oga didn't enter. His workers often stole moments there to
congregate and watch TV. There, Emeka felt most at home.

"Yes, of course I play Ncho," Emeka said, turning back to his game.
He was still curious about the day Phillip had told him to "pay close
attention" to Oga's Lebanese connection.

"I'm surprised to see you here. You're usually working on the car."

"That's my job," Phillip said. "Shall we play?"

"We can, but I have to warn you, I grew up beating my brother at
Ncho." Emeka picked up the seeds and spread them out evenly.

"I think I can chance it," Phillip said as he sat down across from
Emeka. "You go first."

Emeka grabbed his first hand and counted the seeds out. He
glanced at Phillip, still puzzled by him. "Phillip, you know, I never
asked you where you are from."

"I grew up in Umahia."

"It's like I can hear another kind of accent when you speak."

"I lived in the UK for a short time," he said. "I went there to go to school, but things didn't work out as I planned."

"What happened?"

"To keep it short, I worked three jobs at a time to pay living expenses and to pay the girl I married for papers, but I got deported after two years."

Emeka didn't know what to say. Phillip had stated the truth of his ordeal, as if being expelled from Britain was as trivial as being bounced from a party.

"So you're like my brother in a way," Emeka said, shaking his head. "You went to school, but you ended up as a driver."

"I didn't finish school really. I took classes here and there. I was too busy working. So all I have is a distorted accent to show for my schooling abroad. I found this job a month after I got back to Nigeria."

Phillip looked at Emeka. His gaze was steady, calm, and intuitive. Emeka felt he was being read as intently as Oga read the newspaper. "Why did you say what you said to me that day at Oga's business associate's house? Before I got out of the car? You told me to pay attention." Emeka looked back down at the Ncho tray. He still felt Phillip's eyes on him.

"I've been working for Oga a long time. I know the value of every moment spent with him. What you learn in the moment will benefit you in the long run."

"But you're just his driver and errand boy."

"True."

There was a lingering silence. Emeka shifted in his seat. "Why don't you—"

"I need to ask a favor of you," Phillip said, cutting Emeka off.

"What is it?"

Phillip leaned in closer to Emeka. "My brother's wife just had a baby boy." His voice dipped to a throaty whisper.

"Wow, congrats," Emeka said.

"Listen, Oga hasn't paid me for months, so I don't have anything to send to him. You know it's not proper for me, the elder brother, not to send something to him."

Emeka's eyes dimmed as he tilted his head in confusion. "What do you mean Oga hasn't paid you? He hasn't given you your salary?"

"Ah, Oga is always tight with money."

That was news to Emeka. At times he felt the amount of money he was getting could be more, but Oga never withheld his monthly earnings from him. Besides the money, Oga had fully brought Emeka into the fold of the drug game.

"How can he keep your money for months?"

"He doesn't handle you the way he handles everyone else here. For me, for the house help, for anybody who works here, you must manage money when you get it, because you neva know when Oga go hold your small salary." Emeka finally heard Phillip's proud Nigerianness emerge as he spoke pidgin. "When he doesn't pay, he says his accountant will sort out the matter. Can you imagine, his maid Teresa came to him crying. She told him her father died, and she needed money to assist her siblings with the burial back in her hometown. Oga just dey read newspaper. When she finished, he looked at her and told her to go and continue her work. He didn't give her the money until two weeks later."

Emeka couldn't believe it. A wealthy man who stiffed his poor servants.

"How much do you need?"

"Three thousand."

Emeka paused and continued to observe Phillip. Could he trust him? Was he trying to appear like a big man when he crossed his legs in the most sophisticated way with little or no thought or dangled the boss's car keys on his finger as if the car were his own? But here he was, asking for a loan. A proud man would never.

"I will give it to you tonight."

"Thank you. I will start paying you back when I get my salary."

"No wahala. But you know, I have to ask you, why don't you want to do the real work with Oga?"

"What exactly do you consider real work?"

"What Oga does. What I do," Emeka said, thrusting his chest forward.

"After what I went through in the UK, I promised that I would never jeopardize my freedom again."

"But isn't having money freedom?"

"It is. You're right. But once a man falters, he has to be smarter. You see, change happens when you blink. When something seems permanent, it's on the verge of changing."

Emeka counted out his last hand, confused by what Phillip was saying. He was about to win their first round of Ncho, but Phillip had the demeanor of someone who owned the game—as if he had some inside information on what the real outcome would be.

"Listen, Emeka, I think you're sharp. I've seen a few guys in your position with Oga. Oga is a discreet man. Having a figurehead for his operation is as valuable to him as the money he takes. I can sense that you know what is right . . . what is truly right."

"What is right?"

"You know. You absolutely know."

Emeka grew frustrated. "I think you should tell me what you want to say."

"No need. In time, if you are meant to know, you will."

Phillip was like a meandering river. There was no point pushing him further. Instead, he put his last seed in the shallow wooden compartment and realized his win. "I tried to tell you, I'm too good at this game," he said, puffing his chest again.

Phillip smiled. He pressed his lips together and looked down at the board. "Yes, you're quite good."

42

PATIENCE DIDN'T KNOW WHETHER TO BE EXCITED OR nervous when she approached the front gate of Aunty Lola and Bimpe's house. She had missed seeing them as she kept her distance after what had happened at Bimpe's party.

"Patience, how are you?"

Aunty Lola looked surprised to see her when she walked into the den after the house girl let her in.

"I'm fine, Ma. It's been some time. I hope you are okay."

"Yes. Yes. I'm here. What brings *you* here today?" She posed the question as if Patience were new company—as if Patience hadn't spent days talking to her in that very room about her mother and her father and life in general.

"Ma, I'm here to see Bimpe. I'm here to see you too."

"Bimpe is not here, Patience," she said, as if Patience should have known this. "She moved to London. She decided to work on her master's."

"Really? That's good news." Patience felt a sudden sadness rush over her. She had always believed Bimpe would choose London, but she had felt she would be there to see her off when the time came.

"Yes, she was happy. Her friends were all here helping her get her things together. Ade and her girlfriends."

"Ade? Her girlfriends?"

"Yes, they were all here."

"Really?"

"Yes, really. Why?"

"No, Ma, it's fine." Patience couldn't believe what she had heard. She wondered if Bimpe had confronted Ade about the possibility of him cheating. Maybe she did and they worked things out.

"Ade, Nneoma, Edak, Lara, they were all here."

"Nneoma and Edak were here too?" Patience tried to keep calm.

"Yes. Bimpe's friends."

Patience was in shock. How could they have been there after what had happened? She was clear about what she had heard, and she had made it clear to Bimpe.

"Ma, Edak and Nneoma and even Ade, I don't think they are good for Bimpe." Patience felt her voice gain a sense of urgency.

"Patience, I need to talk to you," Aunty Lola said, disregarding her statement.

"Yes, Ma, but did you hear me? I overheard Nneoma and Edak say some things about Ade at the party."

"Bimpe told me some things that don't sit well with me at all. She said you ran away from your father and that you are here moving among some area boys who are doing 419."

Patience froze. How did this become about her? She had never told Bimpe anything about any of the jobs they did. What gave her the right to tell her mother anything, especially something she had no knowledge of?

"She came back from a party one day. She said you were there with those men. She was very upset that you would move with people like that. Patience, I know your father and I know your mother. I know they would not want this life for you."

Patience wanted to scream. What kind of life *did* they want for her? They had only succeeded at making her feel abandoned, disregarded, and afraid.

"I'm sorry, Ma, but Bimpe did not tell you the truth."

"I know you ran away, Patience. I asked people in Ibadan after Bimpe told me about your lifestyle. They said your father has washed his hands of you. They say you left months ago. I'm sorry, but this is unacceptable behavior for a young lady."

"Ma, I came to you for help to get my birth certificate to find my mum. Is that not the responsible thing to do? I haven't seen her in over ten years. I barely know her. I don't know the life she wanted for me. Do you know how that feels?"

"Patience, I don't know. But I know it wouldn't be proper for me to help you do things this way. You're still so young. I can't help you get your documents like this."

"Did you ever try to help me?" Patience said.

"When you came to me, I pitied you. Growing up without a mother is not proper for a young girl. And to see you here, running around Lagos saying you wanted to be a tailor, doing absolutely nothing with your life—I wanted to keep my eye on you. I wanted to encourage you to go the right way. I never wanted to send you to America to go and chase a goose."

There it was: the truth.

And though Aunty Lola had never concealed it, she had never spoken it so plainly until then. She didn't intend to help her get her passport.

She pitied her.

And since she only pitied her, there was no way she loved her, Patience thought. If she loved her, she would help her put the pieces back together, not watch her sort through brokenness while covering her own hands.

Patience felt expended. She had become the subject of Aunty Lola's self-serving good deed. Her poor friend Folami wasn't able to sustain a life in Nigeria the way she had, so she felt sorry for the child she left behind. And yet Aunty Lola had stayed in a marriage she questioned because she didn't want to be the subject of other people's pity.

"I'm sorry, Ma, but it wasn't your pity I wanted nor your pity I asked for. I needed your help."

"Patience, this is not the kind of help I can give you. I'm glad that you were able to meet Bimpe and form a bond with her, but now that she is so shaken by your lifestyle, I don't know if you can be friends with her again."

Patience was stunned but somewhat impressed. Once again, Bimpe had found a way to strike when no battle was being waged against her. She could only feel tall when she reduced someone to their lowest point. When Patience found a crack in Bimpe's perfectly manufactured world, Bimpe went even lower.

Patience was still unsure of God's existence, but she had come to see the devil at play. Bimpe's cruel victory could be only temporary. When light entered a room, darkness no longer had its place. Patience was certain of that.

"Patience, I think you should go home to Ibadan. Talk to your father and have him enroll you in a university. Maybe he can arrange for you to get into UI now."

"Thank you, Ma, but I have to be going." Patience stood and walked out of the room, then out the front door, then through the yard, then out the gate, back into the world. She walked and walked and looked for the nearest bus stop. She didn't wait for anyone to come because nobody would come, not even Chike. Not in that moment.

43

PATIENCE PULLED A LONG GRAY BLANKET OUT OF A BUCKET of damp garments, flicked it in the wind, then draped it over the clothesline Kash had hung for them outside their new flat in Agidingbi.

She wasn't in the mood to wash clothes. All she wanted to do was lie in bed and think about how Bimpe had double-crossed her and how Aunty Lola had pitied her. But washing clothes was her inescapable task for the day. She knew this as soon as she woke up and almost tripped over a pile of jeans and T-shirts Kash had left in the middle of their sitting room.

"Ah, now, Patience, you haven't washed my clothes for me in a while," he said when he noticed her reaction to the mess.

"Tinu, won't you wash your man's clothes?" Patience said to Kash's latest fling.

"Am I his maid?" Tinu crossed her legs and turned to face the eighteen-inch television Kash had bought the day before.

"Patience, you know Tinu now," he whispered to her as he put his arm around her shoulder. "She won't do a good job."

Patience decided not to press the issue for the same reason she always gave in to his requests. Moving in with Kash was an unofficial agreement to take care of him. If she weren't saving her money for America, she would have gotten her own place.

Patience yanked her long, colorful Ankara skirt from the pile of damp clothes—the first thing she had made for herself with her sewing machine. She surveyed the stitching and remembered how slow she was. It had been months since the machine broke. She had promised herself she would fix it when she got money from their first job with Oga.

She never did.

Patience pulled the last item out of the basket. It was Kash's favorite pair of jeans.

She flung them in the air to straighten them out. A small square piece of paper fell from the pocket.

She looked down.

It was a photo.

One of her childhood photos.

Patience bent over and picked it up. She flipped it over and found the word *passport* written on the back. It was her mother's handwriting. She knew it well from her letters and the small inscriptions she had made on the back of other photos and in her novels.

A wave of confusion paralyzed Patience. Then, in a snap, things became clear. She finally understood why Kash continued to discourage her from going to the embassy; why he shot down her hopes of getting to America; and why after he refused to help her get her passport several times, then one day—out of nowhere—he agreed.

She remembered Bose's advice to her. "He's a thief," she said outside by the well.

She hated herself for having trusted him. She had led him to her passport. She had trusted he would bring it to her. How could she have been so naive? Since she was young, she had heard stories of how irresponsible he was and how cunning he became after his father died.

She loved him anyway.

She assumed he loved her the same.

But Kash was yet another person who didn't care about her.

What if her mother was just like everyone else? It was a thought she couldn't bear, so she buried it in the crevices of her shrunken dignity. She had to believe that her mother loved her and wanted to be a part of her life.

Patience gathered her strength and walked back into the flat. She found Kash cuddled up with Tinu on the couch. The room held the stench of stale cigarette smoke.

"What is this?" she said, holding up her photo.

There was a long pause. Tinu looked at Patience in confusion.

"Patience, are you okay?" she said.

Kash stood up and put his hands on his hips.

"What are you doing with that?" he said.

"I found it in your pocket. Why was my passport picture in your pocket? Where is my passport?"

"Listen, I needed some money, *we* needed some money."

"Where is it?"

"I sold it at Oluwole Road. I will give you the money now that I have cash." He pulled his cigarette out of the ashtray and puffed hard and long. He released the smoke through his nose. He fidgeted as he put the cigarette back in the ashtray.

"You sold my passport on the black market? The thing I needed to get to America to see my mother? You sold it because you needed money?"

"You, this spoiled little girl, always crying about your mother and what your father did to you. What about what your father did to me? He stopped paying my school fees. He left me to hustle for myself after my father died. What was I supposed to do, ehn? Should I cry forever? Life is bigger than you being able to go see your mum. We were able to eat that month because everything I buy I share with you since I took you in and supported you despite my limited means."

"Kash, you're calling me spoiled? After all that I've done to take care of you—working as if I'm a house girl!" Patience began to scream. When she stopped, she huffed and puffed and paced the room.

"I was telling you, go back home. How did you expect me to survive on the petty-petty money I was making before we started opening bank accounts, ehn?" he yelled back.

"Okay, okay, it's enough," Tinu said.

"No, it's not enough! Kash, please keep the money. Consider it payment for anything I've ever taken from you. I will no longer be your burden."

Patience walked out and slammed the front door.

44

EMEKA TAPPED HIS FOOT ON THE CAR PEDAL AND TOOK A tight pull from his cigarette. The heat inside the car made his stomach turn. He rolled his window down a bit and peered outside nervously.

"It's good that this car has tinted windows," he said.

"You're turning into Chike," Kash said as he flicked his cigarette ashes into the car's ashtray. "We are fine. The man we sold the house to is in jail. Isn't he the only person who can point us out?"

"Yes, but you never know who else saw us."

So little time had passed since their last job, and yet they were back in Adeniyi Jones, where they had sold the house that had been set on fire, in the same area where the vigilante group had put word out that they were looking for the culprits. Emeka and Kash were parked not too far from the house, waiting for Oga's business associates to make their delivery.

"Don't worry. We went to that house at night. We didn't leave during the day. Nobody saw us." Kash puffed out smoke from his nostrils and rested his head on the window next to him. "It's Patience who I'm thinking about now. She wasn't supposed to know that I sold her passport. She's just too damn spoiled, mehn. Crying over her mummy when she had everything handed to her."

"She's spoiled, yes, but that kind of thing you don't do to your family."

"You dey talk? You diminish your own brother for being a university graduate while we are sitting here as Oga's errand boys."

"Well, because you sold that passport for a few thousand naira, you've made it harder for us to get real money. Now we have to print a fake passport for her when she agrees to do the cocaine job."

"And how do you know she will do the job?"

"What are her options? She staying with Chike now. If they are not broke yet, they will be soon."

"Ehn now, so print the fake passport, jàre."

"Traveling with a fake passport brings more risk. Kash, you're too smart to be this daft."

"Daft? Me? Useless man," Kash said.

A car pulled up next to them. The driver honked and rolled down the passenger side window. There were two men inside. Kash got out of the car and approached the passenger side.

"What's the election outcome?" Kash blurted out the secret question Oga had given them.

"Military victory, of course," they said in unison.

"Oya, where's the money?" Kash said, using the deepest register of his voice, as if having a deeper voice enhanced his muscle mass.

Emeka grew uneasy. Their task for the day was to collect money. But why would Oga send him and Kash, of all people, to Adeniyi Jones, of all places? Why didn't he send Phillip, who usually ran such errands? He wiggled his fingers to shake off his fears. Orders were orders.

The man seated in the passenger seat got out of the car holding a large canvas bag. Kash got out, took the money, and opened the trunk. He put the bag in the trunk as the deliveryman got back into his car. They sped away.

Emeka's heart steadied. Mission accomplished. *Now, get out of the area*, he thought. "Kash, let's go," he yelled from the passenger window.

Kash slammed the trunk shut, then walked to the driver's side and peered through the window. "Just like that. Millions of naira just went from one hand to the next. Emeka, do you really think you can ever get to Oga's level one day?"

"And why not?" he said. Never mind that he could barely eat with a knife and fork at Oga's house, or how he struggled to pronounce the foods Oga's foreign chef made, or how he couldn't fasten the strap on Oga's Rolex, or how he mingled mostly with the house help. If he couldn't act rich, how would he ever be rich? He thought of this often. "In fact, yes, I can get to Oga's level," he said, hoping Kash didn't see beyond his forced bravado.

A gray van sped up and came to a screeching halt. Emeka, still seated in the driver's seat, jerked his head. Two large men jumped out. They grabbed Kash and flung him into the back of their van. Emeka froze. Everything slowed until Kash's piercing screams jolted him out of the car.

"No, no, no, no, no . . . I think you are mistaken!" Emeka yelled. "We are here for work. My uncle lives there. Please, let my friend go."

"Shut up! You see that house?" one of the men said, pointing in the distance. "Your useless friend sold that house. A house he doesn't own. Useless 419 maggot. And look at it now! Go and tell the somebody who sent him that they should come forward. Tell them to bring money or your friend go die. OEC said so, sho gbo?"

They sped off as Emeka looked on. His body went limp.

DURING HIS FRANTIC DRIVE BACK TO OGA'S, EMEKA DECIDED not to tell Chike. Chike would just scold him about his work with Oga and tell Patience. There was nothing either of them could do anyway. Only one person could get Kash back.

Emeka ran up Oga's staircase, missing two and three steps at a time, then barged into Oga's room. Oga and his manservant Gabriel turned to the door.

"Oga . . . Oga," Emeka said between panting breaths. "Oga . . ."

"What is it, you this boy? Speak na."

"Oga . . . they took Kash. The OEC. They took him. They say they want money for him. They want the boss for that job we did on that house."

Oga sipped his tea and placed the cup down as he looked straight into Emeka's eyes. He picked up the cup again.

He sipped once more.

Gabriel sat upright on a wooden stool with Oga's feet in his lap. He rubbed them with the kind of care that made Emeka uncomfortable. But the man had a job to do, and he did it well.

"Gabriel. Oya, leave me and Emeka alone to talk."

"Yes, Sa."

Emeka couldn't believe Oga. After leaving Adeniyi Jones, he had rushed home to tell him Kash had been kidnapped. Where was his panic? Kash, one of his faithful workers, had been kidnapped, yet all he did was sip his tea gingerly.

"Kash is my friend," Emeka said. "They said they will kill him."

Gabriel shut the door. Oga looked up at Emeka and began talking.

"When I was about seventeen or eighteen, I was working in the market selling malu. One day a man walked in to buy. The man looked at me and asked me to come over. I did. He asked how long I had been doing that kind of work. I was ashamed, so I avoided the question. He was clean. I was soaked in cow's blood and shit. He asked me if I could read and write. I told him yes.

"He told me he had a job for me. He said, 'I want you to start writing letters for me. Bring one of your friends too.' I didn't know what kind of letters he was talking about, but I chose my friend Niyi. He and I arrived at the man's house in Ikeja, and we were mesmerized. He had everything we didn't have. When he invited us in, he sat us down and put two letters in our hands.

"We read the letters. They were requests for money by a man who claimed he was an aristocrat exiled in the UK. He claimed he had money stuck in his account in Nigeria. Around that time naira was stronger than the dollar. He said he needed the money to start living well again. He requested that whomever the letter was addressed to help him by sending him five thousand US dollars so he can go about getting the money through a Nigerian who offered to help. In return he would give that person two hundred and fifty thousand once the money was retrieved.

"Our job was to copy that letter over and over again. Our fee would be one hundred naira to split. In those days, that was decent money for a young man. Niyi and I did the job for about a week, and then I started thinking, why should I continue to split one hundred naira?

"One day when we were making our way to his house to work, I met Niyi to take danfo. We played around and spoke about our money. We thought we were rich already. Then when he saw the bus coming he ran toward it as he always did. I stuck out my leg and tripped him. He fell on his face. He screamed that his leg was broken. I ran toward him to show concern. Needless to say, he was out of commission and didn't ask about the job.

"The next time I went back, I did without him. I had Segun, the smartest young man in the neighborhood, copy the letter for me at home. I stuffed several copies in my pants and pulled them out when I got there. I copied the letter as many times as I could. By the end of that day, I gave him my letters and what he thought were Niyi's letters. I told him Niyi couldn't be there, but he was able to do his share of the work. He gave me the usual hundred naira for us to split. I went home and paid Segun ten naira. That was how I got started, and that was my first time learning the importance of self-preservation. In this life, there should be nothing more important to you than you. When you are too concerned with how the next man will eat or survive, you yourself, you will die. It will be a slow death, but you will die. Casualties. Niyi was a casualty; so is Kash. There will always be casualties in this line of work. You have to allow for this kind of thing. Can you accept that?"

Emeka looked at Oga. He didn't shy away or feel uncomfortable. He just stared at him. Oga picked up his tea and sipped again.

"Yes, I can accept that," Emeka said. His voice cracked.

"Furthermore, the job was your job, and you fucked it up," Oga said in between sips. "Kash was caught because of your sloppy work. Why should I pay for that?"

He waved Emeka off.

"Gabriel!" Oga shouted. "Gabriel! Where is this silly boy? Oya, come and continue rubbing my feet."

"I will call him for you." Emeka stood and walked out of the room. A single tear fell from his eye and slowly made its way down his cheek. He wiped it and walked downstairs. "Gabriel, Oga dey call you," he said once he reached the kitchen. He watched as the houseboy rushed out, eager to return to his feet-rubbing duties.

Emeka pressed his hand over his mouth to mask the sound of his weeping.

He sank to the marble floor, took several breaths. This was his fault—Oga was right. Kash was in danger because of him.

He stood and walked out the front door and made his way down Oga's concrete path. He froze when he heard a light but piercing hiss.

"I know what happened to your friend," he heard someone say. Emeka looked around and rubbed his face to eliminate any evidence of tears. He knew that voice well.

"Enter the car. Let's drive out so we can discuss it." Phillip was seated at the wheel of Oga's car with the windows rolled down. He reached over to the passenger side and opened the door.

Emeka hesitated as Phillip started the engine. He looked back at the house, squinting. He decided to get in.

"Who do you think led the OEC to you and Kash at Adeniyi Jones?" Phillip said when they were out of Oga's compound.

"I don't know. They are patrolling that area, so—"

"Emeka, you're a smart fellow. Think about it."

Phillip was relaxed, with one hand on the steering wheel and the other on the back of Emeka's headrest. Emeka was speechless. He had never heard Phillip talk that way. Sinister, though even more worldly and self-aware than he had been the day they had played Ncho. His time in London, mixed with the PhD he had earned in fraud by simply watching Oga for years, had served him well, Emeka thought.

"Crying will not get your friend out of trouble. You need to take action."

"Action?"

"Yes, action," Phillip said. "I can help you . . . if you're willing to uproot the person you idolize. By now, you know what's right, correct?"

Emeka didn't respond. Instead he looked out the window at nothing in particular, hoping to disappear.

45

"PATIENCE, YOU HAVE TO EAT. YOU HAVEN'T HAD ANY-thing since yesterday."

"I'm fine." Patience didn't look away from the plate of beans and plantain Chike had prepared for her. All she could muster was a shake of the head. It was what she had done the whole week she had been staying with Chike, because even lifting her gaze took effort. Her own thoughts had become her biggest disturbance.

The bank jobs, the burned house—all for nothing.

She stabbed one bean at a time as if they were the things she had lost and the things she had never really had.

Her passport. Her mother. Her birth certificate. School. Her father. Bimpe's loyalty. Aunty Lola's help.

She thought of Kash and smashed one bean until its guts oozed out and flattened against her plate.

"Patience, he's your cousin. You know he doesn't have much, but you know he loves you."

Love. She wanted to chew the word and spit it out like fire. And she would breathe her venom onto anyone who dared to mention love in her presence. She imagined even her sister Margaret had an agenda: she would probably be as cruel as Modupe if she didn't have a half sister to feel sorry for.

Love had never been given to her freely.

"Patience, I know you are sad about everything, Kash and Bimpe, and Aunty Lola, but you can still make it to America. We will do that job . . . together. You won't need your passport. Emeka promised to get you a fake one. You will see your mum soon. I will go with you. I'm tired of Nigeria. I'm tired of waiting for something that will never happen. I am tired. Let me go with you. I will take care of you when we get there. We will make a lot of money if we do this job. Patience, you know me . . . *I* love you."

She looked at him and waited for his eyes to divert the way they did whenever he showed real tenderness.

His eyes remained steady, and she found herself loathing him.

"Why now? Why are you *like this* now?" she said, her voice cracking. "What about before? You've known that I've loved you from the beginning."

"I don't know why."

"Chike, you only love me now because you're afraid and you need someone to dump your burdens on." She looked down at the plate of food, picked up her fork, and started poking holes in the plantain.

"Why couldn't you accept that I didn't love you the way you loved me at that time?" he said.

Patience tossed her plate of food on the floor with such force she was surprised that the plate didn't shatter. "What kind of ridiculous question is that?" she said.

"It's the only thing I can say."

His words hit her hard. Yet they brought on an epiphany she wasn't expecting.

She craved love.

He didn't know how to love her.

And even if he did, it would never be enough.

Love was a thing she had never known because for too long she had belonged nowhere and to no one at all.

So she demanded love with no regard for anyone else, not even for herself.

It was time for her to fuel herself. Delight herself. But who would show her how?

"Why was I not good enough for you before?"

"Am I good enough for me? For you? I don't like where I am. I despise who I've become. But I see you now and I can't explain why."

Somehow Patience understood, but tears fell from her eyes like a torrential downpour during rainy season.

When Chike began to clean the food from the floor, she stopped crying. She watched him as he scooped up the beans with his hands and then wiped the floor with a tattered rag. She looked as the residue disappeared from the cracked linoleum.

"I have to go home," she said.

"Will you come back?"

"Yes. I just need to talk to my dad. I need to see him before I decide to do anything. I need to tell him some things."

They were startled by the sudden sound of Emeka barging in through the front door, panicked and jittery.

"Emeka, what is it?" Chike said. "Why do you look like . . . this?"

"Like what?"

"Like you're trying to outrun a ghost."

"I'm fine."

"Okay. Patience and I are here talking," Chike said, annoyed. There was silence as Emeka paced the room.

"Emeka, seriously, what is wrong with you?"

"I just have some things to sort out."

"Did Kash swindle you out of something too?" Chike said.

"Please don't say his name," Patience mumbled.

"Why not? Why shouldn't we say his name? Isn't he our friend? Isn't he your cousin?" Emeka said.

"Calm yourself," Chike said.

"Why should I? Don't we all still need each other? So what if he took your passport?"

Patience was stunned. Emeka had never spoken to her that way. Why was her anger at Kash any of his concern?

"Patience, I'm sorry," Emeka said. "Just . . . just pray for Kash. Pray for him. Pray he finds his way."

"Kash already knows *his* way."

46

"HOW CAN TWO BROTHERS BE QUARRELING LIKE THIS? Ehn? Didn't I teach you to use your common sense?"

Chike looked away from Mama and avoided looking at Emeka, who sat next to him at her table outside her home in Enugu. He couldn't believe his brother had worried her with the details of their fight. Typical Emeka, only thinking of Emeka.

"Mama, don't worry yourself. Me and Emeka are fine. It was just a disagreement."

"Ehn, Emeka, you said Chike beat you. I don't want you behaving like animals." Mama pulled her wrapper from her waist and retied it tighter.

"Good afternoon, Ma. Can I have Butter Mint?" said a teenage boy who had walked up to their mother's table, asking to buy candy. He was her first customer since they had helped Mama set up when they arrived at Enugu two hours before.

"Twenty kobo," she said as she placed the candy into a bag. He paid her and moved on.

"Why would you beat your brother?" she asked Chike in Igbo as she dropped the money into an old tin.

"Mama, Chike and I have settled it," Emeka snapped, and Chike wondered why his brother was still slightly on edge, like the day he barged into their flat asking cryptic questions about Kash. "That's why we came here together. We came together because we've settled everything."

It was as if it was his calling—telling a lie so convincingly, Chike thought. He was ready to do the cocaine job, but Emeka still wasn't his favorite person. He had only agreed to go with him to visit their mum in Enugu so they could witness how much the surgery had changed her situation. She could walk without struggle. No support. Her doctor first had said she would need her cane for a longer stretch of time.

Not Mama.

She had picked up selling goods outside again as soon as the ache from her surgery waned. It was the one detail about her new life that Chike despised. After all their 419, Mama still didn't have enough to retire.

"I hope you will never fight again like that. Your father, ehn, he would not appreciate it. What was it he always told you and Emeka? Ehn, Chike?"

Chike hesitated. The mere thought of his father's relentless counsel sent his emotions from the pit of his belly to the top of his throat. He turned and choked the sensation back down.

"Ehn, Chike? Answer me!"

"Otu onye tuo izu, o gbue ochu," Chike said, still snuffing his own emotions. "Knowledge is never complete. Two heads are better than one."

"Or, Gidi gidi bụ ugwu eze. Unity is strength," Emeka added.

"So you remember, but you beat your brother? And you, you remember, but you left your brother?"

"Mama, we are okay."

"So make sure you go home," she said as she fanned herself with the lid of a plastic container. "Go back to your brother," Mama said to Emeka. "How can you be living in that same Lagos in different places?"

"Mama, don't worry yourself. Chike and I have already started doing business together again."

"Very good. You must work together," she said. Chike and Emeka exchanged looks of discomfort, as if they had just accepted the fact that their work would never be what she intended for them. Would she even forgive them if she knew the truth? Chike looked at Mama again and noticed her tears.

"Every day I thank God that he answered my prayers. Look at my children. They put their money together for me. Your children, too, will do well for you. Continue to support each other. Continue to work together. Look at the good you did together for me. Do you not see me here?"

"Mama, don't cry. We hear you," Emeka said, softening his tone.

Chike stood and pulled his mother from her seat. He bent over, then wrapped his arms around her.

She whispered, "Lead your brother. Do not diminish him. Lead him."

"Yes, Mama," he replied, and Chike wondered if Emeka had heard what she said.

JUST BEFORE DUSK, CHIKE AND EMEKA HELPED MAMA pack up her inventory after serving only five customers for the day. Emeka announced that he was going to take a cab into town to make a phone call and buy a few things.

Chike decided to sit outside alone. He thanked God that the mosquitos weren't out like they normally were in that spot. He sipped a Heineken and looked at passersby, children playing, cars and okadas inching by on the uneven road. He thought of his work and how he was ready to park his own okada for good. He wouldn't be able to rest until his feet touched American soil. *Patience must do this job*, he thought. He remembered when he had been less willing to work with Oga, but she had convinced him because "we have no choice."

An okada drove up carrying Emeka. He got off the motorcycle, paid the driver, and walked toward the house. They locked eyes. Emeka hesitated. Then he propped himself against the exposed cinder block gate.

"Chike, I'm sorry. I'm sorry for our fight." His tone was apologetic, but he still seemed unsettled.

Chike took a long sip of his beer. "Don't worry," he said. "I forgive you. But why did you tell Mama?"

Emeka smiled a timid smile, and Chike realized then that his brother hadn't smiled all day—not even when Mama had cracked jokes about her neighbors. "I called her the day it happened. I was just angry."

They fell silent, but the quarrels between the children down the road echoed in the distance.

"Remember when we used to argue with our friends on the street like that, and Daddy used to come out to settle things?" Emeka said. He pointed toward the children, who had become even more irate.

"Why would I forget, na?" Soothed by the memory, Chike took another sip of beer. "You know I acted like it was embarrassing, but there were times I liked it. I liked when he came out."

The sound of Emeka's laughter warmed him, and he realized he missed his brother more than he knew. "Why would you like when Daddy came out like that? Everybody would be laughing at us after," Emeka said once he caught his breath.

Chike didn't say anything. He wasn't sure why he had appreciated that his father meddled in their affairs with the other kids in the area. Maybe, at that time, some part of him knew his dad wouldn't be there to correct them when they took on riskier pursuits in their adult lives. Or maybe he was just proud of his dad.

"Daddy would just come and destroy our little reputation." Emeka laughed louder. "Daddy. I miss him, mehn."

Chike looked at Emeka and accepted that they would never agree on most things. It was the natural order of their brotherhood, and it was okay.

"Who did you have to call?"

"What do you mean?"

"You took a cab out to make a phone call. Who did you have to call so urgently?"

"Ah, nobody, sha. Just business." Emeka shifted his weight from one foot to another. Chike knew his brother well. He knew something was wrong in his life.

"Emeka, when we do the cocaine job," Chike said, "make me one promise."

"So you'll do the job?" Emeka said.

"I will. I have to. But promise me something."

"What's that?"

"When Patience and I get to America, I will send you some money. Use it to finish that gate. Use it to fix Mama's house. But please seal and paint the gate first."

"Do what Daddy wasn't able to do, isn't it? I will, but I will pay for it myself," Emeka said.

"You've been thinking about Daddy's promise to finish it too?"

"Of course. Every year he wanted to. I'm your elder, so I will finish it."

Chike didn't hug Emeka like he wanted to. It wasn't their way. So he wrapped himself in the comfort of knowing his brother would one day make him proud.

47

"DADDY, I FORGIVE YOU FOR TAKING MY MUM AWAY FROM me. I forgive you, not because you deserve forgiveness—I forgive you so that I can be free."

Patience ran through her speech over and over again as she sat on the bus bound for Ibadan. She couldn't understand why those words made her nervous. She had heard a woman on *Oprah* tell her unrelenting husband she forgave him for putting her through years of physical abuse. She was astonished by the prospect of forgiving someone that way, but something inside her felt it was what she needed to do.

As much as she idolized American culture, the mantra and the whole notion of I-forgive-you-even-though-you're-not-sorry sounded a bit too westernized.

"Hmm, Americans," Patience mumbled. She wasn't sure how a proud Nigerian man like her father would take it. She could hear him dismissing her: "You are telling me that you forgive me? You, a child that I brought into this world, you are saying you forgive me, and you're telling me that your forgiveness is not for my benefit? Are you insane?"

When she looked outside and saw the First Apostolic Church, she knew she was close to her father's compound. Streets that she considered busy during her childhood years were smaller and less hectic. Lagos had turned her eyes inside out. She wondered what New York would feel like to her if she ever got there.

When the bus stopped, Patience got off and started on foot. She ducked when she saw Kusa, her father's gate man, chatting with some of the mallams manning a table of sweets. There was no time for small talk, and she had no intention of explaining to him why she had run away. She picked up speed and looked straight ahead.

Soon she approached the top of the street where her father's off-white house sat. Its silhouette was plump with rounded edges, resembling the sumo wrestlers she saw fighting on TV at Chike's house—supple yet monstrous. She hated everything about the house, from Modupe's control of the daily operations there to her father's swollen pride in its gaudy design. Never mind the fact that most of the area was populated by more modest buildings.

Patience approached the gate and was confronted by an unfamiliar face. It was a new gate man. She had been expecting to see Kusa's son.

"Good evening. I'm Patience, your boss's daughter from Lagos. I'm here to see him."

"Excuse me, madam, but Chief only has one daughter. Please step away from the gate."

"Actually, he has two daughters."

"Chief told me himself that Margaret is his only daughter. Please, I beg, leave this area."

"I will not leave."

"Habu! Habu!" They heard a voice call from the road. "I know the girl. She is Chief's daughter who left." Patience turned and saw Kusa.

"You dis girl, Daddy say you no get respect."

"Kusa, can you remember a time when I no show you respect?"

"Oga said you packed out of the house? Why na, when he dey pamper you and your sister?"

"Kusa, it's too much to explain. Is Daddy home?"

"He dey inside office. I go take you there."

Patience followed Kusa as he stepped through the narrow opening of her father's large black iron gate. She was struck by the beautiful landscaping, none of which had been present when she and Kash came for her passport. The plush green hedges that traced the building appeared as firm as a concrete fence. Palm trees that shot up from the ground stood tall enough to tickle the clouds. The sweet aroma of hibiscus made Patience search for them. She spotted them rooted along the perimeter of the archway leading to a veranda.

Instead of searching for their runaway daughter, her father and stepmother had planted a stunning garden.

Patience wasn't surprised.

Kusa knocked on the front door of the house with a light tap. Not long after, the house girl Fatima answered. She looked like she had seen a person's insides. She tried to speak, but nothing came out of her mouth.

"Fatima, can I see my father?" Patience was done with the small talk about her life. She thanked Kusa and walked past Fatima into the house.

The ceilings were even higher than she remembered, but she decided she wouldn't survey the house any further. She needed to focus on the reason she had come.

Her father's office door was closed. She knocked.

"Who is that?" he said. She decided not to announce herself. She opened the door, and there he was, on the phone, sitting behind his desk wearing a striped polo shirt and facing the side of the room. He didn't look up to see who had entered. His feet remained propped on top of the leather stool next to him. His loafers—brown, suede, and new. Patience wondered if he had just returned from America or London, where he bought most of his clothes.

"Daddy," Patience said to get his attention. He looked at her and then looked away. He continued speaking on the phone.

"As commissioner, I cannot allow that to happen."

Commissioner of finance. Patience wondered how much money he had embezzled so far.

"Listen, someone just walked into my office. We will settle the matter later." He hung up the phone, then picked it up again. He dialed a number. He put the phone back on the receiver, then tried again, still ignoring her.

Patience could hear the obnoxious busy tone. As usual, the telephone system couldn't handle a normal direct call. He tried the number again.

"So you're here for more money after leaving this house and disobeying me?" he said in between dialing each number.

"Daddy, I need . . . your help."

"You don't need me," he said. "What you do when you need money is send Kash to steal from me. Or you go to your mother's former friend in Lagos acting as if you don't have a father. Why are you in my house?"

"Daddy . . . it's not just about money. I'm here . . . I want . . . I need to go to New York."

Her father put the phone down. There was a long menacing silence that she couldn't read.

"You need to go to New York? Okay, so go to New York. Sebi you are on your own. You can do as you please."

"Yes, Daddy, I left your house because you wanted to hold me here. I still feel like you're holding me and you have been since . . . since you made my mum leave." Her candor surprised her, but she was satisfied with her words. "Daddy I know that my mum might be in New York. I know that she moved there when she left Nigeria. Isn't it true?"

"Didn't I tell you not to mention that woman in my house? She made her bed. She fled to America and left you here, and you're asking me about her? Was she the one who paid your school fees? Did she house you? Did she feed you? Why are you in my house if you think I'm holding you?" Patience could hear anger rise in his voice.

"Because I want to know why you've kept her from me." She held her hands together to keep them from shaking. "I know about the letter she wrote me. You never gave it to me. Why?" Patience dabbed her eyes to stop the tears. She didn't want him to see her cry. This was the moment to stand her ground. "I know she took you to court to get custody of me."

"So you think going to court is something? And you are here telling me you went through *my* things and read a letter from your mum. Patience, how did you become like this?"

"Like what, Daddy? Lost? Because I *am* lost, Daddy. I am lost, and you refuse to help me. Why? What did she do to you? How can you keep my own mother from me?" Tired from the struggle, she allowed her tears to fall. More than her lost passport, more than the rejection from the embassy, far beyond her lack of money to get to America, her father's hand had been holding her in place, keeping her from moving beyond her circumstances.

He stood up from his chair, then sat on the desk. He gazed into her eyes. She wanted to look away, but she didn't.

"You want to know about your mum, ehn? She was a selfish woman. Always running her mouth about what she sacrificed to be with me. To have you."

Patience remembered her mum's letter to him and how she used those exact words. Finally he had spoken the truth about her mother.

"She thought that being a celebrity Olympian would be her greatest achievement in life," he said. "I gave her a life as a wife. A mother. She only complained. She only wanted to weigh her ranking in my life as if she should be more. As if she should mean more to me than I mean to myself." He paused. Patience tried to soak up all he said, but he began again.

"You are like her. I can see it already. I've told you before, too much ambition in a woman is unbecoming. You came here to my house after fleeing to tell me you want to go to America to see your mother, and you're now asking me for an explanation. Patience, that Lagos has caused your brain to scatter from your head. You can never know enough about my relationship with your mother. I've done all I can do for you."

Patience was stunned. He spoke of her mother as if she were yet another thing he wanted to conquer. It was how he treated her too, how he treated almost everyone. If ever she should tell him what she had practiced, it was that moment, but she couldn't bring herself to utter the words. *I forgive you, Daddy.* She realized she didn't need to. Those words were for her. She knew her father would never change, so he didn't need to know her heart. She could no longer allow him to keep her trapped.

She would have to be brave like her mother.

She would have to free herself completely.

Patience got up, wiped her tears, and walked out. Modupe, standing not far from her father's office, startled her.

"I did my best for you," Modupe said.

"Your *best*?"

"To raise a child who is not your own, well, it's not a simple thing."

"To be raised by a woman who is not your mother . . . well . . ." She dabbed her eyes again.

Patience walked past Modupe. She opened the front door of the house, then made her way toward her father's outdoor veranda. She pressed her nose against the hibiscus planted in the archway. It smelled as sweet as victory. She plucked one, then another, then another, then several more. She stuffed a few in her purse and one in her braids as she sat down on her father's beautiful pine bench.

"Daddy, I forgive you," she whispered before pressing a flower to her nose again. "I forgive you, not because you deserve forgiveness. I forgive you so that I can be free."

48

PATIENCE PUSHED PAST THE SWARM OF GIRLS WEARING the familiar uniform she wore for three years of her life as a junior student at Our Lady of Good Counsel Secondary School. Their green pinafores reminded her of the times she spent waiting outside the school compound at the start of school breaks, long after her class-mates had been picked up, wondering when or if her father would arrive to bring her home. She had been a junior student then, without Margaret there to quell the loneliness she felt.

She brushed away the pain of the memory and made her way past the entrance to the building where the senior girls were housed. She peered at the faces in the crowd, some familiar. She had no interest in catching up. Her confrontation with her dad, the almost three-hour bus ride from Ibadan to Ogbomosho, a headache brought on by the stress—it was all too much. *Where is Margaret?* she thought.

"Patience, is that you?" she heard someone call out. She turned and saw Margaret's friend Ronke standing across from her.

"In the flesh," Patience said quickly, hoping to avoid a conversation. "Have you seen Margaret? I don't want the reverend sisters to see me."

"She's here. I saw her washing her clothes. A whole senior in SS1, doing her own chores. I told her she should give it to a junior girl. She refused."

"Why punish a junior girl with hard labor?" Patience said.

"Oh, yes, like sister, like sister," she said. "Check for her inside the hostel gate."

Patience passed through the gate, and there was Margaret, bent over her bucket, scrubbing her uniform. She looked up and wiped her brow with the back of her hand.

"Patience . . . ha!" Margaret dropped her clothes in the bucket, ran to Patience, and wrapped her arms around her. Water from her hands dripped down on Patience's skirt before she let go. "I came to you in Lagos, now you come to me. Is this a game we're playing? Did you go to Ibadan? Did you see Mummy and Daddy? There's no way you came all the way to Oyo just to see me."

"Yes, I was there," Patience said.

"So . . . are you going back to UNILAG? Did you tell them you know where your mum is?"

"Margaret, I'm not going back to school."

Margaret paused. Patience looked into her eyes, then looked away. "I came to let you know that I won't be seeing you for some time."

Another weighty silence.

"You figured out how to get yourself to America to see your mum." She pressed her lips together and wiped her wet hands on the iro she had tied around her waist. "Well, I knew you would find your way. I was just hoping it would come after we'd had time to be together in Lagos after I finish school. That place would have been more interesting with me and my sister there together, sha."

"I will write to you."

"You have no choice. How are you getting to Yankee?" she said.

"Well . . ." Patience fidgeted as she thought of what to say. She hadn't prepared what she would tell Margaret when she decided she would do the cocaine job during the bus ride there. She wasn't in school anymore, Chike was barely making any money, she had no family to help her, and there were no options to make the kind of money she needed to get to America. There was no other way for her to move forward. No other way to look for her mum. She and Chike needed a quick solution. This was the only way. "Somebody here gave me and Chike a job in America."

"What kind of work?"

"It's menial work. Nothing I would confess to doing."

"Who cares. As long as you get to America and make enough money to live and eat and find your mum," she said. "Wait, aren't you hungry? Help me finish my clothes. Let's go to the tuck shop to get some ijekuje."

"I've been doing plenty of washing in Lagos for your dear cousin Kash," Patience said. She grabbed her sister's uniform and scrubbed.

"I trust brother Kash to put you to work," Margaret said as she squeezed and draped the clothes on the line outside her room.

If only she knew the other kind of work he had introduced her to, Patience thought.

As they walked toward the tuck shop, Patience pictured what it would be like to swallow capsules of cocaine. The thought made her anxious.

"I'm happy for you. You deserve to know your mum," Margaret said. Patience was comforted by the mention of her mum. The cocaine job would only take a day. Being in her mum's company would be worth it. She had been waiting more than half her life to see her mum again.

"How was your talk with Daddy?"

"Well, let's just say nothing has changed. Our father is and will always be a tyrant."

"Well, of course," Margaret said.

They reached the tuck shop, and Margaret dug into her skirt pocket and pulled out a handful of balled-up money. "What will you have? I will pay."

"No way, Margaret. I know your pocket money isn't like that."

"Well, let's just say I found my mum's stash of money and had my way with it."

Patience noticed how she called Modupe *my* mum and not Mummy, as they normally did. Was she accepting the depth of the divide that had always existed between them—that Modupe was *her* mum?

"Well, since it's money from your mum, I'll have buns, fish rolls, and a Coke."

"Aunty, can we please have two buns, two fish rolls, and two Cokes," Margaret said as she handed the woman manning the tuck shop several naira notes.

"So about this job you'll be doing in America, I hope it's nothing too bad. I mean . . . I hope it's not something that can get you in trouble."

Patience should have known that Margaret—as sharp as she was and as worldly as she wanted to be—would pick up on the possibility of her doing something illegal.

"Of course not. It's just menial labor. That's it."

"Okay," Margaret said as she took the food she had ordered. "So I suppose you'll be sleeping in the hostel with me tonight."

"Yes. No way I'm going back to Lagos tonight."

They walked on and sat on the staircase leading to the classroom. They dug into their bags of food and started eating, the lingering silence between them filled only by the sound of their munching. Patience didn't know what to say. Instead she thought of the cocaine again and the idea of any amount of it bursting in her gut. Her stomach began to turn. She thought of the possibility of getting caught. Would she be sent to a Nigerian prison or an American prison? She hoped it would be an American one. She had heard too many stories about Nigerian jails.

She shook the idea away and scolded herself for even considering prison as part of her future. She and Chike would be victorious. They would do the job and move on with their lives.

Patience turned to Margaret and saw the tears gathering in her eyes before they spilled down her cheeks. Margaret wiped her face.

"Don't start that, Margaret. Why the crying, ehn?"

"I'm okay. I just . . . I just don't want you to forget about me once you remember that I'm not the kind of sister you wanted."

Patience looked away, and the weight of her sister's words bore down on her. Margaret was being unfair. She was already managing enough confusion, from the fight with their dad and thoughts of her next job. Now she needed energy to comfort Margaret.

Patience looked at her half sister again and saw her tears, her melancholy, her care. Patience felt something else.

She felt it without any question of its validity. She loved her sister as fully as her sister loved her.

"Margaret, you've been the kind of sister I've *needed*. You will always be."

Margaret dried her eyes and stared out at the girls roaming the school grounds. Patience gave her a gentle nudge, then they bumped shoulders.

"Let's change the subject," Margaret said. "How's brother Kash treating you besides having you wash his clothes?"

"Our dear brother Kash," Patience said with all the irony she could muster. "You wouldn't even believe me if I told you."

THREE DAYS AFTER PATIENCE RETURNED TO LAGOS, SHE put her sewing machine in her bag and boarded a bus headed to UNILAG. She got off before she reached the campus and walked up the road she had become familiar with before venturing onto dodgier paths. She stopped and gazed across at the tailor. He was there, still seated on his chair at his table sewing. He didn't look up. He continued with his work.

She thought of what Kash had told her and grew nervous. If she brought the machine back to the tailor, the man would cause a scene and blame her for breaking it.

She would confront him anyway, come what may.

She took a deep breath and moved across the street.

"Good afternoon," she said.

"Good afternoon," he said, though he didn't look up at her. "Have you started selling clothes?"

Patience was stunned that he knew it was her. "No . . . I haven't. The machine you sold me broke . . . I mean, you sold me a broken machine," she said. "Sa, why na? Was I not sincere about my desire to sew?"

The man finished his stitching and looked up at her, his eyes still a strong crimson color. "Where is it?" he said.

"I have it here. In my bag."

"Bring it."

She pulled it out and gave it to him. He set it down on the far corner of his table. He grabbed a screwdriver and opened the plate under the needle. He examined it. He blew into it, and Patience saw a cloud of dust lift. He grabbed a small brush from his tools and circled it around the inside of the plate, then screwed it back on. Then he pried open the entire machine. Patience watched as his veiny hands went to work—tightening, unscrewing, dusting before he put the machine back together.

"Ẹ jọọ, Iya Munsurat," he yelled to the woman at the stationery printing shop next door. The roar of her generator pumping electricity into the store almost drowned him out.

"Ẹ jọọ, I need light."

"Yes, Sa," the woman said.

Her employee came out and ran a long extension cord his way. When he plugged Patience's machine into the socket, she realized why his manual machine was more valuable to him. Kash was right that she was naive.

He turned her machine on, then placed some fabric under the needle and turned the knob. Patience was startled by the sound of the needle moving up and down, forming a straight stitch along his scrap of fabric.

"Just like that?" she said.

"Take it. Go and use it again."

"What is your price, Sa?"

"No price," he said as he pulled his chair back in front of his machine. "Just send the power back to Iya Munsurat there."

Patience held the extension cord in her hand, stunned.

The tailor sat down and resumed his work.

49

MAYOWA SAT UP IN HIS BED AND MARVELED AT THE LIGHT
that spilled in through the window as his father's favorite song filtered
through the bedroom door.

The sweet sound of Sunny Ade declaring his appreciation to God
for life's treasures was Mr. Adeshina's go-to whenever he wanted to
give thanks for an extraordinary occasion. He had played the song the
day he returned to Nigeria after spending three long years in London
working on his master's degree in marketing. He had played it the
day Mayowa's mother was released from the hospital after the doctors
removed a benign tumor from her ovaries. Mayowa also remembered
faintly hearing the song play above the chitchat of his parents' closest
friends, who had come to congratulate him the day he finished at the
University of Ibadan.

Although Mayowa always welcomed the tune, he didn't need to be
reminded that they were celebrating something grand. From the start
of the year he had been striking off the passing days on the MKO
Abiola campaign calendar he had taped on the wall next to his bed. At
the stroke of midnight, he had already crossed off June 12 and scribbled
Election Day over the entire calendar before he drifted off to sleep.

The aroma of his mother's corned beef, onion, and tomato omelet
filtered into his room and made his stomach rumble.

He had his bath, then threw on his green-white-green campaign polo. He ironed his button-down shirt. He would take it to the office and change into it in case his father allowed him to do TV interviews to discuss Abiola's impending victory.

He had a lot to say.

He would be the perfect voice for the youth of Nigeria, he thought. He would talk about how Abiola's presidency would inspire his generation to be better than they knew. He would say his peers could look to economic change, infrastructure change, jobs. Why should a good man like Chike be subjected to driving an okada after earning a degree in engineering? He wondered if Chike would stand near him during such an interview. He was excited that his friend had agreed to spend the day with him at the campaign headquarters to help. They would ring in the victory together.

Mayowa ran downstairs and saw his thirteen-year-old and fifteen-year-old sisters, Ibukun and Teniola, in the sitting room. He jumped in front of the television they were glued to and started dancing.

"Brother Mayowa, please! We are missing our program!" Teniola said.

"It's election day, and you're watching this nonsense," he said.

"Mayowa, leave your sisters alone, ah-ahn," his mother yelled from the kitchen. She playfully swatted him with a rag when he walked in and stole a kiss from her.

"You this boy," she said.

"Mummy, it's election day!" he said.

"Oya, go and buy my newspaper," his father said. "We need to be going soon so we can vote before we go to the office."

When Mayowa made his way outside, he saw his neighbors, Mr. Oni and Mr. Adeniji, discussing the election.

"There's our good man," Mr. Oni said as he pointed to Mayowa.

"Ah-ahn, you should be at MKO's place by now."

"We will be going soon," Mayowa said.

He thought of how the two men had questioned the possibility of an Abiola victory when talk of him running for the presidency began. It was Mayowa's father who had convinced them that Abiola was serious and determined to change things. And yet Mayowa still remembered when his father had been like the men he needed to persuade, because theirs was a generation that had become accustomed to political brokenness.

A bitter memory, watching his dad settle in the bosom of hopelessness brought on by his brother's misfortune—a four-year prison sentence for writing about Buhari in the paper.

And then one day Mr. Adeshina reunited with Abiola, his old classmate from Baptist Boys' High School in Abeokuta. Mayowa wondered how one man was able to lift the burdens his father had carried for so long.

Mayowa made his way to the closest stall in the neighborhood and grabbed the newspaper from the front table.

"Na wa o, today is the day," Mr. Odusanya, the shop owner, said.

"Yes, o. Today is the day."

"Tell your papa if he wants to celebrate the day he should come and buy all the shayo from me."

"I will tell him," Mayowa said as he slipped him the money for the newspaper. He glanced at the headlines:

DAY OF VICTORY FOR ABIOLA?

THE DAWN OF NIGERIA'S DEMOCRACY

He flipped the newspaper to look below the fold and noticed a bittersweet headline:

ELECTIONS TO COMMENCE DESPITE PREVIOUS HIGH
COURT INJUNCTION TO CANCEL DUE TO CORRUPTION

"These people dey craze," Mr. Odusanya said as Mayowa frowned at the headline. "High Court na enemy of progress. We will have a fair election today. There will be democracy."

"Amen," Mayowa said, brushing off his worries over the previous ruling to kill the elections. "The government will continue to do the right thing." Mayowa was sure of it. He knew if his belief was strong enough Abiola would be president. Never mind all the talk of the military's plans to derail their promise of democracy. Never mind the Babangida Must Stay campaign that many analysts said was gaining traction. Certainly never mind the close call two days prior when the high court ruled to cancel the elections due to supposed corruption. They still had no evidence of foul play on the part of Abiola or his opponent, because there was no foul play.

Mayowa's father believed that all would continue to work in Abiola's favor, and because his father believed it, Mayowa believed it too.

"Make sure you take plenty photos at the campaign office. You must document this day well-well," Mr. Odusanya said.

"Yes, Sa." Mayowa tilted his body forward as a sign of respect to the old man before he made his way back home. When he stepped back through his parents' gate, he noticed his father sitting in their patio chair. Mayowa handed him the paper and sat next to him.

"Daddy, the paper is still talking about how the high court wanted to cancel the elections. Can you imagine?"

"Don't worry about that. Today is a new day. Don't allow your faith to diminish." Mr. Adeshina scanned the front of the paper, then rolled it up and propped it under his armpit.

"Mayowa, I'm so proud of the work you've done on this campaign. You've been diligent and very protective of Abiola's agenda. It will all pay off soon."

"Amen, Daddy."

"I prayed for this day for many, many years, but I never imagined how it would be," his dad said, lowering the newspaper and staring off into the distance. "In 1966, military coup; 1975, military coup with no plan to return to democracy; 1976, 1983, military coup, military coup. Ah-ahn," Mr. Adeshina said as his voice dipped. "In the beginning when the military took over, they would come out acting civilized as if they were going to do good for the country. Our people would celebrate, excited for a new day, not knowing that the military would destroy this place. Reporters were beaten and thrown in jail; my own brother, thrown in prison. Babangida devalued our money to practically nothing with no positive outcome."

Mayowa shuddered at his father's emphasis of the word *practically.*

"Enough is enough," his father continued. "I'm glad I'm alive to witness this. I'm glad my son will witness this."

Mayowa bowed his head and grinned. He realized then that seeing his father happy came first for him. He never wanted to see him in tears again. Once was enough, though sometimes he relived the day his dad came home from the bank, bloody and beaten, military officers the aggressors.

His father's crime: not queuing up at a bank.

Mr. Adeshina stood and brushed off his slacks as his driver revved the engine of the car.

"My son," he said, facing Mayowa, "let's go vote."

BY THE TIME MAYOWA AND HIS FATHER ARRIVED AT ABIOLA'S campaign headquarters, Chike was waiting outside on his okada. The three men walked in together and found the main room buzzing with men sitting close to the television, laughing and chatting about how MKO was already defeating Tofa.

Reporters wandered around thrusting tape recorders in the face of anyone who looked capable enough to answer questions about how Abiola was feeling. The man himself was said to be out and about, first to cast his vote, then to meet with select press outlets. Mayowa said he would wait to do an interview until the victory was announced.

It was a lot to take in, and Mayowa couldn't tame his excitement. The happenings in the room made him go back and forth between dancing and scanning news channels to find out what they were reporting.

"This is overwhelming," Mayowa said after hours had passed. "We know he will win, so why don't they just announce it now!"

"Let's go to Allen Avenue for ice cream," Chike said.

"Yes, o. I need a break."

Chike drove them on his motorcycle to Mr. Biggs, not far from the campaign headquarters.

"I want vanilla," Chike said once they reached the counter.

"Chocolate for me," Mayowa said.

"In a matter of hours Nigeria will be a democracy led by Abiola. Can you imagine?" Mayowa said, wide-eyed. They sat down, holding their ice cream cones, a fitting symbol of the sweetness that consumed Lagos that day.

"All of my father's hard work is paying off now. Nigeria will be a better place. I'm telling you, with Abiola beginning our democracy, our political structure will have the potential to rival the Western world in the next ten years."

"Speaking of the Western world, I want to let you know now that I will be going to America with Patience," Chike said. "I went to the American Embassy, and I was able to get my visa for an extended stay."

"Wow." Mayowa paused and licked his ice cream. "How extended will your stay be?"

"I'm not sure, but I will come back. I just want to explore the world outside Nigeria for now."

Chike couldn't bring himself to tell Mayowa that he got his visa after he agreed to do the cocaine job.

"Make sure you don't stay long. Look at what the polls are showing today. Abiola will win, o." His intensity returned at his utterance of Abiola's name.

Chike was mildly excited about the potential of the election. He was tired of hoping. He was ready to act. Going to America would be the first step. "Mayowa . . . I've never asked you . . . why are you so excited about Nigeria and Abiola?"

"Because of my dad." Mayowa licked his ice cream around the edges of the cone. "We have to work to find solutions—that's what he always says. When he started working with Abiola, he became a different person. Before he would read the newspaper and complain, 'Ah, Nigeria ti baj ẹ.' To see him like that, so defeated, mehn . . ." he said, trailing off. "Then Abiola came around with his philosophy, and my dad changed. I saw the difference in his eyes. Then he told me something I will never forget. He said, 'Mayowa, I believe my generation has failed you in so many ways. We think a lot about the money, the personal plots of land, and possessions we want our children to inherit from their fathers, but we don't think about the country we are passing down. We didn't fight for you and your mates. We've watched the military bulldoze the country. You are the future, and Abiola is the answer to our biggest mistakes.'"

"Wow." Chike was impressed by Mayowa's dad's candor.

"Anyway, sha, I love Abiola because I think one day I can be president of Nigeria if he can be," Mayowa said. He stood up and threw his shoulders back jokingly.

"Look at this useless man," Chike said.

"Useless, ke. I am the future of this nation. Bow at my feet."

They laughed and laughed, then licked their ice cream in a hurry as it began to melt down their hands.

50

CHIKE DIDN'T CARE THAT HE WAS SPEEDING. HE WASN'T worried he would fall into a gutter. He ripped through traffic on his okada like he was living out his last days. If he crashed into anyone on the road, he would blame it on the victim for getting in his way.

It was the Lagos way of settling accidents anyway.

He needed to get to Mayowa's house. He would try him there first. Was he there with his father watching the news? Everyone was watching the news. It was because of the news that Chike was speeding. It was because of the news that he needed to see Mayowa.

Before he jumped on his okada to embark on his frantic ride, he and Patience had sat on the couch as they watched Babangida annul the results of the June 12 election.

"Fellow Nigerians, it is true that by the canceled presidential election, we all found the nation at a peculiar bar of history . . ." he said. *"In the circumstance, the administration had no option than to respond appropriately to the unfortunate experience of terminating the presidential election."*

Those were the words that Chike remembered most from the president's address. He told the nation that the election had been rigged. It was a lie. The people of Nigeria knew this. The country hadn't seen a freer and fairer election.

But hope couldn't live in Nigeria.

Abiola had run his campaign on hope. That sentiment had been so easily erased.

Chike pulled up to Mayowa's house. The mallam who sold sweets out front whistled for his attention.

"Mayowa and his papa no dey for house."

"Where are they?"

"I don't know."

"When did they leave?"

"One hour's time."

"Have you seen the news?"

"Yes."

"Did Mayowa and his papa see what happened?"

"Mayowa dey cry as he dey enter car. He dey see am."

Chike hopped back on his okada and sped toward Abiola's headquarters.

CHIKE PARKED HIS MOTORCYCLE NEAR THE EDGE OF Abiola's sprawling compound. There were hundreds of people lined up chanting, "MKO is president!" Chike saw a somewhat clear path to the gate.

"What are you doing here?" said one of the two men who guarded the gate.

"I'm here to see Mayowa and his dad. Mayowa is my friend."

"Nobody else can enter the compound. Carry your okada and go."

"Is Chief Abiola inside?"

"I said carry your bike and go!" the man shouted.

Chike decided not to press further. The annulment of the elections pricked at everyone's emotions. Abiola was probably inside strategizing his next move.

Chike would try to find Mayowa another day.

51

"PHILLIP, GO TELL THIS GIRL TO COME DOWNSTAIRS. AH-ahn, what is taking her so long, jàre?"

"Oga, no vex, I will call her to come down," Phillip replied.

"Hurry o, so we can get back home before these silly protesters find their way to this side. Abeg, nobody should vandalize my car because of Abiola."

"Yes, Oga." Phillip looked at the passenger seat where Emeka sat and gave him an approving nod. Emeka turned away. Phillip clicked the automatic button to unlock the car doors, then ran toward the modest house Oga had built for his girlfriend, Tope.

"All these people rioting, it's funny, o," Emeka said, looking back at Oga from the front seat. "I had been saying it, the military will never allow democracy."

"Indeed," Oga said as he read the front page of *The Punch* newspaper. ELEVEN FOUND DEAD AT ABIOLA RIOTS was the top headline.

Emeka fiddled with his tie and tapped his foot. He pressed the dial on the radio, then stopped when he heard Naughty by Nature's "Hip Hop Hooray." The song was a welcome tune to calm his nerves—not too slow, not too hard core, like his favorite Dr. Dre song, "Nuthin' but a 'G' Thang." He needed a fluffier song to settle his body. He looked down at his watch. Five twenty-five. He looked out the rear window. He tapped his foot again.

He belted out "Hooray" from the song's chorus.

"This music is nonsense," Oga said.

Emeka looked at his watch and out the back window again.

"Oga, please, I want to go and buy minerals and biscuits from the mallam on that side. What can I collect for you?"

"I'm okay. Hurry up. Phillip should be down soon with Tope."

Emeka opened the door, then clicked the automatic button to lock them all. He shut his door and hesitated for a moment. He looked down the street toward the rear of the car, where he heard the voices of a few men. They were carrying things, but he couldn't see what. He turned to walk toward the top of the road, where several mallams sold goods from stalls and rickety wooden tables.

"Give me cabin biscuit and orange Fanta."

"Make you drink am for dis side," the mallam said, handing him his drink. "Give me my bottle when you drink am finished so I can put am for crate."

Emeka paid him and opened the bottle with his teeth. He took a swig, then turned to look at Oga's car as three men approached it. One knocked on the window. Oga rolled it down. They exchanged words.

In a matter of seconds several men, some who wore Ọmọ Èkó Congress T-shirts, abbreviated as OEC in bold letters, surrounded the car carrying large wooden sticks. One had a gun. Another carried a tire around his shoulder. They exchanged words with Oga, who was still seated in the back seat of the car with the window down. Oga gripped the car roof and tried to climb out of the window. Two men blocked him.

"I'm locked inside, help me! Emeka, are you there?" he screamed. "Do you know who I am? Get away from my car!"

Emeka stood behind a few men who had gathered at the stall. He couldn't move his legs. Onlookers kept their distance, knowing what was coming.

The men began to shake the car. Glass broke. Emeka's heart began to beat faster when he saw them light the tire, then plop it on top of Oga's cracked windshield. When Emeka heard Oga scream, his body grew so numb he didn't realize when the bottle of orange Fanta slid from his grip and smashed on the ground.

Emeka couldn't watch anymore. He looked around at the crowd, which was engrossed in the incident, including the mallam, who didn't seem to care about his broken Fanta bottle.

"If he's a thief, they should just kill him straight!" one man shouted from the crowd.

Emeka managed to lift his feet and walk toward the main road. There he started running and didn't stop until he got to the bus stop half a mile away. Phillip, sitting on the side of the road, looked up at Emeka and stood as he approached. Emeka stopped and panted to catch his breath.

"What happened?" Phillip said. "Is everything okay?"

"It's done," Emeka said in between breaths. "Oga is gone."

52

TWO WEEKS BEFORE OGA'S DEATH, PHILLIP AND EMEKA
had sat in the comfort of their boss's plush BMW and drafted a plan
to get rid of him.

The car had become their meeting place to map out steps to right
Oga's wrongs and forge their new partnership. Kash had already been
released by the OEC by then. To buy his freedom, Emeka and Phillip
took a large chunk of money from Oga's safe.

Their next step: hand Oga over to the OEC.

They went over the plan ad nauseam to make sure they were both
in sync.

"We cannot make any mistakes," Emeka said as he bit his fingernails.

"Don't worry," Phillip reassured him.

Phillip broke the plan down like this: "The day Oga goes to Tope's
house, we will send an area boy to the OEC to give them Oga's exact
location and expected time of arrival."

Emeka's face fell. He hoped Tope would be okay.

"Emeka, please settle your mind about Tope's situation," Phillip
said. "Didn't she know that being Oga's girlfriend would destroy her
life at some point?"

Emeka knew they had no choice—they had to tell the OEC that

Tope had told Oga that the Onabanjos wouldn't be home when he sold their house.

"The OEC only ran her out of Lagos. I made them promise not to beat her."

"What if they did anyway?"

"What did Oga tell you? Casualties, right?"

"Right."

"Next thing: I will click the child safety locks on the back doors before it's time for us to go to Tope's place. Emeka, make sure you sit in the front seat so you don't get locked in the back with him."

"Won't he notice if I don't sit next to him like I always do?"

"I said he won't notice," Phillip said.

"But if he does?"

"Oga won't notice because he keeps his head in his newspapers."

"Okay," Emeka said.

"Oga will get impatient and tell me to go knock on Tope's door, not knowing that she's probably hiding in her mum's village in Abeokuta." Phillip snickered.

"Then I will come up with a reason to get out of the car when it's time for the OEC to confront Oga," Emeka said.

"Yes . . . I think we know what happens at that point, right?"

"Right," Emeka said. He took a deep breath and pictured the end of the plan. Would the OEC burn Oga alive in the car or would they drag him out and torture him? Emeka shuddered at the thought, but he had no choice. He remembered how lifeless Kash had become since his release from OEC captivity.

God only knows what they did to him.

He would help Kash get back on his feet after the next job was done—the most important job he'd ever do.

"The next day we will go see Kenny, our Lebanese friend," Phillip said. "We will tell him Oga is gone. Emeka, imagine . . . once we get rid of Oga, the cocaine job is yours. Let's not fuck up."

They had told Kenny about the bounty on Oga's head and they had asked Kenny to let Emeka take the lead in getting the cocaine to America.

Kenny was skeptical at first.

Giving a whole trafficking job to someone so inexperienced?

"There are other people ready and willing to do a job like this. Why would I need you, Emeka?" Kenny said.

"You can find someone else, but remember, we are using an American citizen as our first mule," Emeka said, masking his nerves as he spoke. "American mules are paid more. You got a big discount. Oga knew that, and you know that."

Emeka didn't know if Kenny knew that Patience would be using a fake American passport that bore her real name, but Patience was still a real American, and that was their biggest advantage.

Kenny took a bite of the coconut he was fiddling with, then paused. Emeka could see him thinking.

"Hmph, it's amazing, right? . . . How an American passport is a ticket to roam the world with no problem," he said. "Okay, we can make a deal. I told Oga to be careful with his petty theft. He didn't listen."

That they were able to pull it off still felt like a miracle to Emeka. Phillip, on the other hand, was so confident in the plan that Emeka wondered if he had been mapping out the details before they ever met.

"Oga doesn't care about us," Phillip had said as he drove Emeka around the day Kash was kidnapped and he found Emeka in tears outside Oga's compound. "He doesn't care that these crazy vigilante people can kill any one of us or kidnap us. He sent you and Kash to the area for an errand. Kash never came back. I know he put out a description of Kash to the people there saying he was responsible for the fire."

"How do you know that?" Emeka said, his eye sockets still aching from crying. He felt his forehead wrinkle as his suspicions seeped in.

"I've been working for Oga for too long. I know how he thinks, and I know that right now you are skeptical. But listen, it's time . . ."

"Time for what?"

"First, we have to pay the OEC part of the money they want," Phillip said.

"Where will we get that kind of money?"

"Oga keeps bundles of money in three of his large safes in the house. I know the combination to all three."

"Why haven't you robbed him in all this time?"

"I'm not a thief. I leave that sort of work to Oga and men like you. And stealing money from Oga won't put him out of business. A man who doesn't take care of the people who work for him should be handled. This is the only way. Kash is an ordinary pawn. The OEC wants to remove the mastermind from Lagos. Let's give them the mastermind," Phillip said.

"I can't do it," Emeka said.

"You think it is only you the OEC knows? These people will find your brother and your mother."

Emeka realized then that Phillip knew where Chike lived since Phillip had driven him there for a visit one day. What if he turned on him and told the vigilantes where to find his brother?

"Okay, I'm listening."

"If they remove Oga, we can promise them that there's a new boss who will take over all of Oga's operations. That boss will never steal houses in that area."

"Why is putting in a new boss even their concern?"

"Because once there's a shift in power in any operation, it wipes the slate clean. They will feel like they have a hand in deciding the order of things in Oga's former dealings."

"Who will step in?"

"You will."

"Me, no, no, no!"

"Think about it. If you take over, Emeka, you will have Oga's operation and you can run it how you want. The OEC go handle Oga, and you go chop everything he leaves behind."

"I'm not ready to do that. Oga is teaching me. How can we do this to him?"

Emeka wished he and Chike hadn't fought the night he left home. And he wished he had never moved in with Oga. It was better when he could make money doing the work while maintaining a bit of distance from it.

"Why are you doing this? What do you want?" Emeka said.

"I want half the money for each job. We will be like partners."

"Didn't you say you're not a thief?"

"I'm not. You will do all the illegal work. I will be your driver. That is my work. It's a raise in my salary that Oga never pays on time anyway."

"That's a big raise. An overpaid driver."

"If we take Oga down together, we reap the reward together."

Emeka was reluctant, but he knew he was in too deep. Kash had been kidnapped by men willing to kill him. Chike would disown him if ever he found out. And his dream of running an operation like Oga's was dangling before him. All he had to do was reach out and take it. He would become the man he envisioned. He would finally rid himself of the disgrace of lack. Why should he wait to seize his good fortune?

"Okay," Emeka had said. "How do we take down Oga?"

53

"MILITARY MUST GO! MILITARY MUST GO!"

Chike listened and ran toward the demonstrators as their chants journeyed far beyond their physical presence. Never did he think he would have the urge to see them in action until he felt the way he felt in that moment.

A week had passed since the election had been annulled, and the crowds of protesters in the streets of Lagos grew like bamboo—rapidly even under the poorest of circumstances. It was scorching, though some days rain flooded the streets. Marchers, strikers, activists, and riffraff all came anyway. Those with good intentions came to demand an end to military dictatorship.

They were tired. Chike was tired too.

Those who came to riot threw stones and set fire to cars and loose tires. They blocked roads and harassed passersby. Stories of police being beaten to death made headlines.

Chike still hadn't heard from Mayowa, and he had a short time to prepare for his departure to America. He needed something to assuage the pinch in his gut. He needed to see the men fighting and marching and chanting and screaming and setting things ablaze.

He needed to feel alive in Nigeria, alive in his skin. So he followed their voices.

Abiola had been addressing his supporters since the annulment, calling himself Nigeria's "only elected president." *A brave man*, he thought.

He imagined Mayowa's dad had his hands full as one of his top aides, so he tried to convince himself that Mayowa was fine. Still, he was worried.

Patience, who normally calmed him down, didn't do much to ease his concern. "With all that's going on outside, you should keep trying to find Mayowa," she said. "You have to see him before we go to America."

So he rode out again to search for his friend. He had heard about the areas that were swarming with mobs who acted like they had nothing to live for. Some were out to shed blood to make a point. He avoided those streets. This made it harder for him to get to Mayowa's place.

When he pulled up to the house, he barely knocked his motorcycle's kickstand into place before seeing Mayowa's dad speed out of their gate.

"Mr. Adeshina!" Chike shouted.

The man stopped the car. "Chike, I cannot find Mayowa! Have you seen him?"

"No, Sa. I came to see if he was home."

"Please, if you see that boy, tell him I'm looking for him!" Mr. Adeshina said this just before he took off in his car.

As he sped along familiar streets on his bike, he heard the chants of the protesters.

"Solidarity forever! Solidarity forever!"

He got closer and felt an even stronger tug toward the mayhem. The crowd's unity set off a whirlwind that lifted the foundation underneath his feet—a tornado pulling Chike in.

Then he saw them.

He was struck by their size. They stomped, they marched, they threw sticks and tires, they broke the windshields of motorists who dared to venture their way.

His heart began to beat to the drum of their will. How could he be so hypnotized and afraid at the same time?

And finally, he came alive.

They sang songs that put corrupt leaders on trial in the only court of law they controlled—the streets of Lagos:

Gbogbo won lo lowonbe
Gbogbo won lo lowonbe
Bi Nigeria ṣe daru
Nigeria de daru

They gathered to push over an abandoned car, its windows already broken. When it hit the ground, they all cheered. Police officers on the scene took formation in preparation for an inevitable battle. They were armed but outnumbered by the masses, which grew more and more anxious as the streets boiled from the heat. The demonstrators changed their tune:

Babangida 419, Maryam na cocaine pusher!

Chike was struck by the song calling the first lady a cocaine pusher as he stood on the sidelines, ready to make a break for it whenever the police decided to make a move. He remembered what Emeka had told him about top government officials being a part of the cocaine trade. Was it true?

A man ripped off his shirt, set it on fire, and threw it toward the barricade of police. The flaming shirt fell short and landed on the invisible line that kept the officers and crowd apart.

A loud blast came from a rifle pointed at the sky by one officer. The man who had thrown the flaming T-shirt bolted. Protesters ran him down, forcing him to stand his ground. An angry member of the mob grabbed him and slapped him. A war was breaking out. Police charged at the crowd as they went blow for blow.

Then in the midst of the chaos Chike spotted Mayowa. At first he thought his eyes were deceiving him, but he knew his friend too well.

Mayowa looked confused. First he ran into the middle of the street, then he looked back and ran to another corner. Chike moved toward him, keeping his eyes fixed on him. Before he could get to him, the crowd swallowed him up.

Chike ran faster.

The mob, even more manic.

Some started jumping.

Police began to swing.

Tear gas engulfed the air.

Chike was blinded. He covered his face and stumbled toward the concrete median that separated traffic. He took the fetal position and covered his head.

After what felt like an eternity, he peeked out of his shirt. The crowd had dispersed. He saw some in the distance, still chanting, still marching. Some were being flung around like rag dolls by police holding guns. Chike stood and looked where he had first seen Mayowa. He ran toward the area, then saw his friend lying on the pavement, his shirt torn, his face bloody.

"Mayowa! It's me, Chike! Mayowa! Somebody, help!"

INSIDE MAYOWA'S HOSPITAL ROOM, CHIKE ONLY ALLOWED himself to stand near the wall. Something was supposed to spill from him, he thought as he looked at Mayowa, who lay in his bed a few feet away, fully conscious but mute. Chike wanted to comfort him. He wanted to approach the bed, but he sensed that his friend needed space.

Mr. Adeshina appeared in the room, frantic, several hours after Chike had paid part of the bill to have Mayowa checked in. No money, no entry, the hospital officials had told them and several others who appeared to have been wounded during the demonstrations.

"Mayowa, when I left you home today, I told you not to join those boys who were rioting. Now look at your face!" Mr. Adeshina said with tears in his eyes.

Mayowa said nothing.

"I'm talking to you! You cannot be a part of the violence. We want people to protest, but you can't do it alone with riffraff."

"I'm sorry, Daddy," Mayowa mumbled, barely looking at him.

"Let me go and talk to your doctor about when you can come home."

When Mr. Adeshina left the room, Chike sat on the edge of Mayowa's bed. "I'm sorry I couldn't help you."

Chike sensed that shame had stolen its way into Mayowa's heart, though he had done nothing wrong. In fact, he had done everything right. He had believed in the promise of democracy. What he got in return was three broken ribs and a dislocated jaw.

"When are you leaving for America?" Mayowa mumbled.

"We are leaving next week."

"If you don't come back to Nigeria . . ." Mayowa took a long pause and put his hand on his jaw. "I would understand."

54

CHIKE'S APARTMENT RESEMBLED A WORKSHOP OF SORTS.
A pot of okra stew, antidiarrheal capsules, balloons, gloves, and bricks
of cocaine were spread across the tables and chairs.

Emeka's hands trembled as he put scoops of cocaine into the fingertips of plastic gloves. He cut each bud that amounted to a gram, tied
the ends, and glued them shut. He added another layer of plastic, then
repeated the process. Trails of powder settled into the faded green
carpet as he ranted on about how a Lebanese man named Sammi had
shown him what to do.

"This has to be perfect," he said.

"Emeka, we know," Patience said. "You've told us a thousand times."

"Brotha, stop worrying yourself," Chike said. "We are ready to get
this done."

Patience felt nerves take over the pit of her stomach. They were the
kind of nerves that made her want to take the diarrheal prevention
pills before it was time. Reality had set in as she surveyed what she
was about to ingest.

And something about the way Emeka was handling the job rubbed
her the wrong way. He was clumsy and fidgety. He kept dropping the
gloves as he tried to insert the small cocaine packets he was creating,
yet he stressed there was no room for error. He didn't look like a man

who was able to take down one of the most notorious crooks in Lagos, as he had told them. Maybe that was to his benefit, since most people still believed members of the OEC had acted alone in cornering Oga for what had happened to that house. Many debated whether Oga was really dead or just had been pushed out of town.

"Emeka, when should we begin the process?" Patience said. They had three hours until their flight to America. Somewhere beneath her nerves was a sensational joy. She couldn't believe the day had finally come.

"We will start soon since we need to be at the airport in two hours' time," he said. "First, let's go over the rules.

"Rule number one: It's an international flight, so the airline will serve you food. If your flight attendant asks you what you want to eat, choose a meal. When she serves you, I suggest you don't eat it, just pretend to. Put napkins on the food tray, then reseal it when it's time to trash it. Don't let your flight attendant hold the food when she comes around asking for trash; just throw it in the bag. We don't want the airline people to be suspicious about you not eating."

"Why shouldn't we eat?" Patience said as she paced the room. "It's a seven-hour flight to London before we get to America." She wished they had gone over the rules earlier.

"Do you want to shit the product out?" Emeka said. "Make sure you still take food, because if you refuse to eat, they will suspect you and alert customs.

"Rule number two: If for some reason you start shitting in the airplane and some of the product comes out, you will need to wash the packets in the bathroom and swallow them again."

"Oh my God!" Chike frowned in disgust. "I don't think I can do that, I beg."

"Jikonata onwe gi! Don't be a fool!" Emeka shouted. "If you don't do it, you will get caught and go to jail because you are afraid of eating a little of your own shit!"

"Okay!" Chike said.

"Rule number three: You have to be calm at all times. Carrying seven hundred grams of blow in your belly will be uncomfortable, but you cannot let customs see you sweating or complaining about any physical problems or anything at all. That's how some people get caught.

"Rule number three . . ."

"You already said rule number three," Patience said.

"Oh, yes . . . yes . . . I mean rule number four: When you reach New York, go straight to your hotel. You will eat this chocolate and wait for the cocaine to come out with your shit. Wash it well, well. Then put it in that bag," he said, pointing to the carry-on bag packed with their things before handing them a sheet of paper with the contact's details. "You will go to this address to drop it off."

"Well, at least we get to eat some chocolate when we get to our destination," Patience said.

"Chocolate? You're thinking about chocolate?" Emeka said. "Listen, don't come and fuck this thing up, o. This is my first job with Kenny. Let's get this done so you and Chike can go and live your lives away from Nigeria's madness and I can start making millions."

The mention of her and Chike living together in peace somehow melted her nerves and gave her the perspective she needed. In the end, she was sure it would all be worth it.

EMEKA DROVE DOWN THE EXPRESSWAY HEADING FOR Murtala Muhammed Airport. He looked out of the window often, slid his palms up and down the steering wheel. He turned the radio on, turned the radio off.

With all of his talk of being the boss and being a rich man, he had finally achieved it, but it all seemed like more than he was prepared to take on. In time he would grow comfortable, but she and Chike wouldn't be there to witness his evolution.

Out of everyone, Patience had expected Chike to be the nervous one, but he seemed calm. Elated even.

"Ahhhhh, tune!!!" he said from the front seat. He cranked the volume. Dr. Dre's "Nuthin' but a 'G' Thang" burst from the speakers.

"Chike, I beg, this is too loud," Emeka said, lowering the volume. "We need to be careful. Protesters are still around doing crazy things, o."

"Emeka, don't worry. We are on our way out."

"Let's get you out safely."

Chike cranked the speakers to near capacity. He rapped Snoop Dogg's part and pumped his fist as if he hadn't just swallowed nearly a kilo of cocaine. Patience had to admit, it wasn't as hard as she had thought it would be—they popped one antishit capsule and one cocaine bag dipped in a bowl of slippery blended okra stew. Each ball went down easily.

They reached the expressway, and Patience spotted the airport. They were almost there.

"See airport, o!" Chike said.

"Chineke, look." Emeka pointed out the front windshield. It was a police roadblock.

"Don't worry. We will give them money and be on our way," Chike said. Patience shifted in her seat. She took out two hundred naira so she would be ready. She felt her heart pounding above her belly full of cocaine.

"Just don't tell them you are traveling," Emeka said, rubbing the steering wheel again. "Let me talk to them."

Emeka slowed the car down and turned the music off. One officer stayed near their patrol car as the other approached them.

"Boss, how now?" Emeka said.

Patience diverted her eyes when he stared at her in the back seat. She looked at him again and found him still glaring. Chike watched their awkward exchange.

"Officer, what is the issue?" Chike said.

"You're going to the airport. Why?" the officer shifted his gaze to the front seat and curled his lip.

"We are going to get our brother. He went to Ghana," Emeka said.

"Ghana, eh hen," the officer said, nodding. "What business does he have in Ghana?"

"He is a trader," Emeka said.

"What is he trading?"

"I'm sorry, Officer, what is the relevance of the questions you're asking?" Patience said.

"Look at this fine girl. You dey question me?" He laughed. "Open the boot," he said, pointing toward the trunk before he walked to the back of the car.

"He will see our luggage," Patience whispered. "Drive away, Emeka."

"Are you mad? If we drive, they will chase us and find us at the air-port before you board your flight. I told you I would talk to him, but you had to open your mouth. We will let him see the trunk, and then we will give him money." Emeka popped the trunk. The officer hesitated, then laughed. He walked back to the front door.

"You get heavy bags for car but you say your brother traveled to Ghana," he said. "Everybody, commot for this car."

The officer's partner flagged down other cars to wait their turn to be harassed. Passengers from two cars got out and looked at Chike, Emeka, and Patience.

"Officer, we have something for you and your colleague," Emeka said, moving his hand toward his pocket.

"I said commot for this car," he yelled. He pulled his rifle from his back and held it in his hand like a cane.

Emeka and Patience got out of the car. Chike didn't.

"If you don't commot for that car, you will see . . ."

"Chike, get out of the car!" Emeka said.

Chike got out and stood next to his brother.

The officer walked toward Patience and stood in front of her. "Where are you going?" His bad breath made her eyes water. "I said, where are you going?"

"We are not going anywhere. We told you we are going to pick up our brother. The clothes there are for somebody."

"This your story doesn't make sense." He grabbed her arm.

"Officer, my brother said we have something for you. Why can't you just take the money, ehn?" Chike said. "Isn't it money you want? It's always money you useless people want!"

"Ah-ahn, you dey shout on me, an officer, saying we dey take illegal bribes?" he shouted as if he was appalled by the truth being spoken aloud. "You want to go and riot at the airport!" the officer said. "You are criminals!"

"No, Sa, we don't want to riot. We're just going to collect our brother," Emeka said.

"Friday! Friday!" the officer yelled to his partner. "Come and take the clothes from this trunk for evidence."

Friday ran to the trunk, snatched their suitcases, and put them in the back seat of the police car.

"It's not fair! Leave them!" Patience heard passengers from the other halted cars plead for them.

"Why would you take our clothes?" Patience said. She felt her palms dampen. Tears streamed from her eyes without warning.

"I like you," the officer said, moving back toward Patience. He grabbed her waist with one hand and pulled her in closer, still holding his rifle in the other hand.

Patience was disgusted, then she noticed Chike moving toward the police officer. She thought her eyes were deceiving her when Chike grabbed the officer's gun. Chike and the officer began to yell, each struggling for control. There were pleas coming from the crowd. Then Patience saw Officer Friday walk over to his partner.

The policeman managed to snatch the gun away. Chike put his

353

hands up in defeat. "I said it. You people are here to riot," the police officer said. "You're here to disturb the peace in this country."

"Peace?" Chike yelled in amusement. "How can we have peace in this country when—"

The blast of a single gunshot interrupted Chike. In a silent panic, Patience and Emeka began to search their bodies for bullet holes and blood.

Neither of them had been hit.

"Chike!" Emeka said as he saw his brother sink to the ground, holding his midsection. Officer Friday stood behind Chike, still pointing the rifle he had just fired.

Patience began to scream.

Both officers ran to their car and sped off.

Passengers from other cars fled the scene. One man ran to them. He held Chike's head up and surveyed his wound.

"Drive him to the hospital now or he won't survive this."

Emeka lifted his brother's body and placed him in the back seat of the shiny black BMW he had taken from Oga's collection. "Patience! Patience, get in the car!" he yelled. Patience barely made it into the passenger seat before Emeka sped off.

When they arrived at the nearest hospital, Patience placed her hand on Chike's heart. It was still beating. She began to pray. "Let him live. Protect him," she pleaded.

An awkward and unfamiliar conversation with God—that and her tears were all she had to give.

She felt useless.

If only hope was something she could hold in her hand. She would put it on Chike's wound, remove the bullet he had taken, and seal the hole shut—a hole that hadn't existed minutes before.

But she knew hope more than anyone—an elusive desire, a prerequisite for patience.

Patience didn't want to hope. Chike didn't have the time.

Emeka parked the car in front of the small hospital. He lifted his brother from the back seat and ran toward the gated entrance. A security guard halted them.

"What is this?" he said.

"My brother has been shot. He needs medical attention," Emeka said.

"Please, can we get him some assistance?" Patience said between sobs.

"Let me go and call the doctor to come and survey this issue." The guard stood and strolled toward the entrance of the hospital. Patience and Emeka looked at each other, puzzled.

Minutes later, a doctor emerged. He peered at Chike's body. "I'm sorry, but I cannot have a gunshot victim here. Carry this problem away from my hospital. We cannot allow riffraff here for treatment."

"What do you mean riffraff? He is dying!" Patience yelled.

"This is my brother," Emeka said. "He is not riffraff. He is my brother. You need to treat him. You *will* treat him."

"I will not treat him. If you're out participating in a riot, then you reap what you sow. In fact, your brother has transcended. He can't be saved."

Emeka looked at the doctor, then into his brother's vacant eyes. He placed Chike's body on the dusty road in front of the hospital and knelt beside him. Patience looked on, emotionless. She heard Emeka's faint sobs in between the doctor's demands to remove Chike's body from the road in front of his hospital. After that, it was as if everything went silent. Patience looked at Chike, the only man she had ever loved and who had learned to love her the same. He was now a life wasted. His spirit, his beliefs, his efforts—gone.

55

PATIENCE LOOKED UP AT THE RED BRICK BUILDING ON
Monroe Street in Brooklyn as a gentle rain sprinkled from the placid
blue sky. The clean, earthy air offered a remedy of calm to the streets,
creating a rare mood in New York. She couldn't think of a more beautiful day to knock on her mother's door.

It had been two months since her arrival in the city—two months
since the woman at the public library had told her to search the telephone books for her mother's address. And so she did for the first
month. Fifteen Folami Adewales were listed in different parts of the
city.

Patience called them all and visited some. None was her mother.

What a task it was, looking for a lost person in New York.

Such a small place, packed so tightly with people across five areas
that seemed worlds apart.

One day Patience thought about her mum's maiden name, and
there she was, listed in a tattered telephone book under a Brooklyn
address—the only Folami Bayonle.

When Patience saw a woman standing outside the red brick home
for the first time, she turned and made her way back underground to
the subway—back to the hotel that had become her home in Manhattan. The woman was her mother. She had to be.

Why didn't Patience confront her? It was what she had been waiting for, working for, risking her life for. But she hadn't expected to see the woman with someone else, someone she seemed attached to.

During the second month of her stay, Patience left her hotel room for good and rented a room not far from her mother's address.

She lost count of how many times she had gone to the red brick house and looked at it from a comfortable distance. She would see the woman she knew was her mother put her arm around a boy who looked no older than ten. The woman smiled at the boy often, frowned at him often, and appeared more vigilant on the days he rode his bike on the cracked pavement.

When Patience thought she had mustered up enough courage, she crossed the street and started toward the house just before the woman emerged from the front door with the boy. Patience watched as the woman bent toward him and wiped the mucus from his nose. She had turned and walked away in a hurry.

Now Patience walked up the stairs of the red brick building and felt her legs grow stiff. She managed to reach the door, lift her arm, and then ball up her fist. She hesitated. What if the woman didn't recognize her? Patience wondered how irreversibly that would hurt her. But she would never know if she didn't allow herself to knock on the door.

So she did. She knocked.

No answer.

She knocked harder.

No answer. Then she noticed a doorbell. *How could I have missed the doorbell?* she thought.

She rang it.

She heard a woman's voice call out, "Coming!"

She felt a presence behind the door. She knew someone was there, looking through the peephole. If it was her mother, would she recognize her daughter through such a narrow view after a decade-long separation?

It didn't matter. The door opened.

The woman stood before Patience. She looked at her as if air had left her body.

Her mother said nothing, then she was about to say something but didn't.

Patience knew the woman didn't say anything because she knew—she knew she was Patience and Patience was hers.

Patience said nothing, then she was about to say something, then the words left her. She didn't need those words anymore. Her mother spoke first.

"Patience?" Her narrow eyes grew to their capacity, almost the size of an American nickel.

"Yes," Patience said, feeling the weight of possible rejection lift from her body. The woman was surely her mother. Her eyes gave her away—just a touch darker than chestnut and wide-set like Patience's. She looked at the woman's hands as she clasped them together to express her disbelief. She remembered those hands, though they had aged slightly. How those hands would stroke her cheeks and gather her plaited hair in ponytails. How she would polish her own lengthy nail beds taupe, then blow them dry.

They stood gazing at each other until her mother broke the long silence. "Would you like to come inside?" she said, uttering her words carefully, as if she wasn't sure how Patience felt.

"Yes, please," Patience said. Tears fell from her eyes. Her emotions startled her. She was only supposed to allow herself to cry after having a long conversation with her mother, because then she would know where they stood, but her mother's mere presence filled her body with wonder and excitement and pain. Patience thought about Chike, her beloved Chike—who had succumbed to merely her memory of home—her father, Margaret, Kash, and all she had done to leave Nigeria to arrive at this very spot.

"Please don't cry," her mother said. She grabbed Patience and wrapped her arms around her. She held her tightly and gripped her long braids from behind. When Patience's sobs subsided into calming breaths, she discovered that the woman she had come to reunite with smelled of cocoa butter and lavender—a subtle detail that made her mother even more real.

The woman broke their embrace and led her into her living room off the side from her narrow foyer. If Patience had come here when she first arrived in New York, she would have compared the massiveness of her father's mansion to the simplicity of her mother's place. But she had seen enough of New York to know that the inside of the red brick dwelling, with its narrow doorways and compact sitting room, was decent living in Brooklyn. Inside there was a display of photos and books in a wall unit, a small-screen television with some sort of video game consul sitting above it.

"Sit. Please," her mother said with a stiff smile as if she was trying to mask her true state. "Do you like tea? I'm quite a tea drinker."

"I remember that."

They were silent, and they gazed at each other.

"Yes. I will take some tea," Patience said, shaking the moment off.

Her mother walked out, and Patience surveyed the room. She rose from the slender wooden chair, upholstered with what appeared to be cowhide. She looked at her mother's cherry wall unit. There she noticed photos of the little boy. Dressed in a baseball uniform, he held a bat confidently. Patience looked for a photo of herself. There wasn't one.

"Do you like sugar in your tea?" her mother said as she put a tea-kettle and mug on the center table.

"Yes, I love sugar in my tea."

Folami lifted the lid, spooned sugar granules into the teacups, and stirred.

"Sugar cubes are better," Patience said. "It's one of the things I miss about home. Two cubes was always enough. In America, all the cafés give you loose sugar. It's not the same."

"I never thought of that," her mother said with a smile that seemed more relaxed. She ran her fingers through the back of her straight bob-length hair.

Patience smiled a nervous smile at Folami, who sat across from her, then lifted her teacup and drank to avoid having to counter the silence with some sort of talk. Folami did the same. Patience watched her mother—how she gripped the cup as if she were cradling a crystal ball in her palm.

"So . . ." her mum said. Patience imagined that she wanted her to initiate the conversation about the massive elephant in their midst.

"What do you think, Mum? I'm here," Patience said, still fighting the shakes.

"Well . . . I'm thinking so much." Folami rubbed her forearm as she gripped her cup in one hand. "It's too much to say just like that."

Her mother wiped her eyes, and Patience noticed then that she had been crying.

"I have the letter you wrote me."

"You . . . have the letter? So you read the letter?" Her mother seemed surprised.

"Daddy never gave it to me, but I found it." She decided not to tell her she had read the one she had written to her father too.

"I'm not surprised." Her mother pursed her lips.

"So you didn't just leave. You tried to get custody of me, right?"

"How do you know that?"

"In your letter. You said it without saying it. Then your old friend, Aunty Lola. She found me and told me things."

"Ah, Lola! Doesn't she live right there in Ibadan?" she said as she wiped away the rest of her tears.

"She lives in Lagos now. But when she was in Ibadan, Daddy didn't let her visit me."

"Oh." Folami's expression melted into a blank stare. She stood and walked out of the room. Patience wanted to follow. Instead she sat and sipped her tea and swallowed her grief. She had already cried once. She needed a break.

Her mother returned to the room after several minutes. She smoothed down her dress and sat down.

"Yes, it's true. I went to court. I fought to get you back. Your daddy by then had a lot of money, and he didn't give me anything once he made me leave. But even if I had had enough money, I believe he would have still won that case," she said through a deep sigh. "He's a man of influence, you know?"

"Yes, I know," Patience said. She fell quiet, digesting what her mother had said. A man of prominence would have his way and alter people's lives just because he could.

"Do you mind if I lie down here?"

Folami frowned. "Yes, of course. I mean, no, I don't mind. Go ahead. Are you okay?"

"Yes, I'm fine."

Patience lay down on the brown couch. She closed her eyes to clear her mind of all the things she wanted to say. She couldn't believe that she had been in her mum's presence for only a little while and she was already falling apart. She scolded herself for her lack of control. She felt a hand rest on her thigh.

"I know you have a lot of questions. I have a lot to say. If you want to rest or even take a nap, you can," her mother said with the same soothing voice that Patience remembered from her girlhood. "Right now it's about noon. I will be leaving the house around 2:30. You can come with me, or you can stay and continue to rest."

"Why didn't you stay in Nigeria? He put you out of the house, but you could have stayed in Nigeria," Patience said.

She sat up and looked at her mother. The woman took a deep breath and looked into her eyes again.

"I left Nigeria because of him," Folami replied, pointing at a photo of the boy.

"He is not your half brother," her mother said, her shoulders more relaxed. Patience was puzzled. "His name is Dayo, and Dayo is your brother fully. He is your father's son."

Patience was speechless.

"I was pregnant when I left Nigeria. When I went to court to fight for custody of you, my mother told me to wear big dresses to conceal my belly. If your father could take you away from me, he would be able to take my baby once he was born. People thought I went crazy when I left Nigeria. I was somewhat out of my mind because I had to leave you, Patience. But I had to protect at least one of my children."

Patience was quiet as she took in the news. She had always wanted a life with her mother. Dayo hadn't been deprived of that. She envied him. She resented him. Then she remembered her life in Nigeria—the pain of not knowing who she was and of feeling like an outsider in a family that was supposed to be her own. She was happy Dayo didn't have to experience what she had.

Patience stood and walked over to her mother's display of photos. She surveyed all of Dayo's school portraits and sports trophies. She pictured herself sitting at one of his games, cheering for him.

She felt her mother's presence at her side. Her mother pulled out Patience's hand and placed a small four-by-six frame in her palm. It was a photograph of the two of them—her mother dressed in an Ankara skirt and blouse, Patience in a yellow romper. She must have been about eight years old. They were holding hands in front of their old bungalow in Ibadan.

"Dayo has seen this photo so many times. I tell him he has a sister," she said with tears in her eyes. "I stayed away from Nigeria because I didn't want anybody to find out about Dayo. But every single blessed day, I hoped for this," her mother said with an intense squint in her eyes. "That somehow we would reunite. That you would find us."

Patience held the photo and wandered back to the couch. *Find us.* She repeated her mother's words in her mind a few times.

"In your letter to me you said one day we would meet again and when we did, I would know what you'd added to our lives. Were you talking about him?"

"Yes. I was talking about Dayo."

Patience sat down, stared at the photo her mum gave her, and wept again.

PATIENCE AWOKE GROGGY. SHE RUBBED HER EYES AND sat up on the couch. She didn't know when she had fallen asleep or how. But she was still holding the photo of her and her mum in her hand. She imagined that her tears had induced her slumber. Or maybe it was everything that had led up to that day. She was exhausted.

"How did you sleep?" her mother said, lowering the book she was reading.

"Okay." Patience observed her. She realized then how much her mother still looked like an athlete—her face chiseled behind her dark, chin-length bob, her arms toned, her midsection solid and upright. "Are you still a runner?"

"You remember that?" her mother said. "I'm not anymore . . . not professionally. I still run for exercise, and I teach my students how to run. I'm an athletic coach at a university here. This was my way of not giving up on my dream," she said, then smiled a half smile.

Patience felt her resentment return. Her mum had continued to pursue a dream while she, Patience, was left behind in Nigeria wondering what had happened to her. Then she thought of Aunty Lola, who had given up her dream of interior design, and Modupe, who had buried her identity in being the wife of a wealthy man. She believed she could allow herself to be proud of her mother's strong will. Just not fully in that moment.

"You know I wanted to go to the Olympics. That was my dream. But then I got pregnant with you."

"So . . . I was a mistake."

"No . . . no, you were unplanned," her mother said. Patience wondered how *unplanned* and *mistake* were any different. "I was a star runner, I was still a student, and I didn't know if your father was good for me. He was always a very complicated man."

"How did you meet?" Patience said. She wondered how a woman could settle for a complicated man. Then she remembered Chike and how much she had worked to make things work with him.

"At Howard, I was standing in line waiting to register for classes. He approached me because he heard the registrar say my name, so he knew I was Nigerian. Then we found out we were both from Ibadan."

Her mother shook her head and mashed her lips together as if she was fond of the memory. "Then he invited me to one of his Nigerian student union meetings. That was when I noticed his arrogance. He called the group his 'ship.' I skipped the meetings for some time after that."

Patience thought of how her mother had softened her Nigerian accent when she said the word *skipped*. It was the way an American would say it. Her mum had blended in.

"But then it got cold in DC, and I was homesick, so I went to his meeting looking for fellow Nigerians. I was really busy with track practice, but I made time for it."

"So how did you . . . ?"

"Start dating your daddy?"

"Yes."

"There was something very electric about his presence, so I decided to chance it. I wasn't the best runner at first. I lost every single race during my first semester. But once I started winning my races, your dad . . . well, that's when he started to change. He didn't seem interested in being the boyfriend of the famous girl in school."

Patience was quiet as she took in what her mother had said. She looked around the room again, then fixed her gaze on one of Dayo's photos. He resembled her father so much—his square jawline, his pout, his frame. She wondered how she hadn't noticed at first.

"What are your interests, Patience?" her mother said.

"I like to sew." She had never felt so comfortable telling anyone else. "I want to go to Parsons School of Design. They say it's not an easy school to get into. I heard that everybody in this New York thinks they are a top designer."

Her mother giggled a fluttery giggle, and Patience remembered her natural elegance when she tilted her head ever so slightly as she laughed.

"Just apply. If you don't get in, just apply to another school."

Patience admired her mother's confidence.

"Patience, let's continue to talk in the car as we go pick up Dayo," her mother said with a new urgency in her voice.

Patience hesitated. That was where her mum needed to be by 2:30. Patience wasn't sure she wanted to go. Was she ready for him? She couldn't believe she was so nervous about meeting a child.

"Shall we?" her mother said again. She stood and grabbed her keys.

"Okay."

"Where do you live?" her mother said as she sped down Fulton Street, heading west in her Toyota Camry.

"I live not too far from you. I rent a room in East New York."

"I see."

There was silence, and Patience wondered if her mother wanted her to stay with her and Dayo. If she offered, she would turn her down. Patience felt she needed her own space—her own life away from the adults who had shaped her with their bad decisions.

"What school does Dayo go to?" Patience said, hoping to deflect from her mum entertaining the thought if she already was, though a small part of her needed to avoid the possibility of her mother not offering to house her.

"He's at a private school near one of the universities in downtown Brooklyn. He's in fifth grade now. You would think he's heading to college next year. He's very bright."

Her mother grinned and blinked, visibly captivated by the thought of her son.

"How's your half sister? Margaret?"

"She's fine. She's my sister, not my half sister."

"Oh. I assume you've gotten along well with her over the years," Folami said stiffly.

"Very well. She's been the one consistent person in my life." Patience hoped her comment sounded like a subtle jab, because it was. "We take care of each other."

"I'm happy you have her. I'm happy you have each other." Her mother shifted uncomfortably in her seat.

Patience didn't know what to do with what she felt. Her mum had always been the perfect picture of a woman in her mind.

But now she was just a regular woman.

Flawed and part of the biggest disappointment of her life.

The car sped on, and she looked up at a billboard. The man in a cologne ad reminded her of her father, with his square face, bearded chin, and solid build.

This didn't surprise her.

She had seen her father's face all over New York: from the men on Wall Street to the working-class types riding the subways from Manhattan to the outer boroughs during rush hour.

She didn't miss him. She just knew that he was there, home in Ibadan, and that even with all the space and strain between them, he was her father still.

She glanced at her mum, who kept her eyes steady on the road. Then at her hands on the steering wheel. The large veins reminded her that she was the woman who once had read to her and braided her hair and mothered her. But so much time had passed between them, and she still didn't know why.

She needed to know why.

"Mum . . ."

"Yes . . . Patience." Folami smiled, and Patience knew she did because she had called her Mum. Patience didn't know what else to call her.

"Why? Why did Daddy throw you out of the house that day? I remember that day. I was there. I saw him and Uncle Timi throw you out. I remember you cried. You screamed. You called my name. But I still don't know why." Patience felt an eager tear take up space in her left eye.

Folami was quiet. She kept driving, but she slowed down, then parked near a fire hydrant in front of a residential block.

Patience surveyed the rows of buildings. "Is his school here?" she said, still unable to say her new brother's name out loud.

"No. I just . . . I haven't had to repeat this story to anyone in a very long time. It's not a story that I'm proud of."

"I will try to be understanding," Patience said, and she was proud of herself for not making her mother a concrete promise.

"There was a fight."

"What do you mean a fight? He hit you?" Patience looked at her mum eagerly.

"No. That wasn't it."

"So what happened?"

"So much happened," her mother said as she let out an audible breath. "When I found out he was with Modupe . . . and she had Margaret . . ." Her voice trailed off at the mention of both names. She stared through the windshield as if she were watching her past replay on it.

"I wasn't surprised because I suspected it. Yes, I was hurt. His family never treated me well. Kashimawo's father, Timi, was too concerned with your daddy's money. He thought I was somehow going to block his inheritance from your dad, not knowing that your dad was fed up with taking care of him. Your father's aunt Bukky, who raised them . . . she was a traditional woman. In fact, she was quite cruel. And one day I was just fed up."

She shook her head and bit down on her bottom lip. Her eyes bared a deep-seated pain. Patience wished she could comfort her, but she didn't have the energy.

"What happened?"

"Ikokore happened. I hate ikokore—yam full of oil. Imagine me being taught to make it." She snickered through her tight frown as if it were a must to find an amusing part to her story.

"I don't understand."

"One day your dad sent your aunt Bukky to teach me how to cook ikokore. That was his mum's favorite dish from her hometown, and she cooked it for him and Timi often before she died. I wasn't doing things the way Aunty Bukky liked, so she started abusing me like she always did. 'Useless girl, you can't cut simple yam.' I ignored her. She kept going and said Kolade was planning to throw me out and bring Modupe in. I prayed, asking God to keep me. But you know . . ." she said, trailing off again. "The devil prevailed that day when I slapped her face."

"You slapped her?" Patience said, somewhat bewildered and somewhat in awe.

"I did. I slapped her. Then I slapped her again and again and again. It was only God that saved her when Kolade came home and pulled me off her. I yelled at him. He yelled at me. Then I went to pick you up. When we got to the house, you ran in like you always did. I saw you staring out of the window when your dad and his brother were tossing my things outside. They threw me out that day with no option to see you again."

Once more, there was silence in the car, and Patience realized then that there could never have been a good enough reason for their separation. She could picture her father feeling violated by her mother's nerve in laying hands on his aunt, who was like his mum, yet he could so easily excuse his own infidelity as normal. Patience felt a deep sense of solidarity and sympathy for her mother again.

"I'm not proud of that day. I regret it. I wish I had taken you and left Kolade before that day. I wish I had never moved back to Nigeria with him. I've wished these things every day of my life since then. I am so sorry, Patience. You deserved better."

Folami's silent tears fell, and Patience remained emotionless. She looked at her mum, whose tears transformed her perfect face into that of a sweaty marathon runner.

"I understand," Patience said. "Let's go. Let's go pick up Dayo before you're late."

Dayo—his name was actually pleasant to say.

Her mum hushed and looked at Patience. She reached toward the back seat of the car and grabbed a roll of paper towels that sat next to a dragon toy and a coloring book. She dried her eyes. She put the car in drive and pressed the gas.

"How did Modupe . . . how did she treat you?" her mother said.

"If you ask her, she'll say she did the best she could."

"What does that really mean?"

"Well, it's not an easy thing to explain, but growing up, she didn't treat me the way she would her own daughter, and I knew I couldn't try to see her as a mum to me even if I wanted to."

Her mother glanced at her, then turned to face the road again.

"Patience, I know it may be a bit too soon for me to be offering you any advice, but if I may . . . please choose wisely whenever you decide to give any man your time. Our people value marriage, but if you don't choose a person who will add to your life in a healthy way, you will find yourself tired, unhappy, and broken even. I don't want that for you."

Her mother paused as if she expected her to respond. Patience had nothing meaningful to say. Choosing a man was the furthest thing from her mind.

"Do you have a boyfriend now?"

Patience thought of Chike and found herself annoyed by the question. What could she possibly say? *Mum, I had a boyfriend, but I don't have a boyfriend anymore because he was killed on our way to the airport just so I could see you again and so he could begin to live his destiny.*

Who knew his destiny would be an early death?

Patience thought of her last moments with Chike's lifeless body, as Emeka drove around aimlessly until he remembered that she would need to purge the cocaine before it killed her. When she did purge, it felt as if her own life had dropped out of her body. Her numbness remained the next morning when Phillip drove them to Kenny's house to present Chike's body as proof of how the plan had gone awry. Kenny's breath smelled of tobacco when he sat close to her and told her she would be working for him because Emeka and Phillip had "fucked everything up." She watched, still numb, as Phillip and Emeka carried Chike's body out Kenny's back door, the blood on his shirt thick and muddy-red as if tinned tomato had been smeared all over him. She didn't ask where they were taking him, or what they would do to him.

And that was it. She still couldn't believe their ending.

"I don't have a boyfriend," Patience told her mum.

"No problem, just face your studies for now, right?"

"Right," Patience said.

"You have to build your life brick by brick. And you shouldn't allow an unworthy someone to change your course."

Patience thought of the irony of her mother telling her to do what she had been trying to do since she left her father's house.

There was a long pause. Patience sensed her mother was thinking of what to say.

"Have you been following Abiola's story?" she finally said. "Such a shame how the military won't let democracy prevail."

"Yes. I saw him speak at a rally not too far from UNILAG when I was there." Patience closed her eyes, forgetting that she didn't want to tell her mother much about her life in Lagos.

"So you were a student at UNILAG?"

"Yes . . . briefly."

"Why did you leave?"

"There were too many strikes. It's like I was not there at all."

"So is your father paying for you to go to Parsons?"

"There's a boutique downtown. I just applied to work there. Hopefully . . . you know." She ignored the bit about her father. She had no intention of telling her she had run away.

"Oh, well . . . I love your independence, but if you ever need anything, remember I'm your mother. I will do my best for you."

Patience was quiet again. She didn't even know how to ask her mother for anything. She imagined it would be harder than begging for money from strangers on the roadside.

"How's Kashimawo? He must be a professional by now."

"You can say that," Patience said, thinking of her cousin, a professional thief once kidnapped and now a shell of his former self. "Kash is very enterprising. He had to be after Daddy stopped giving him money."

"Hmmm, that Kash was always so clever. Your daddy is not the only person who can be successful, you know? You and your cousin are just as capable."

They *were* capable before the ground they toiled had become a sinkhole, burying them alive. Were they capable of forgiving their own missteps and beginning anew? Patience wasn't sure.

Silence fell between her and her mum, and she imagined herself filling those gaps with meaningless mother-daughter conversation that didn't conjure up painful memories—the kind Margaret and Modupe shared or Bimpe and Aunty Lola often had. One day she and her mother would have that. Knowing this made Patience sad because it was yet another thing in her life she would have to wait for.

And yet she was proud and hopeful because she had made their future together more than a possibility.

"Patience, I forgot to ask . . . how did you get here? How did you get to America?"

Patience stared at the windshield, this time watching her own past replay as she avoided eye contact with her mum.

"Mummy," she said before a deep sigh and a long pause. "That is a story for another time."

ACKNOWLEDGMENTS

This book wouldn't have been possible without the encouragement and guidance of so many people.

Nana Ekua Brew-Hammond, you are one of the many writers who inspired me to dare to write a novel. Thank you for helping me polish up my manuscript and for putting it into the right hands. It's a privilege to share this honor with you.

To my editor, Rakesh Satyal, you guided me so seamlessly through this process in the midst of a pandemic. Thank you for being so easy to work with, for believing in this novel, and for encouraging me to add a sprinkle here and there until this book was just right.

To my husband, Kunle Ayodeji, thank you for guarding my heart and stirring my desire to create. I love you beyond words.

Thank you to my mother, Sinot Ishola, for believing in me, loving me, and rooting for me so passionately. My sister, Lola Ishola, I hear your cheers for me. I love and cherish you both. To my father, Raufu Bayo Ishola, I am lucky to have grown up listening to you tell stories late at night. I knew then who I could become. I miss you.

To the young people in my life: My daughter, Teju, you inspire me to remember the miracles of life. Dream big and don't ever lose your fiery imagination and curiosity. Tomi, my charming son, thank you for keeping me on my toes. My nephew, Anthony, I am so taken by your love and care for me and our entire family. You're such a blessing. Camille, my dear niece, rock this world with your strong will and poise.

ACKNOWLEDGMENTS

Thank you to my friends who've inspired me and supported me and my work over the years: Funmi Bamishigbin, Tosi Rigby, Adeola Fayehun, Dionna Matlock, Dana Oliver, Djenny Passé, Johnette Reed, Audra West. Arao Ameny, thank you for taking the time to read the early version of this story and for your detailed notes and suggestions.

I am grateful to have picked the brains of Marlene Nwabuisi, Omoyele Sowore, Malcolm Fabiyi, Kunle Ayodeji, and Adeola Fayehun. I was better equipped to write this story because of your insight and encouragement.

I am also grateful to Hafsat Abiola and Joanna Lipper for sharing part of Moshood Kashimawo Abiola's story in *The Supreme Price*, a documentary about Mrs. Kudirat Abiola. That piece allowed me to gauge his influence even further and watch a streamlined account of the various speeches he gave in Nigeria as he campaigned for the presidency in 1993.

Thank you all. May your own aspirations take form and exceed your expectations.

A NOTE FROM THE COVER DESIGNER

Patience is a young woman on the precipice of becoming a truly independent adult, ready to take risks and claim a life of her own in a formidable world. With the cover, I hoped to capture a moment when Patience might be feeling the fear-laced thrill of that transition most keenly: she's stepping out onto the streets of Lagos at night, with a whole host of possibilities sprawling before her, ready to let the brightness of the lights invite her in or lead her astray.

Sara Wood

Here ends Abi Ishola-Ayodeji's
Patience Is a Subtle Thief.

The first edition of this book was
printed and bound at LSC Communications
in Harrisonburg, Virginia, March 2022.

A NOTE ON THE TYPE

The text of this novel was set in Minion, a serif typeface designed by Robert Slimbach and released by Adobe Systems
in 1990. Inspired by late Renaissance-era type, Minion's
name stems from the traditional naming system for type
sizes, in which minion is between nonpareil and brevier.
Designed for body text, Minion is classic yet condensed
in style, achieving a harmonious balance between the size
of letters. It is a standard font in many Adobe programs,
making it one of the most popular typefaces used in books.

HARPERVIA

An imprint dedicated to publishing international voices,
offering readers a chance to encounter other lives and other
points of view via the language of the imagination.